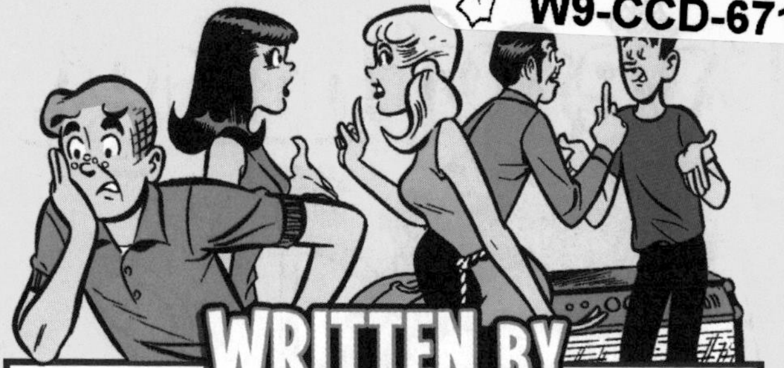

WRITTEN BY

Frank Doyle, Al Hartley,
George Gladir & Dick Malmgren

ART BY

Harry Lucey, Al Hartley, Bob Bolling, Bob White,
Dan DeCarlo, Bill Vigoda, Gus Lemoine, Samm Schwartz,
Mario Acquaviva, Jon D'Agostino, Chic Stone,
Marty Epp, Rudy Lapick, Bill Yoshida & Barry Grossman

This book contains some material that was originally created in a less socially sensitive time in our society and reflects attitudes that may be interpreted as being unacceptable today. The stories are reprinted here without alteration for historical reference.

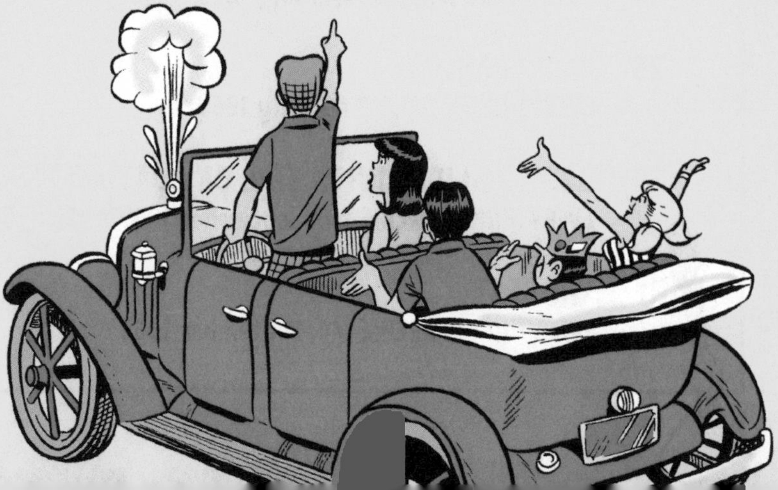

Everything's Archie

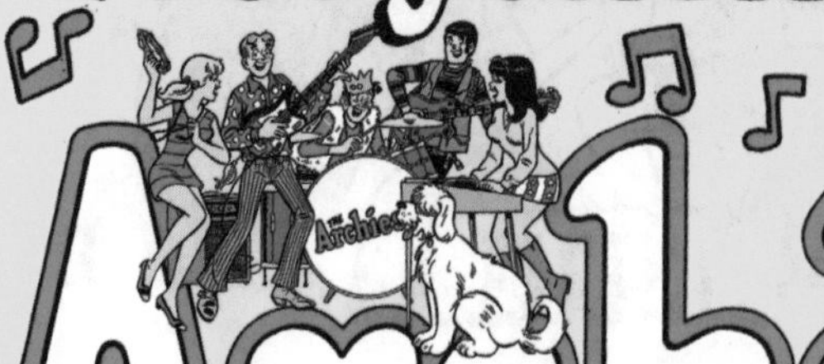

TABLE OF CONTENTS

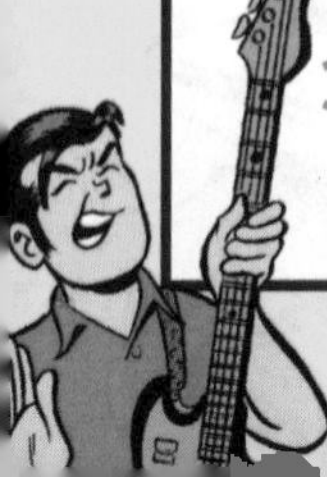

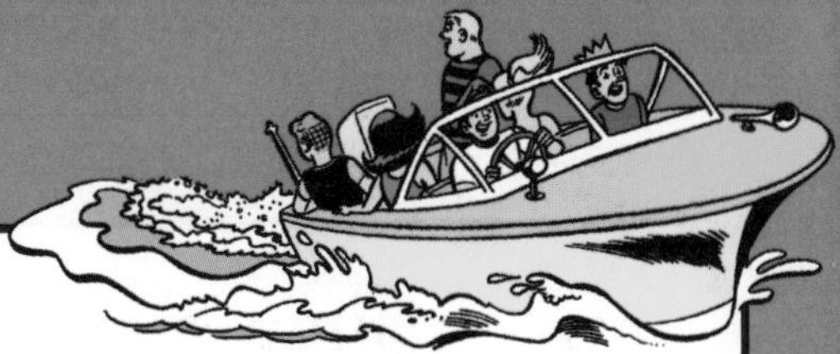

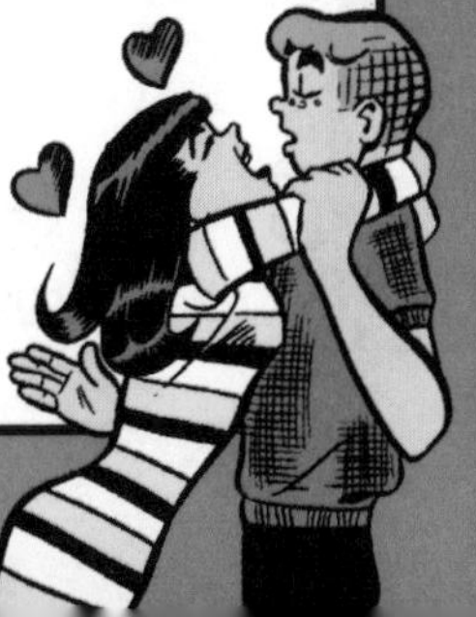

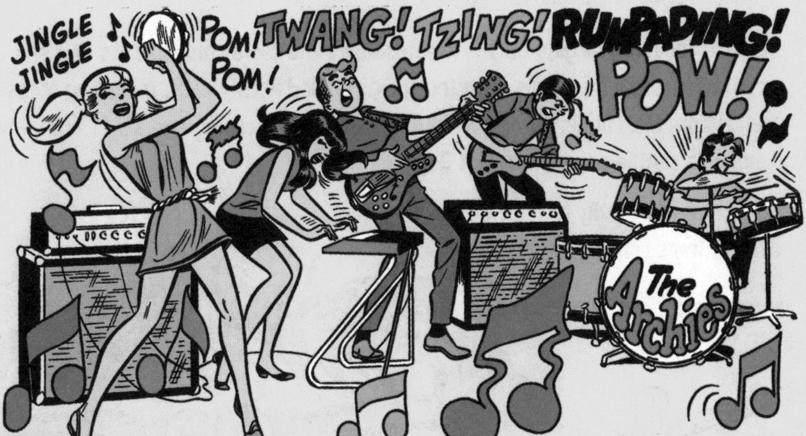
JINGLE JINGLE
POM! POM!
TWANG! TZING! RUMPADING!
POW!
The Archies

Everything's Archie

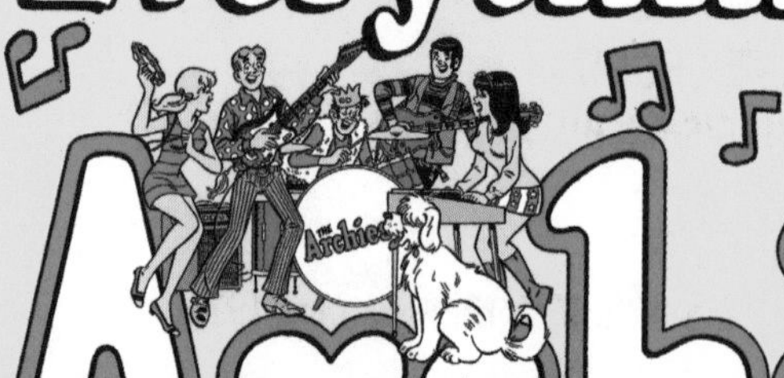
The Archies

Everything's Archie was a comic series that ran from 1969 to 1991 and originally served as a vehicle for showcasing the newly-created band The Archies, as featured on the Saturday morning cartoon *The Archie Show* produced by Filmation for CBS. *Everything's Archie* was also the name of the second studio album released by The Archies, which featured the hit single "Sugar, Sugar."

The *Everything's Archie* comic, which was part of the *Archie Giant* series, followed the exploits of The Archies as they meet record execs, attend music festivals and play gigs all while balancing their regular high school hijinks, adding in a dash of drama, and even solving a mystery or two! The series even had the characters visiting Filmation–the actual animation studio that produced *The Archie Show*!

Despite focusing largely on The Archies band, the series also has its fair share of hilarity and adventures starring the extended Archie cast, including Moose and Dilton, Mr. Lodge, some of the Riverdale High faculty and staff and even Jughead's canine companion, Hot Dog!

Now let's get ready to rock because everything's coming up Archie!

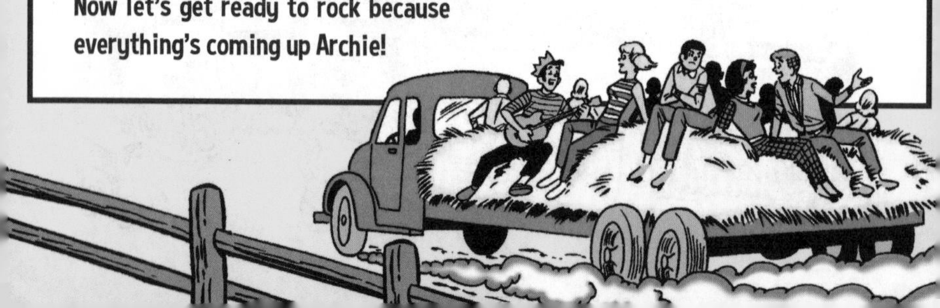

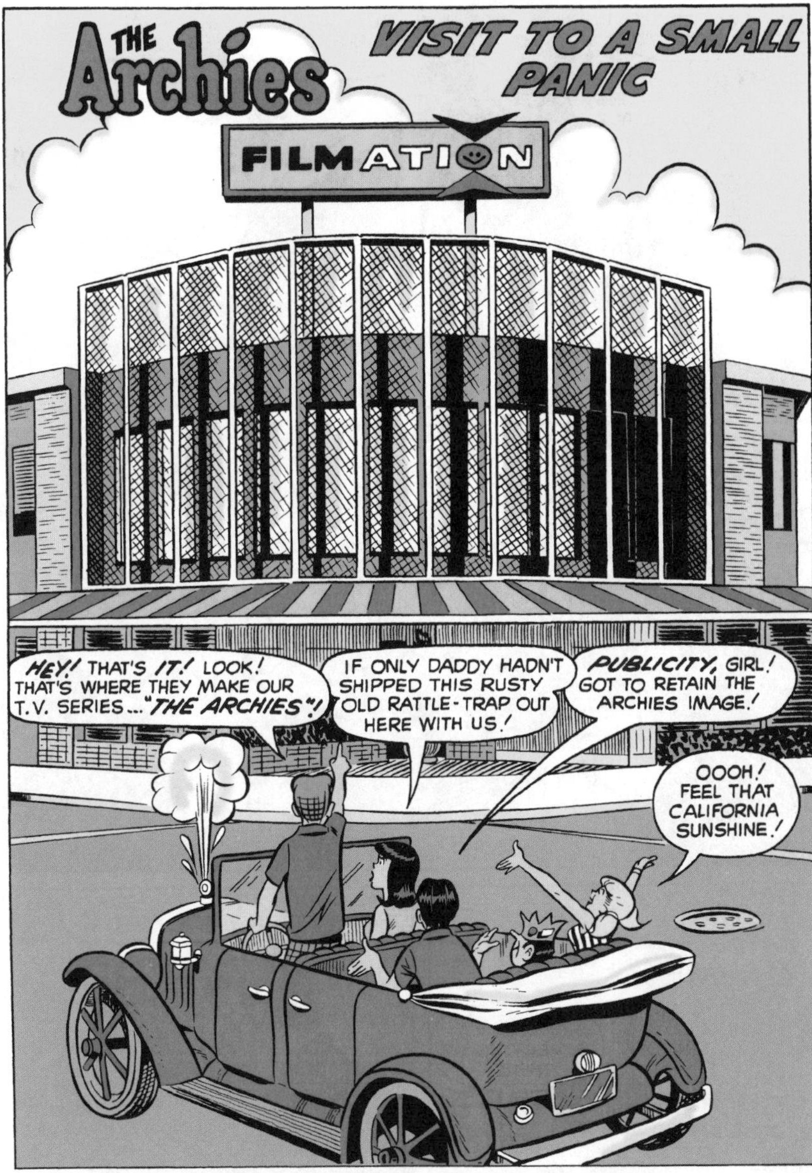
THE Archies
VISIT TO A SMALL PANIC
FILMATION
HEY! THAT'S IT! LOOK! THAT'S WHERE THEY MAKE OUR T.V. SERIES ... "THE ARCHIES"!
IF ONLY DADDY HADN'T SHIPPED THIS RUSTY OLD RATTLE-TRAP OUT HERE WITH US!
PUBLICITY, GIRL! GOT TO RETAIN THE ARCHIES IMAGE!
OOOH! FEEL THAT CALIFORNIA SUNSHINE!

Story: Frank Doyle Pencils: Harry Lucey
Inks: Marty Epp Letters: Bill Yoshida Colors: Barry Grossman

Originally printed in EVERYTHING'S ARCHIE #1, MAY 1969

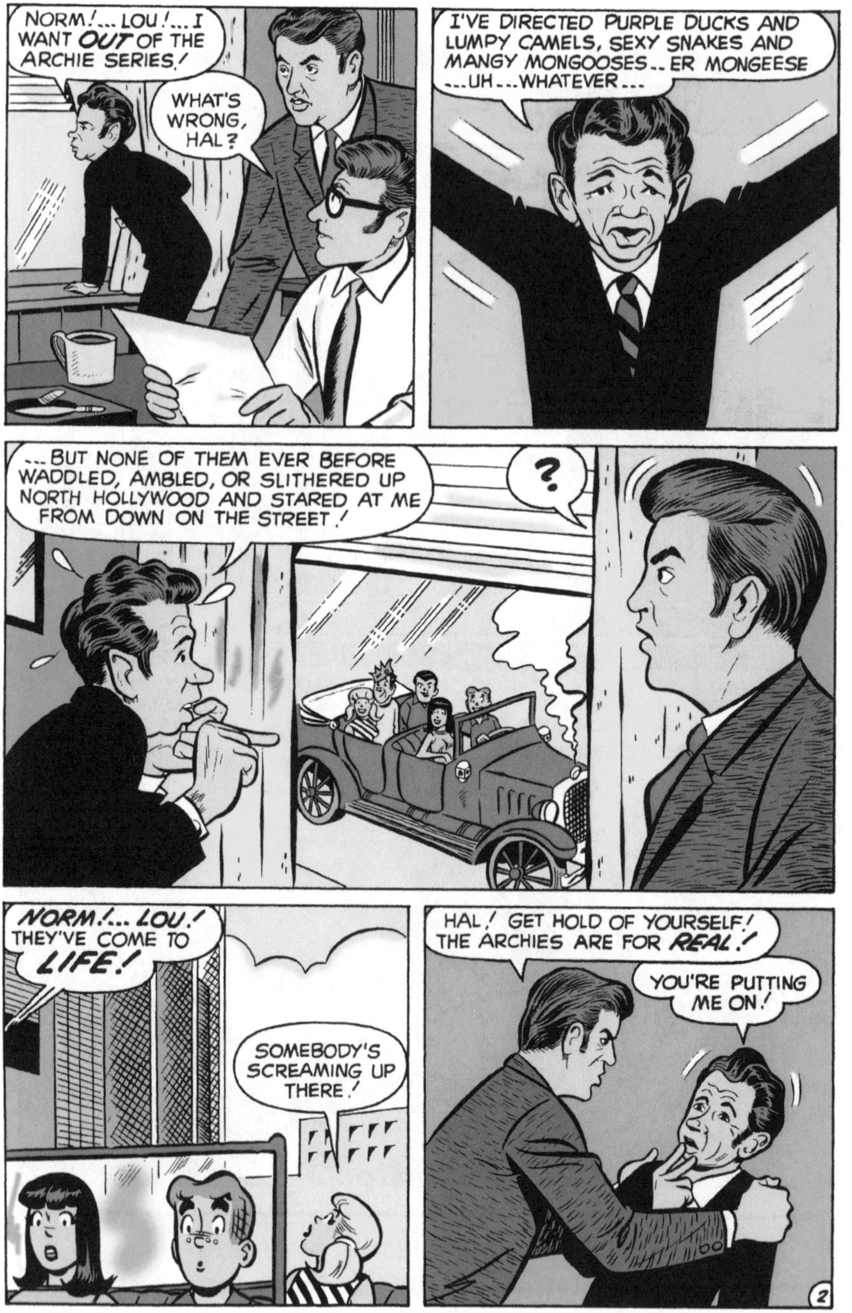
NORM!... LOU!... I WANT OUT OF THE ARCHIE SERIES!
WHAT'S WRONG, HAL?
I'VE DIRECTED PURPLE DUCKS AND LUMPY CAMELS, SEXY SNAKES AND MANGY MONGOOSES.. ER MONGEESE ...UH...WHATEVER...
...BUT NONE OF THEM EVER BEFORE WADDLED, AMBLED, OR SLITHERED UP NORTH HOLLYWOOD AND STARED AT ME FROM DOWN ON THE STREET!
?
NORM!... LOU! THEY'VE COME TO LIFE!
SOMEBODY'S SCREAMING UP THERE!
HAL! GET HOLD OF YOURSELF! THE ARCHIES ARE FOR REAL!
YOU'RE PUTTING ME ON!
2

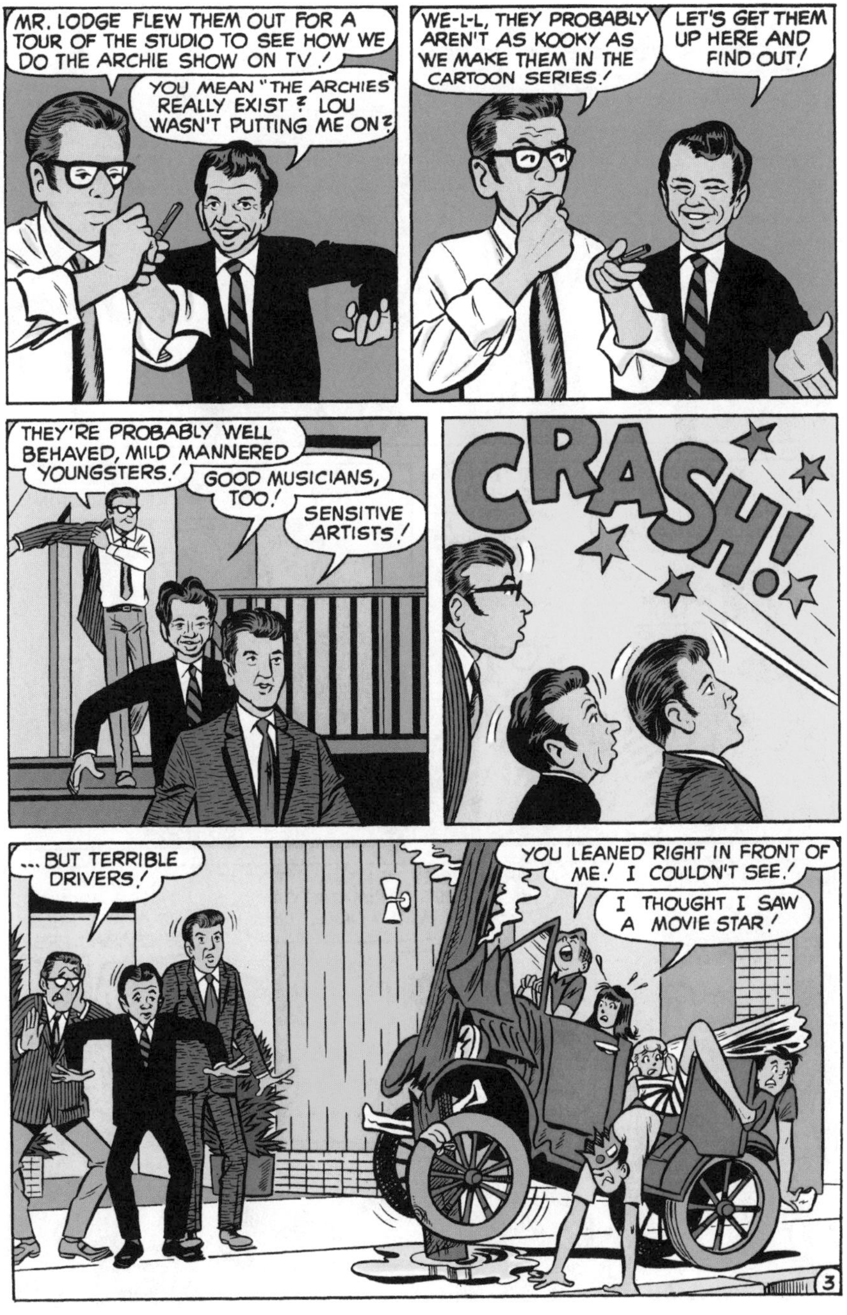
MR. LODGE FLEW THEM OUT FOR A TOUR OF THE STUDIO TO SEE HOW WE DO THE ARCHIE SHOW ON TV!
YOU MEAN "THE ARCHIES" REALLY EXIST? LOU WASN'T PUTTING ME ON?
WE-L-L, THEY PROBABLY AREN'T AS KOOKY AS WE MAKE THEM IN THE CARTOON SERIES!
LET'S GET THEM UP HERE AND FIND OUT!
THEY'RE PROBABLY WELL BEHAVED, MILD MANNERED YOUNGSTERS!
GOOD MUSICIANS, TOO!
SENSITIVE ARTISTS!
CRASH!
... BUT TERRIBLE DRIVERS!
YOU LEANED RIGHT IN FRONT OF ME! I COULDN'T SEE!
I THOUGHT I SAW A MOVIE STAR!
3

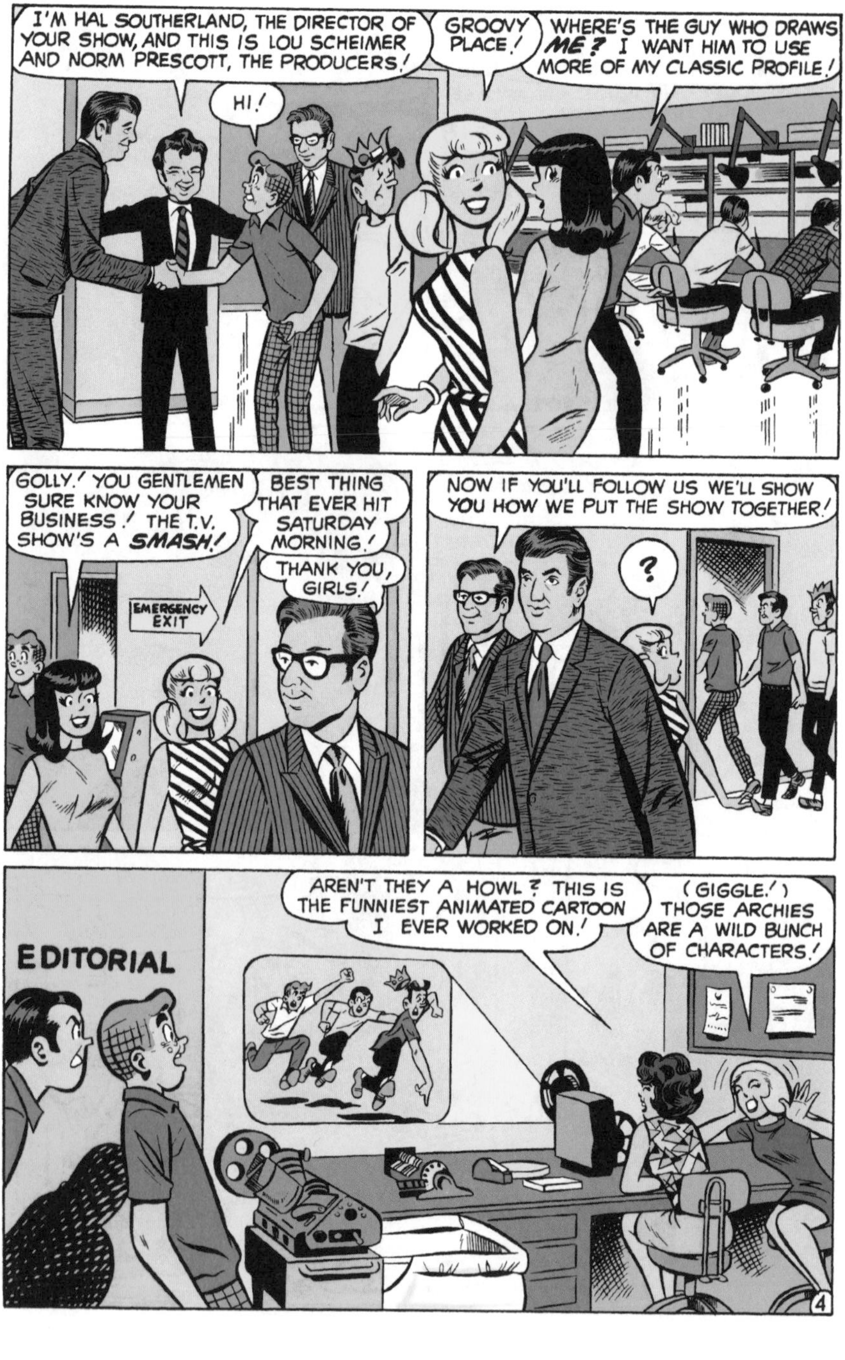
I'M HAL SOUTHERLAND, THE DIRECTOR OF YOUR SHOW, AND THIS IS LOU SCHEIMER AND NORM PRESCOTT, THE PRODUCERS!
GROOVY PLACE!
WHERE'S THE GUY WHO DRAWS ME? I WANT HIM TO USE MORE OF MY CLASSIC PROFILE!
HI!
GOLLY! YOU GENTLEMEN SURE KNOW YOUR BUSINESS! THE T.V. SHOW'S A SMASH!
BEST THING THAT EVER HIT SATURDAY MORNING!
THANK YOU, GIRLS!
EMERGENCY EXIT
NOW IF YOU'LL FOLLOW US WE'LL SHOW YOU HOW WE PUT THE SHOW TOGETHER!
?
AREN'T THEY A HOWL? THIS IS THE FUNNIEST ANIMATED CARTOON I EVER WORKED ON!
(GIGGLE!) THOSE ARCHIES ARE A WILD BUNCH OF CHARACTERS!
EDITORIAL
4

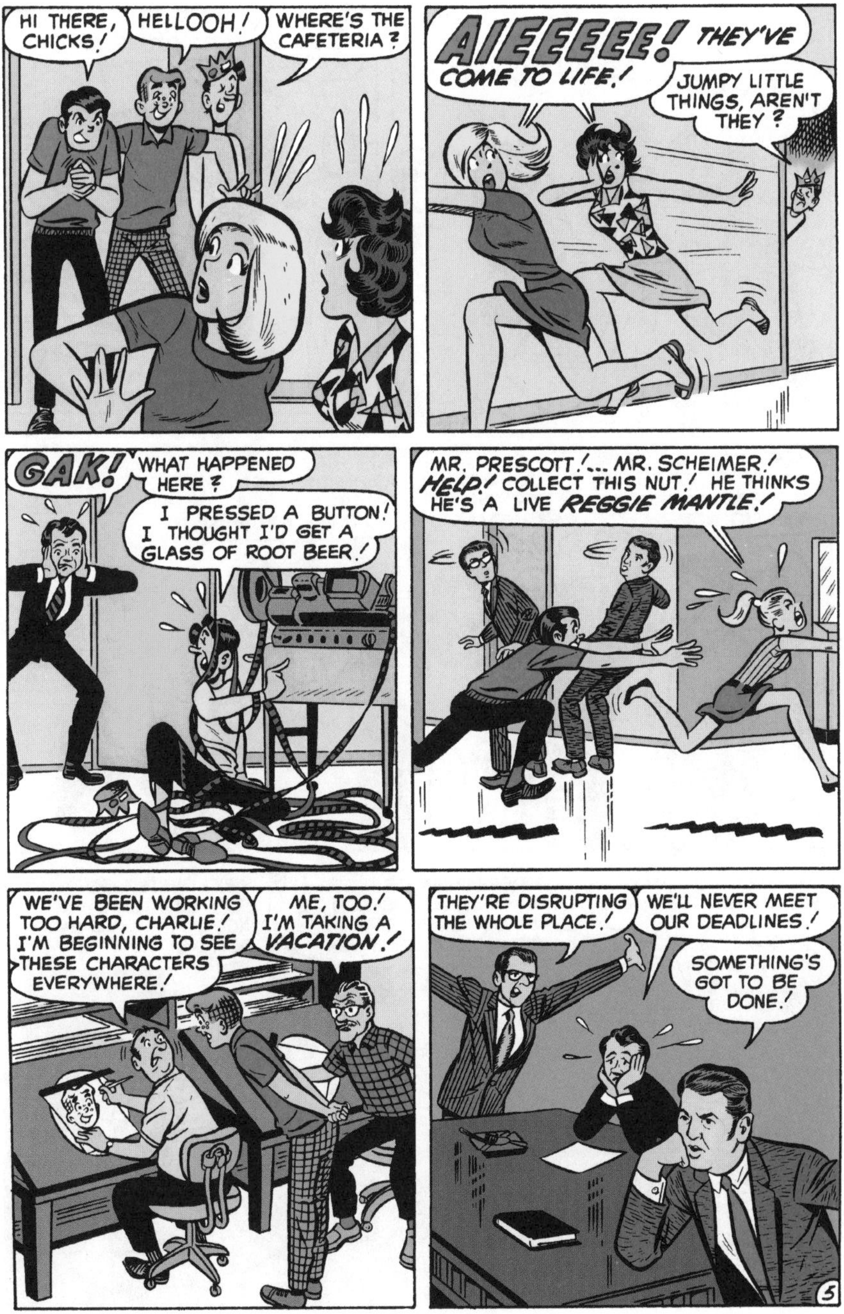
HI THERE, CHICKS!
HELLOOH!
WHERE'S THE CAFETERIA?
AIEEEEE! THEY'VE COME TO LIFE!
JUMPY LITTLE THINGS, AREN'T THEY?
GAK!
WHAT HAPPENED HERE?
I PRESSED A BUTTON! I THOUGHT I'D GET A GLASS OF ROOT BEER!
MR. PRESCOTT!... MR. SCHEIMER! HELP! COLLECT THIS NUT! HE THINKS HE'S A LIVE REGGIE MANTLE!
WE'VE BEEN WORKING TOO HARD, CHARLIE! I'M BEGINNING TO SEE THESE CHARACTERS EVERYWHERE!
ME, TOO! I'M TAKING A VACATION!
THEY'RE DISRUPTING THE WHOLE PLACE!
WE'LL NEVER MEET OUR DEADLINES!
SOMETHING'S GOT TO BE DONE!
5

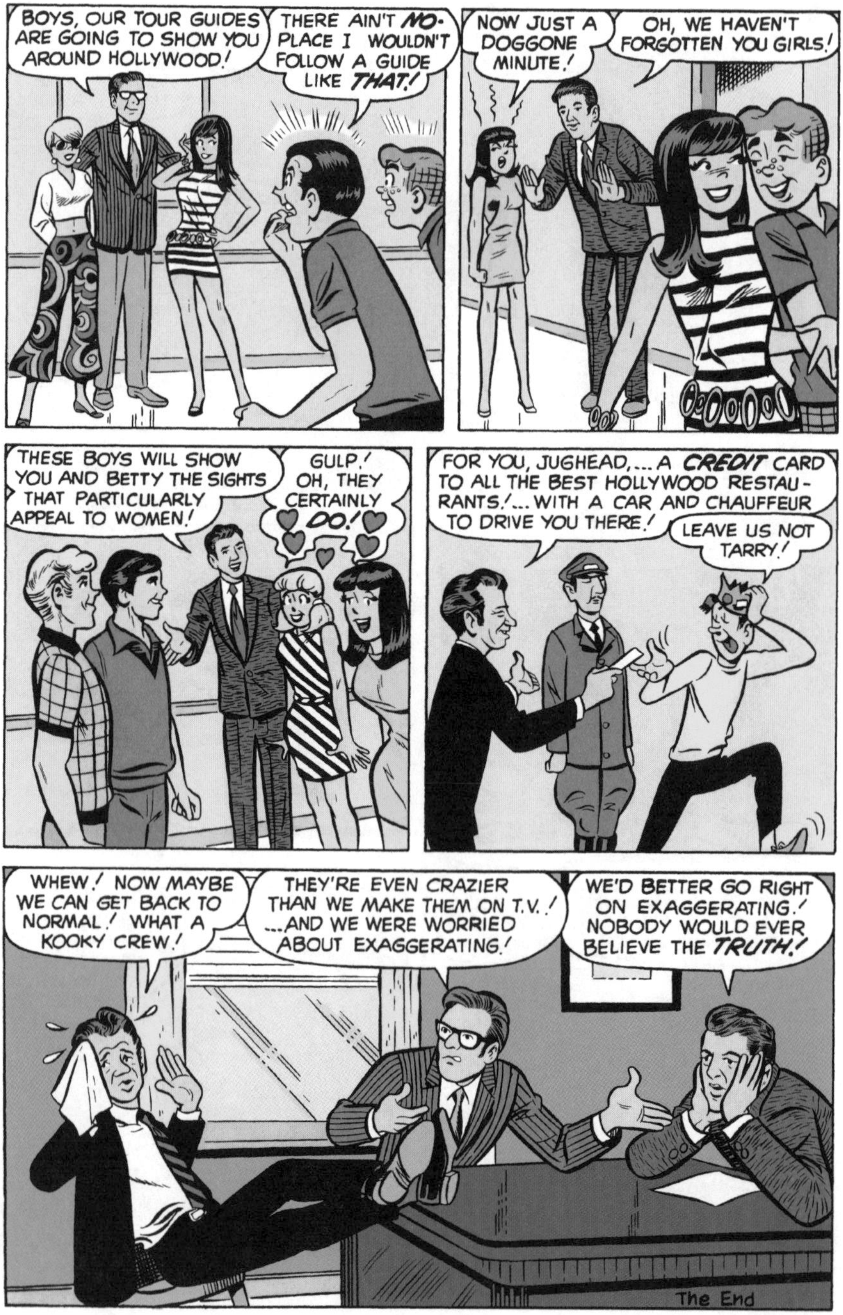
BOYS, OUR TOUR GUIDES ARE GOING TO SHOW YOU AROUND HOLLYWOOD!
THERE AIN'T NO-PLACE I WOULDN'T FOLLOW A GUIDE LIKE THAT!
NOW JUST A DOGGONE MINUTE!
OH, WE HAVEN'T FORGOTTEN YOU GIRLS!
THESE BOYS WILL SHOW YOU AND BETTY THE SIGHTS THAT PARTICULARLY APPEAL TO WOMEN!
GULP! OH, THEY CERTAINLY DO!
FOR YOU, JUGHEAD,... A CREDIT CARD TO ALL THE BEST HOLLYWOOD RESTAU-RANTS!... WITH A CAR AND CHAUFFEUR TO DRIVE YOU THERE!
LEAVE US NOT TARRY!
WHEW! NOW MAYBE WE CAN GET BACK TO NORMAL! WHAT A KOOKY CREW!
THEY'RE EVEN CRAZIER THAN WE MAKE THEM ON T.V.! ...AND WE WERE WORRIED ABOUT EXAGGERATING!
WE'D BETTER GO RIGHT ON EXAGGERATING! NOBODY WOULD EVER BELIEVE THE TRUTH!
The End

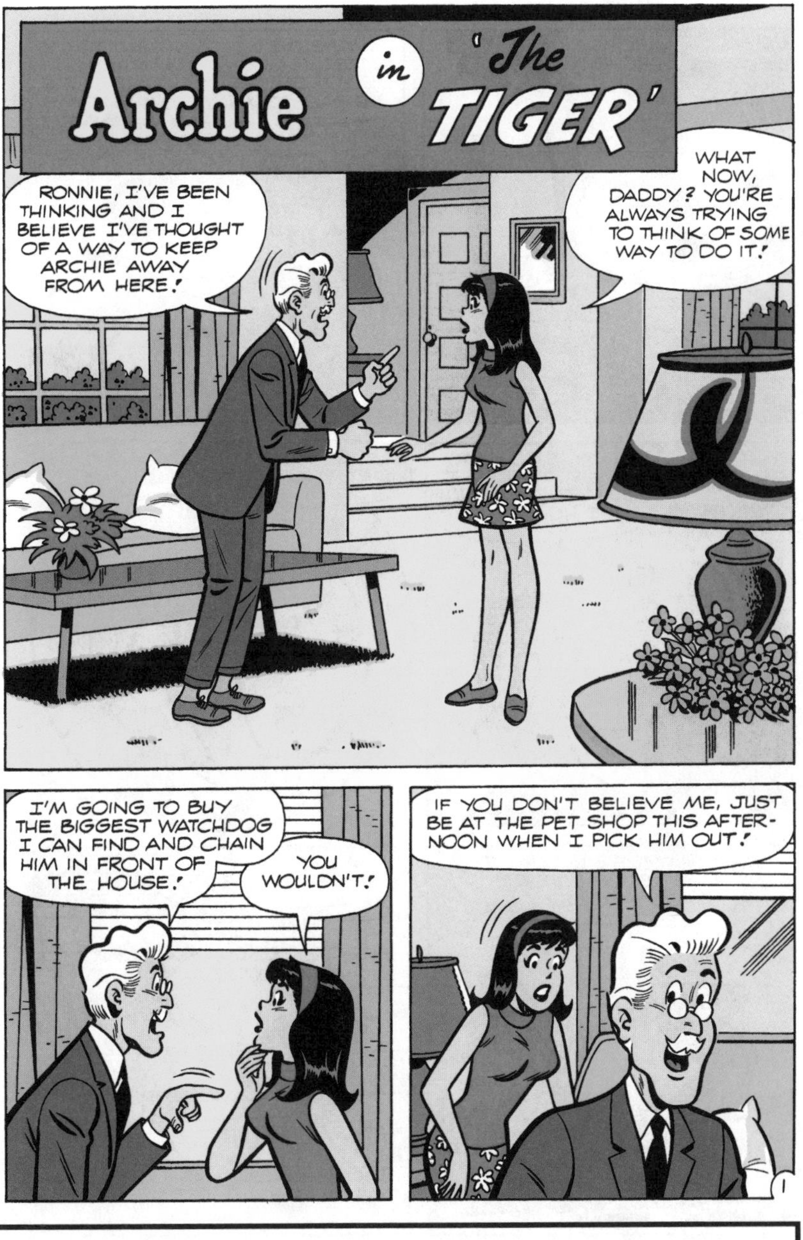
Archie in 'The TIGER'
RONNIE, I'VE BEEN THINKING AND I BELIEVE I'VE THOUGHT OF A WAY TO KEEP ARCHIE AWAY FROM HERE!
WHAT NOW, DADDY? YOU'RE ALWAYS TRYING TO THINK OF SOME WAY TO DO IT!
I'M GOING TO BUY THE BIGGEST WATCHDOG I CAN FIND AND CHAIN HIM IN FRONT OF THE HOUSE!
YOU WOULDN'T!
IF YOU DON'T BELIEVE ME, JUST BE AT THE PET SHOP THIS AFTER-NOON WHEN I PICK HIM OUT!
1

Story & Pencils: Al Hartley   Inks & Letters: Jon D'Agostino

Originally printed in EVERYTHING'S ARCHIE #1, MAY 1969

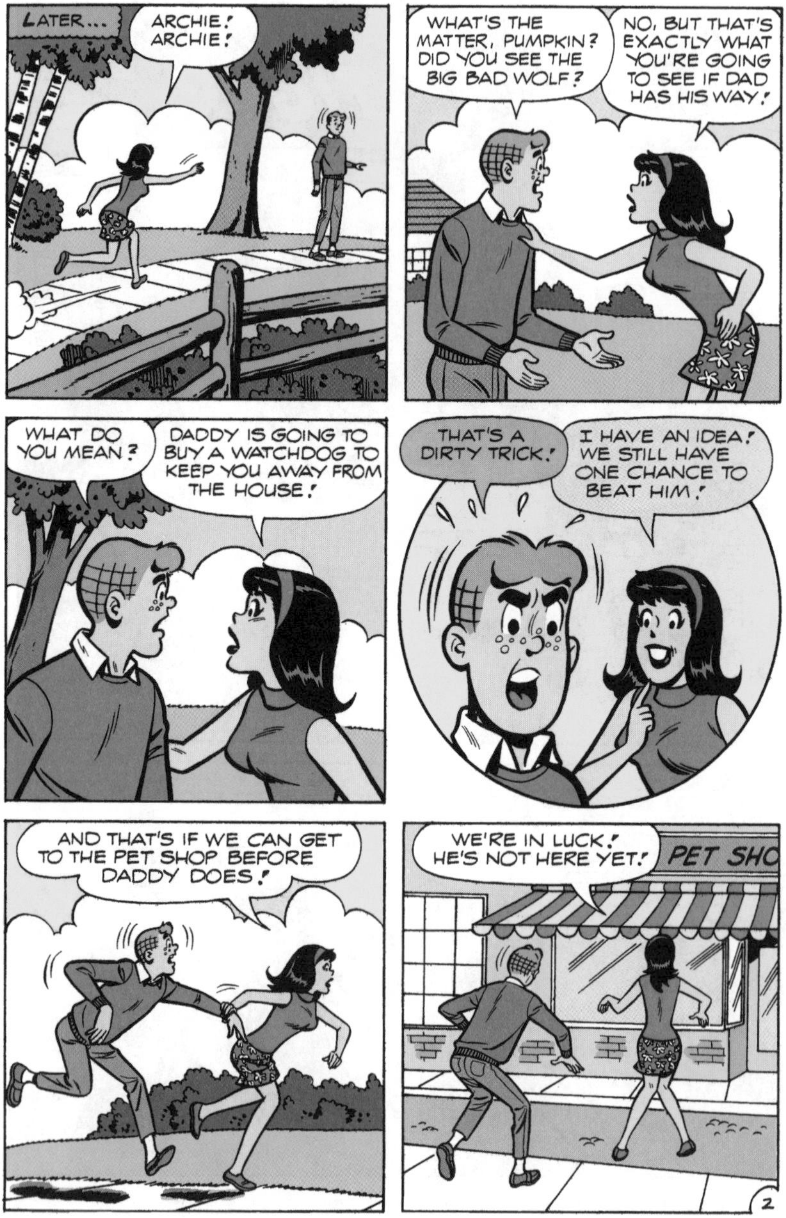
LATER...
ARCHIE! ARCHIE!
WHAT'S THE MATTER, PUMPKIN? DID YOU SEE THE BIG BAD WOLF?
NO, BUT THAT'S EXACTLY WHAT YOU'RE GOING TO SEE IF DAD HAS HIS WAY!
WHAT DO YOU MEAN?
DADDY IS GOING TO BUY A WATCHDOG TO KEEP YOU AWAY FROM THE HOUSE!
THAT'S A DIRTY TRICK!
I HAVE AN IDEA! WE STILL HAVE ONE CHANCE TO BEAT HIM!
AND THAT'S IF WE CAN GET TO THE PET SHOP BEFORE DADDY DOES!
WE'RE IN LUCK! HE'S NOT HERE YET!
PET SHO
2

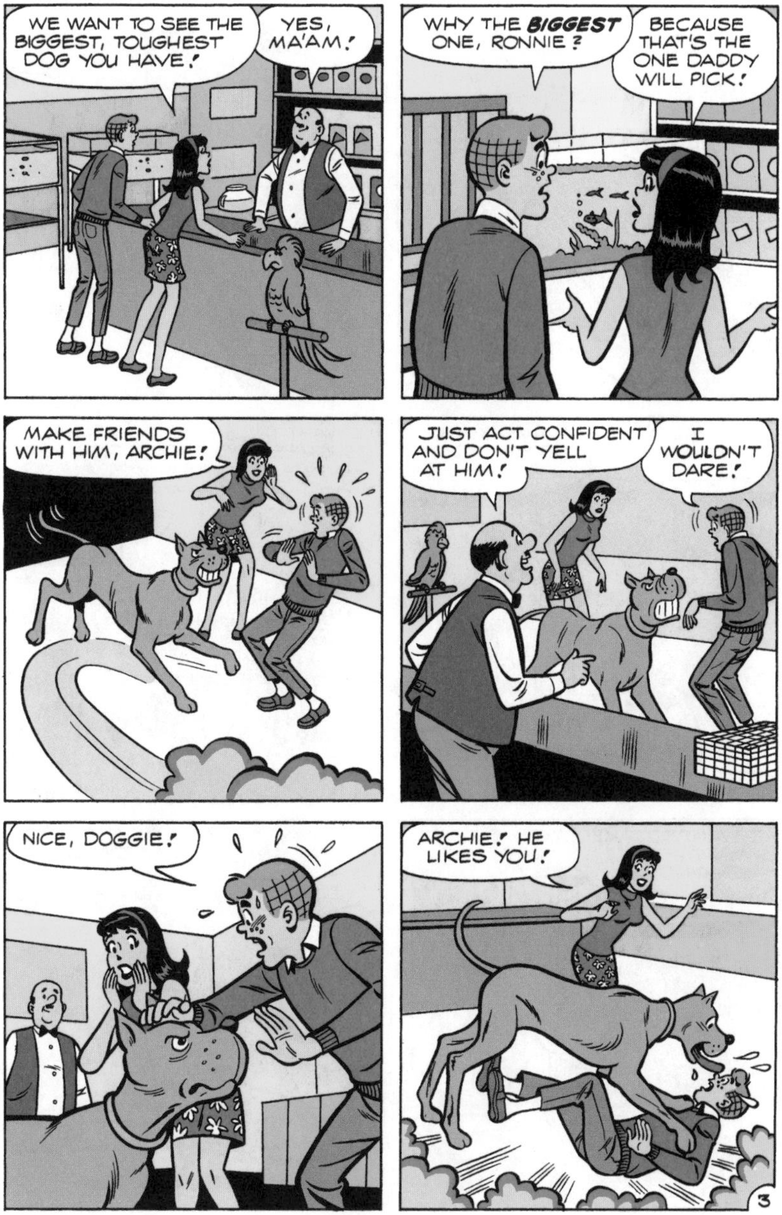
WE WANT TO SEE THE BIGGEST, TOUGHEST DOG YOU HAVE!
YES, MA'AM!
WHY THE BIGGEST ONE, RONNIE?
BECAUSE THAT'S THE ONE DADDY WILL PICK!
MAKE FRIENDS WITH HIM, ARCHIE!
JUST ACT CONFIDENT AND DON'T YELL AT HIM!
I WOULDN'T DARE!
NICE, DOGGIE!
ARCHIE! HE LIKES YOU!
3

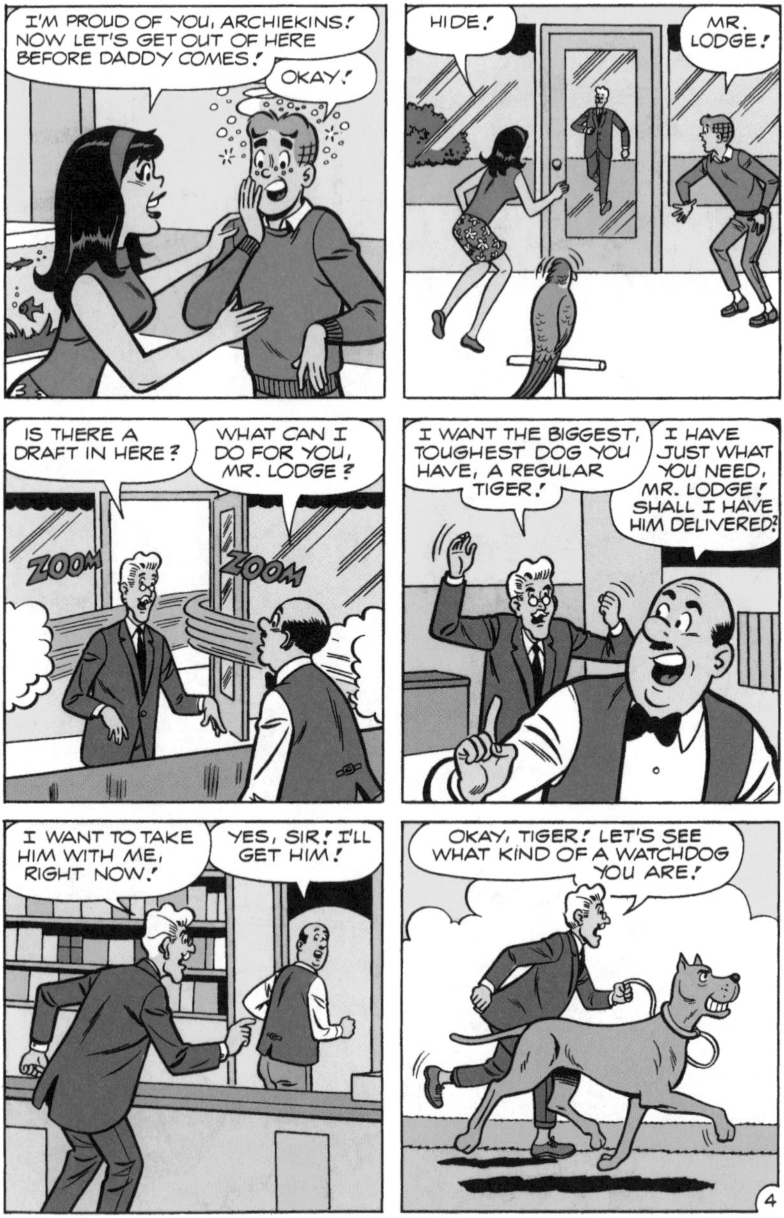
I'M PROUD OF YOU, ARCHIEKINS! NOW LET'S GET OUT OF HERE BEFORE DADDY COMES!
OKAY!
HIDE!
MR. LODGE!
IS THERE A DRAFT IN HERE?
WHAT CAN I DO FOR YOU, MR. LODGE?
ZOOM
ZOOM
I WANT THE BIGGEST, TOUGHEST DOG YOU HAVE, A REGULAR TIGER!
I HAVE JUST WHAT YOU NEED, MR. LODGE! SHALL I HAVE HIM DELIVERED?
I WANT TO TAKE HIM WITH ME, RIGHT NOW!
YES, SIR! I'LL GET HIM!
OKAY, TIGER! LET'S SEE WHAT KIND OF A WATCHDOG YOU ARE!
4

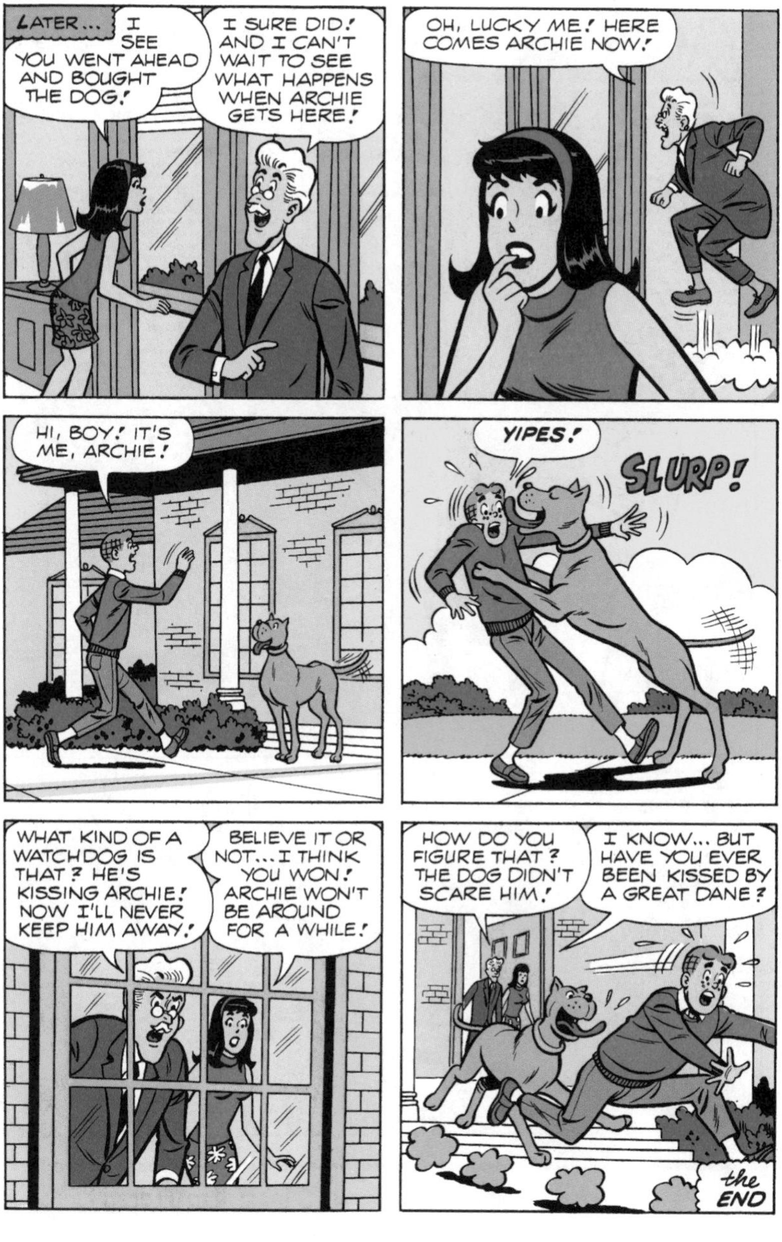
LATER...
I SEE YOU WENT AHEAD AND BOUGHT THE DOG!
I SURE DID! AND I CAN'T WAIT TO SEE WHAT HAPPENS WHEN ARCHIE GETS HERE!
OH, LUCKY ME! HERE COMES ARCHIE NOW!
HI, BOY! IT'S ME, ARCHIE!
YIPES!
SLURP!
WHAT KIND OF A WATCHDOG IS THAT? HE'S KISSING ARCHIE! NOW I'LL NEVER KEEP HIM AWAY!
BELIEVE IT OR NOT... I THINK YOU WON! ARCHIE WON'T BE AROUND FOR A WHILE!
HOW DO YOU FIGURE THAT? THE DOG DIDN'T SCARE HIM!
I KNOW... BUT HAVE YOU EVER BEEN KISSED BY A GREAT DANE?
the END

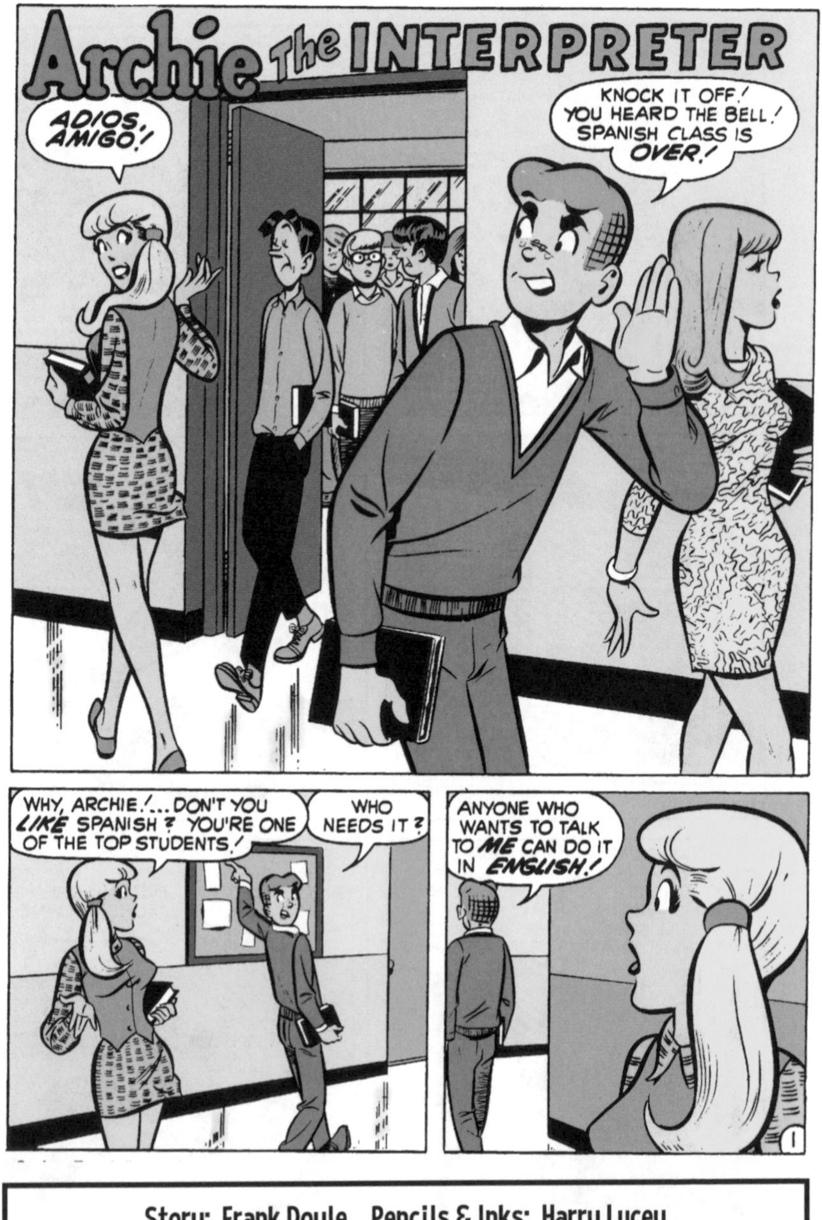
Archie the INTERPRETER
ADIOS, AMIGO!
KNOCK IT OFF! YOU HEARD THE BELL! SPANISH CLASS IS OVER!
WHY, ARCHIE!... DON'T YOU LIKE SPANISH? YOU'RE ONE OF THE TOP STUDENTS!
WHO NEEDS IT?
ANYONE WHO WANTS TO TALK TO ME CAN DO IT IN ENGLISH!
1

Story: Frank Doyle   Pencils & Inks: Harry Lucey
Letters: Bill Yoshida   Colors: Barry Grossman

Originally printed in EVERYTHING'S ARCHIE #2, JULY 1969

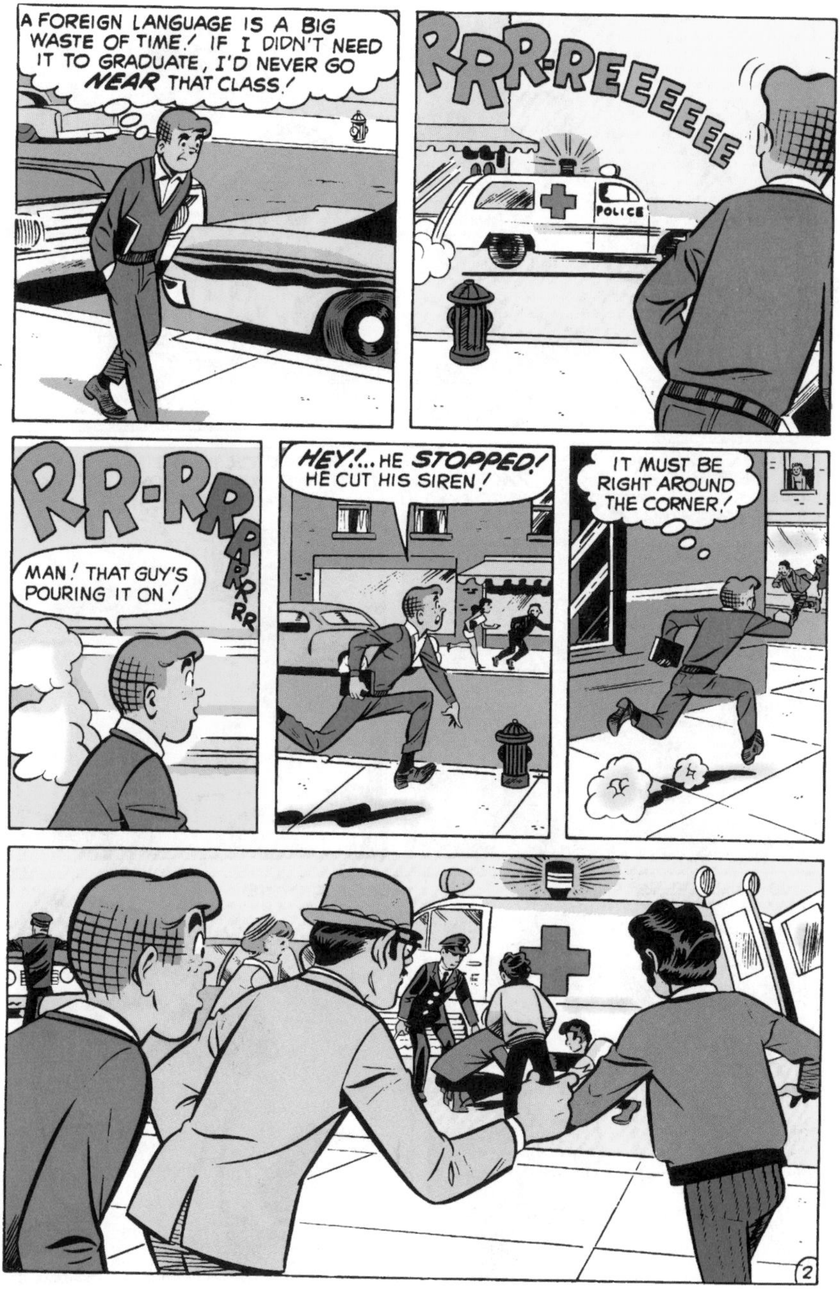
A FOREIGN LANGUAGE IS A BIG WASTE OF TIME! IF I DIDN'T NEED IT TO GRADUATE, I'D NEVER GO NEAR THAT CLASS!
RRR-REEEEEEE
POLICE
RR-RRRRRRR
MAN! THAT GUY'S POURING IT ON!
HEY!... HE STOPPED! HE CUT HIS SIREN!
IT MUST BE RIGHT AROUND THE CORNER!
2

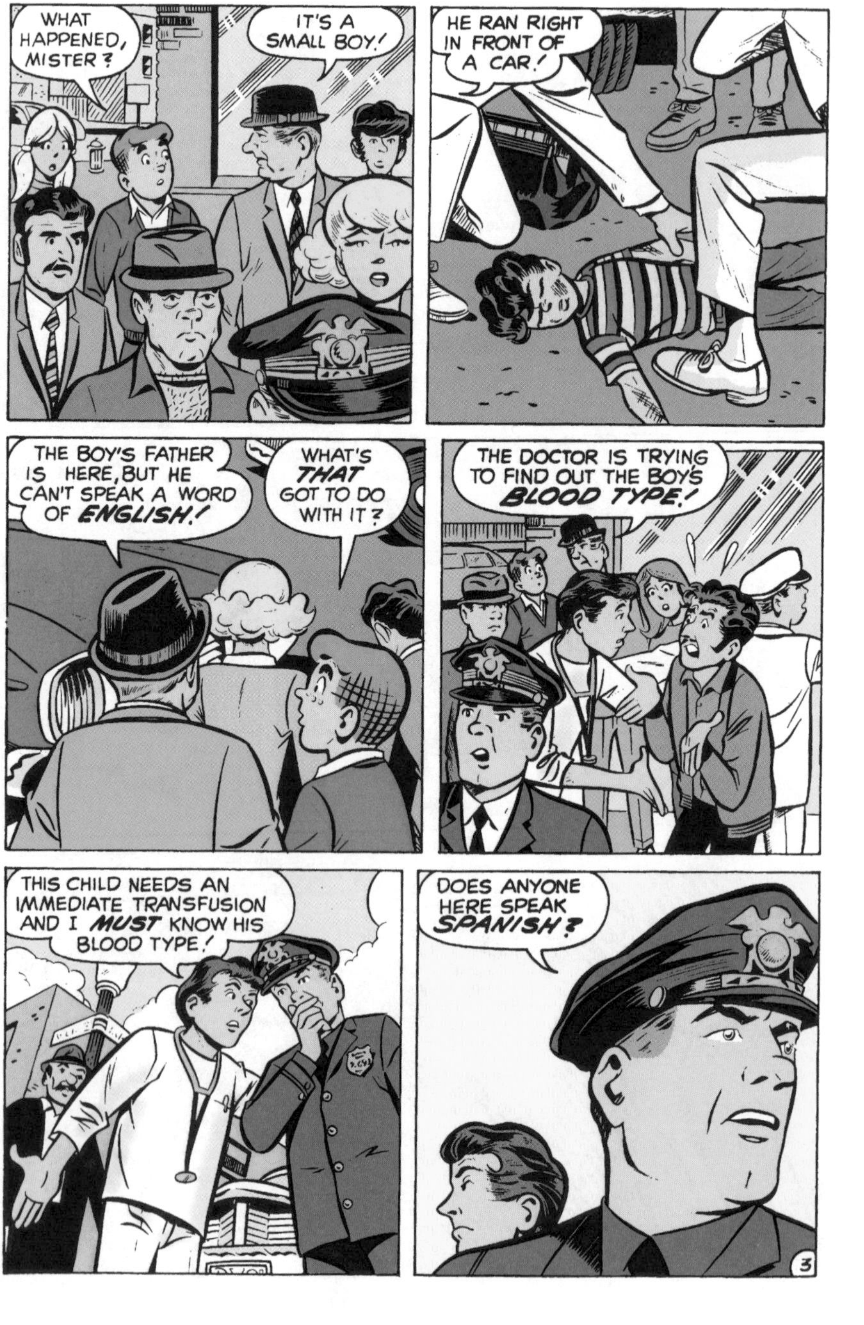
WHAT HAPPENED, MISTER?
IT'S A SMALL BOY!
HE RAN RIGHT IN FRONT OF A CAR!
THE BOY'S FATHER IS HERE, BUT HE CAN'T SPEAK A WORD OF ENGLISH!
WHAT'S THAT GOT TO DO WITH IT?
THE DOCTOR IS TRYING TO FIND OUT THE BOY'S BLOOD TYPE!
THIS CHILD NEEDS AN IMMEDIATE TRANSFUSION AND I MUST KNOW HIS BLOOD TYPE!
DOES ANYONE HERE SPEAK SPANISH?
3

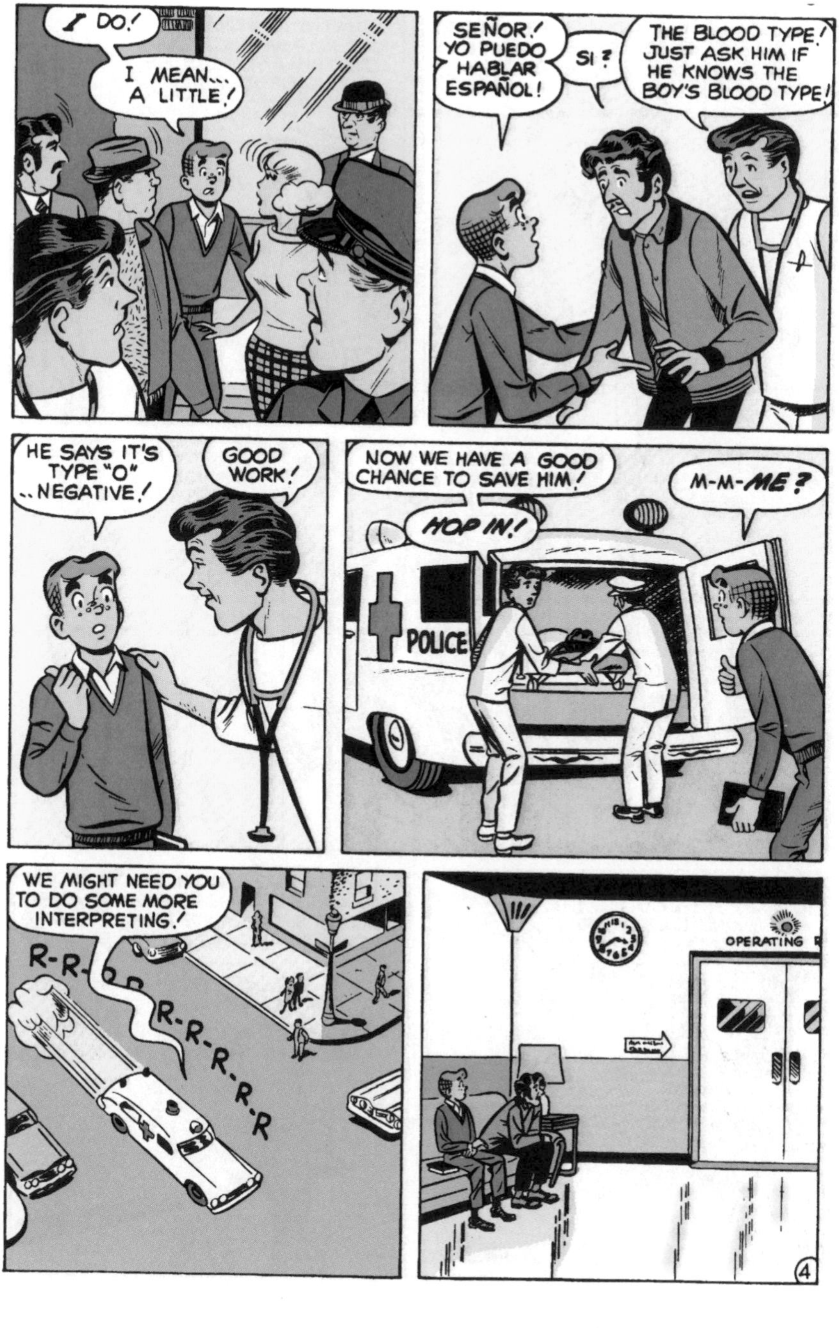
I DO!
I MEAN... A LITTLE!
SEÑOR! YO PUEDO HABLAR ESPAÑOL!
SI?
THE BLOOD TYPE! JUST ASK HIM IF HE KNOWS THE BOY'S BLOOD TYPE!
HE SAYS IT'S TYPE "O" ..NEGATIVE!
GOOD WORK!
NOW WE HAVE A GOOD CHANCE TO SAVE HIM!
HOP IN!
M-M-ME?
POLICE
WE MIGHT NEED YOU TO DO SOME MORE INTERPRETING!
R-R-R-R
R-R-R-R-R-R
OPERATING R
4

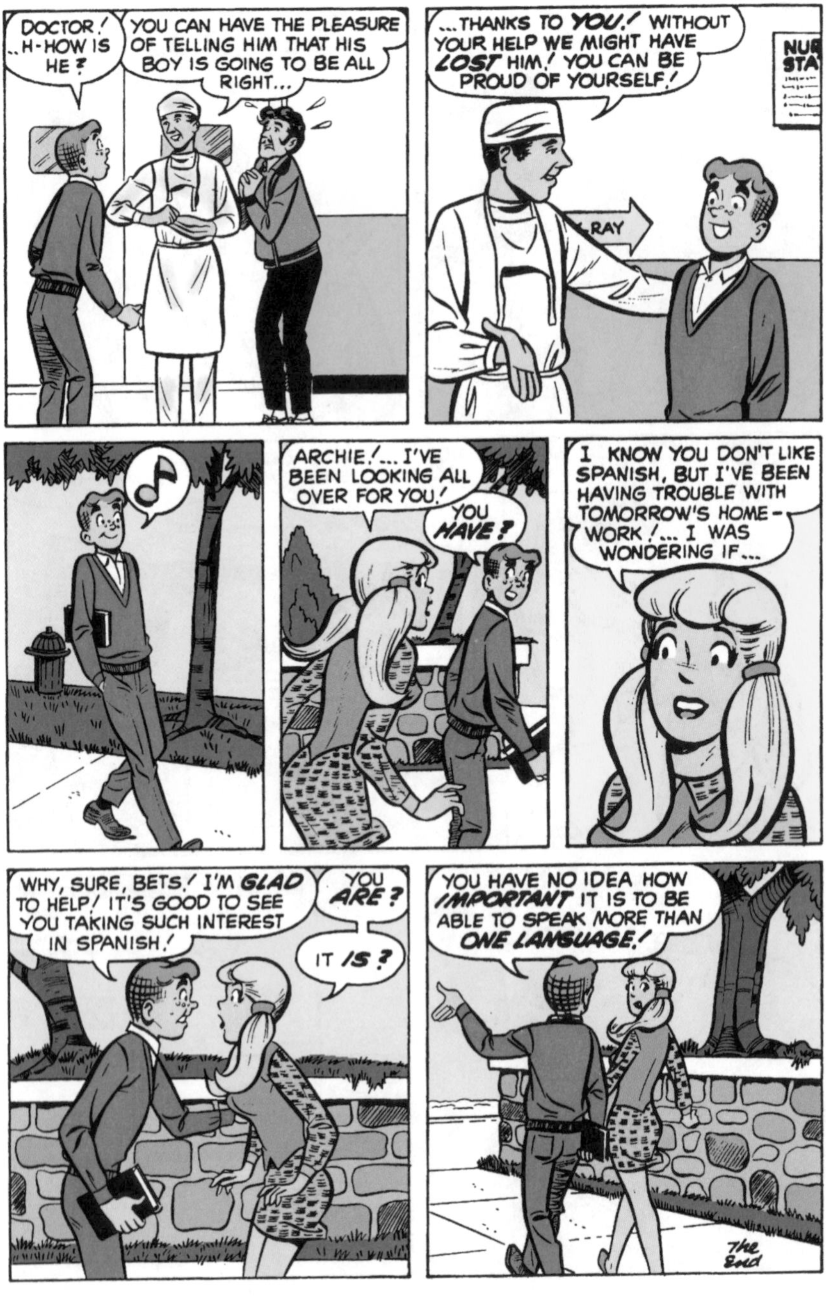
DOCTOR! ..H-HOW IS HE?
YOU CAN HAVE THE PLEASURE OF TELLING HIM THAT HIS BOY IS GOING TO BE ALL RIGHT...
...THANKS TO YOU! WITHOUT YOUR HELP WE MIGHT HAVE LOST HIM! YOU CAN BE PROUD OF YOURSELF!
NUR STA
RAY
ARCHIE!... I'VE BEEN LOOKING ALL OVER FOR YOU!
YOU HAVE?
I KNOW YOU DON'T LIKE SPANISH, BUT I'VE BEEN HAVING TROUBLE WITH TOMORROW'S HOME-WORK!... I WAS WONDERING IF...
WHY, SURE, BETS! I'M GLAD TO HELP! IT'S GOOD TO SEE YOU TAKING SUCH INTEREST IN SPANISH!
YOU ARE?
IT IS?
YOU HAVE NO IDEA HOW IMPORTANT IT IS TO BE ABLE TO SPEAK MORE THAN ONE LANGUAGE!
The End

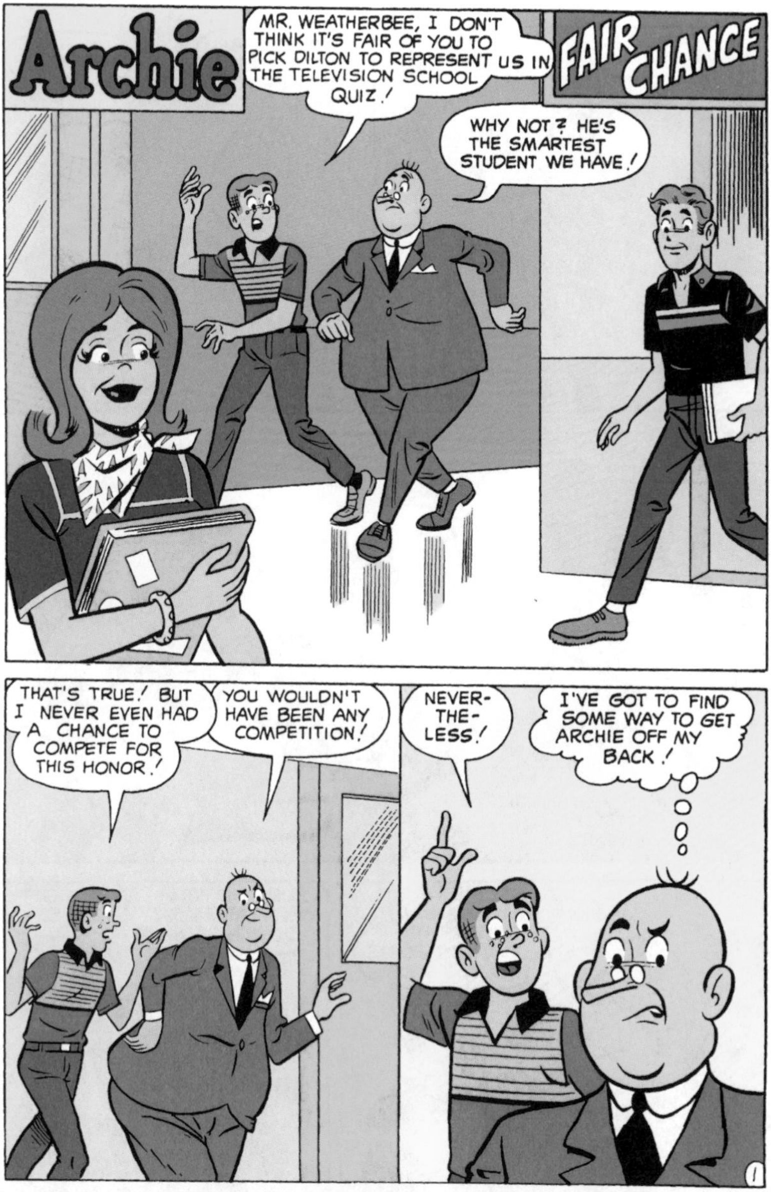
Archie
FAIR CHANCE
MR. WEATHERBEE, I DON'T THINK IT'S FAIR OF YOU TO PICK DILTON TO REPRESENT US IN THE TELEVISION SCHOOL QUIZ!
WHY NOT? HE'S THE SMARTEST STUDENT WE HAVE!
THAT'S TRUE! BUT I NEVER EVEN HAD A CHANCE TO COMPETE FOR THIS HONOR!
YOU WOULDN'T HAVE BEEN ANY COMPETITION!
NEVER-THE-LESS!
I'VE GOT TO FIND SOME WAY TO GET ARCHIE OFF MY BACK!
1

Story: Frank Doyle Pencils & Inks: Bob Bolling
Letters: Bill Yoshida Colors: Barry Grossman

Originally printed in EVERYTHING'S ARCHIE #2, JULY 1969

26

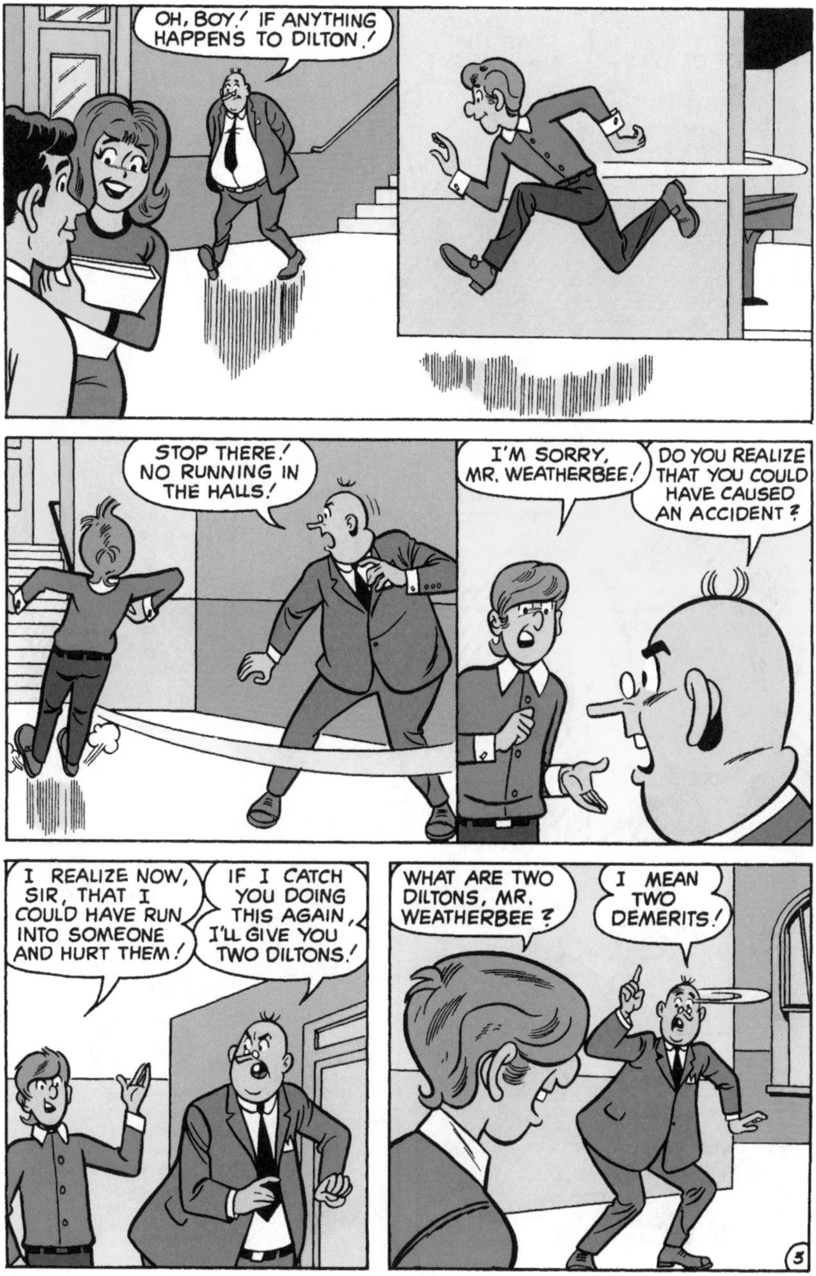
OH, BOY! IF ANYTHING HAPPENS TO DILTON!
STOP THERE! NO RUNNING IN THE HALLS!
I'M SORRY, MR. WEATHERBEE!
DO YOU REALIZE THAT YOU COULD HAVE CAUSED AN ACCIDENT?
I REALIZE NOW, SIR, THAT I COULD HAVE RUN INTO SOMEONE AND HURT THEM!
IF I CATCH YOU DOING THIS AGAIN, I'LL GIVE YOU TWO DILTONS!
WHAT ARE TWO DILTONS, MR. WEATHERBEE?
I MEAN TWO DEMERITS!
5

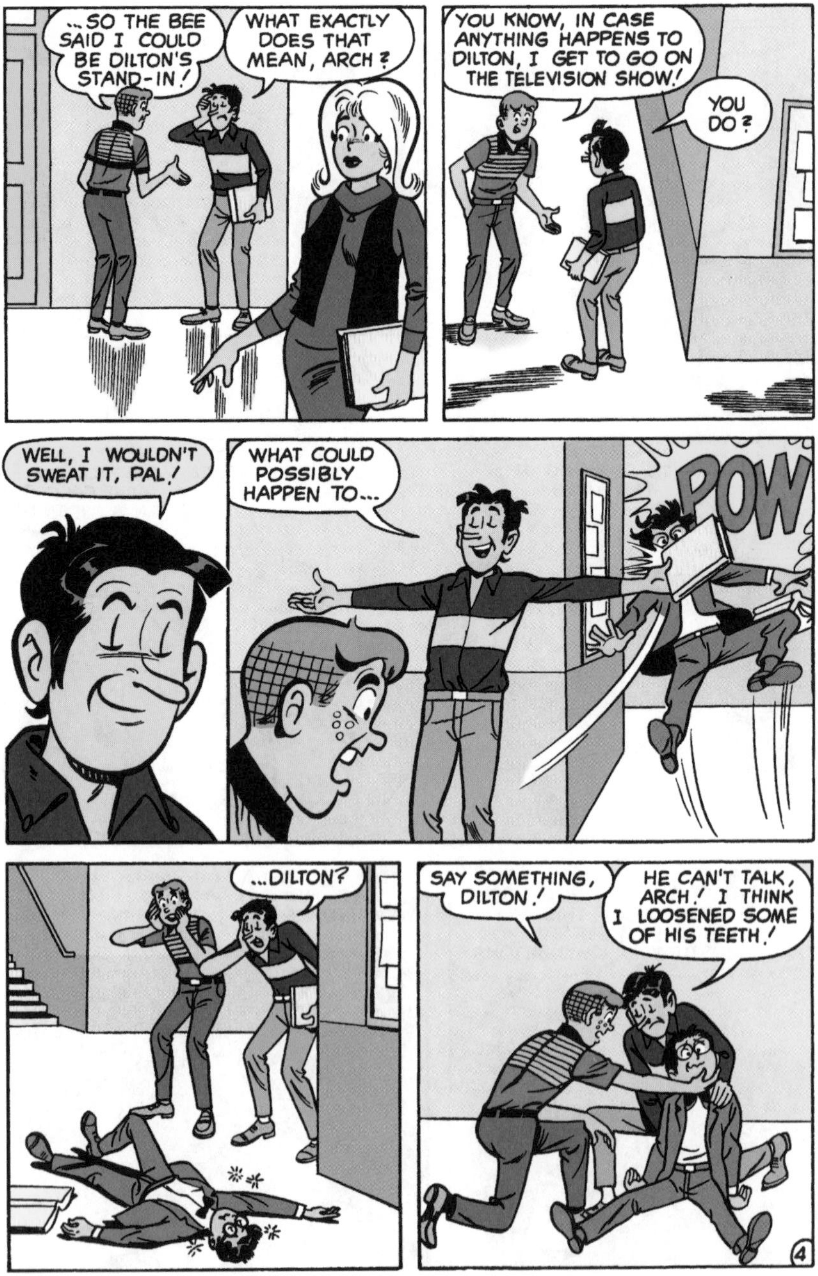
...SO THE BEE SAID I COULD BE DILTON'S STAND-IN!
WHAT EXACTLY DOES THAT MEAN, ARCH?
YOU KNOW, IN CASE ANYTHING HAPPENS TO DILTON, I GET TO GO ON THE TELEVISION SHOW!
YOU DO?
WELL, I WOULDN'T SWEAT IT, PAL!
WHAT COULD POSSIBLY HAPPEN TO...
POW
...DILTON?
SAY SOMETHING, DILTON!
HE CAN'T TALK, ARCH! I THINK I LOOSENED SOME OF HIS TEETH!
4

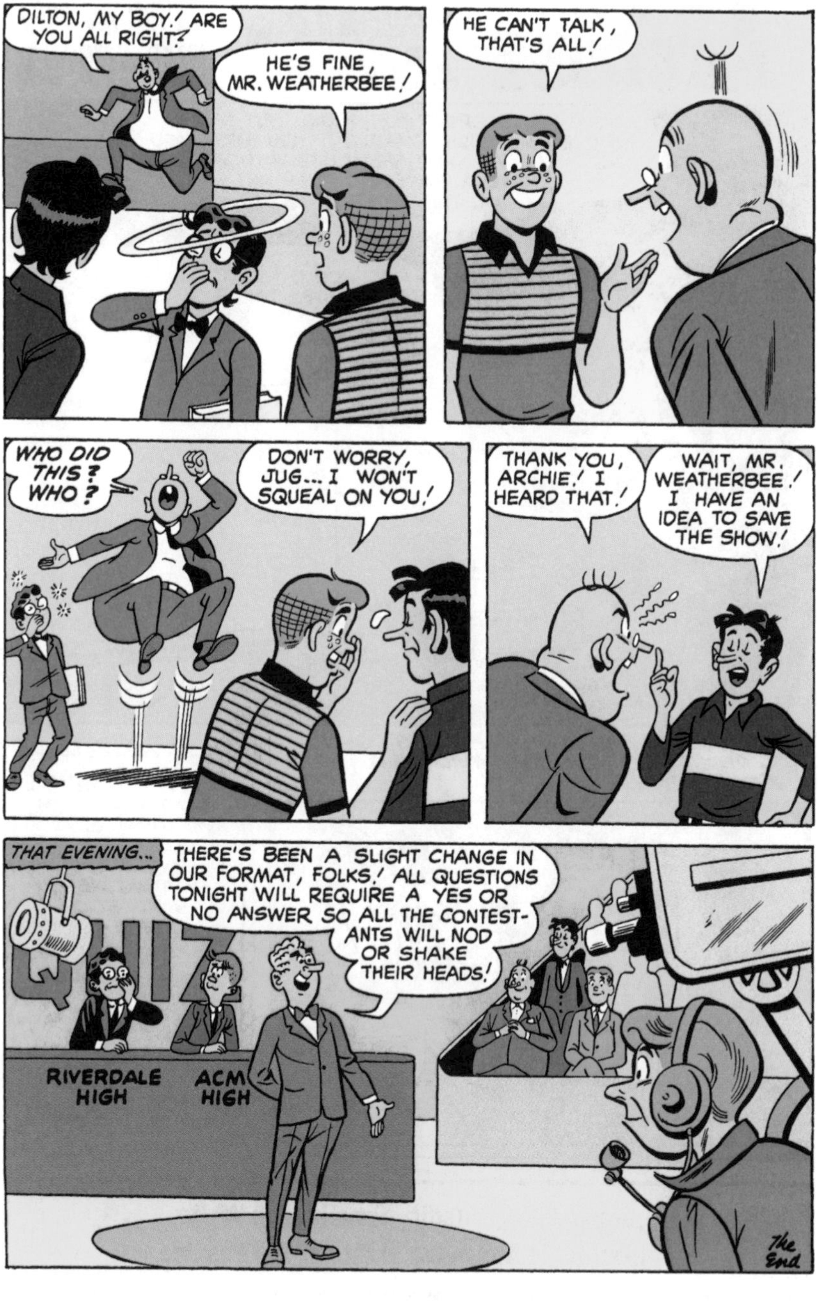
DILTON, MY BOY! ARE YOU ALL RIGHT?
HE'S FINE, MR. WEATHERBEE!
HE CAN'T TALK, THAT'S ALL!
WHO DID THIS? WHO?
DON'T WORRY, JUG... I WON'T SQUEAL ON YOU!
THANK YOU, ARCHIE! I HEARD THAT!
WAIT, MR. WEATHERBEE! I HAVE AN IDEA TO SAVE THE SHOW!
THAT EVENING...
THERE'S BEEN A SLIGHT CHANGE IN OUR FORMAT, FOLKS! ALL QUESTIONS TONIGHT WILL REQUIRE A YES OR NO ANSWER SO ALL THE CONTESTANTS WILL NOD OR SHAKE THEIR HEADS!
QUIZ
RIVERDALE HIGH
ACM HIGH
The End

THE Archies SAFETY SLIDES WITH "TIPS ON BOATING"

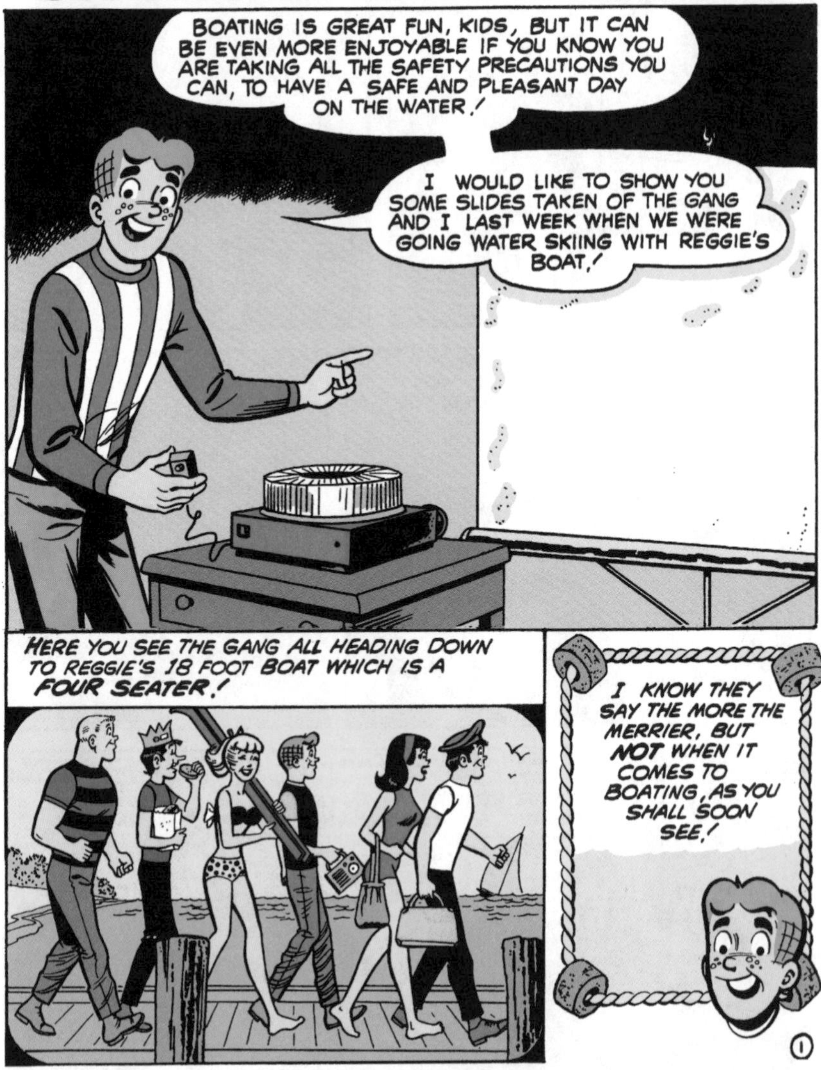
BOATING IS GREAT FUN, KIDS, BUT IT CAN BE EVEN MORE ENJOYABLE IF YOU KNOW YOU ARE TAKING ALL THE SAFETY PRECAUTIONS YOU CAN, TO HAVE A SAFE AND PLEASANT DAY ON THE WATER!
I WOULD LIKE TO SHOW YOU SOME SLIDES TAKEN OF THE GANG AND I LAST WEEK WHEN WE WERE GOING WATER SKIING WITH REGGIE'S BOAT!
HERE YOU SEE THE GANG ALL HEADING DOWN TO REGGIE'S 18 FOOT BOAT WHICH IS A FOUR SEATER!
I KNOW THEY SAY THE MORE THE MERRIER, BUT NOT WHEN IT COMES TO BOATING, AS YOU SHALL SOON SEE!
1

Story: George Gladir Pencils: Bob White
Inks: Mario Acquaviva Letters: Bill Yoshida

Originally printed in EVERYTHING'S ARCHIE #4, SEPTEMBER 1969

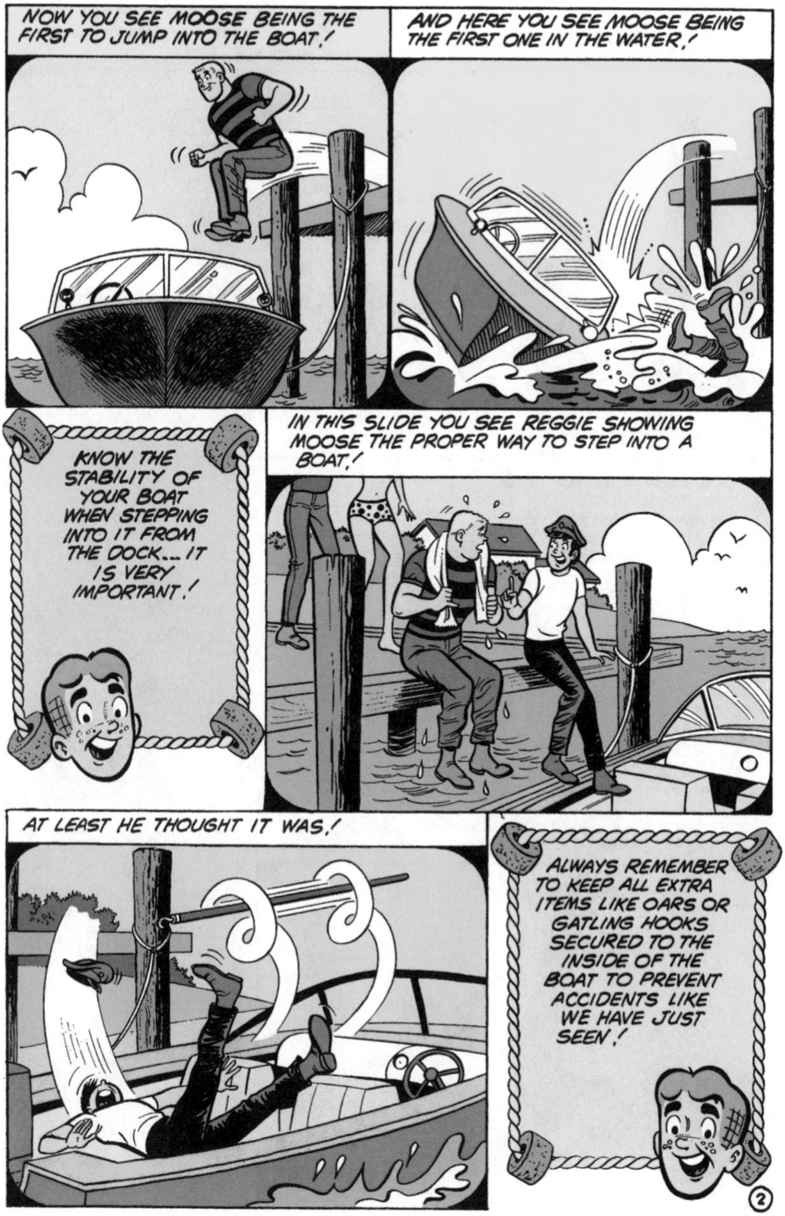
NOW YOU SEE MOOSE BEING THE FIRST TO JUMP INTO THE BOAT!
AND HERE YOU SEE MOOSE BEING THE FIRST ONE IN THE WATER!
KNOW THE STABILITY OF YOUR BOAT WHEN STEPPING INTO IT FROM THE DOCK... IT IS VERY IMPORTANT!
IN THIS SLIDE YOU SEE REGGIE SHOWING MOOSE THE PROPER WAY TO STEP INTO A BOAT!
AT LEAST HE THOUGHT IT WAS!
ALWAYS REMEMBER TO KEEP ALL EXTRA ITEMS LIKE OARS OR GATLING HOOKS SECURED TO THE INSIDE OF THE BOAT TO PREVENT ACCIDENTS LIKE WE HAVE JUST SEEN!
2

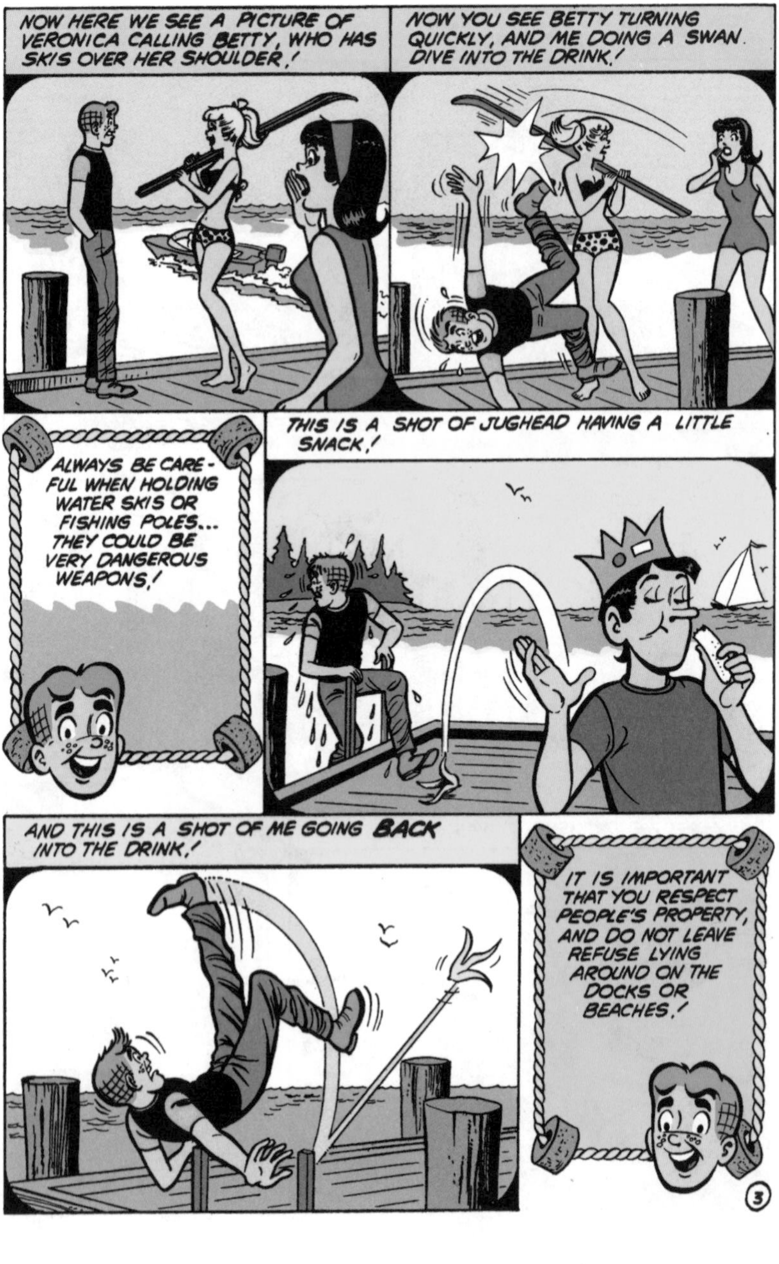
NOW HERE WE SEE A PICTURE OF VERONICA CALLING BETTY, WHO HAS SKIS OVER HER SHOULDER!
NOW YOU SEE BETTY TURNING QUICKLY, AND ME DOING A SWAN DIVE INTO THE DRINK!
ALWAYS BE CAREFUL WHEN HOLDING WATER SKIS OR FISHING POLES... THEY COULD BE VERY DANGEROUS WEAPONS!
THIS IS A SHOT OF JUGHEAD HAVING A LITTLE SNACK!
AND THIS IS A SHOT OF ME GOING BACK INTO THE DRINK!
IT IS IMPORTANT THAT YOU RESPECT PEOPLE'S PROPERTY, AND DO NOT LEAVE REFUSE LYING AROUND ON THE DOCKS OR BEACHES!
3

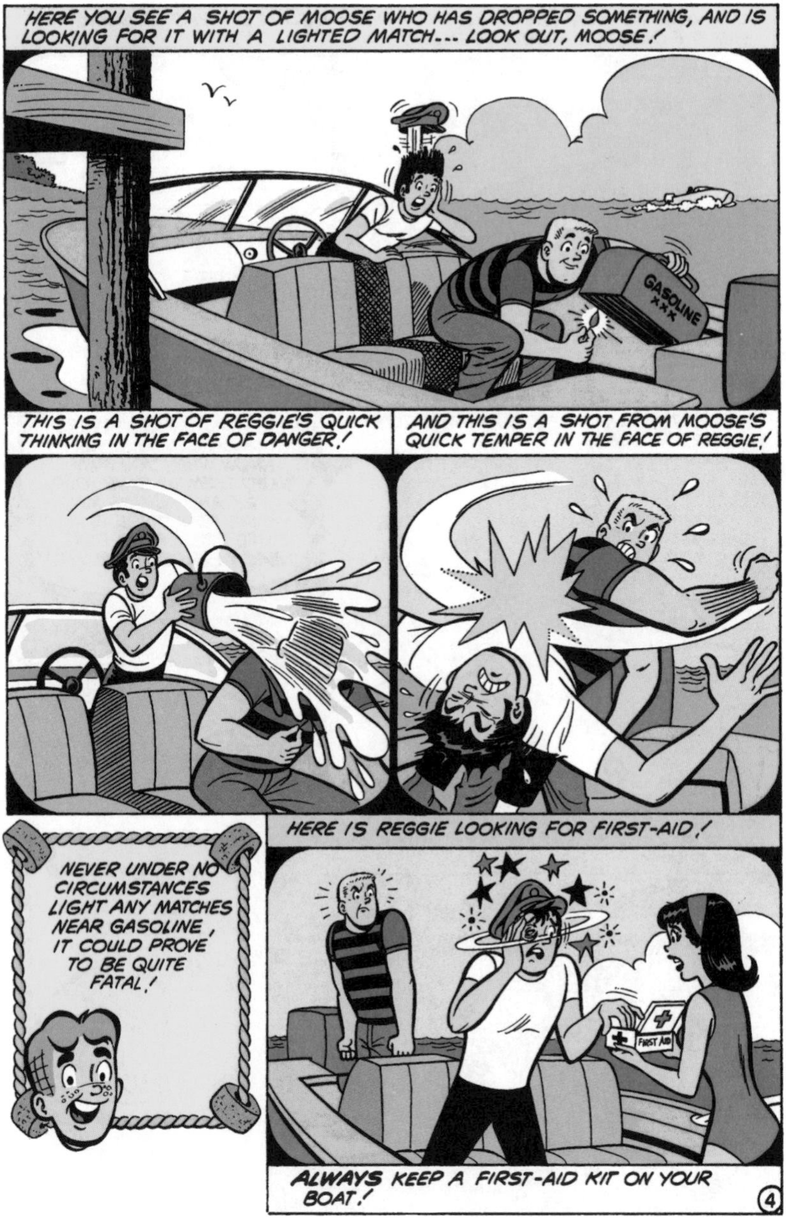
HERE YOU SEE A SHOT OF MOOSE WHO HAS DROPPED SOMETHING, AND IS LOOKING FOR IT WITH A LIGHTED MATCH... LOOK OUT, MOOSE!
GASOLINE XXX
THIS IS A SHOT OF REGGIE'S QUICK THINKING IN THE FACE OF DANGER!
AND THIS IS A SHOT FROM MOOSE'S QUICK TEMPER IN THE FACE OF REGGIE!
HERE IS REGGIE LOOKING FOR FIRST-AID!
NEVER UNDER NO CIRCUMSTANCES LIGHT ANY MATCHES NEAR GASOLINE, IT COULD PROVE TO BE QUITE FATAL!
FIRST AID
ALWAYS KEEP A FIRST-AID KIT ON YOUR BOAT!
4

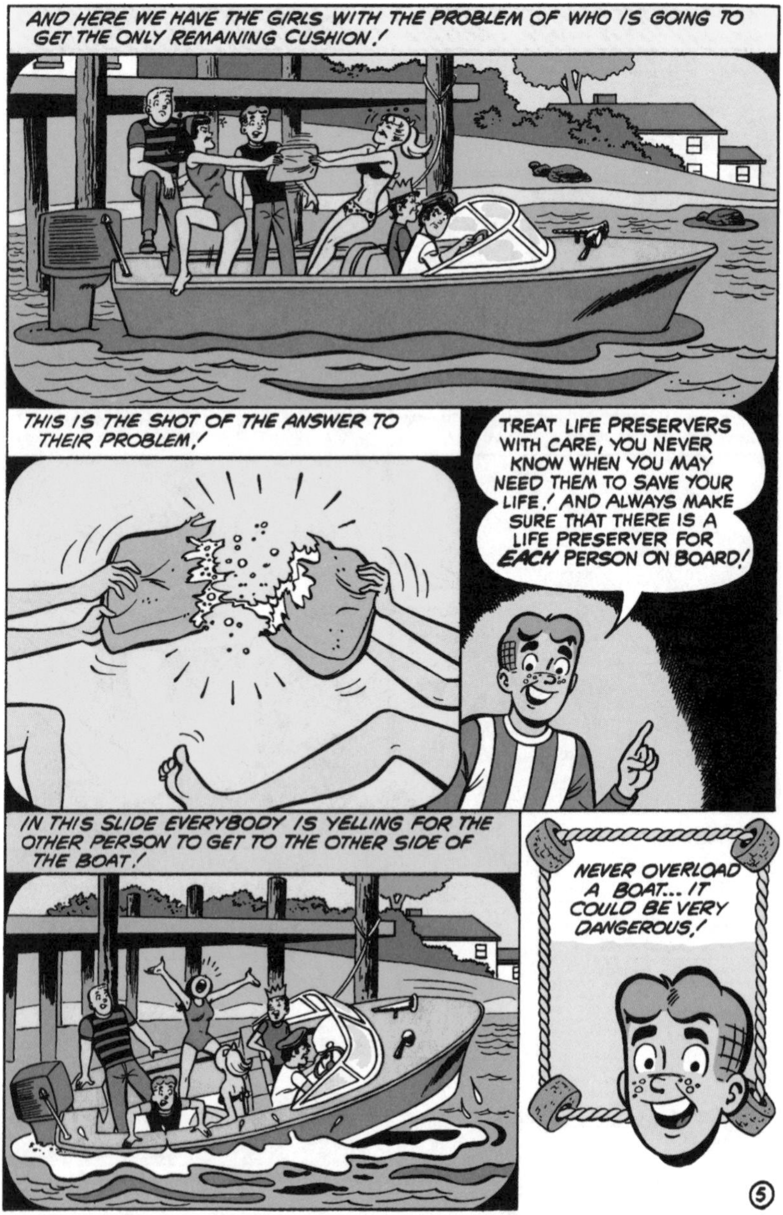
AND HERE WE HAVE THE GIRLS WITH THE PROBLEM OF WHO IS GOING TO GET THE ONLY REMAINING CUSHION!
THIS IS THE SHOT OF THE ANSWER TO THEIR PROBLEM!
TREAT LIFE PRESERVERS WITH CARE, YOU NEVER KNOW WHEN YOU MAY NEED THEM TO SAVE YOUR LIFE! AND ALWAYS MAKE SURE THAT THERE IS A LIFE PRESERVER FOR EACH PERSON ON BOARD!
IN THIS SLIDE EVERYBODY IS YELLING FOR THE OTHER PERSON TO GET TO THE OTHER SIDE OF THE BOAT!
NEVER OVERLOAD A BOAT... IT COULD BE VERY DANGEROUS!
5

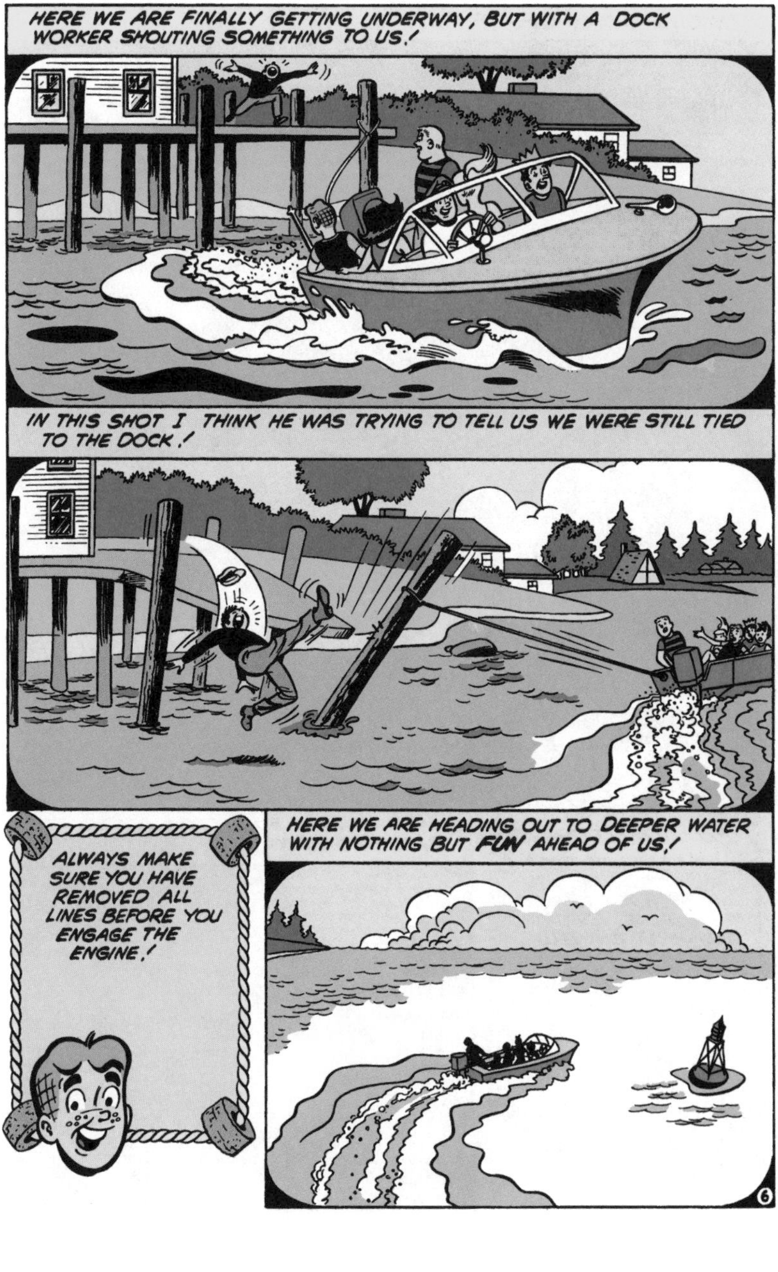
HERE WE ARE FINALLY GETTING UNDERWAY, BUT WITH A DOCK WORKER SHOUTING SOMETHING TO US.!
IN THIS SHOT I THINK HE WAS TRYING TO TELL US WE WERE STILL TIED TO THE DOCK.!
ALWAYS MAKE SURE YOU HAVE REMOVED ALL LINES BEFORE YOU ENGAGE THE ENGINE.!
HERE WE ARE HEADING OUT TO DEEPER WATER WITH NOTHING BUT FUN AHEAD OF US.!
6

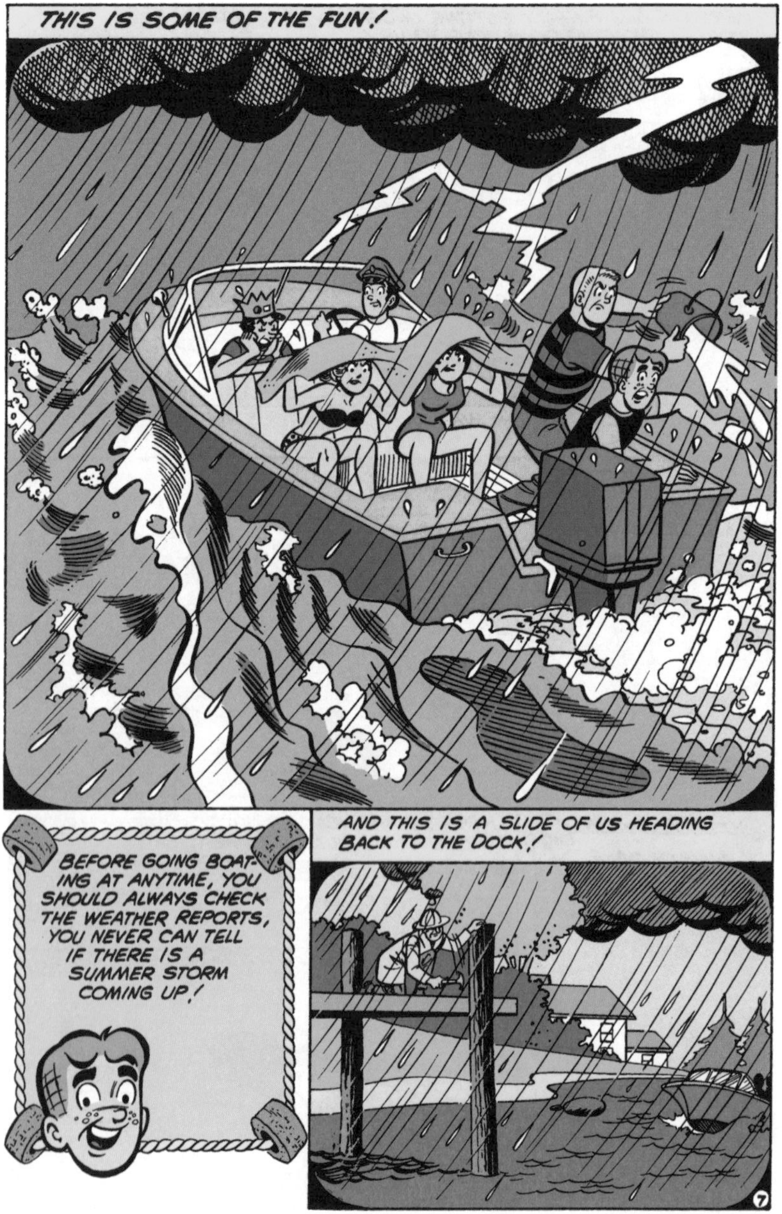
THIS IS SOME OF THE FUN!
BEFORE GOING BOATING AT ANYTIME, YOU SHOULD ALWAYS CHECK THE WEATHER REPORTS, YOU NEVER CAN TELL IF THERE IS A SUMMER STORM COMING UP!
AND THIS IS A SLIDE OF US HEADING BACK TO THE DOCK!

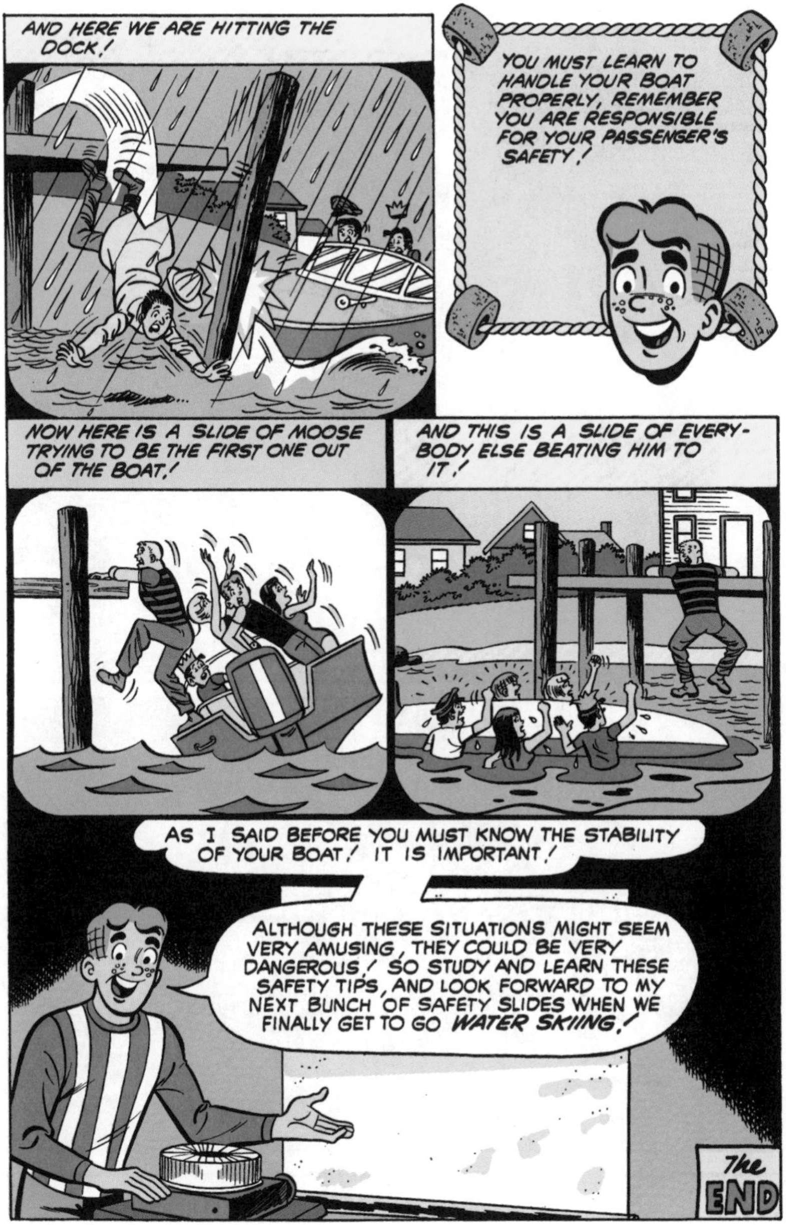
AND HERE WE ARE HITTING THE DOCK!
YOU MUST LEARN TO HANDLE YOUR BOAT PROPERLY, REMEMBER YOU ARE RESPONSIBLE FOR YOUR PASSENGER'S SAFETY!
NOW HERE IS A SLIDE OF MOOSE TRYING TO BE THE FIRST ONE OUT OF THE BOAT!
AND THIS IS A SLIDE OF EVERY-BODY ELSE BEATING HIM TO IT!
AS I SAID BEFORE YOU MUST KNOW THE STABILITY OF YOUR BOAT! IT IS IMPORTANT!
ALTHOUGH THESE SITUATIONS MIGHT SEEM VERY AMUSING, THEY COULD BE VERY DANGEROUS! SO STUDY AND LEARN THESE SAFETY TIPS, AND LOOK FORWARD TO MY NEXT BUNCH OF SAFETY SLIDES WHEN WE FINALLY GET TO GO WATER SKIING!
The END

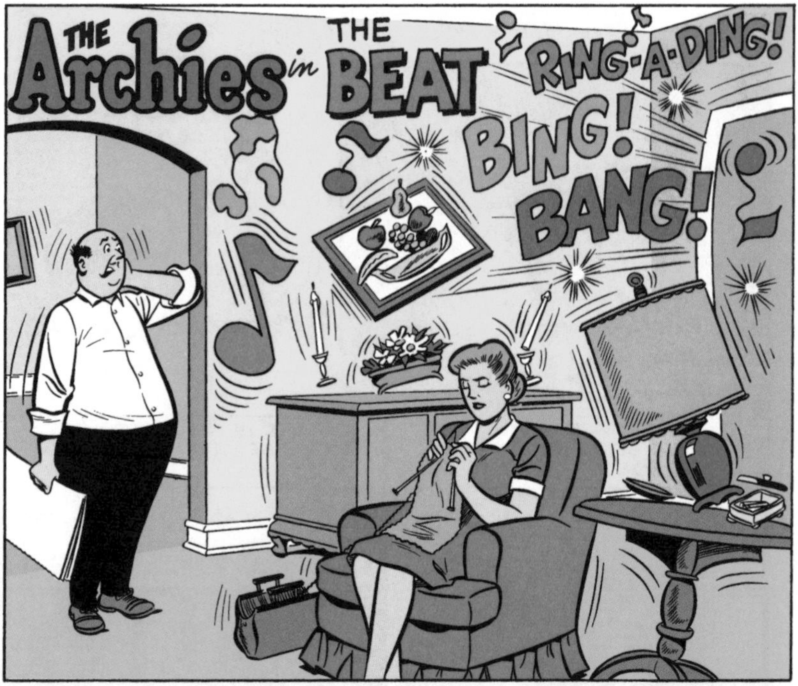
THE Archies in THE BEAT
RING-A-DING!
BING!
BANG!

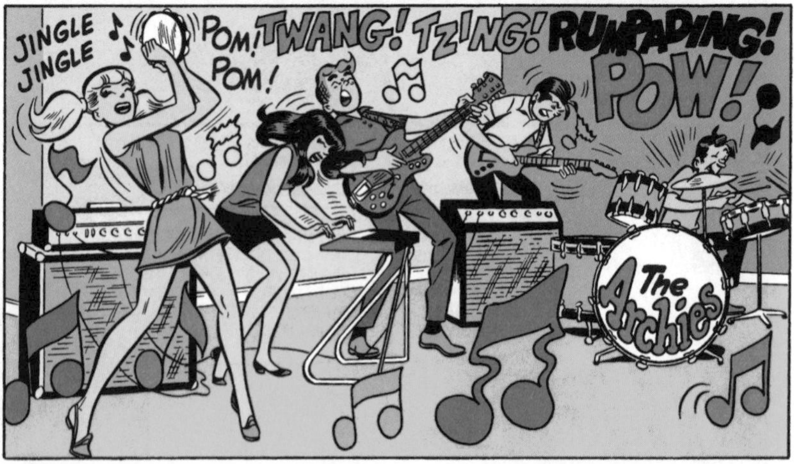
JINGLE JINGLE
POM! POM!
TWANG!
TZING!
RUMPADING!
POW!
The Archies

Story: Frank Doyle Pencils: Harry Lucey
Inks: Mario Acquaviva Letters: Bill Yoshida

Originally printed in EVERYTHING'S ARCHIE #4, SEPTEMBER 1969

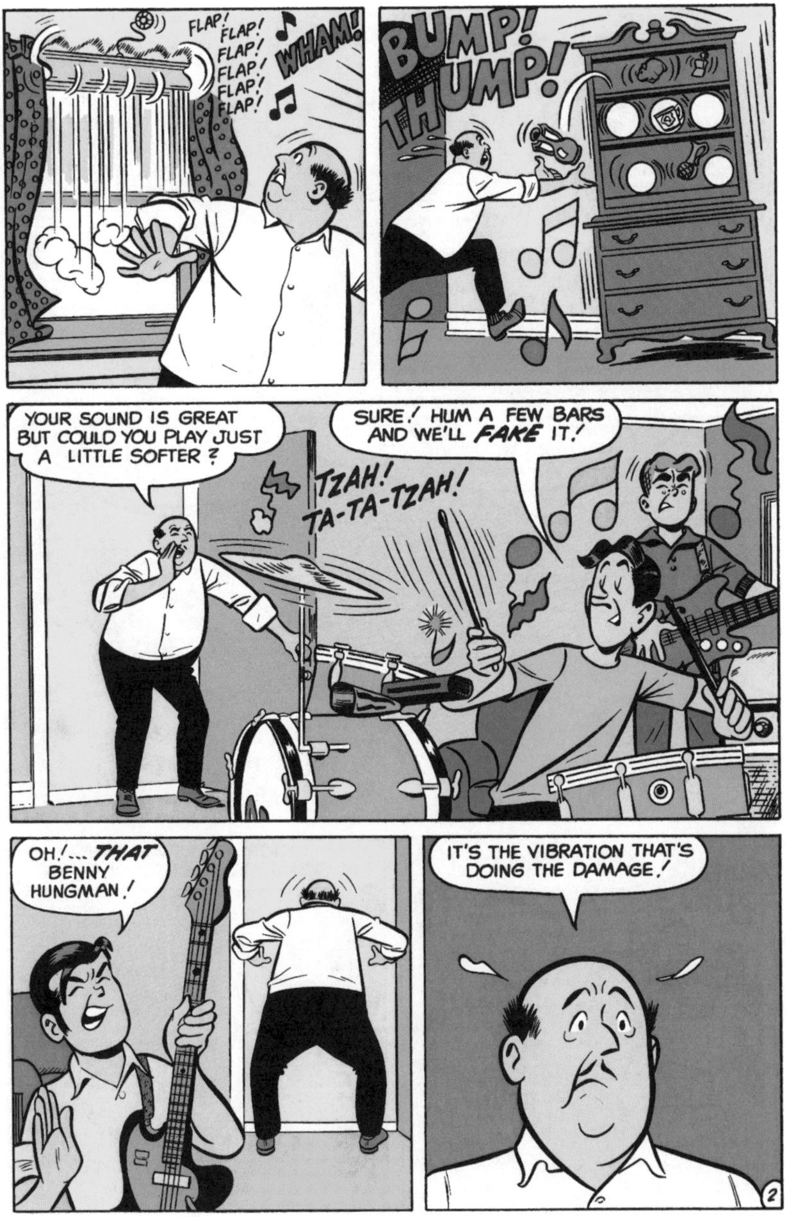
FLAP! FLAP! FLAP! FLAP! FLAP! FLAP!
WHAM!
BUMP! THUMP!
YOUR SOUND IS GREAT BUT COULD YOU PLAY JUST A LITTLE SOFTER ?
SURE! HUM A FEW BARS AND WE'LL FAKE IT!
TZAH! TA-TA-TZAH!
OH!... THAT BENNY HUNGMAN!
IT'S THE VIBRATION THAT'S DOING THE DAMAGE!
2

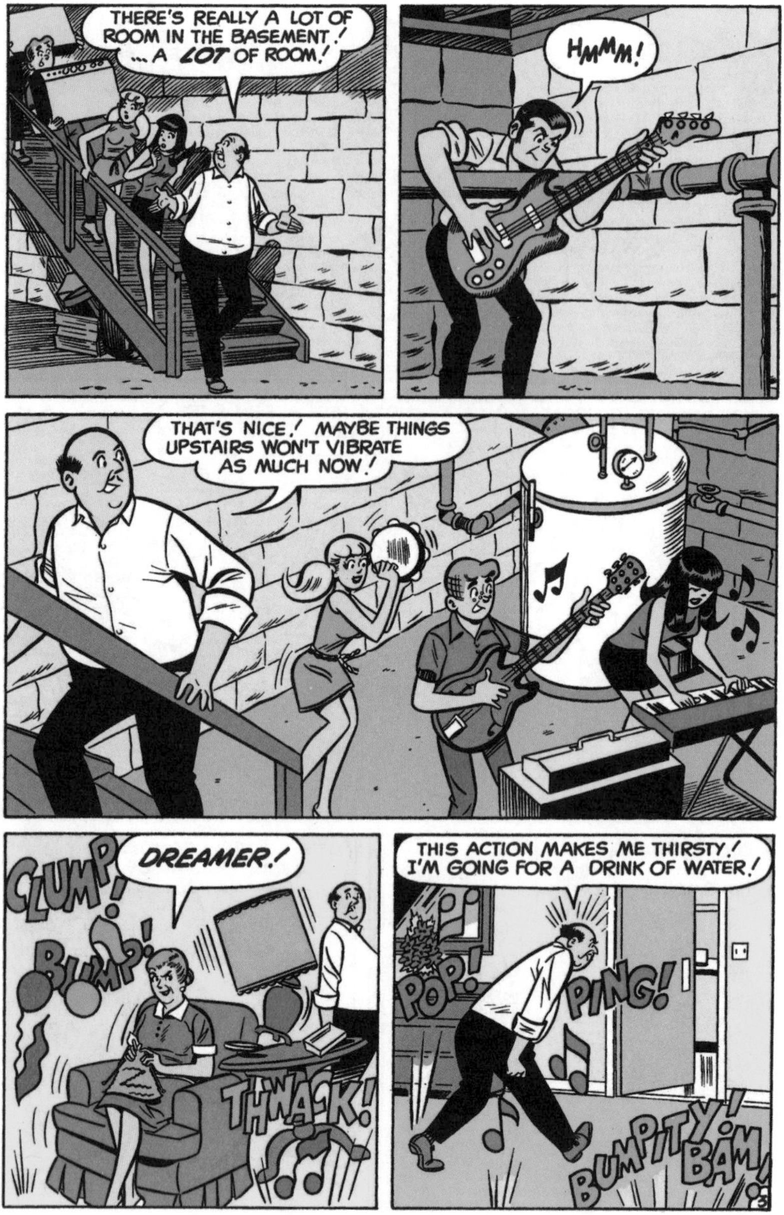
THERE'S REALLY A LOT OF ROOM IN THE BASEMENT! ...A LOT OF ROOM!
HMMM!
THAT'S NICE! MAYBE THINGS UPSTAIRS WON'T VIBRATE AS MUCH NOW!
CLUMP!
DREAMER!
BUMP!
THWACK!
THIS ACTION MAKES ME THIRSTY! I'M GOING FOR A DRINK OF WATER!
POP!
PING!
BUMPITY!
BAM!

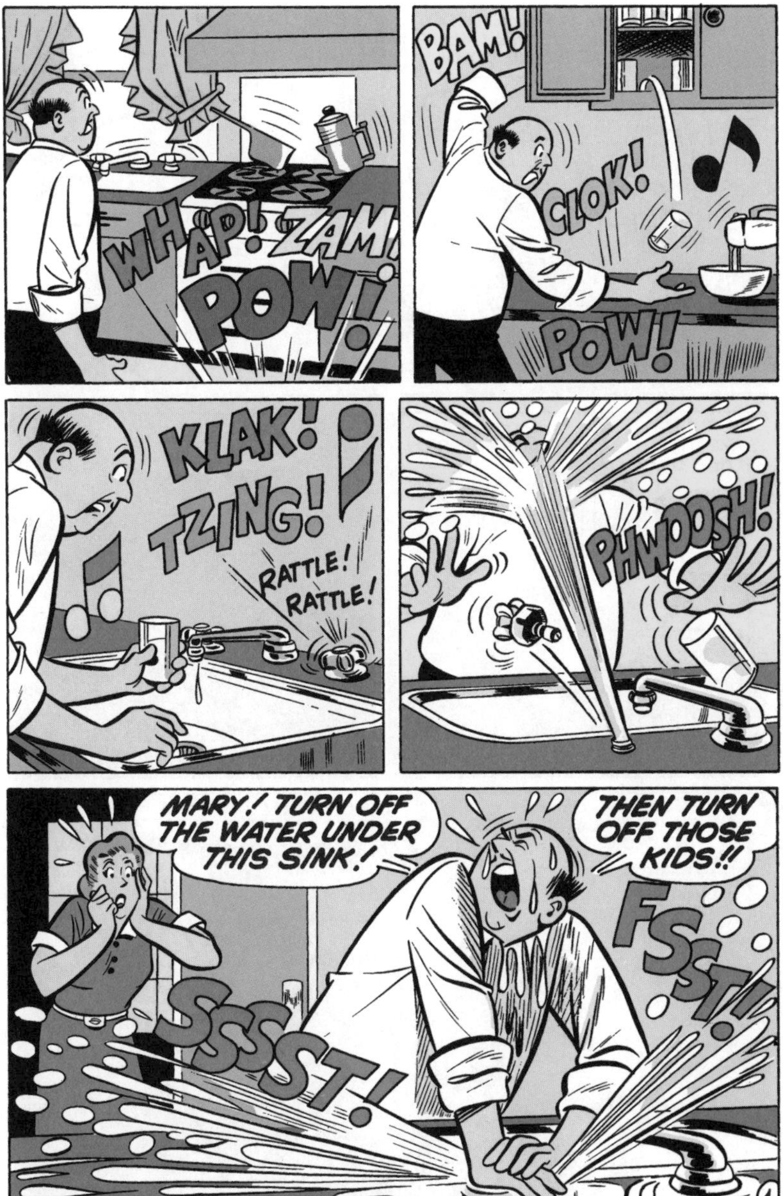
WHAP! ZAM!
POW!!
BAM!
CLOK!
POW!
KLAK!
TZING!
RATTLE! RATTLE!
PHWOOSH!
MARY! TURN OFF THE WATER UNDER THIS SINK!
THEN TURN OFF THOSE KIDS!!
FSST!!
SSSST!
4

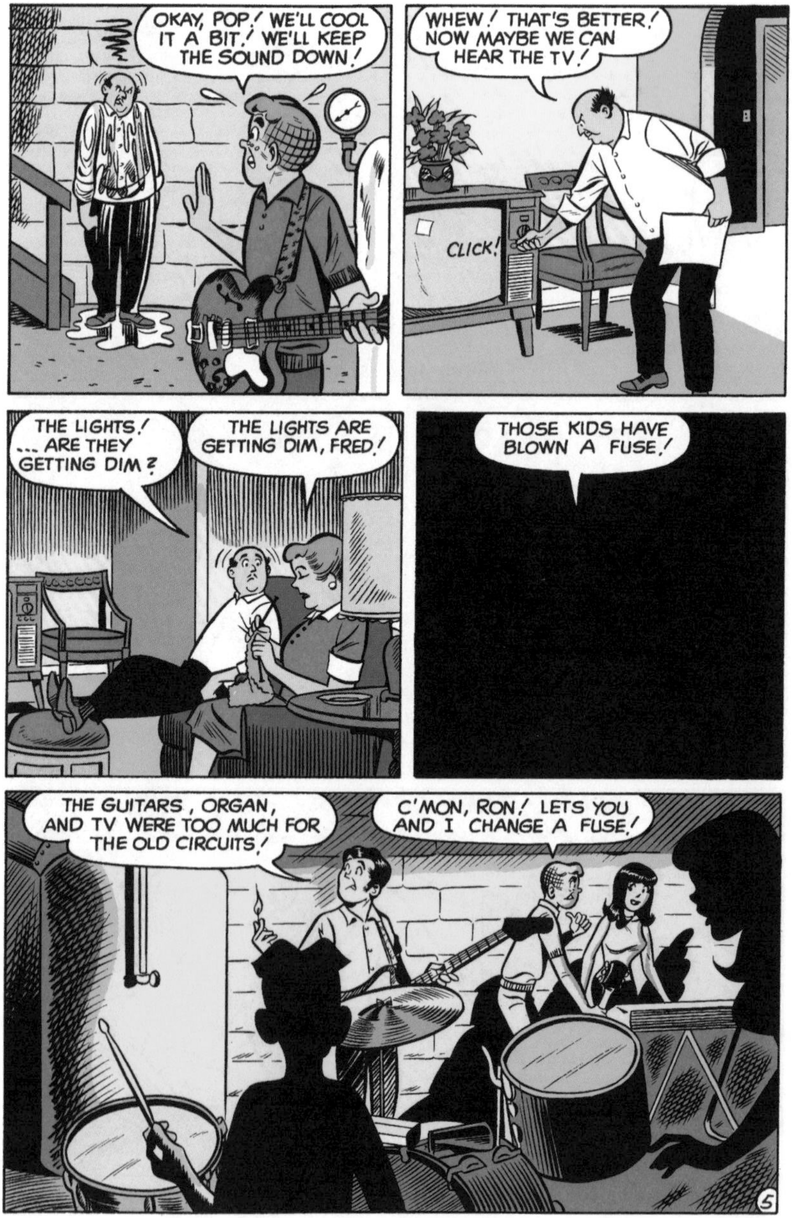
OKAY, POP! WE'LL COOL IT A BIT! WE'LL KEEP THE SOUND DOWN!
WHEW! THAT'S BETTER! NOW MAYBE WE CAN HEAR THE TV!
CLICK!
THE LIGHTS! ... ARE THEY GETTING DIM?
THE LIGHTS ARE GETTING DIM, FRED!
THOSE KIDS HAVE BLOWN A FUSE!
THE GUITARS, ORGAN, AND TV WERE TOO MUCH FOR THE OLD CIRCUITS!
C'MON, RON! LETS YOU AND I CHANGE A FUSE!
5

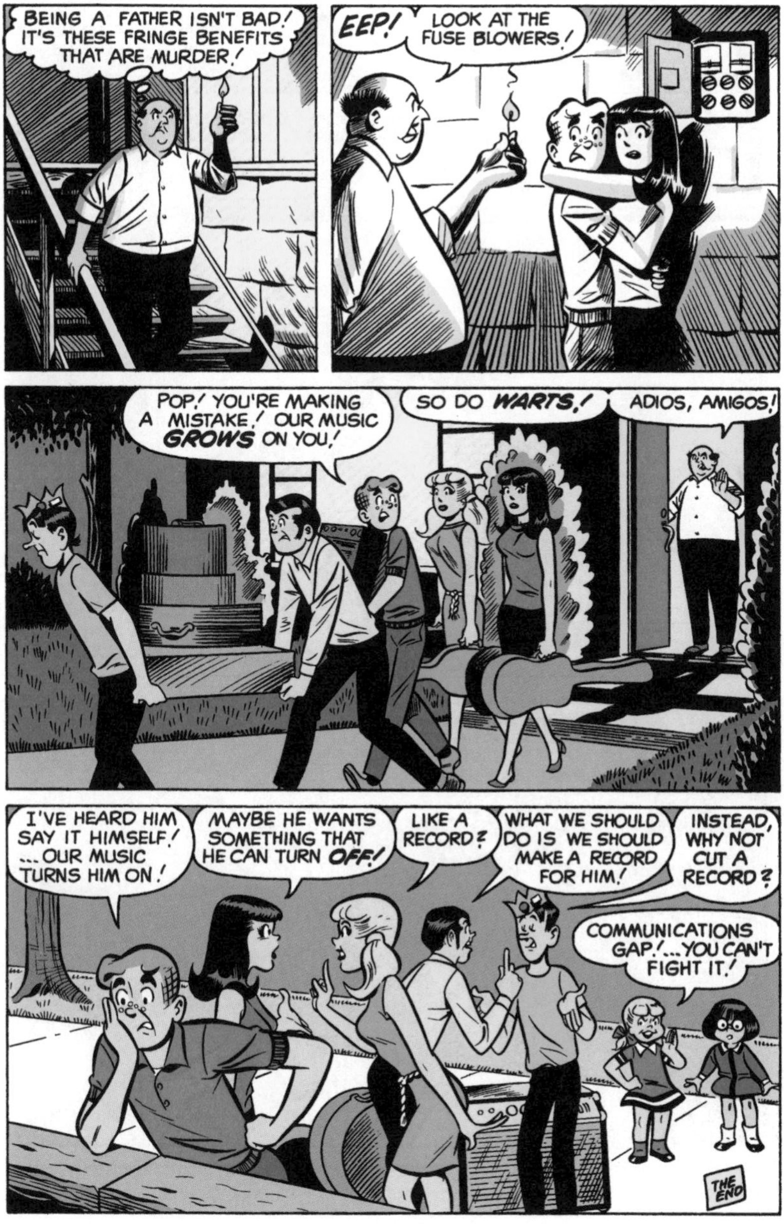
BEING A FATHER ISN'T BAD! IT'S THESE FRINGE BENEFITS THAT ARE MURDER!
EEP!
LOOK AT THE FUSE BLOWERS!
POP! YOU'RE MAKING A MISTAKE! OUR MUSIC GROWS ON YOU!
SO DO WARTS!
ADIOS, AMIGOS!
I'VE HEARD HIM SAY IT HIMSELF! ...OUR MUSIC TURNS HIM ON!
MAYBE HE WANTS SOMETHING THAT HE CAN TURN OFF!
LIKE A RECORD?
WHAT WE SHOULD DO IS WE SHOULD MAKE A RECORD FOR HIM!
INSTEAD, WHY NOT CUT A RECORD?
COMMUNICATIONS GAP!...YOU CAN'T FIGHT IT!
THE END

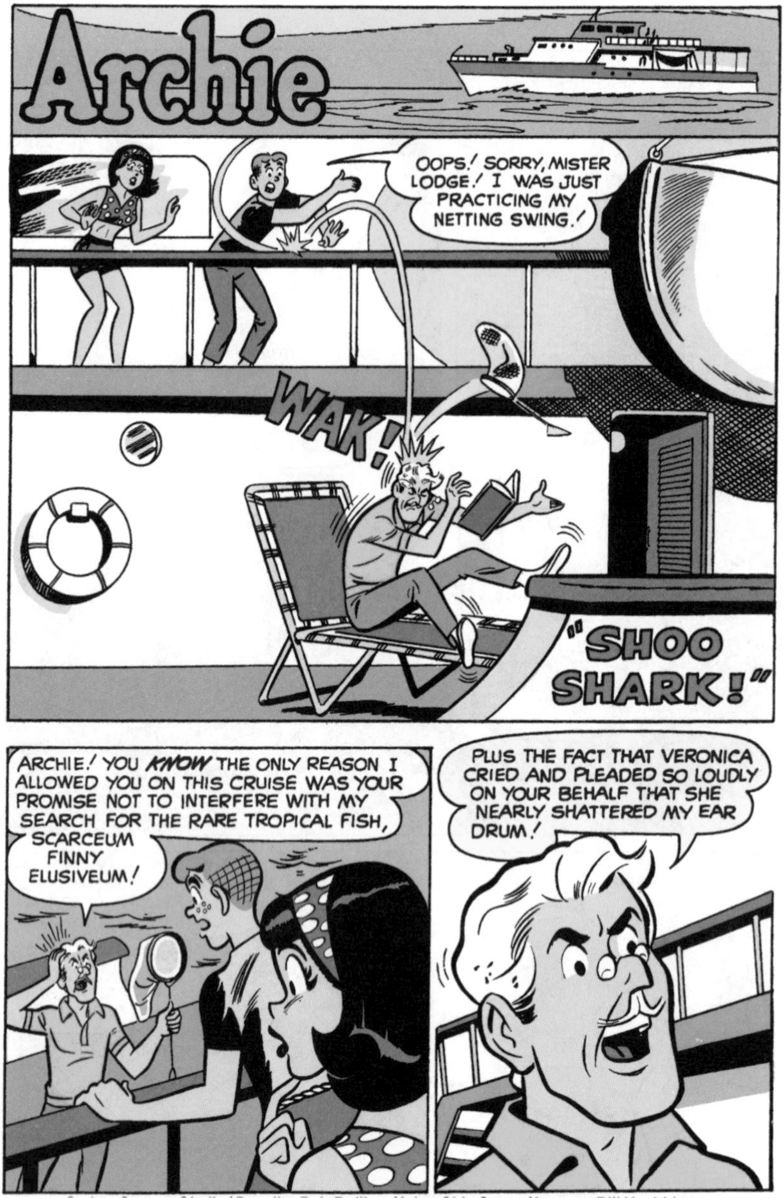
Archie
OOPS! SORRY, MISTER LODGE! I WAS JUST PRACTICING MY NETTING SWING!
WAK!
"SHOO SHARK!"
ARCHIE! YOU KNOW THE ONLY REASON I ALLOWED YOU ON THIS CRUISE WAS YOUR PROMISE NOT TO INTERFERE WITH MY SEARCH FOR THE RARE TROPICAL FISH,
SCARCEUM FINNY ELUSIVEUM!
PLUS THE FACT THAT VERONICA CRIED AND PLEADED SO LOUDLY ON YOUR BEHALF THAT SHE NEARLY SHATTERED MY EAR DRUM!

Story: George Gladir Pencils: Bob Bolling
Inks: Chic Stone Letters: Bill Yoshida

Originally printed in EVERYTHING'S ARCHIE #5, NOVEMBER 1969

...AND I CAN'T DIVE WITH A SHATTERED EARDRUM!

POOR DADDY. HIS S.U.E. MEANS SO MUCH TO HIM!

SUE? YOUR UPSTAIRS MAID! IS SHE HERE, TOO?

NO, SILLY! S.U.E.! SOCIETY OF UNDERWATER EXPLORERS! FORMED EXCLUSIVELY OF MILLION-AIRES! DADDY'S THE ONLY MEMBER WHO HASN'T LECTURED TO THE SOCIETY ON ANY OF HIS EXPLOITS.... THAT'S WHY FINDING THAT RARE TROPICAL FISH IS SO IMPORTANT TO HIM!

SOME MILLIONAIRES HAVE IT ROUGH!

BY THE WAY, ARCHIE, SWEETS, I HAVE A *SURPRISE* FOR YOU!

GROOVY! WHAT IS IT?

IT'LL BE FINISHED TOMORROW!

?

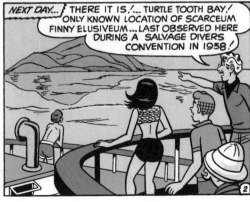

NEXT DAY... THERE IT IS!... TURTLE TOOTH BAY! ONLY KNOWN LOCATION OF SCARCEUM FINNY ELUSIVEUM...LAST OBSERVED HERE DURING A SALVAGE DIVERS CONVENTION IN 1958!

2

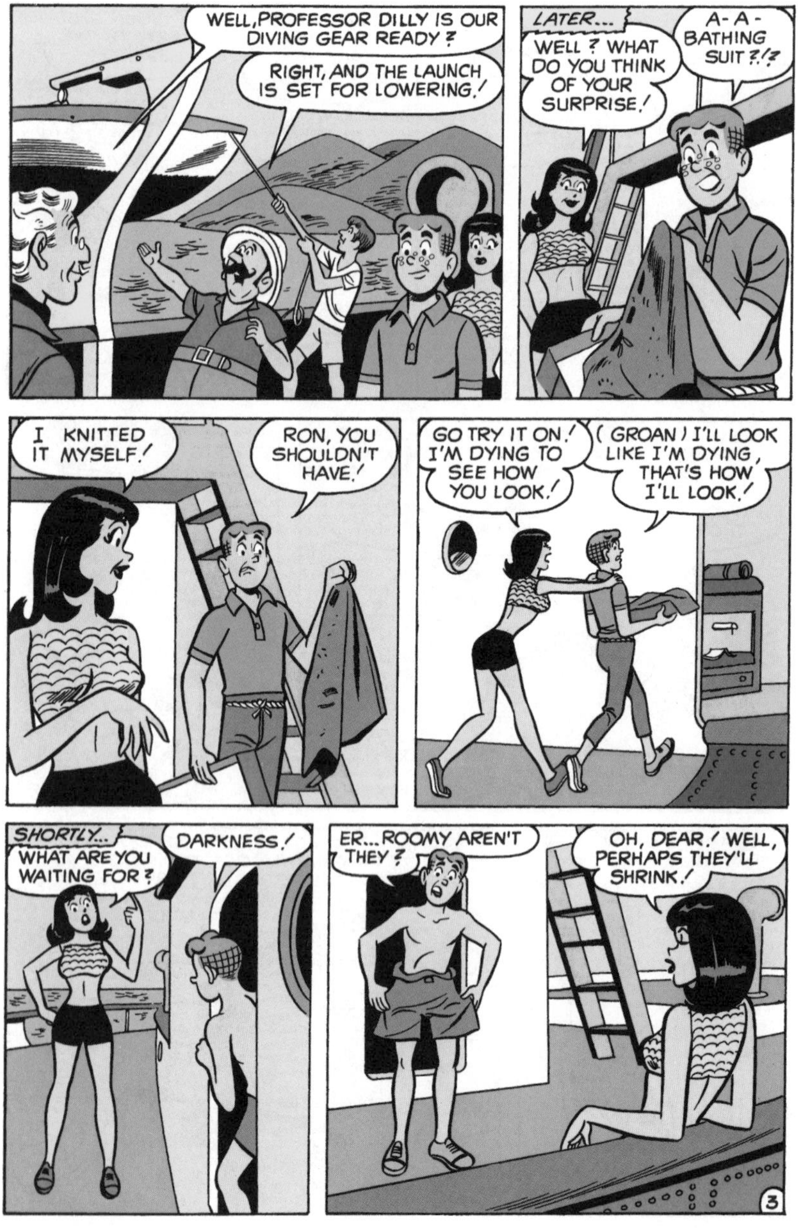
WELL, PROFESSOR DILLY IS OUR DIVING GEAR READY ?
RIGHT, AND THE LAUNCH IS SET FOR LOWERING!
LATER...
WELL ? WHAT DO YOU THINK OF YOUR SURPRISE!
A- A- BATHING SUIT ?!?
I KNITTED IT MYSELF!
RON, YOU SHOULDN'T HAVE!
GO TRY IT ON! I'M DYING TO SEE HOW YOU LOOK!
(GROAN) I'LL LOOK LIKE I'M DYING, THAT'S HOW I'LL LOOK!
SHORTLY...
WHAT ARE YOU WAITING FOR ?
DARKNESS!
ER... ROOMY AREN'T THEY ?
OH, DEAR! WELL, PERHAPS THEY'LL SHRINK!
3

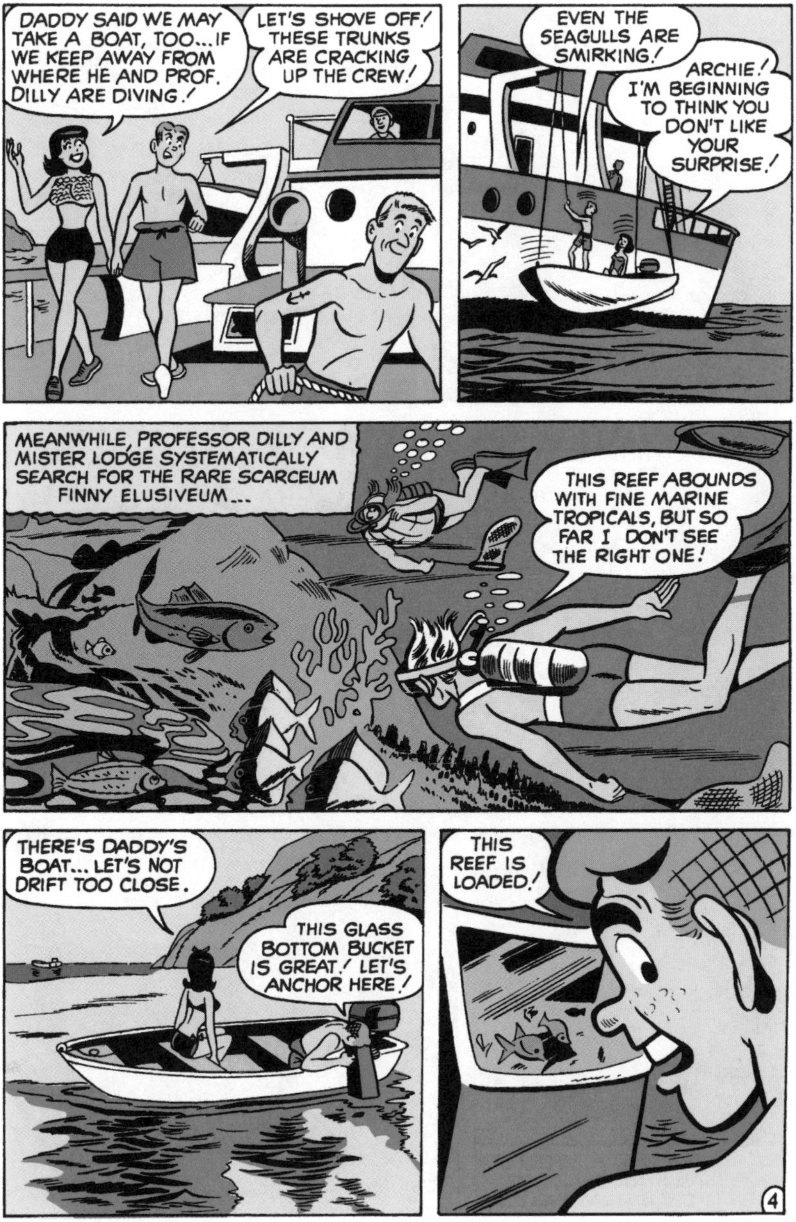
DADDY SAID WE MAY TAKE A BOAT, TOO... IF WE KEEP AWAY FROM WHERE HE AND PROF. DILLY ARE DIVING!
LET'S SHOVE OFF! THESE TRUNKS ARE CRACKING UP THE CREW!
EVEN THE SEAGULLS ARE SMIRKING!
ARCHIE! I'M BEGINNING TO THINK YOU DON'T LIKE YOUR SURPRISE!
MEANWHILE, PROFESSOR DILLY AND MISTER LODGE SYSTEMATICALLY SEARCH FOR THE RARE SCARCEUM FINNY ELUSIVEUM...
THIS REEF ABOUNDS WITH FINE MARINE TROPICALS, BUT SO FAR I DON'T SEE THE RIGHT ONE!
THERE'S DADDY'S BOAT... LET'S NOT DRIFT TOO CLOSE.
THIS GLASS BOTTOM BUCKET IS GREAT! LET'S ANCHOR HERE!
THIS REEF IS LOADED!
4

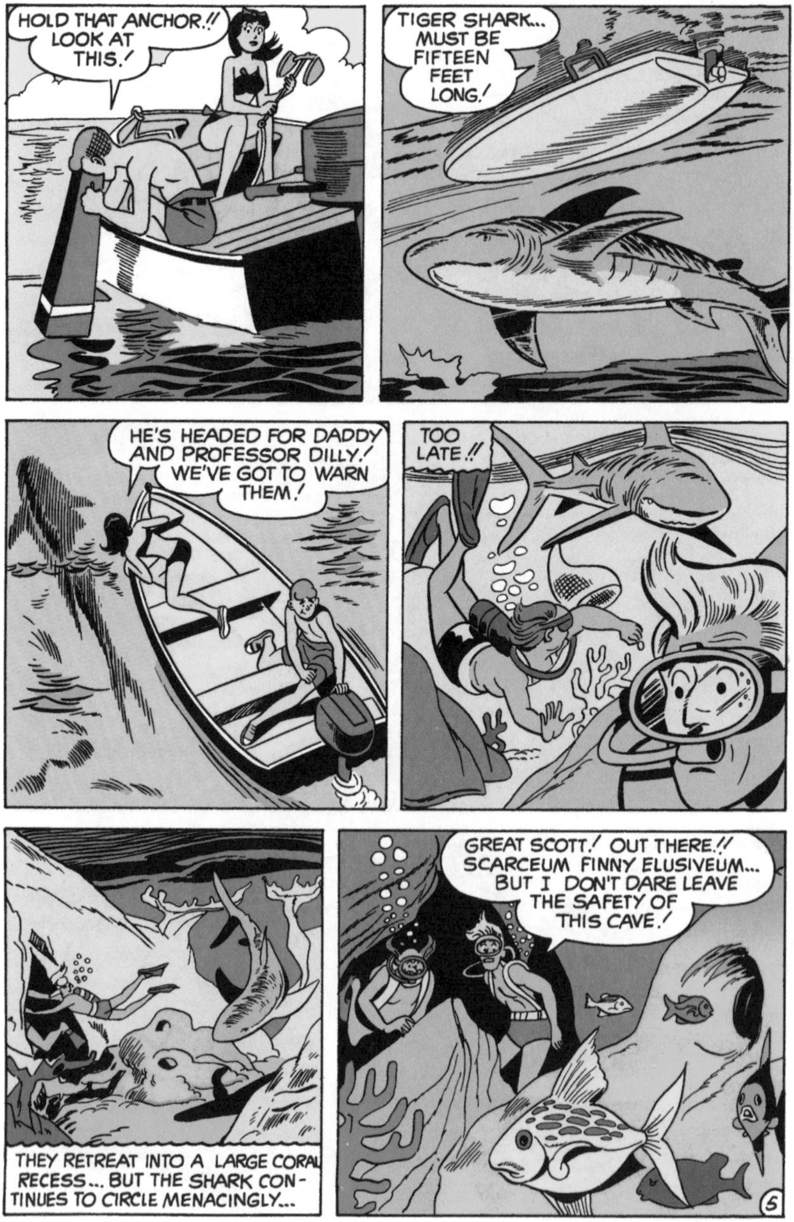
HOLD THAT ANCHOR.!! LOOK AT THIS.!
TIGER SHARK... MUST BE FIFTEEN FEET LONG.!
HE'S HEADED FOR DADDY AND PROFESSOR DILLY.! WE'VE GOT TO WARN THEM.!
TOO LATE.!!
THEY RETREAT INTO A LARGE CORAL RECESS... BUT THE SHARK CON-TINUES TO CIRCLE MENACINGLY...
GREAT SCOTT.! OUT THERE.!! SCARCEUM FINNY ELUSIVEUM... BUT I DON'T DARE LEAVE THE SAFETY OF THIS CAVE.!
5

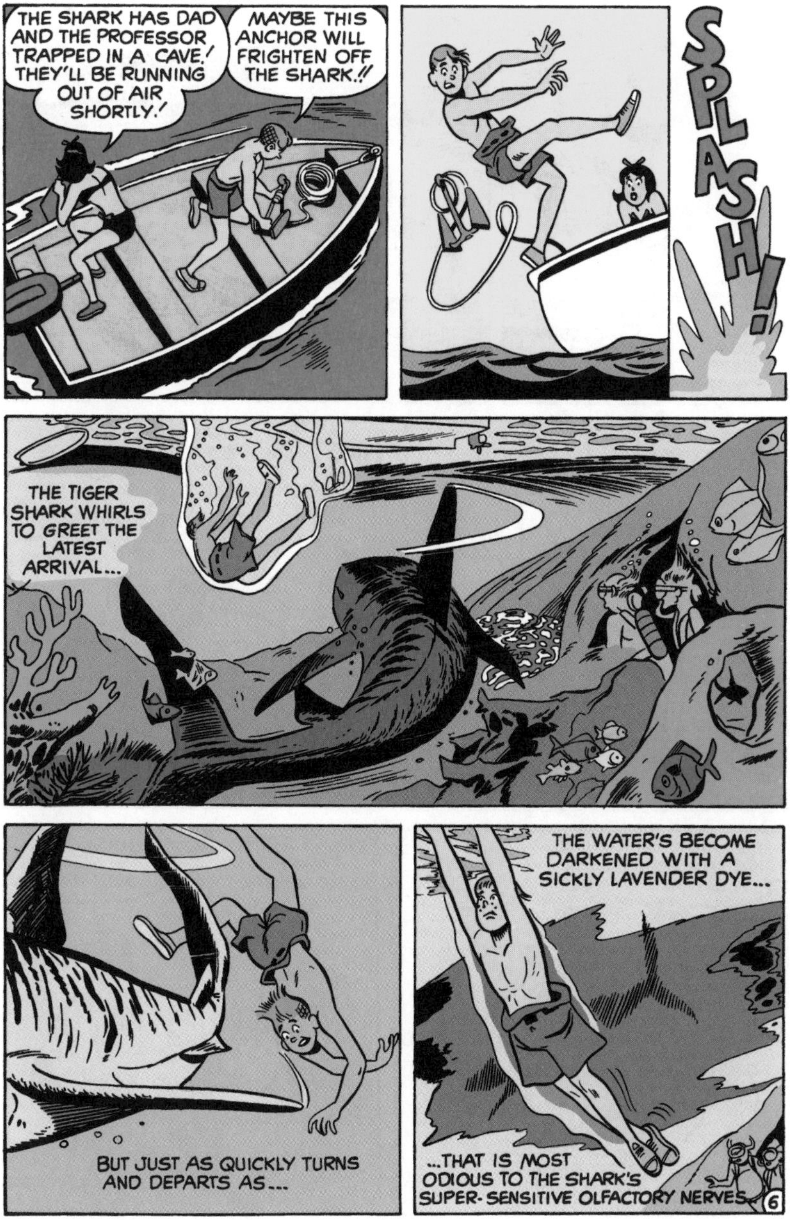
THE SHARK HAS DAD AND THE PROFESSOR TRAPPED IN A CAVE! THEY'LL BE RUNNING OUT OF AIR SHORTLY!
MAYBE THIS ANCHOR WILL FRIGHTEN OFF THE SHARK!!
SPLASH!
THE TIGER SHARK WHIRLS TO GREET THE LATEST ARRIVAL...
BUT JUST AS QUICKLY TURNS AND DEPARTS AS...
THE WATER'S BECOME DARKENED WITH A SICKLY LAVENDER DYE...
...THAT IS MOST ODIOUS TO THE SHARK'S SUPER-SENSITIVE OLFACTORY NERVES.
6

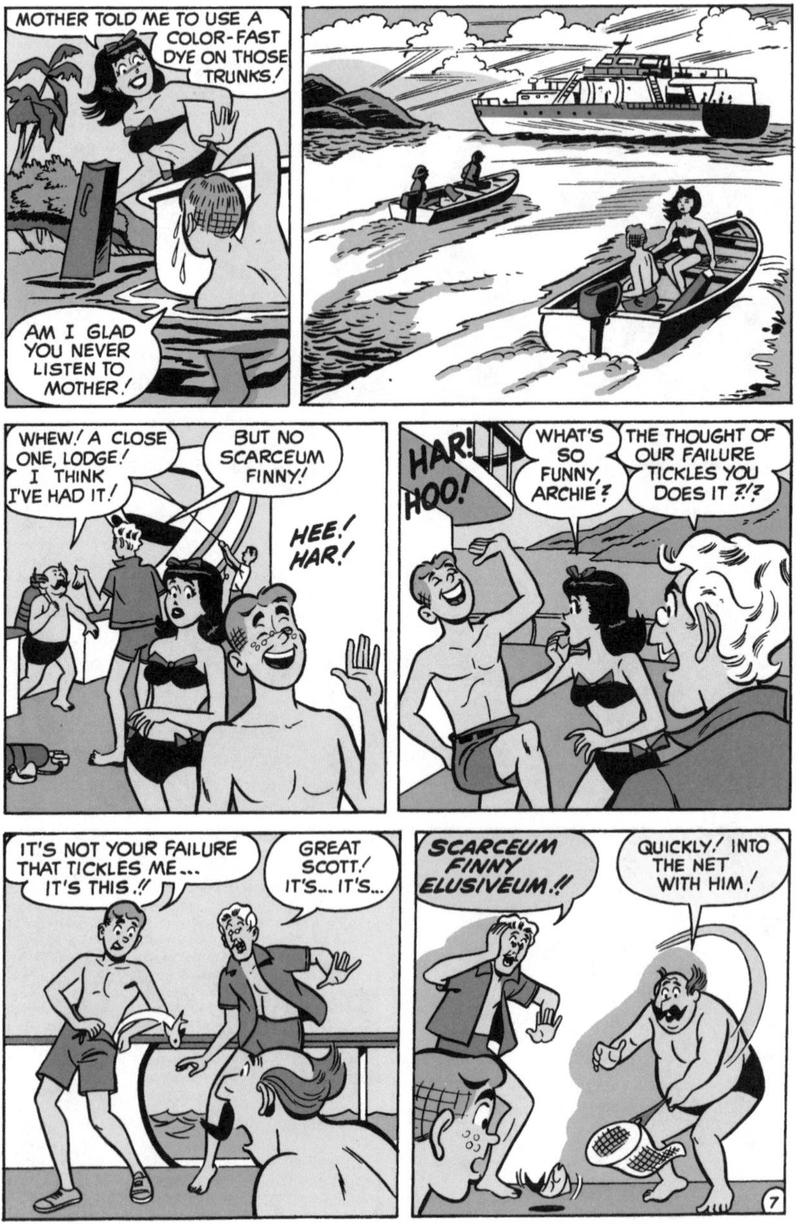
MOTHER TOLD ME TO USE A COLOR-FAST DYE ON THOSE TRUNKS!
AM I GLAD YOU NEVER LISTEN TO MOTHER!
WHEW! A CLOSE ONE, LODGE! I THINK I'VE HAD IT!
BUT NO SCARCEUM FINNY!
HEE! HAR!
HAR! HOO!
WHAT'S SO FUNNY, ARCHIE?
THE THOUGHT OF OUR FAILURE TICKLES YOU DOES IT ?!?
IT'S NOT YOUR FAILURE THAT TICKLES ME... IT'S THIS.!!
GREAT SCOTT! IT'S... IT'S...
SCARCEUM FINNY ELUSIVEUM.!!
QUICKLY! INTO THE NET WITH HIM!
7

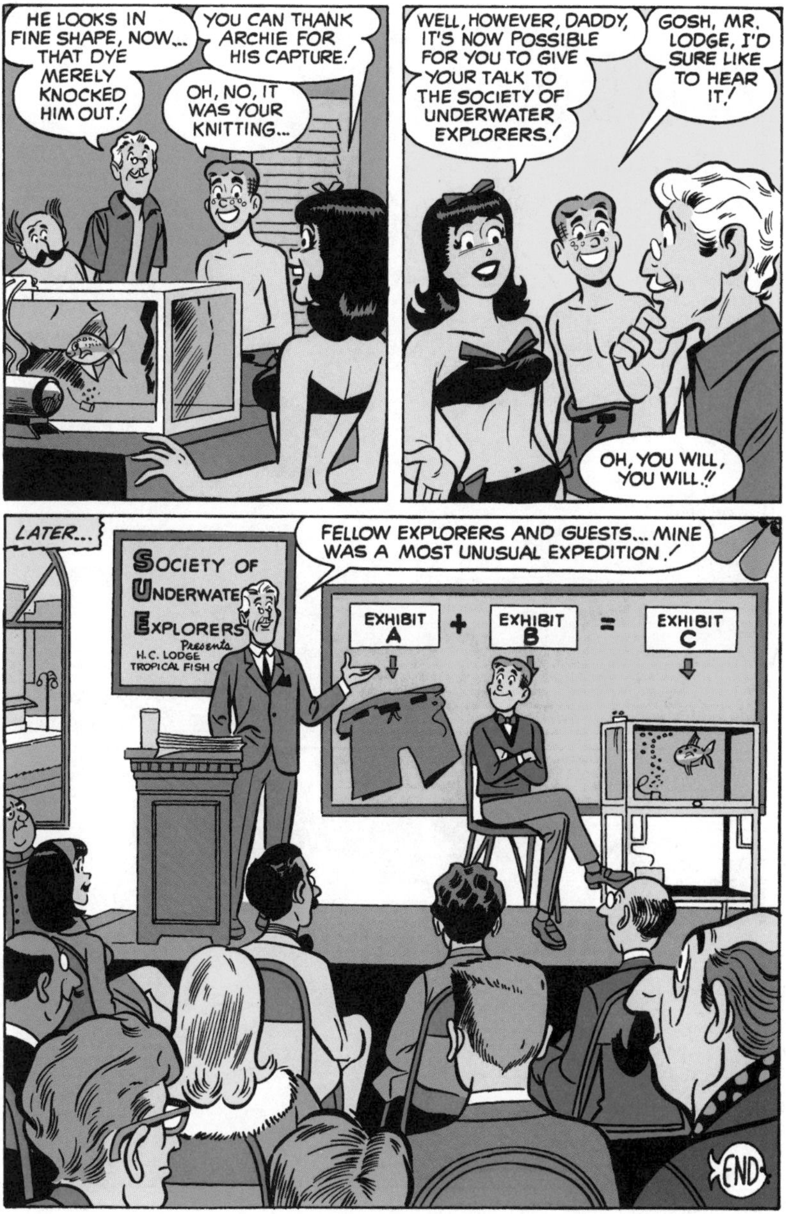
HE LOOKS IN FINE SHAPE, NOW... THAT DYE MERELY KNOCKED HIM OUT!
YOU CAN THANK ARCHIE FOR HIS CAPTURE!
OH, NO, IT WAS YOUR KNITTING...
WELL, HOWEVER, DADDY, IT'S NOW POSSIBLE FOR YOU TO GIVE YOUR TALK TO THE SOCIETY OF UNDERWATER EXPLORERS!
GOSH, MR. LODGE, I'D SURE LIKE TO HEAR IT!
OH, YOU WILL, YOU WILL!!
LATER...
FELLOW EXPLORERS AND GUESTS... MINE WAS A MOST UNUSUAL EXPEDITION!
SOCIETY OF UNDERWATE EXPLORERS Presents H.C. LODGE TROPICAL FISH C
EXHIBIT A
EXHIBIT B
EXHIBIT C
END

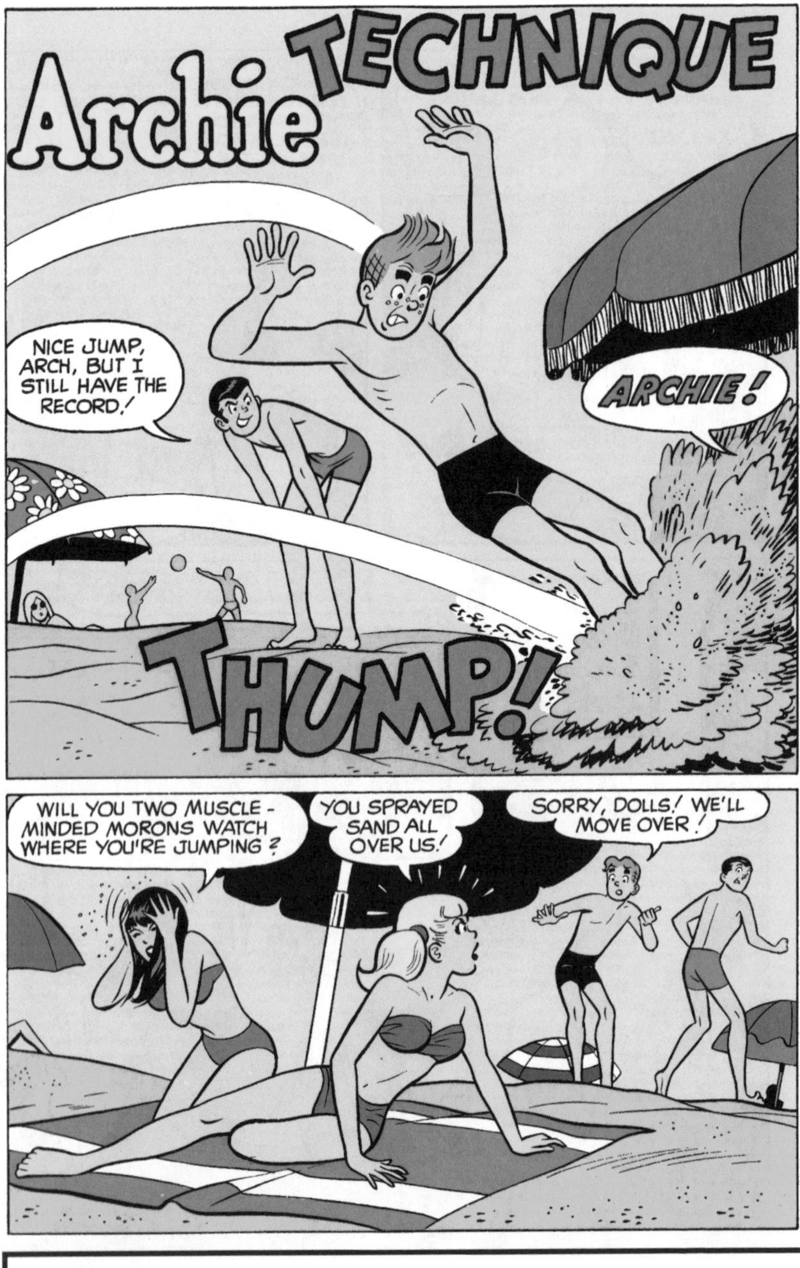
Archie
TECHNIQUE
NICE JUMP, ARCH, BUT I STILL HAVE THE RECORD!
ARCHIE!
THUMP!
WILL YOU TWO MUSCLE-MINDED MORONS WATCH WHERE YOU'RE JUMPING?
YOU SPRAYED SAND ALL OVER US!
SORRY, DOLLS! WE'LL MOVE OVER!

Story: Frank Doyle Pencils: Harry Lucey Letters: Bill Yoshida

Originally printed in EVERYTHING'S ARCHIE #5, NOVEMBER 1969

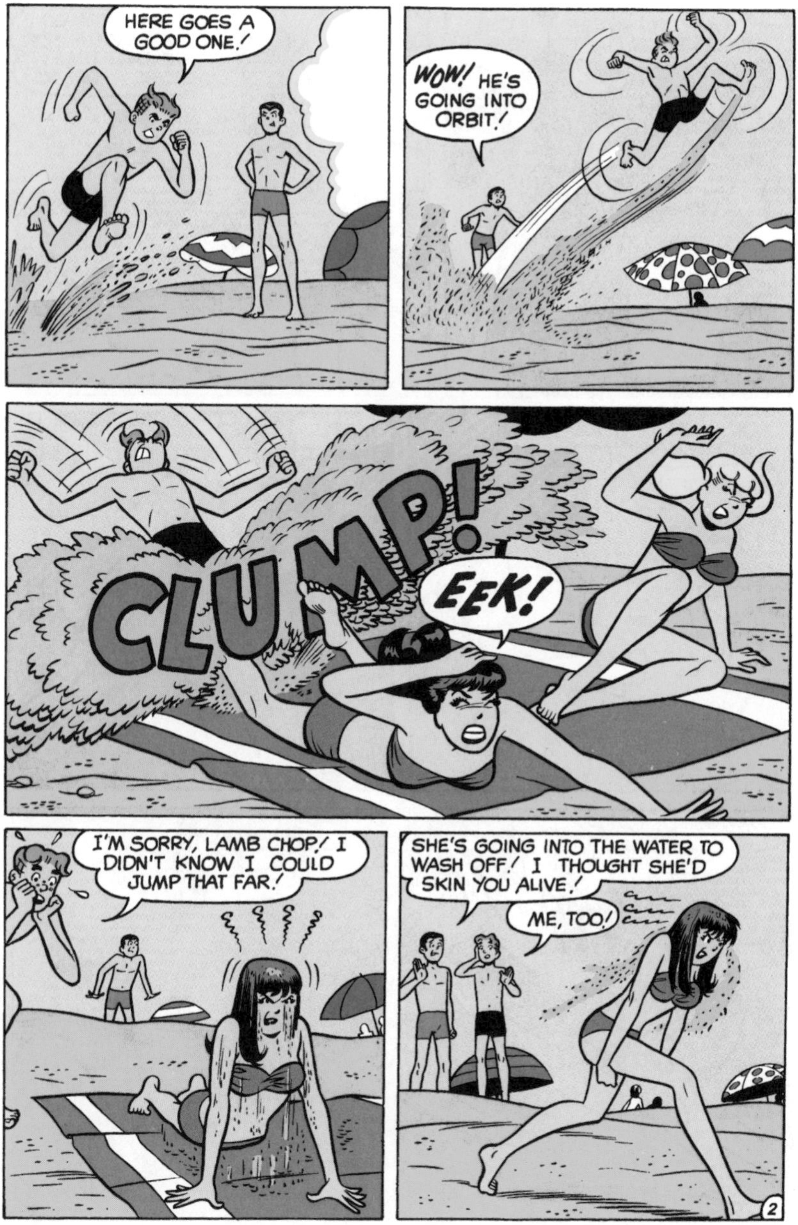
HERE GOES A GOOD ONE!
WOW! HE'S GOING INTO ORBIT!
CLUMP!
EEK!
I'M SORRY, LAMB CHOP! I DIDN'T KNOW I COULD JUMP THAT FAR!
SHE'S GOING INTO THE WATER TO WASH OFF! I THOUGHT SHE'D SKIN YOU ALIVE!
ME, TOO!
2

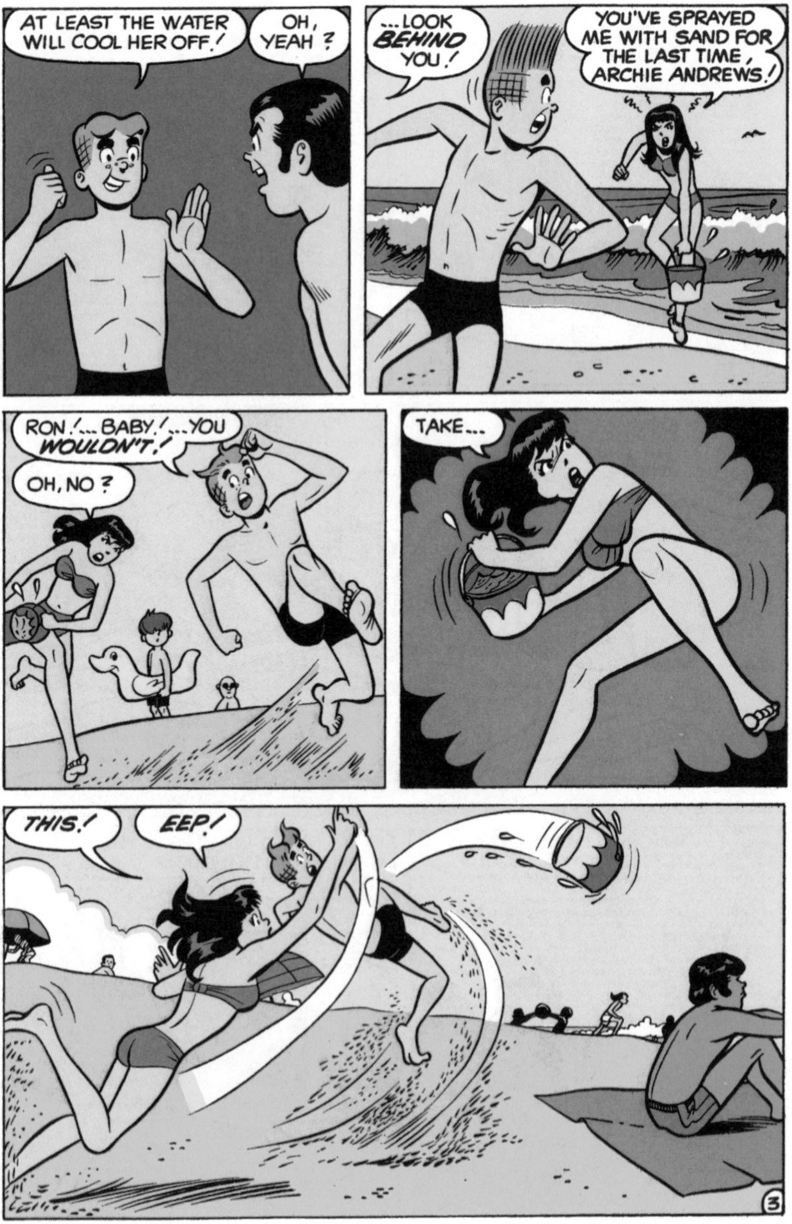
AT LEAST THE WATER WILL COOL HER OFF!
OH, YEAH ?
...LOOK BEHIND YOU!
YOU'VE SPRAYED ME WITH SAND FOR THE LAST TIME, ARCHIE ANDREWS!
RON!...BABY!...YOU WOULDN'T!
OH, NO ?
TAKE...
THIS!
EEP!
3

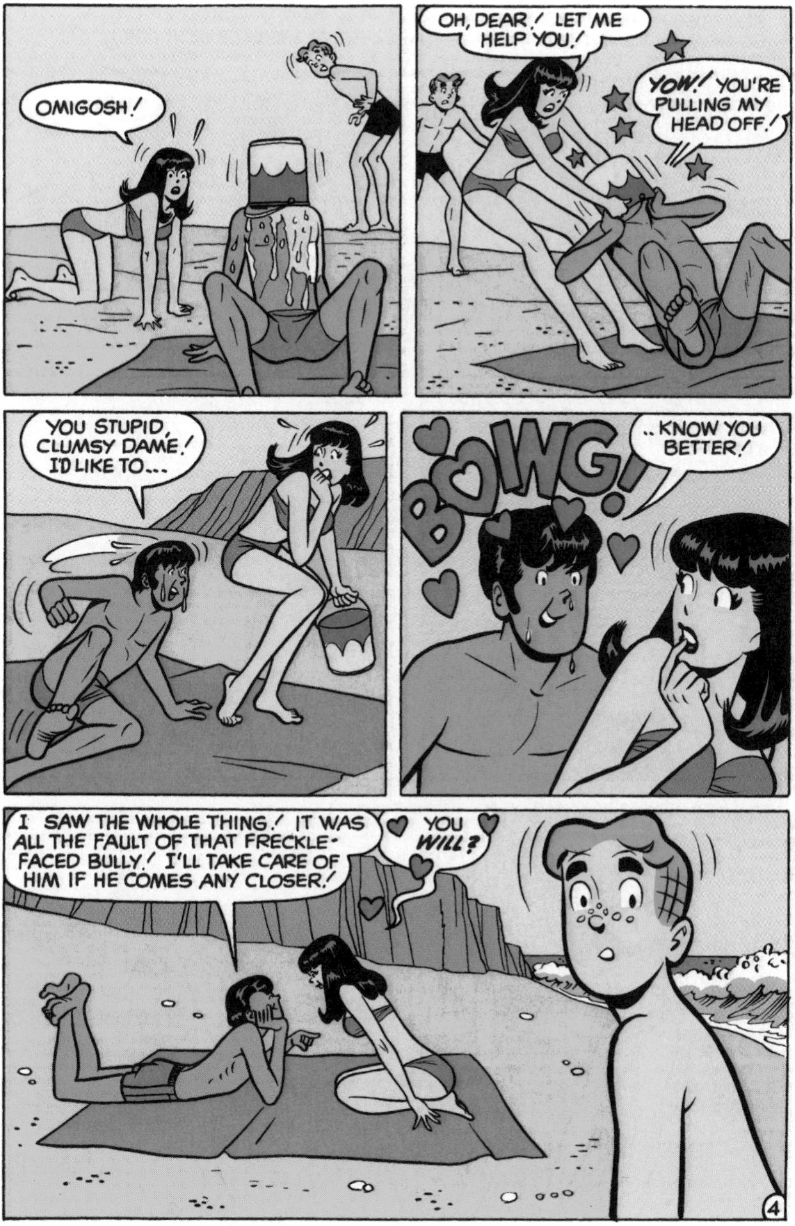
OMIGOSH!
OH, DEAR! LET ME HELP YOU!
YOW! YOU'RE PULLING MY HEAD OFF!
YOU STUPID, CLUMSY DAME! I'D LIKE TO...
BOING!
..KNOW YOU BETTER!
I SAW THE WHOLE THING! IT WAS ALL THE FAULT OF THAT FRECKLE-FACED BULLY! I'LL TAKE CARE OF HIM IF HE COMES ANY CLOSER!
YOU WILL?
4

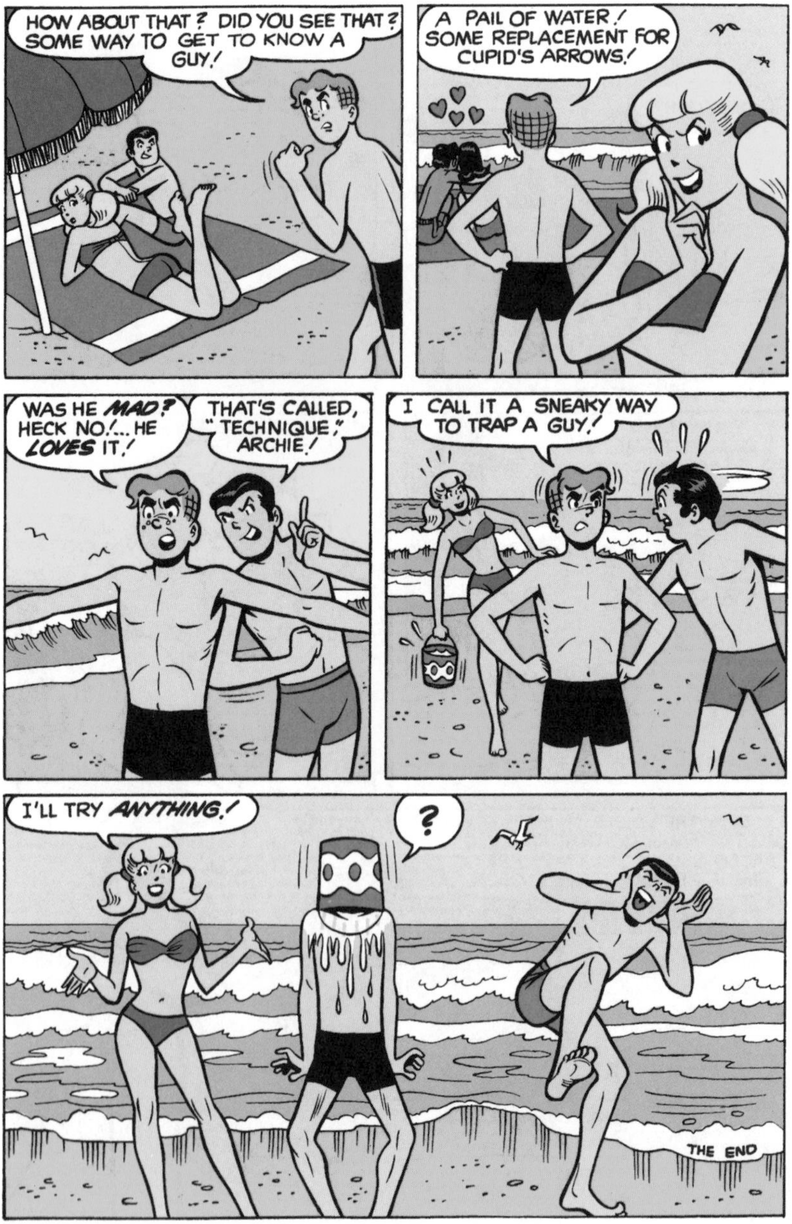
HOW ABOUT THAT? DID YOU SEE THAT? SOME WAY TO GET TO KNOW A GUY!
A PAIL OF WATER! SOME REPLACEMENT FOR CUPID'S ARROWS!
WAS HE MAD? HECK NO!...HE LOVES IT!
THAT'S CALLED, "TECHNIQUE," ARCHIE!
I CALL IT A SNEAKY WAY TO TRAP A GUY!
I'LL TRY ANYTHING!
?
THE END

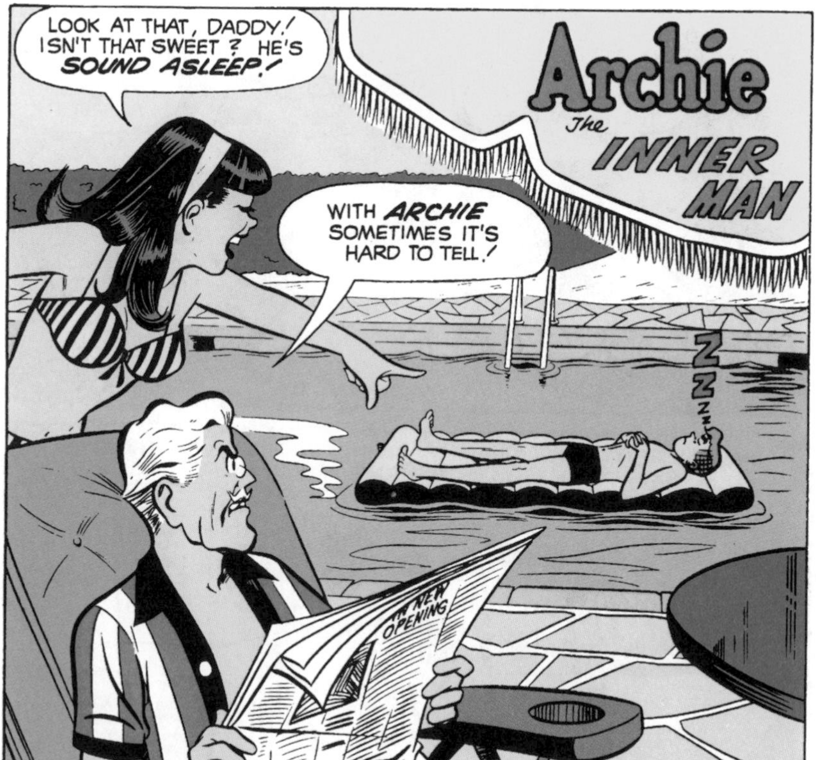
LOOK AT THAT, DADDY! ISN'T THAT SWEET? HE'S SOUND ASLEEP!
Archie
The INNER MAN
WITH ARCHIE SOMETIMES IT'S HARD TO TELL!
Z Z Z

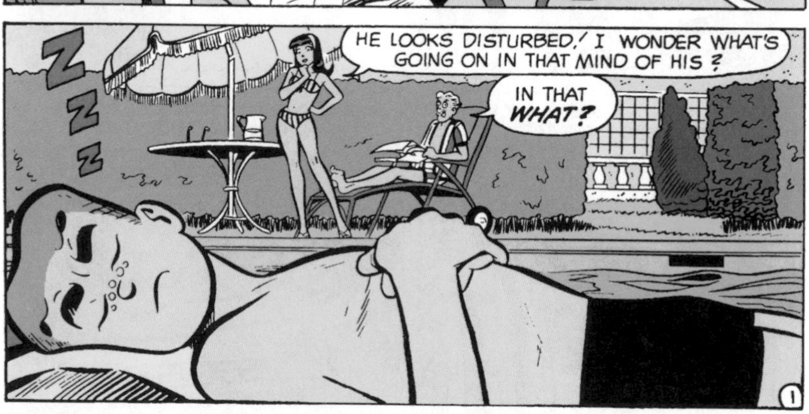
Z Z Z
HE LOOKS DISTURBED! I WONDER WHAT'S GOING ON IN THAT MIND OF HIS?
IN THAT WHAT?
1

Story: Frank Doyle Pencils: Harry Lucey
Inks: Marty Epp Letters: Bill Yoshida

Originally printed in EVERYTHING'S ARCHIE #5, NOVEMBER 1969

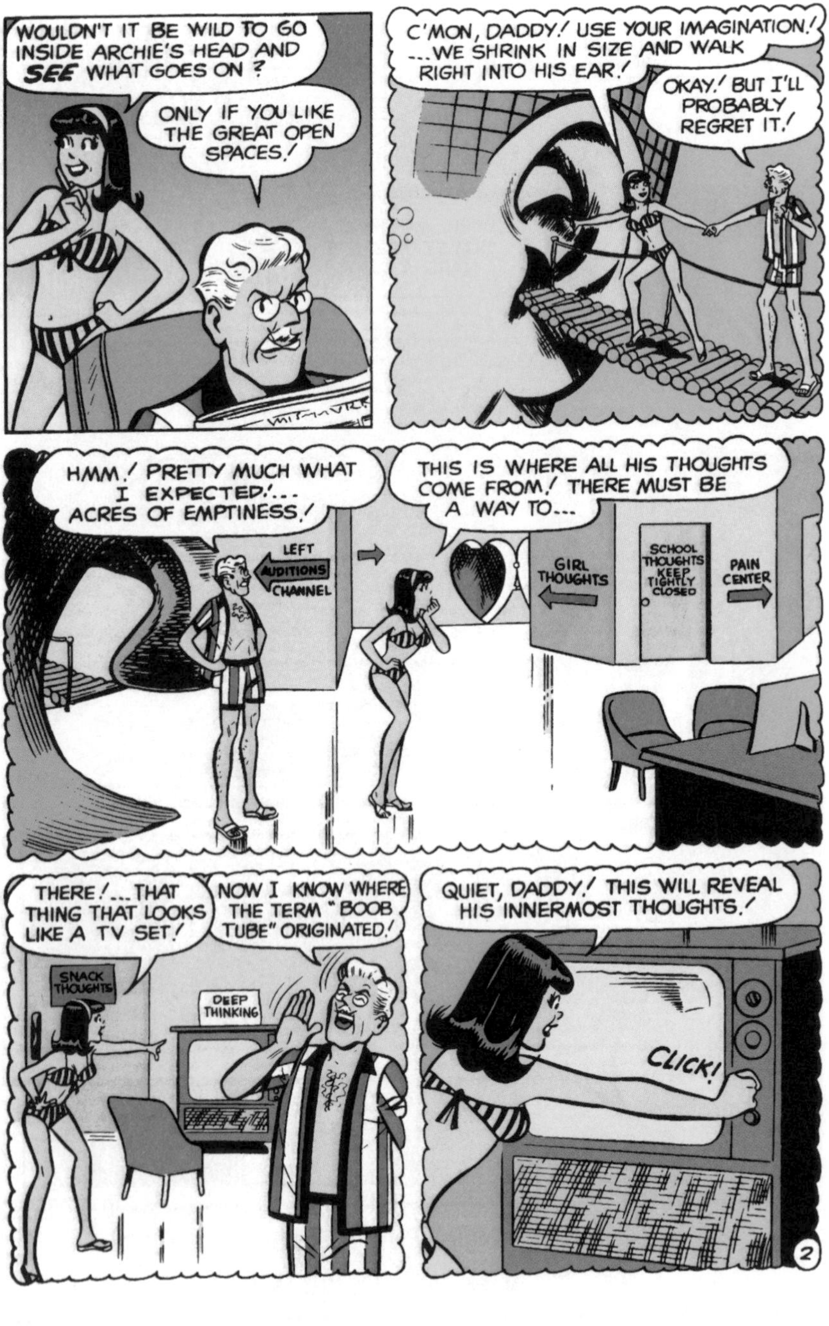
WOULDN'T IT BE WILD TO GO INSIDE ARCHIE'S HEAD AND SEE WHAT GOES ON ?
ONLY IF YOU LIKE THE GREAT OPEN SPACES!
C'MON, DADDY! USE YOUR IMAGINATION! ...WE SHRINK IN SIZE AND WALK RIGHT INTO HIS EAR!
OKAY! BUT I'LL PROBABLY REGRET IT!
HMM! PRETTY MUCH WHAT I EXPECTED!... ACRES OF EMPTINESS!
THIS IS WHERE ALL HIS THOUGHTS COME FROM! THERE MUST BE A WAY TO...
LEFT
AUDITIONS
CHANNEL
GIRL THOUGHTS
SCHOOL THOUGHTS KEEP TIGHTLY CLOSED
PAIN CENTER
THERE!... THAT THING THAT LOOKS LIKE A TV SET!
NOW I KNOW WHERE THE TERM "BOOB TUBE" ORIGINATED!
SNACK THOUGHTS
DEEP THINKING
QUIET, DADDY! THIS WILL REVEAL HIS INNERMOST THOUGHTS!
CLICK!
2

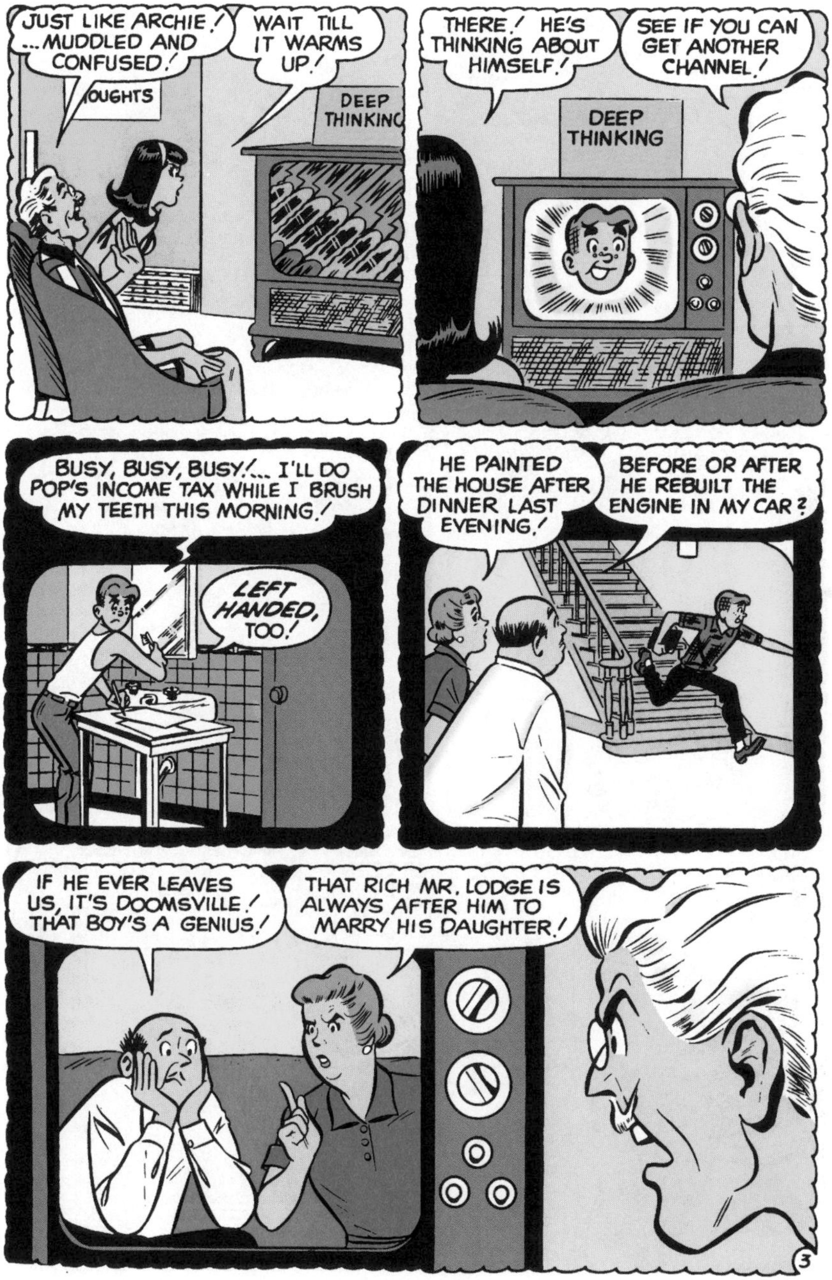
JUST LIKE ARCHIE! ...MUDDLED AND CONFUSED!
WAIT TILL IT WARMS UP!
OUGHTS
DEEP THINKING
THERE! HE'S THINKING ABOUT HIMSELF!
SEE IF YOU CAN GET ANOTHER CHANNEL!
DEEP THINKING
BUSY, BUSY, BUSY!... I'LL DO POP'S INCOME TAX WHILE I BRUSH MY TEETH THIS MORNING!
LEFT HANDED, TOO!
HE PAINTED THE HOUSE AFTER DINNER LAST EVENING!
BEFORE OR AFTER HE REBUILT THE ENGINE IN MY CAR?
IF HE EVER LEAVES US, IT'S DOOMSVILLE! THAT BOY'S A GENIUS!
THAT RICH MR. LODGE IS ALWAYS AFTER HIM TO MARRY HIS DAUGHTER!
3

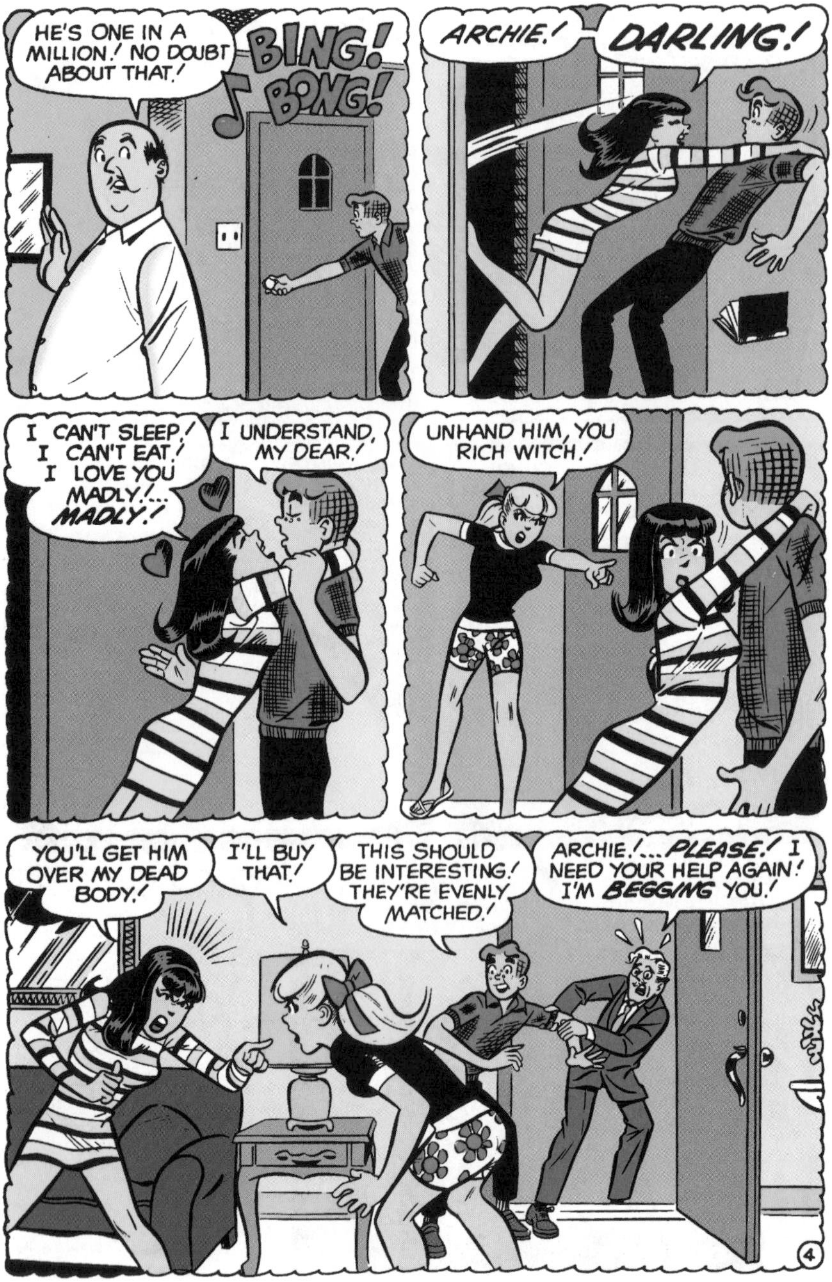
HE'S ONE IN A MILLION! NO DOUBT ABOUT THAT!
BING! BONG!
ARCHIE!
DARLING!
I CAN'T SLEEP! I CAN'T EAT! I LOVE YOU MADLY!... MADLY!
I UNDERSTAND, MY DEAR!
UNHAND HIM, YOU RICH WITCH!
YOU'LL GET HIM OVER MY DEAD BODY!
I'LL BUY THAT!
THIS SHOULD BE INTERESTING! THEY'RE EVENLY MATCHED!
ARCHIE!... PLEASE! I NEED YOUR HELP AGAIN! I'M BEGGING YOU!
4

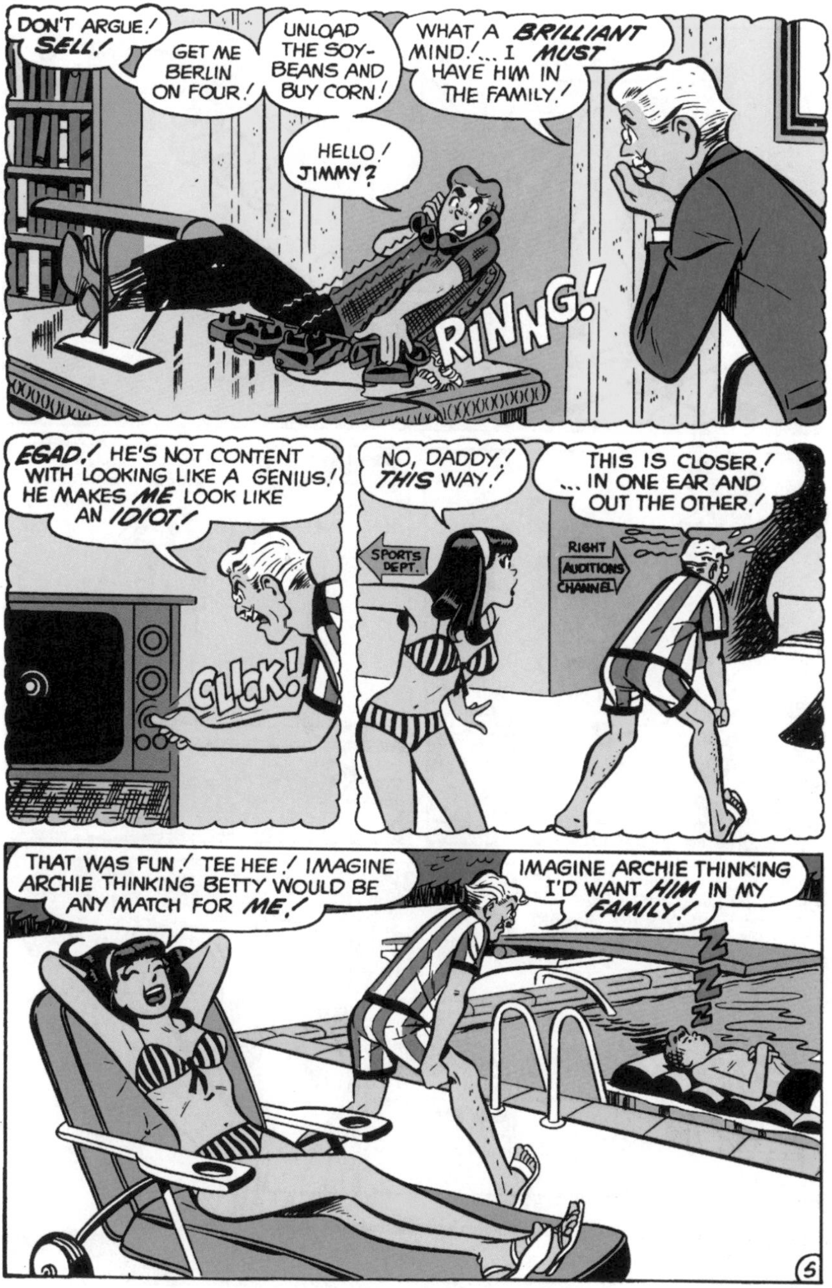
DON'T ARGUE! SELL!
GET ME BERLIN ON FOUR!
UNLOAD THE SOY-BEANS AND BUY CORN!
WHAT A BRILLIANT MIND!... I MUST HAVE HIM IN THE FAMILY!
HELLO! JIMMY?
RINNG!
EGAD! HE'S NOT CONTENT WITH LOOKING LIKE A GENIUS! HE MAKES ME LOOK LIKE AN IDIOT!
CLICK!
NO, DADDY! THIS WAY!
SPORTS DEPT.
THIS IS CLOSER! ... IN ONE EAR AND OUT THE OTHER!
RIGHT AUDITIONS CHANNEL
THAT WAS FUN! TEE HEE! IMAGINE ARCHIE THINKING BETTY WOULD BE ANY MATCH FOR ME!
IMAGINE ARCHIE THINKING I'D WANT HIM IN MY FAMILY!
Z Z Z
5

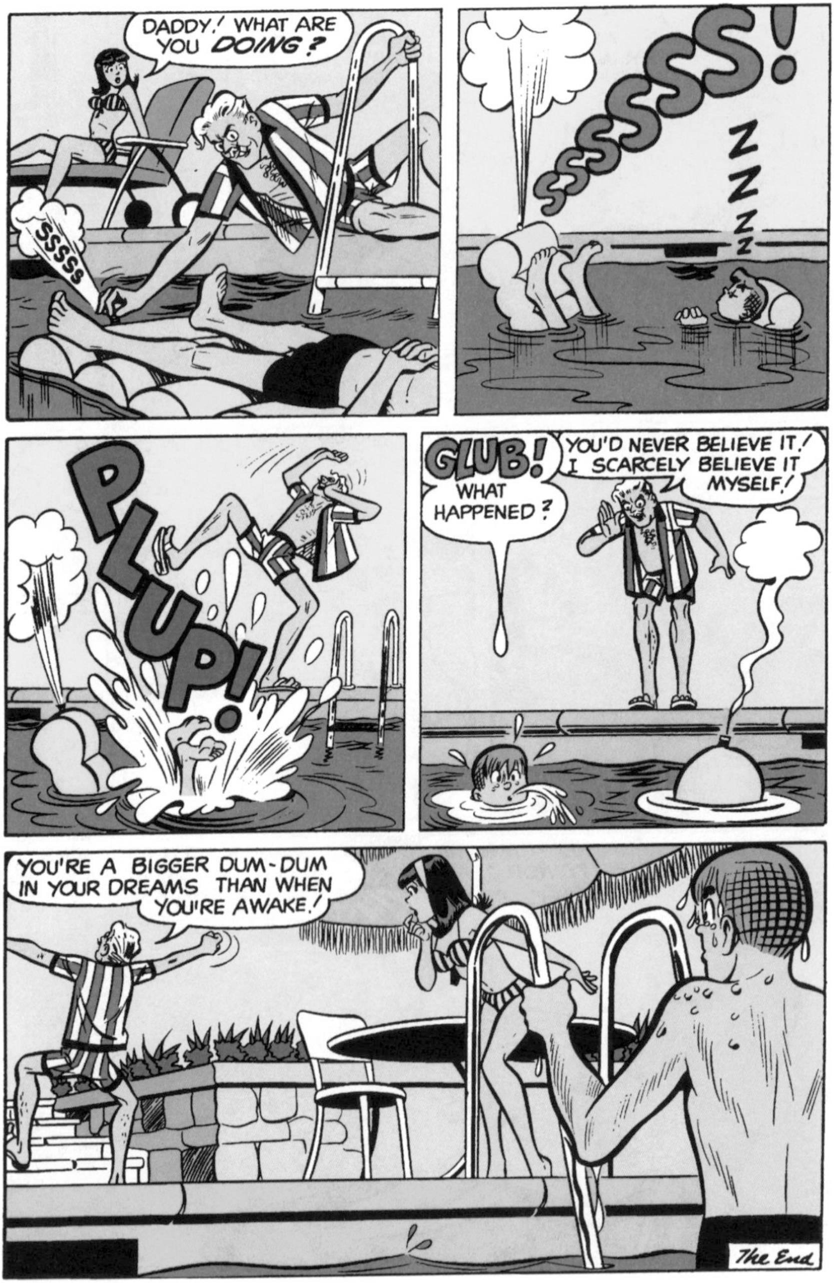
DADDY! WHAT ARE YOU DOING?
SSSSS
SSSSSS!
Z Z Z Z
PLUP!
GLUB! WHAT HAPPENED?
YOU'D NEVER BELIEVE IT! I SCARCELY BELIEVE IT MYSELF!
YOU'RE A BIGGER DUM-DUM IN YOUR DREAMS THAN WHEN YOU'RE AWAKE!
The End

Archie in "SAY CHEESE"

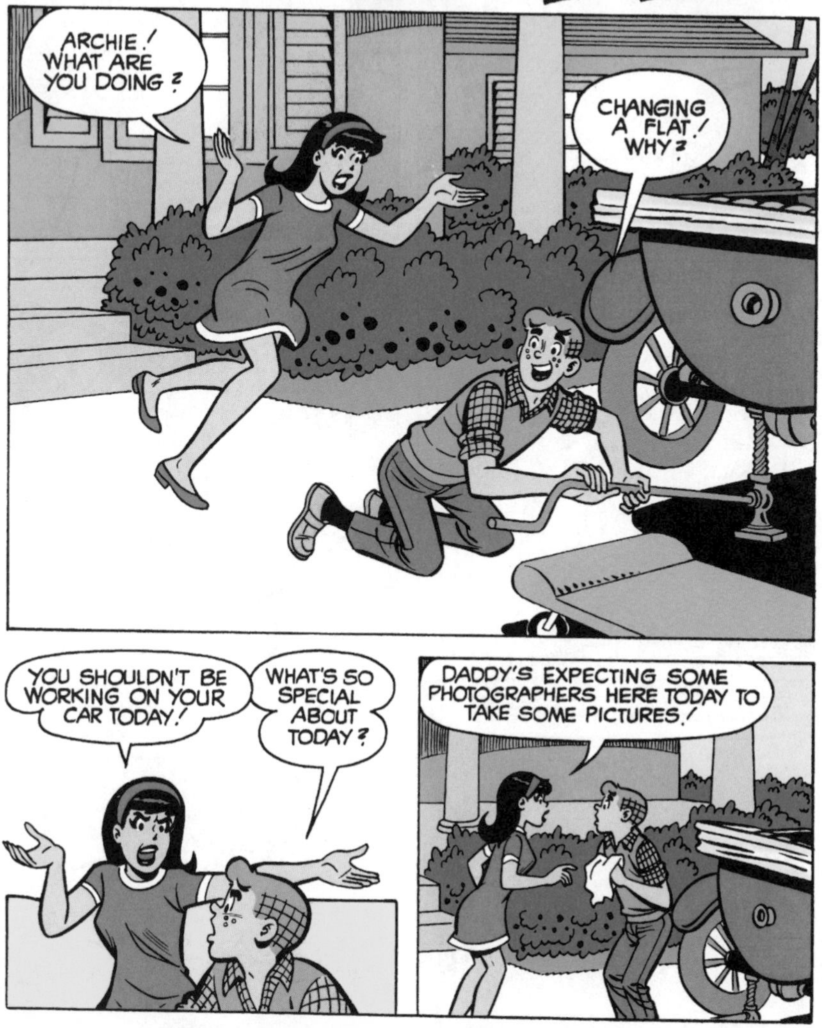
ARCHIE! WHAT ARE YOU DOING?
CHANGING A FLAT! WHY?
YOU SHOULDN'T BE WORKING ON YOUR CAR TODAY!
WHAT'S SO SPECIAL ABOUT TODAY?
DADDY'S EXPECTING SOME PHOTOGRAPHERS HERE TODAY TO TAKE SOME PICTURES!

Story & Pencils: Al Hartley Letters: Bill Yoshida

Originally printed in EVERYTHING'S ARCHIE #6, JANUARY 1970

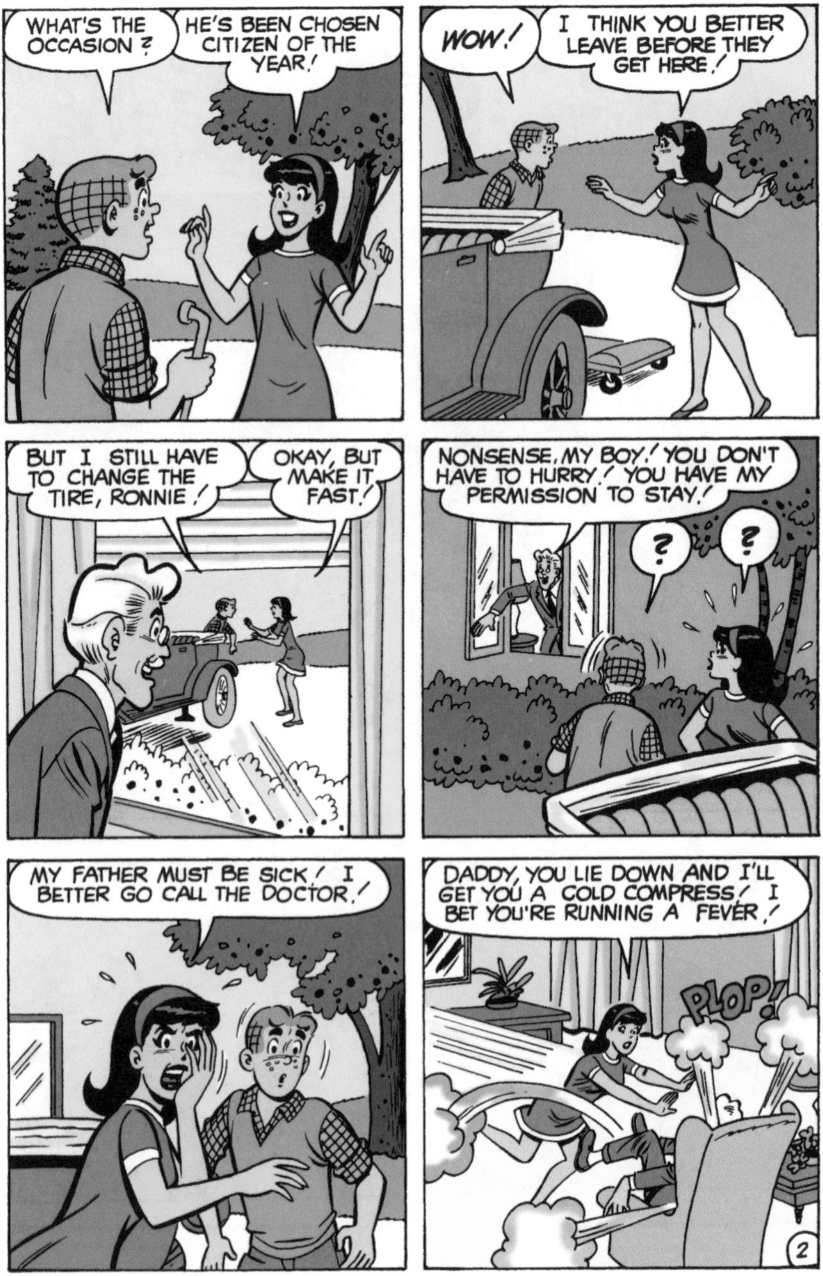
WHAT'S THE OCCASION ?
HE'S BEEN CHOSEN CITIZEN OF THE YEAR!
WOW!
I THINK YOU BETTER LEAVE BEFORE THEY GET HERE!
BUT I STILL HAVE TO CHANGE THE TIRE, RONNIE!
OKAY, BUT MAKE IT FAST!
NONSENSE, MY BOY! YOU DON'T HAVE TO HURRY! YOU HAVE MY PERMISSION TO STAY!
?
?
MY FATHER MUST BE SICK! I BETTER GO CALL THE DOCTOR!
DADDY, YOU LIE DOWN AND I'LL GET YOU A COLD COMPRESS! I BET YOU'RE RUNNING A FEVER!
PLOP!
2

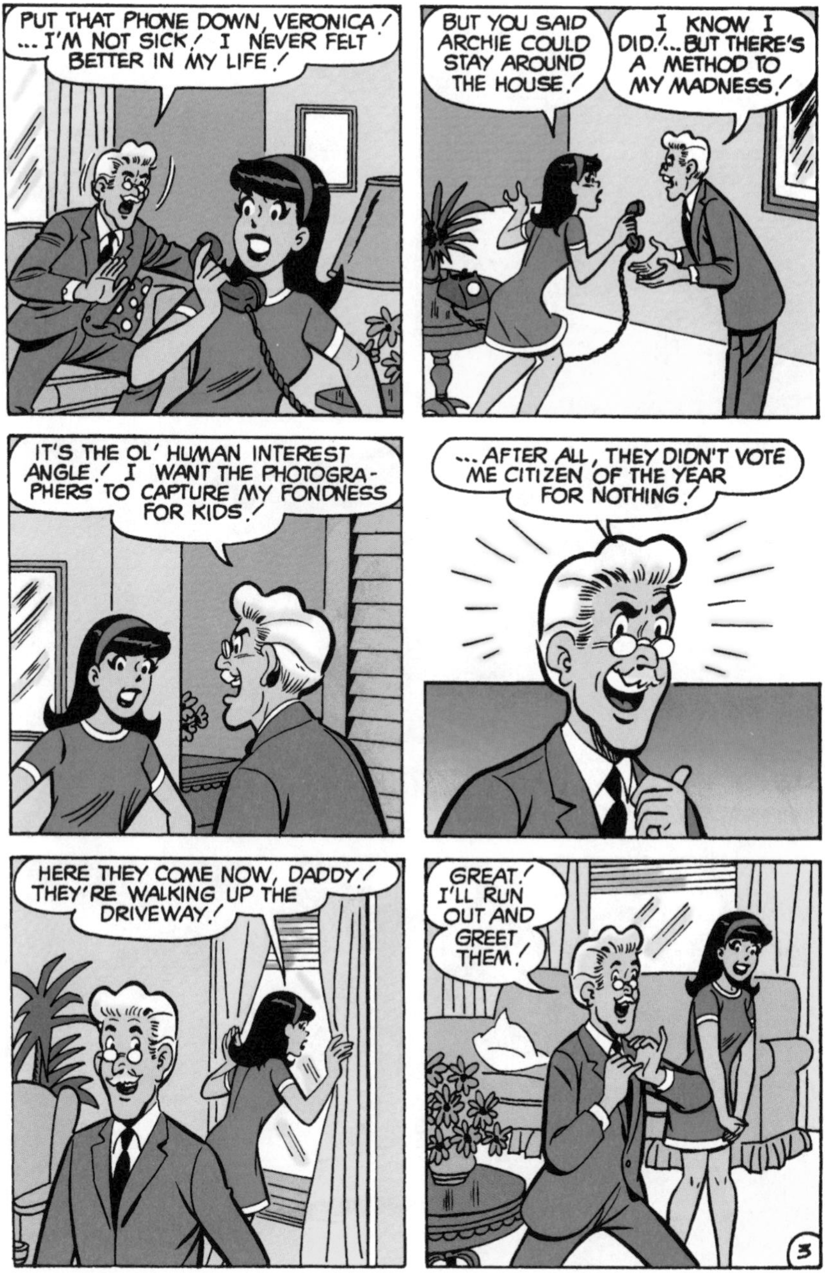
PUT THAT PHONE DOWN, VERONICA! ... I'M NOT SICK! I NEVER FELT BETTER IN MY LIFE!
BUT YOU SAID ARCHIE COULD STAY AROUND THE HOUSE!
I KNOW I DID!... BUT THERE'S A METHOD TO MY MADNESS!
IT'S THE OL' HUMAN INTEREST ANGLE! I WANT THE PHOTOGRA-PHERS TO CAPTURE MY FONDNESS FOR KIDS!
...AFTER ALL, THEY DIDN'T VOTE ME CITIZEN OF THE YEAR FOR NOTHING!
HERE THEY COME NOW, DADDY! THEY'RE WALKING UP THE DRIVEWAY!
GREAT! I'LL RUN OUT AND GREET THEM!
3

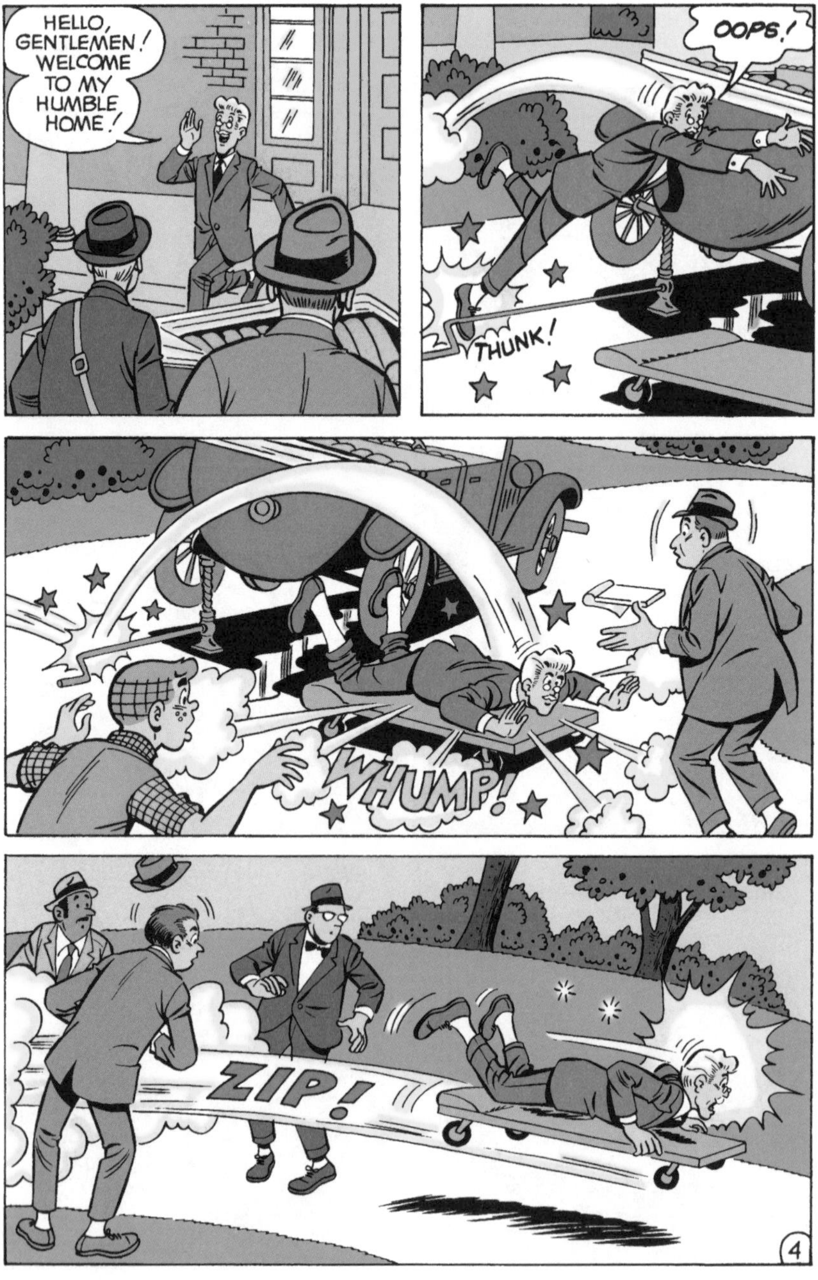
HELLO, GENTLEMEN! WELCOME TO MY HUMBLE HOME!
OOPS!
THUNK!
WHUMP!
ZIP!
4

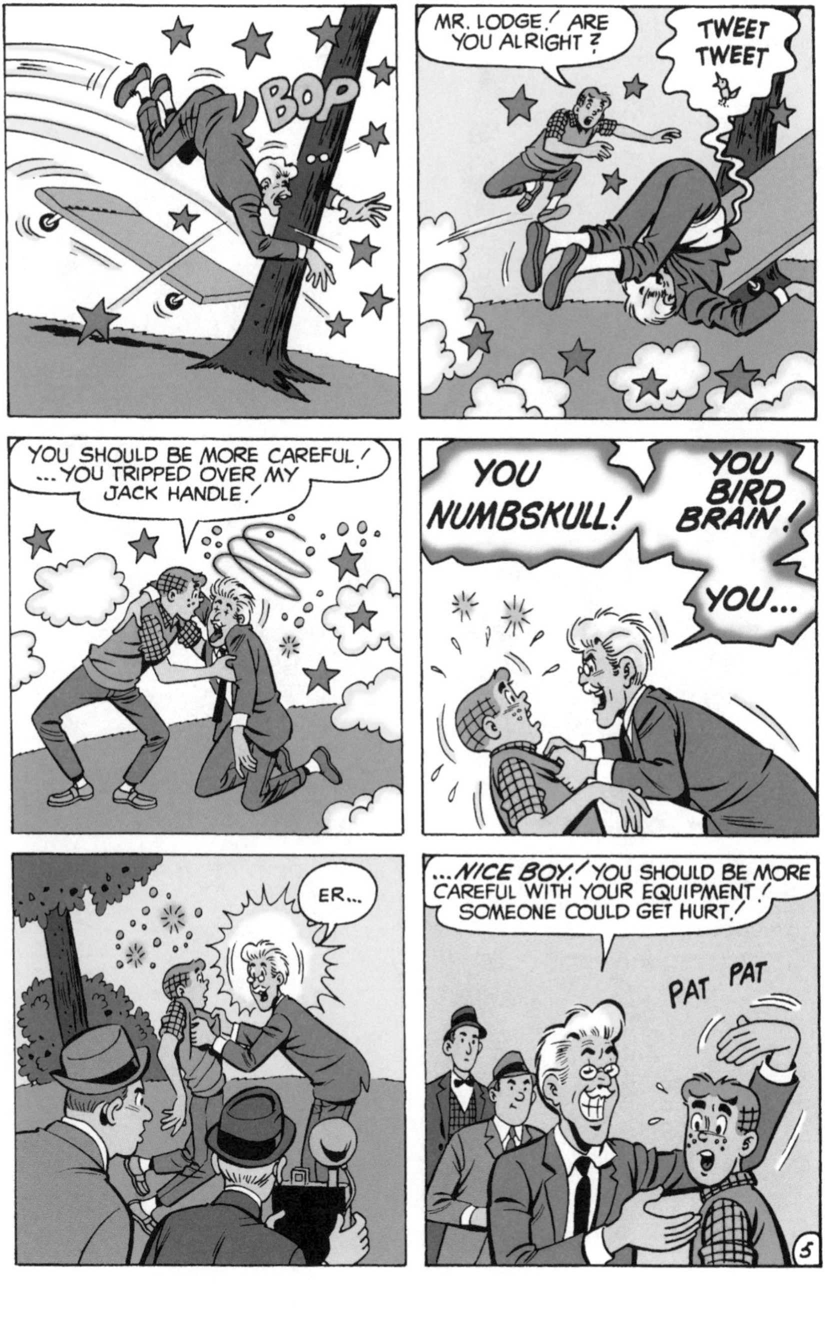
BOP
MR. LODGE! ARE YOU ALRIGHT?
TWEET TWEET
YOU SHOULD BE MORE CAREFUL! ...YOU TRIPPED OVER MY JACK HANDLE!
YOU NUMBSKULL!
YOU BIRD BRAIN!
YOU...
ER...
...NICE BOY! YOU SHOULD BE MORE CAREFUL WITH YOUR EQUIPMENT! SOMEONE COULD GET HURT!
PAT PAT
5

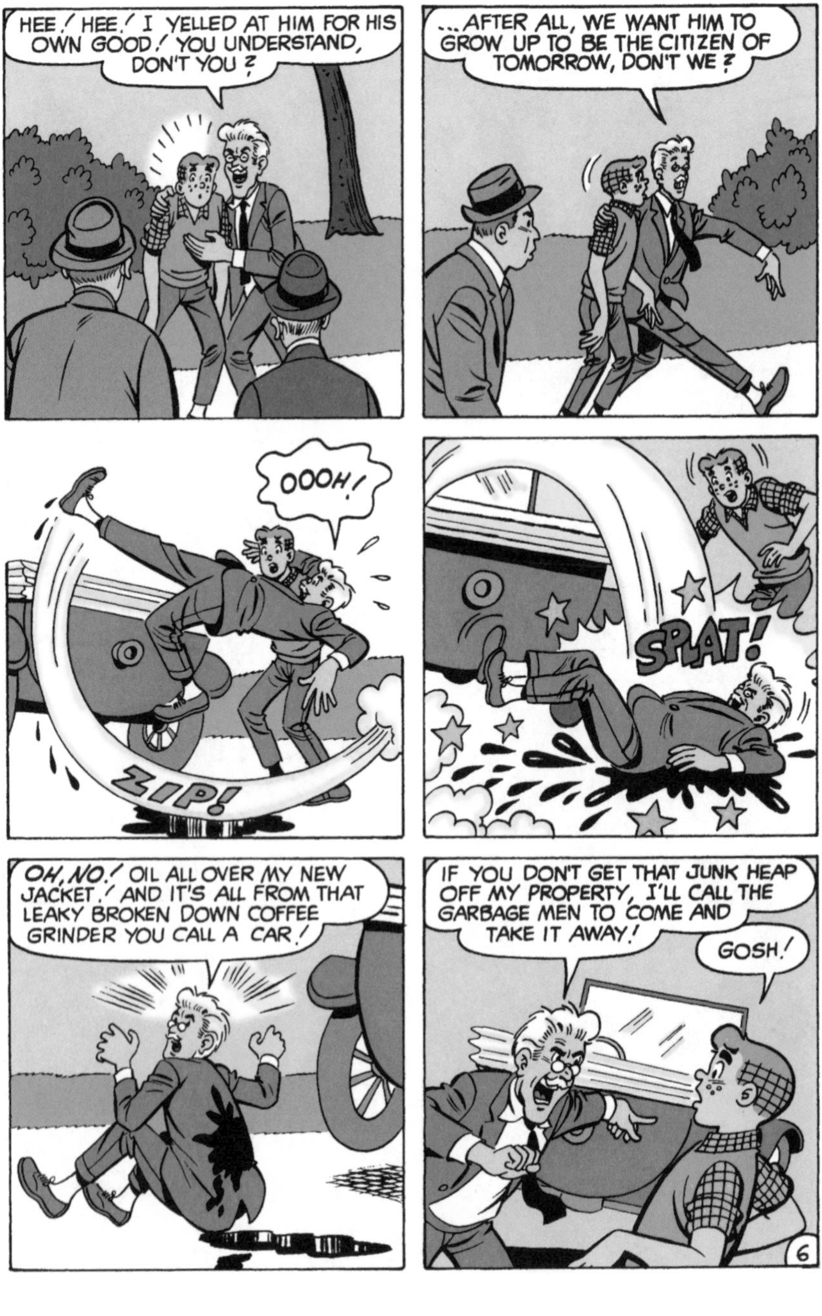
HEE! HEE! I YELLED AT HIM FOR HIS OWN GOOD! YOU UNDERSTAND, DON'T YOU ?
...AFTER ALL, WE WANT HIM TO GROW UP TO BE THE CITIZEN OF TOMORROW, DON'T WE ?
OOOH!
ZIP!
SPLAT!
OH, NO! OIL ALL OVER MY NEW JACKET! AND IT'S ALL FROM THAT LEAKY BROKEN DOWN COFFEE GRINDER YOU CALL A CAR!
IF YOU DON'T GET THAT JUNK HEAP OFF MY PROPERTY, I'LL CALL THE GARBAGE MEN TO COME AND TAKE IT AWAY!
GOSH!
6

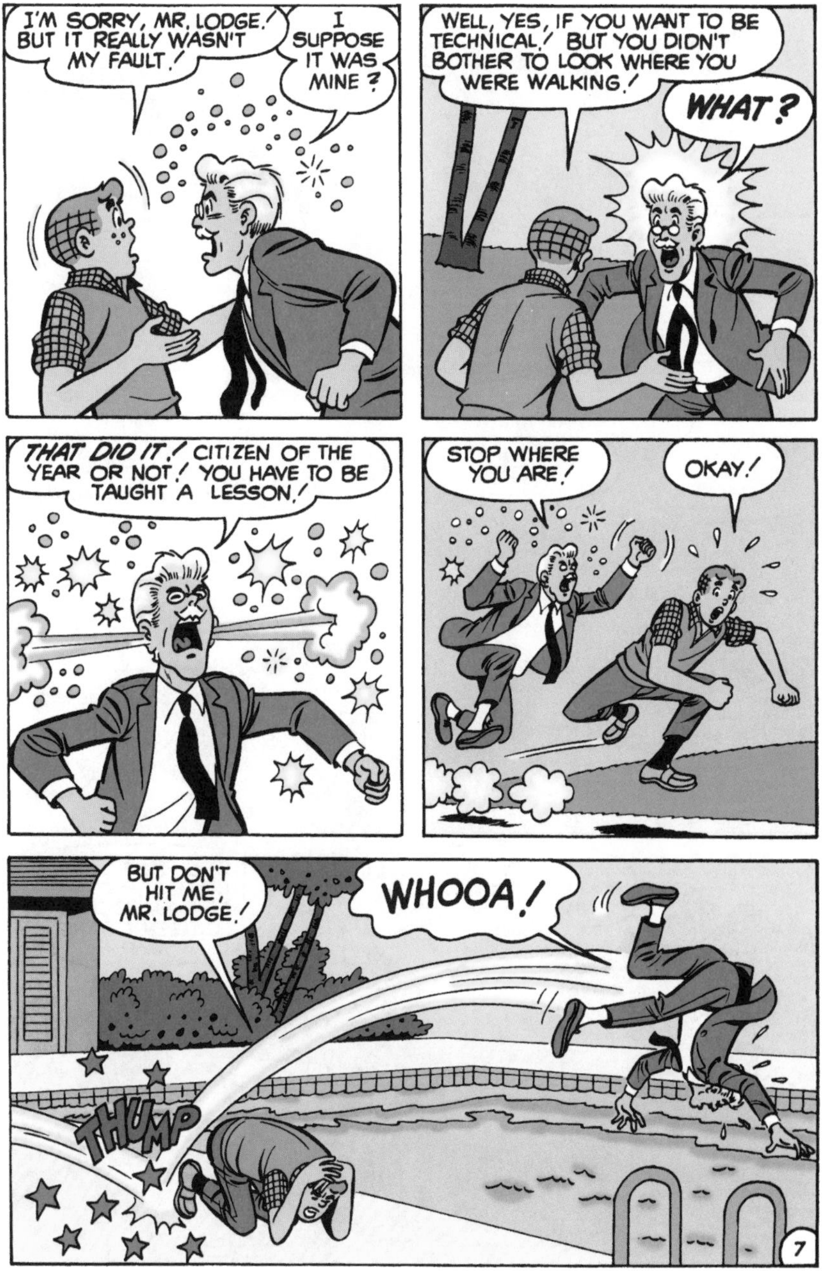
I'M SORRY, MR. LODGE! BUT IT REALLY WASN'T MY FAULT!
I SUPPOSE IT WAS MINE ?
WELL, YES, IF YOU WANT TO BE TECHNICAL! BUT YOU DIDN'T BOTHER TO LOOK WHERE YOU WERE WALKING!
WHAT ?
THAT DID IT! CITIZEN OF THE YEAR OR NOT! YOU HAVE TO BE TAUGHT A LESSON!
STOP WHERE YOU ARE!
OKAY!
BUT DON'T HIT ME, MR. LODGE!
WHOOA!
THUMP
7

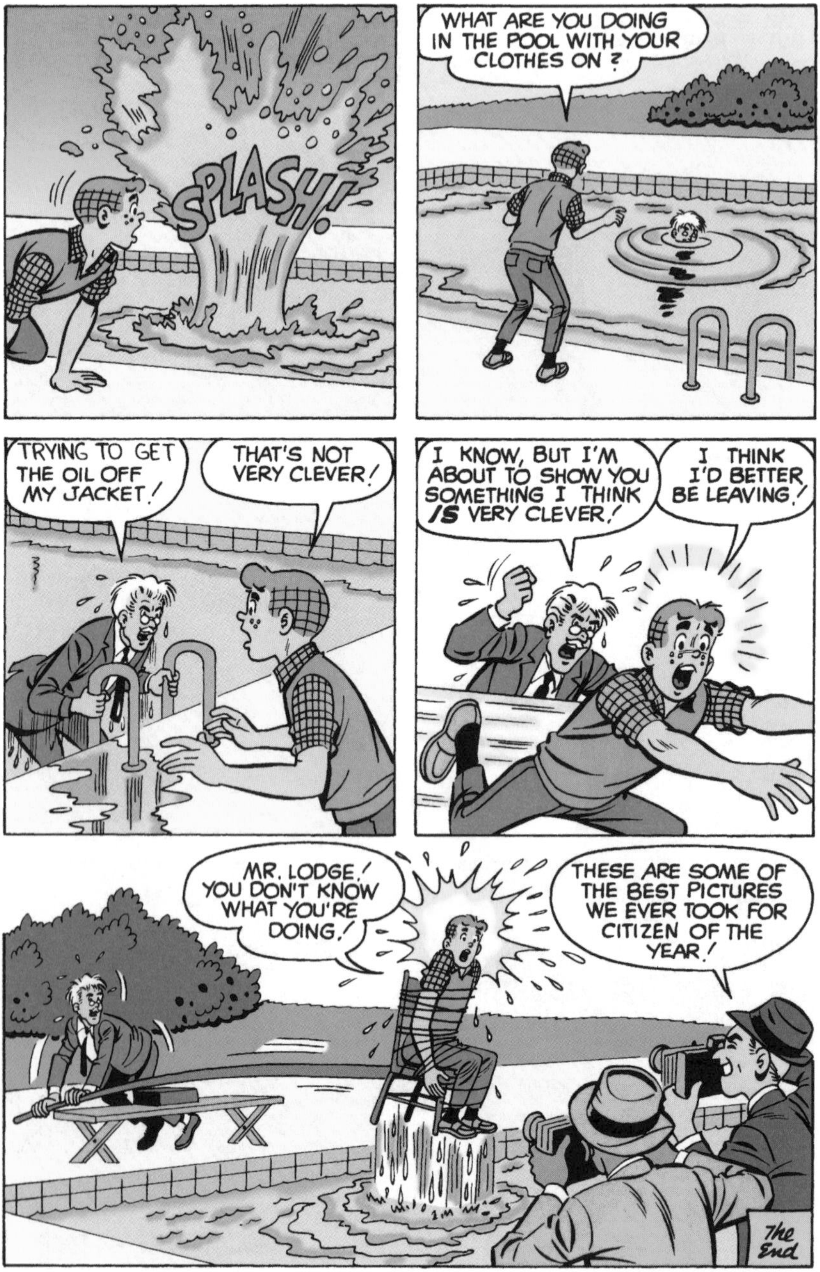
SPLASH!
WHAT ARE YOU DOING IN THE POOL WITH YOUR CLOTHES ON ?
TRYING TO GET THE OIL OFF MY JACKET!
THAT'S NOT VERY CLEVER!
I KNOW, BUT I'M ABOUT TO SHOW YOU SOMETHING I THINK IS VERY CLEVER!
I THINK I'D BETTER BE LEAVING!
MR. LODGE! YOU DON'T KNOW WHAT YOU'RE DOING!
THESE ARE SOME OF THE BEST PICTURES WE EVER TOOK FOR CITIZEN OF THE YEAR!
The End

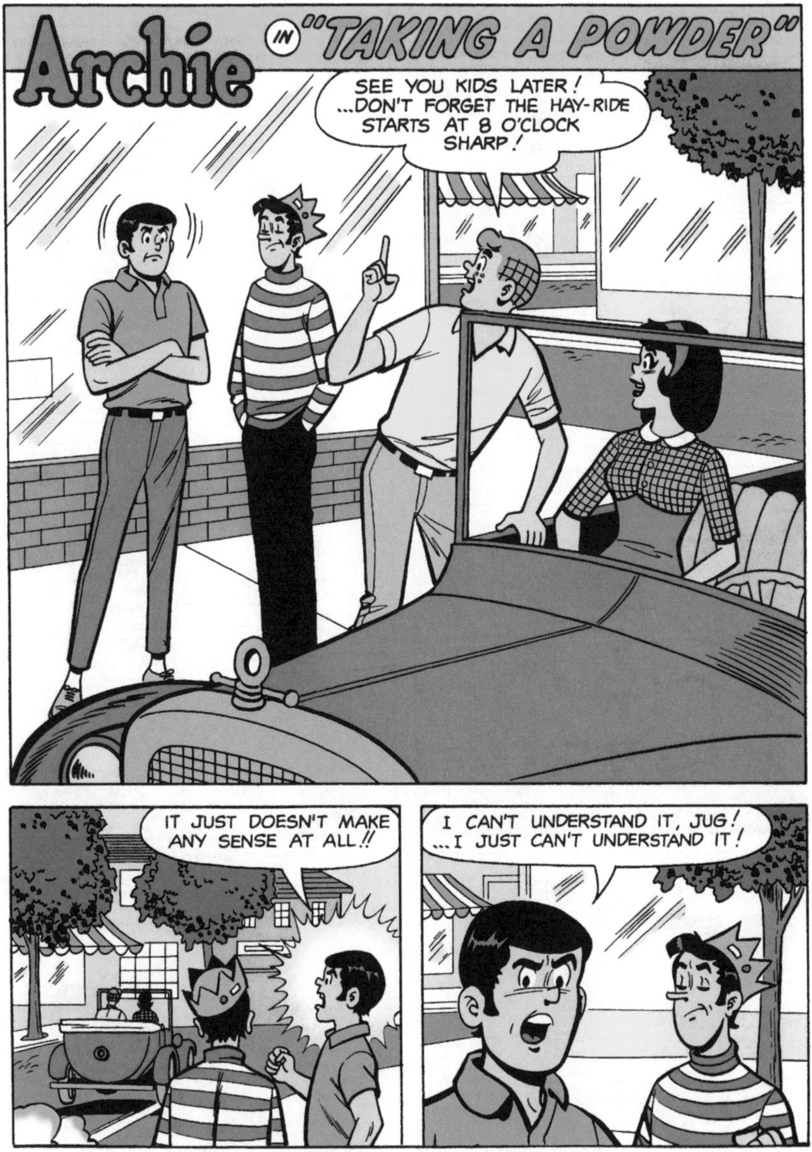
Archie
IN "TAKING A POWDER"
SEE YOU KIDS LATER! ...DON'T FORGET THE HAY-RIDE STARTS AT 8 O'CLOCK SHARP!
IT JUST DOESN'T MAKE ANY SENSE AT ALL!!
I CAN'T UNDERSTAND IT, JUG! ...I JUST CAN'T UNDERSTAND IT!

Story & Pencils: Al Hartley

Inks: Jon D'Agostino Letters: Bill Yoshida

Originally printed in EVERYTHING'S ARCHIE #6, JANUARY 1970

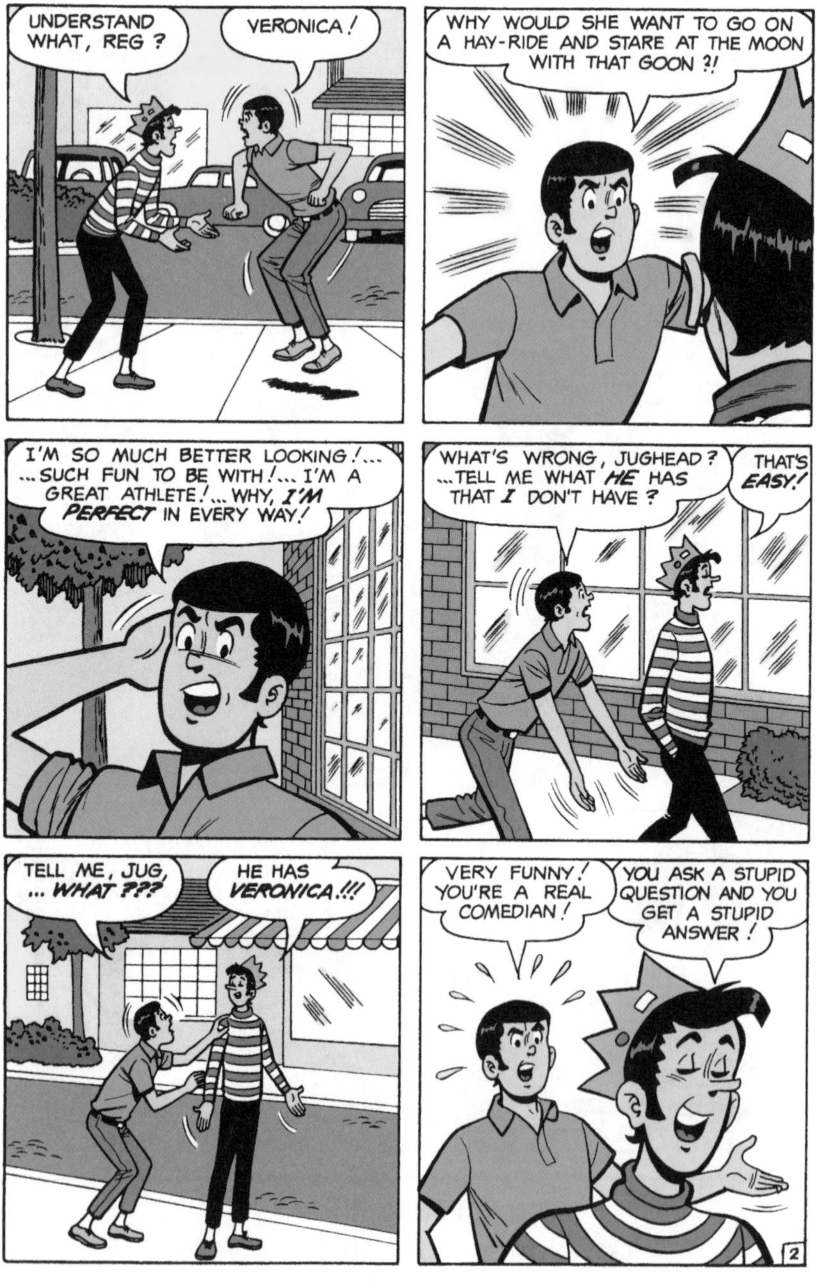
UNDERSTAND WHAT, REG ?
VERONICA !
WHY WOULD SHE WANT TO GO ON A HAY-RIDE AND STARE AT THE MOON WITH THAT GOON ?!
I'M SO MUCH BETTER LOOKING !... ...SUCH FUN TO BE WITH !... I'M A GREAT ATHLETE !... WHY, I'M PERFECT IN EVERY WAY !
WHAT'S WRONG, JUGHEAD ? ...TELL ME WHAT HE HAS THAT I DON'T HAVE ?
THAT'S EASY !
TELL ME, JUG, ... WHAT ???
HE HAS VERONICA !!!
VERY FUNNY ! YOU'RE A REAL COMEDIAN !
YOU ASK A STUPID QUESTION AND YOU GET A STUPID ANSWER !
2

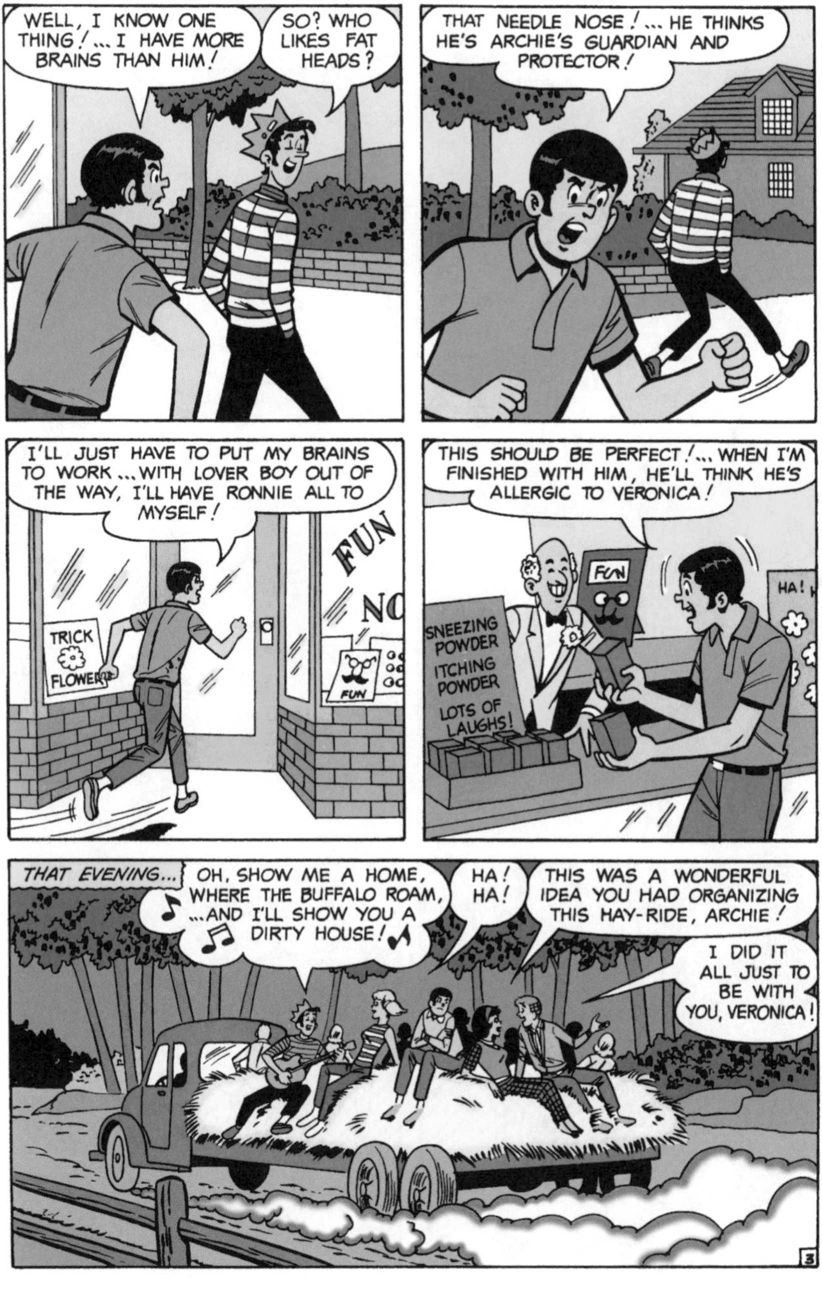
WELL, I KNOW ONE THING! ... I HAVE MORE BRAINS THAN HIM!
SO? WHO LIKES FAT HEADS?
THAT NEEDLE NOSE! ... HE THINKS HE'S ARCHIE'S GUARDIAN AND PROTECTOR!
I'LL JUST HAVE TO PUT MY BRAINS TO WORK ... WITH LOVER BOY OUT OF THE WAY, I'LL HAVE RONNIE ALL TO MYSELF!
FUN
NO
TRICK FLOWER
FUN
THIS SHOULD BE PERFECT! ... WHEN I'M FINISHED WITH HIM, HE'LL THINK HE'S ALLERGIC TO VERONICA!
FUN
HA!
SNEEZING POWDER
ITCHING POWDER
LOTS OF LAUGHS!
THAT EVENING...
OH, SHOW ME A HOME, WHERE THE BUFFALO ROAM, ...AND I'LL SHOW YOU A DIRTY HOUSE!
HA! HA!
THIS WAS A WONDERFUL IDEA YOU HAD ORGANIZING THIS HAY-RIDE, ARCHIE!
I DID IT ALL JUST TO BE WITH YOU, VERONICA!
3

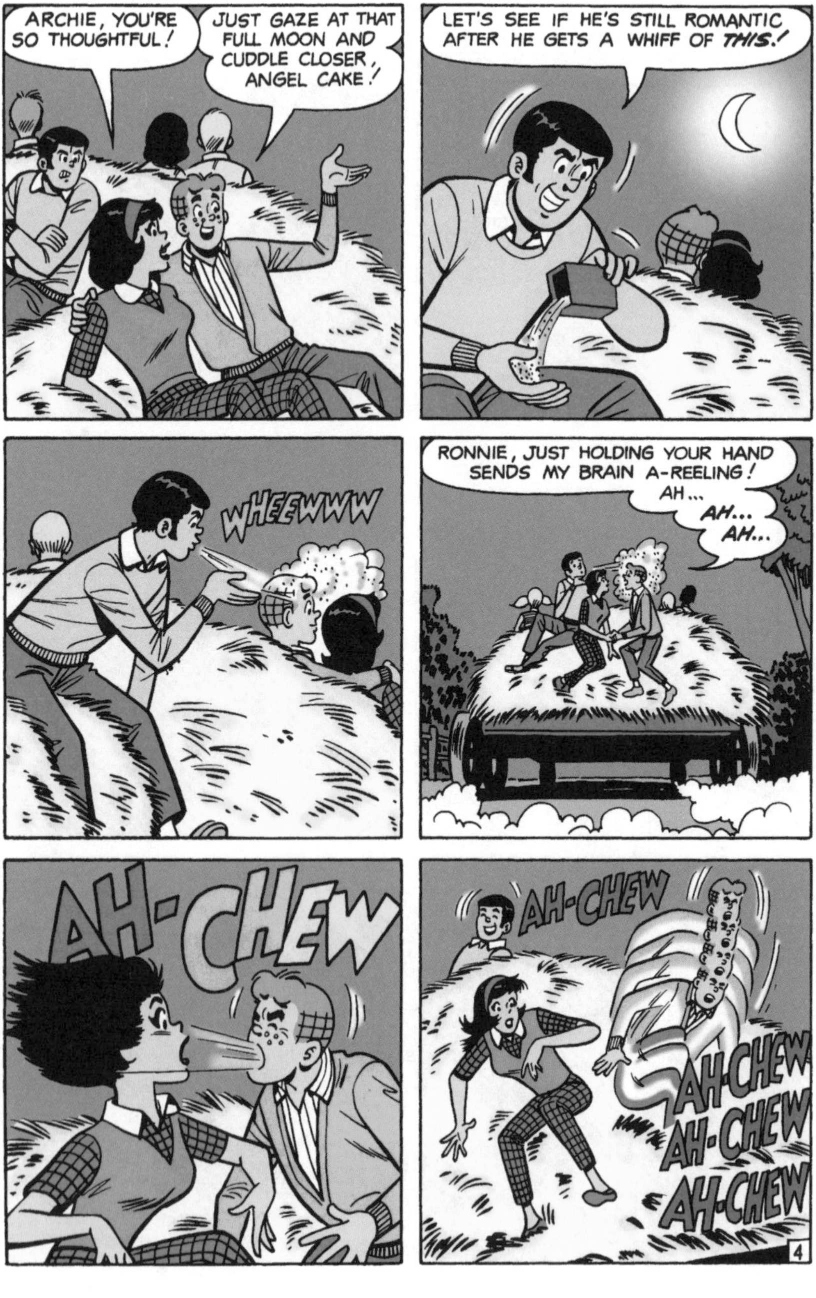
ARCHIE, YOU'RE SO THOUGHTFUL!
JUST GAZE AT THAT FULL MOON AND CUDDLE CLOSER, ANGEL CAKE!
LET'S SEE IF HE'S STILL ROMANTIC AFTER HE GETS A WHIFF OF THIS!
WHEEWWW
RONNIE, JUST HOLDING YOUR HAND SENDS MY BRAIN A-REELING! AH... AH... AH...
AH-CHEW
AH-CHEW
AH-CHEW
AH-CHEW
AH-CHEW
4

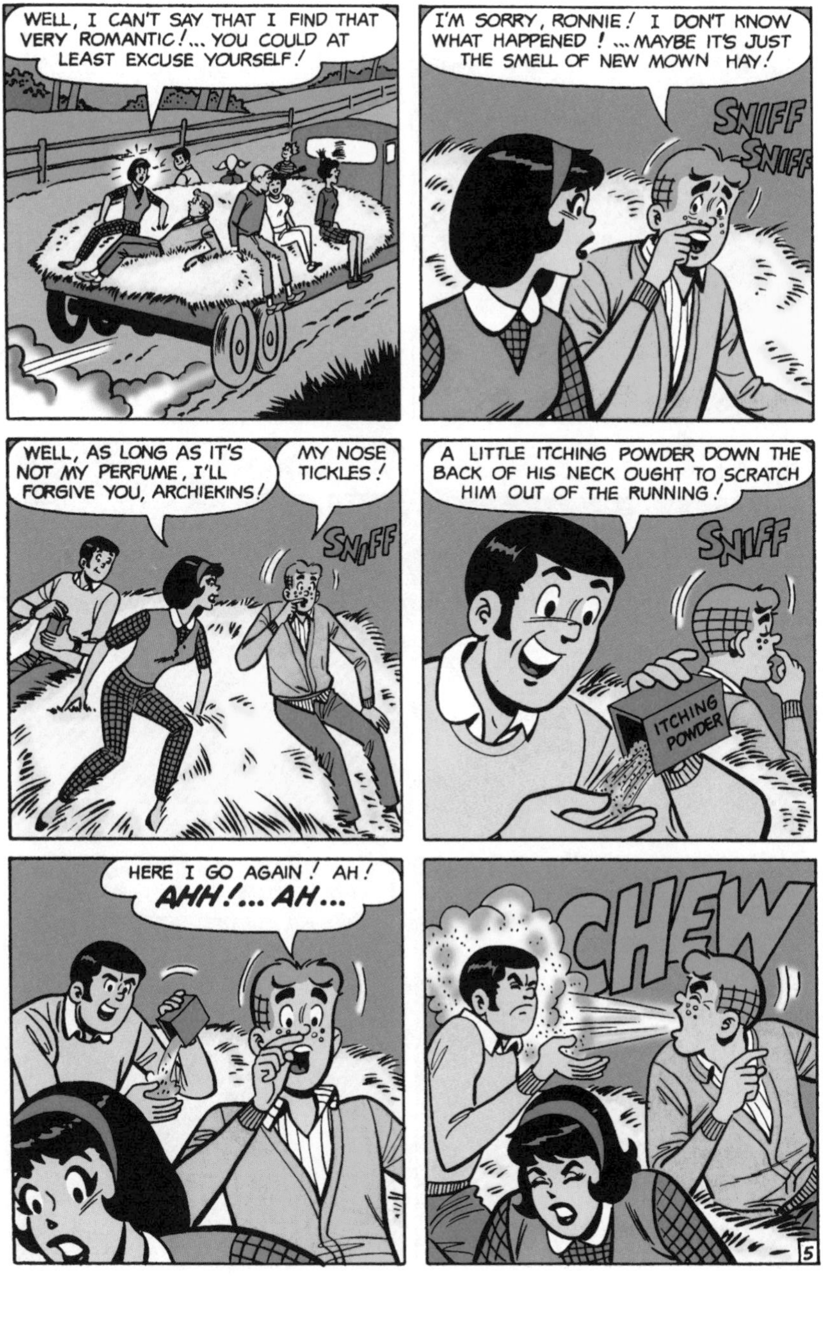
WELL, I CAN'T SAY THAT I FIND THAT VERY ROMANTIC!... YOU COULD AT LEAST EXCUSE YOURSELF!
I'M SORRY, RONNIE! I DON'T KNOW WHAT HAPPENED! ... MAYBE IT'S JUST THE SMELL OF NEW MOWN HAY!
SNIFF SNIFF
WELL, AS LONG AS IT'S NOT MY PERFUME, I'LL FORGIVE YOU, ARCHIEKINS!
MY NOSE TICKLES!
SNIFF
A LITTLE ITCHING POWDER DOWN THE BACK OF HIS NECK OUGHT TO SCRATCH HIM OUT OF THE RUNNING!
SNIFF
ITCHING POWDER
HERE I GO AGAIN! AH!
AHH!... AH...
CHEW
5

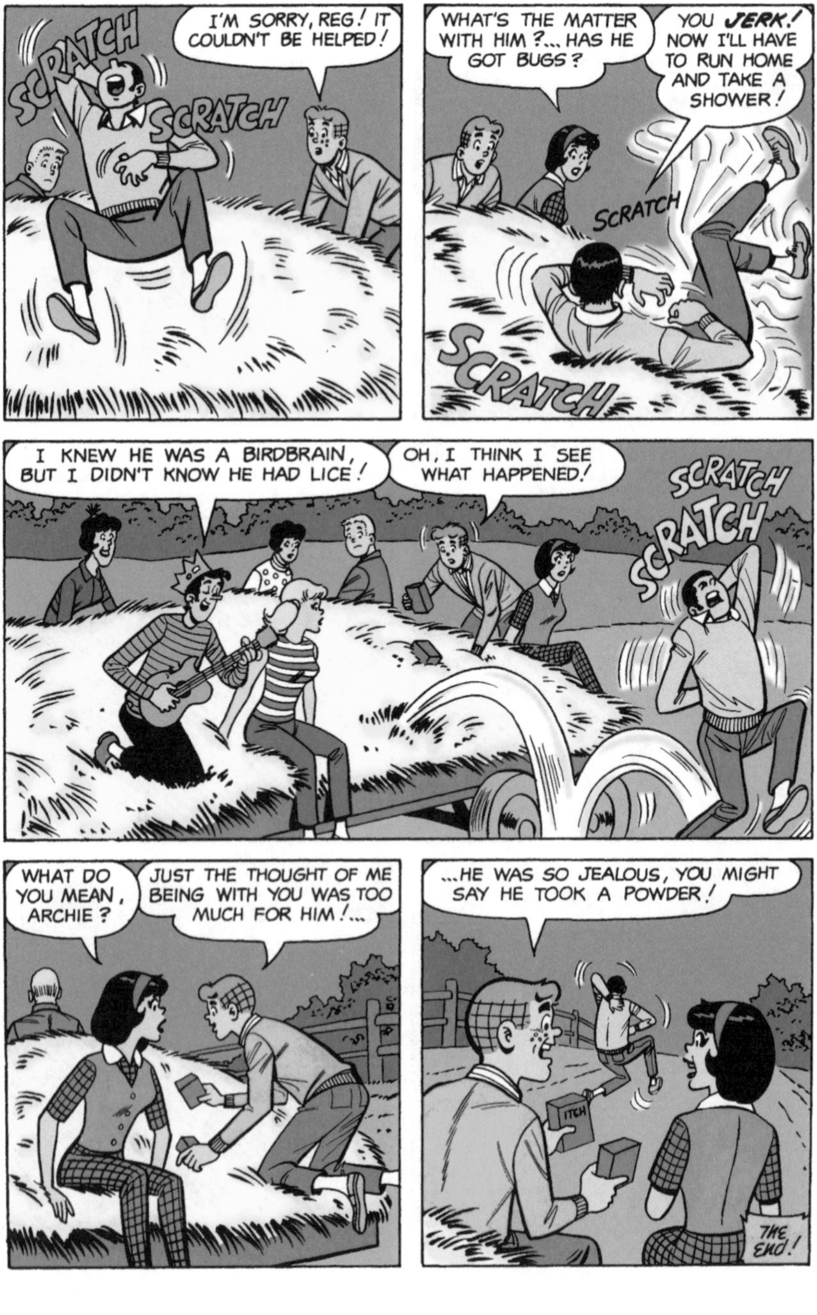
SCRATCH
SCRATCH
I'M SORRY, REG! IT COULDN'T BE HELPED!
WHAT'S THE MATTER WITH HIM?... HAS HE GOT BUGS?
YOU JERK! NOW I'LL HAVE TO RUN HOME AND TAKE A SHOWER!
SCRATCH
SCRATCH
I KNEW HE WAS A BIRDBRAIN, BUT I DIDN'T KNOW HE HAD LICE!
OH, I THINK I SEE WHAT HAPPENED!
SCRATCH
SCRATCH
WHAT DO YOU MEAN, ARCHIE?
JUST THE THOUGHT OF ME BEING WITH YOU WAS TOO MUCH FOR HIM!...
...HE WAS SO JEALOUS, YOU MIGHT SAY HE TOOK A POWDER!
ITCH
THE END!

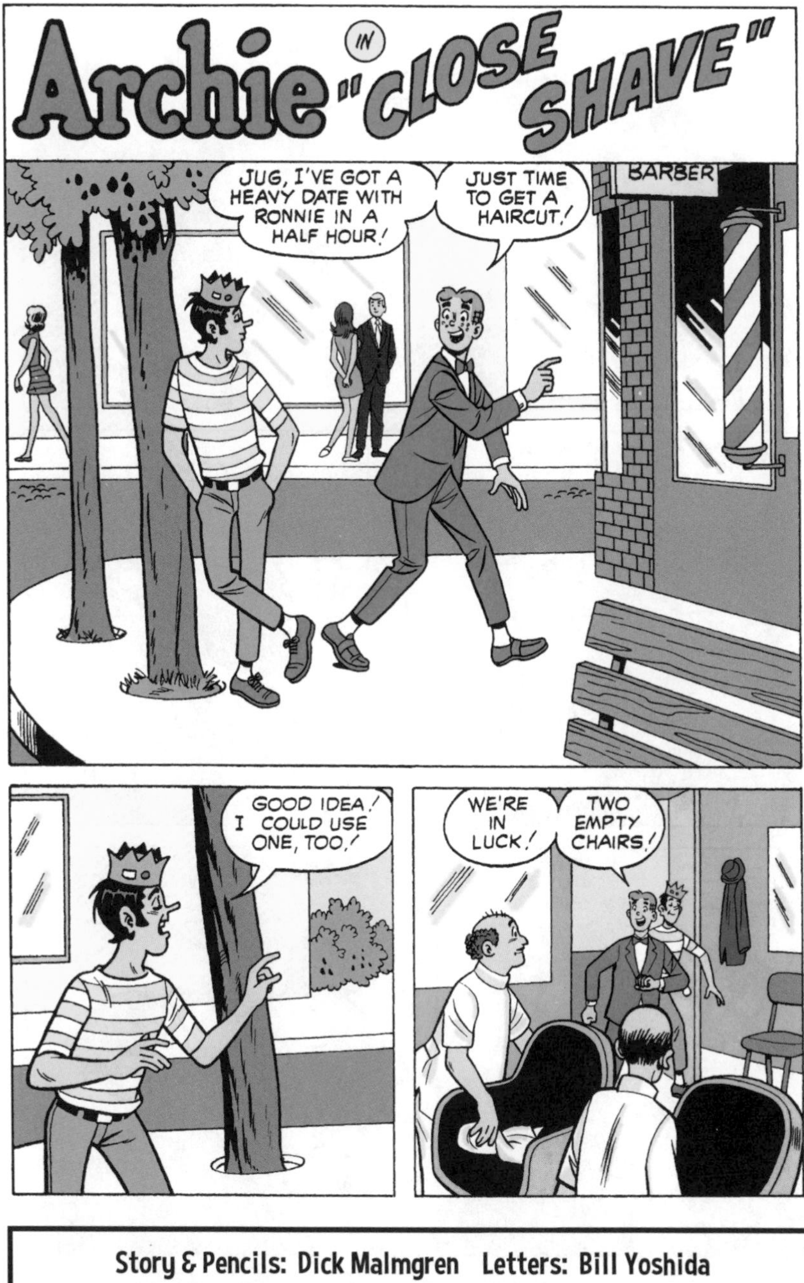
Archie
IN
"CLOSE SHAVE"
JUG, I'VE GOT A HEAVY DATE WITH RONNIE IN A HALF HOUR!
JUST TIME TO GET A HAIRCUT!
BARBER
GOOD IDEA! I COULD USE ONE, TOO!
WE'RE IN LUCK!
TWO EMPTY CHAIRS!

Story & Pencils: Dick Malmgren Letters: Bill Yoshida

Originally printed in EVERYTHING'S ARCHIE #6, JANUARY 1970

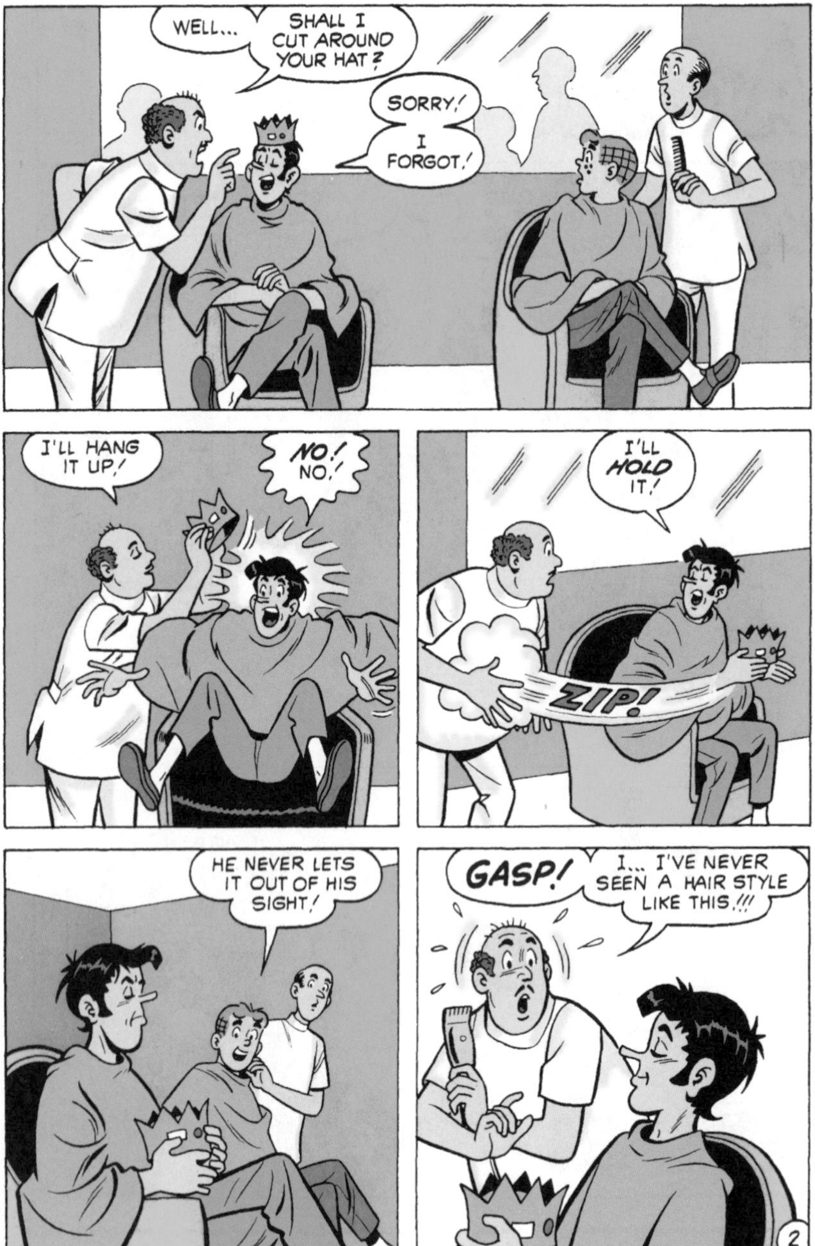
WELL...
SHALL I CUT AROUND YOUR HAT?
SORRY!
I FORGOT!
I'LL HANG IT UP!
NO! NO!
I'LL HOLD IT!
ZIP!
HE NEVER LETS IT OUT OF HIS SIGHT!
GASP!
I... I'VE NEVER SEEN A HAIR STYLE LIKE THIS!!!
2

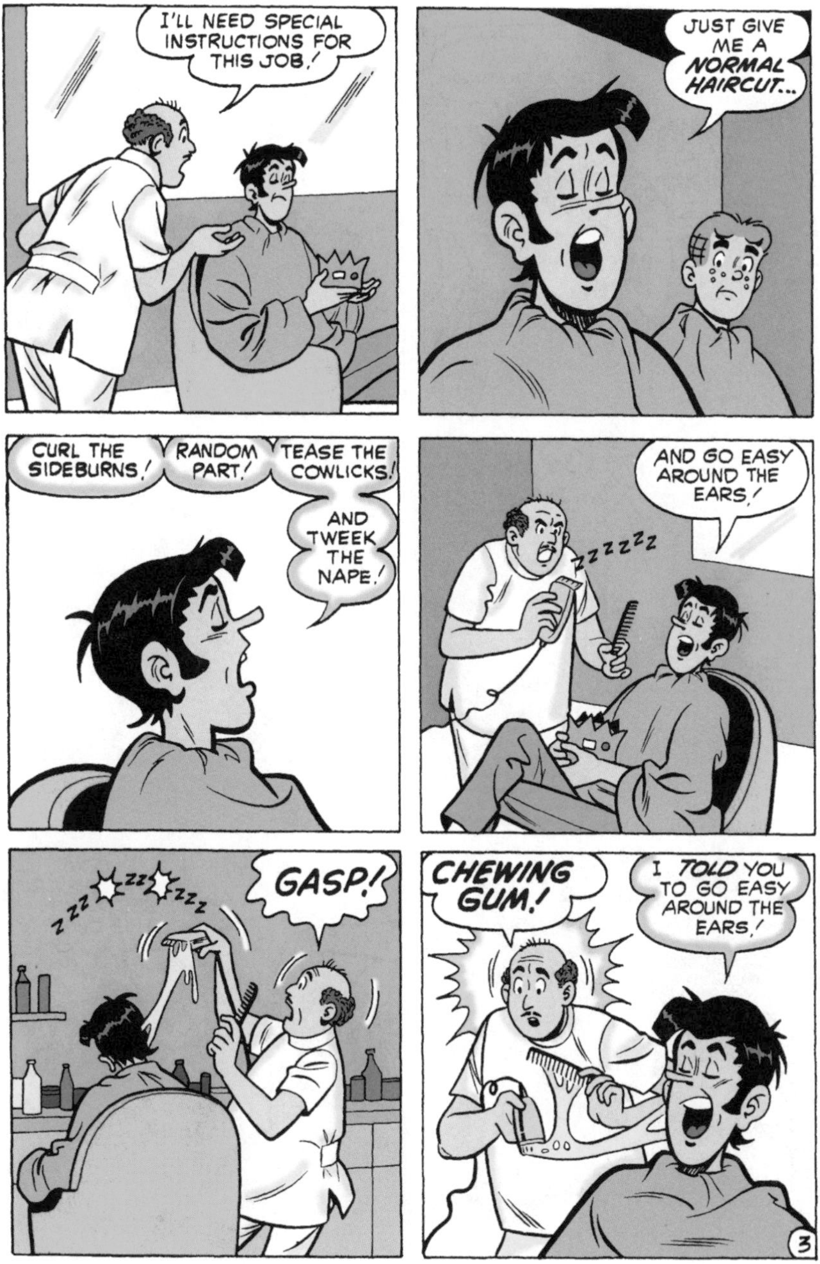
I'LL NEED SPECIAL INSTRUCTIONS FOR THIS JOB!
JUST GIVE ME A NORMAL HAIRCUT...
CURL THE SIDEBURNS!
RANDOM PART!
TEASE THE COWLICKS!
AND TWEEK THE NAPE!
AND GO EASY AROUND THE EARS!
ZZZZZZ
ZZZ ZZ ZZZ
GASP!
CHEWING GUM!
I TOLD YOU TO GO EASY AROUND THE EARS!
3

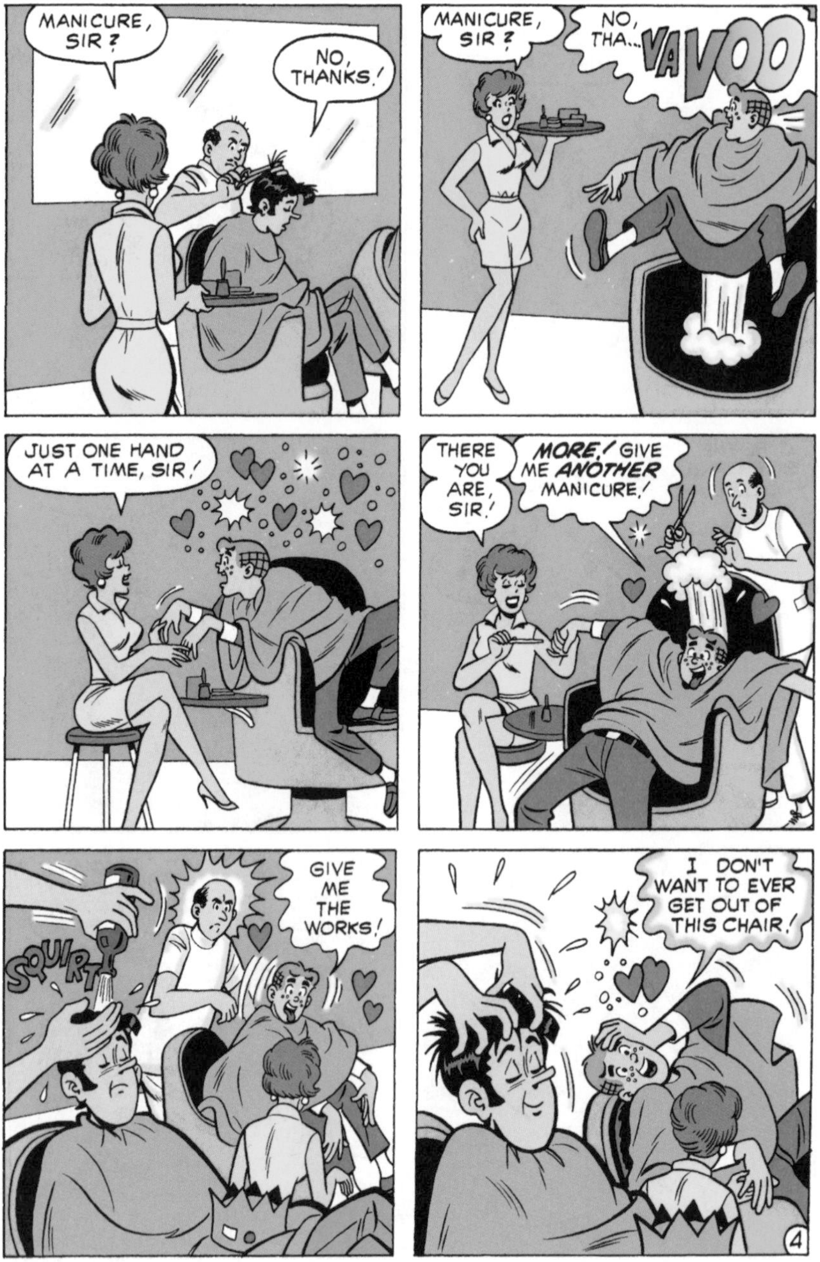
MANICURE, SIR?
NO, THANKS!
MANICURE, SIR?
NO, THA...
VAVOOM
JUST ONE HAND AT A TIME, SIR!
THERE YOU ARE, SIR!
MORE! GIVE ME ANOTHER MANICURE!
SQUIRT
GIVE ME THE WORKS!
I DON'T WANT TO EVER GET OUT OF THIS CHAIR!
4

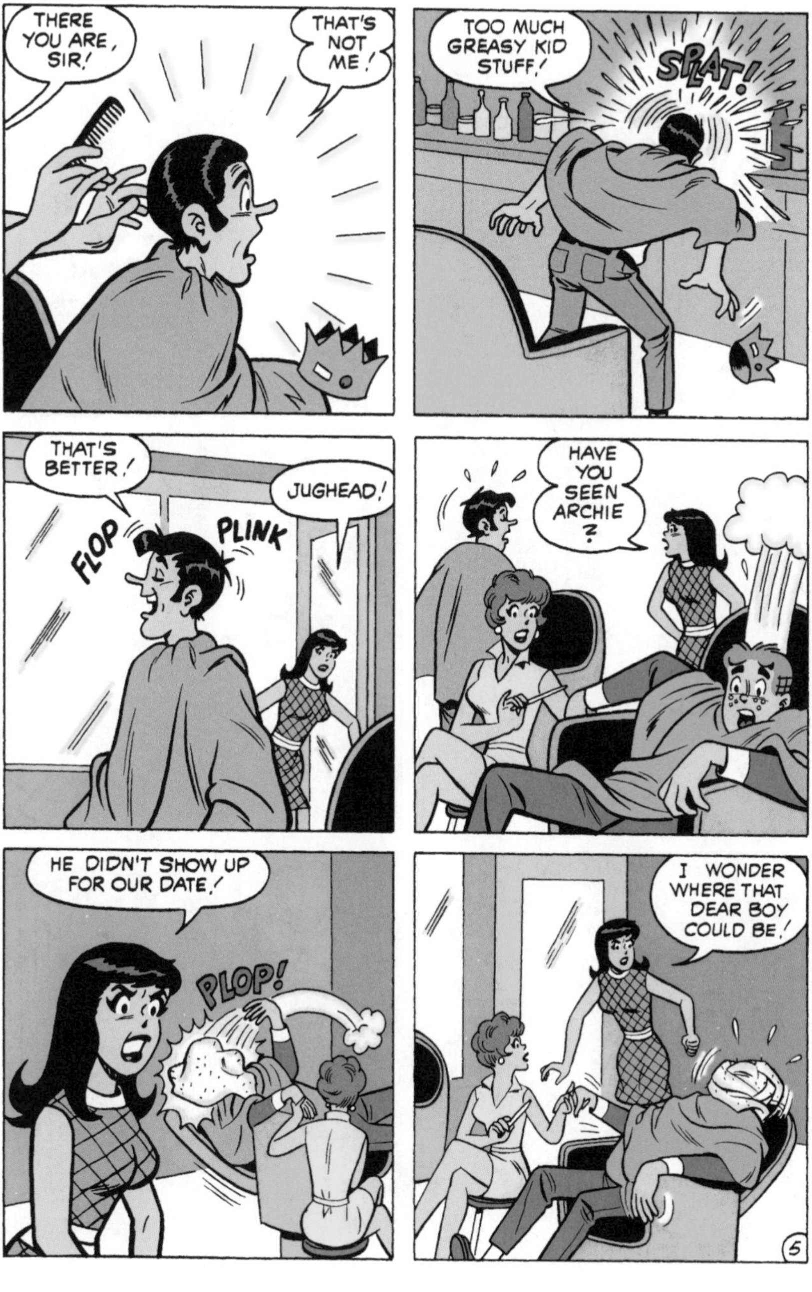
THERE YOU ARE, SIR!
THAT'S NOT ME!
TOO MUCH GREASY KID STUFF!
SPLAT!
THAT'S BETTER!
FLOP
PLINK
JUGHEAD!
HAVE YOU SEEN ARCHIE?
HE DIDN'T SHOW UP FOR OUR DATE!
PLOP!
I WONDER WHERE THAT DEAR BOY COULD BE!
5

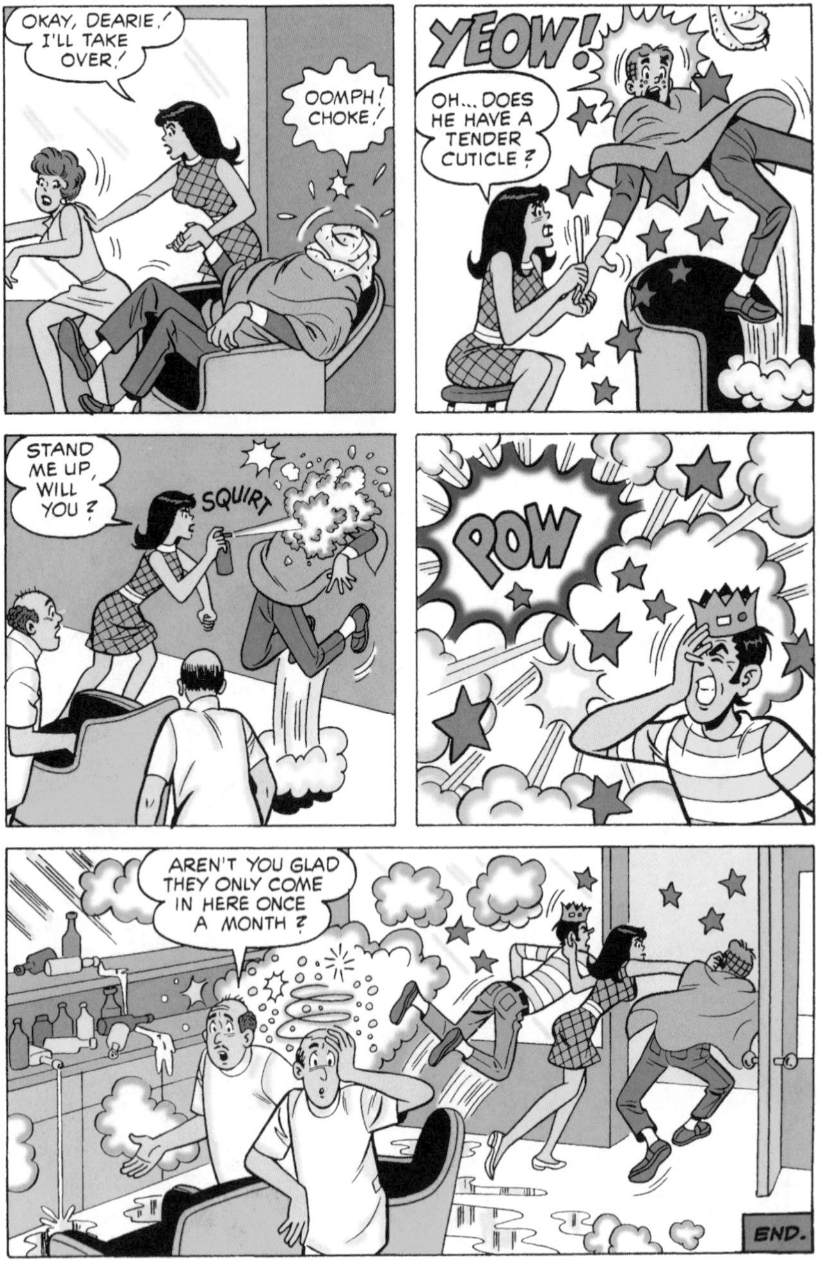
OKAY, DEARIE! I'LL TAKE OVER!
OOMPH! CHOKE!
YEOW!
OH... DOES HE HAVE A TENDER CUTICLE?
STAND ME UP, WILL YOU?
SQUIRT
POW
AREN'T YOU GLAD THEY ONLY COME IN HERE ONCE A MONTH?
END.

Everything's Archie in "Fair Play"

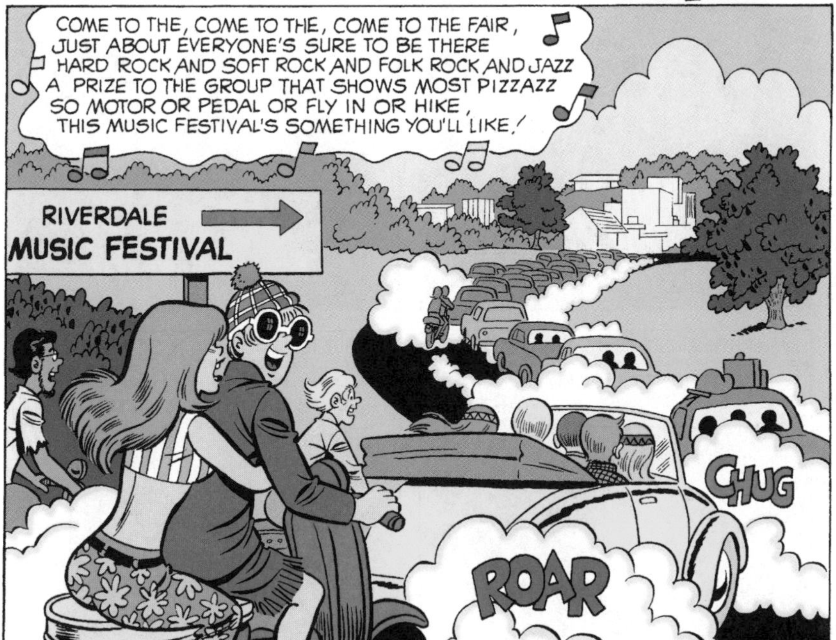
COME TO THE, COME TO THE, COME TO THE FAIR,
JUST ABOUT EVERYONE'S SURE TO BE THERE
HARD ROCK AND SOFT ROCK AND FOLK ROCK AND JAZZ
A PRIZE TO THE GROUP THAT SHOWS MOST PIZZAZZ
SO MOTOR OR PEDAL OR FLY IN OR HIKE,
THIS MUSIC FESTIVAL'S SOMETHING YOU'LL LIKE!
RIVERDALE MUSIC FESTIVAL
CHUG
ROAR

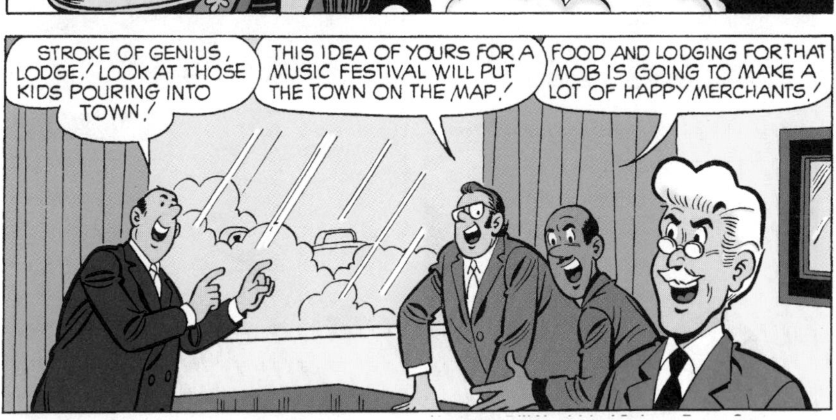
STROKE OF GENIUS, LODGE! LOOK AT THOSE KIDS POURING INTO TOWN!
THIS IDEA OF YOURS FOR A MUSIC FESTIVAL WILL PUT THE TOWN ON THE MAP!
FOOD AND LODGING FOR THAT MOB IS GOING TO MAKE A LOT OF HAPPY MERCHANTS!

Story & Pencils: Al Hartley Inks: Jon D'Agostino
Letters: Bill Yoshida Colors: Barry Grossman

Originally printed in EVERYTHING'S ARCHIE #7, APRIL 1970

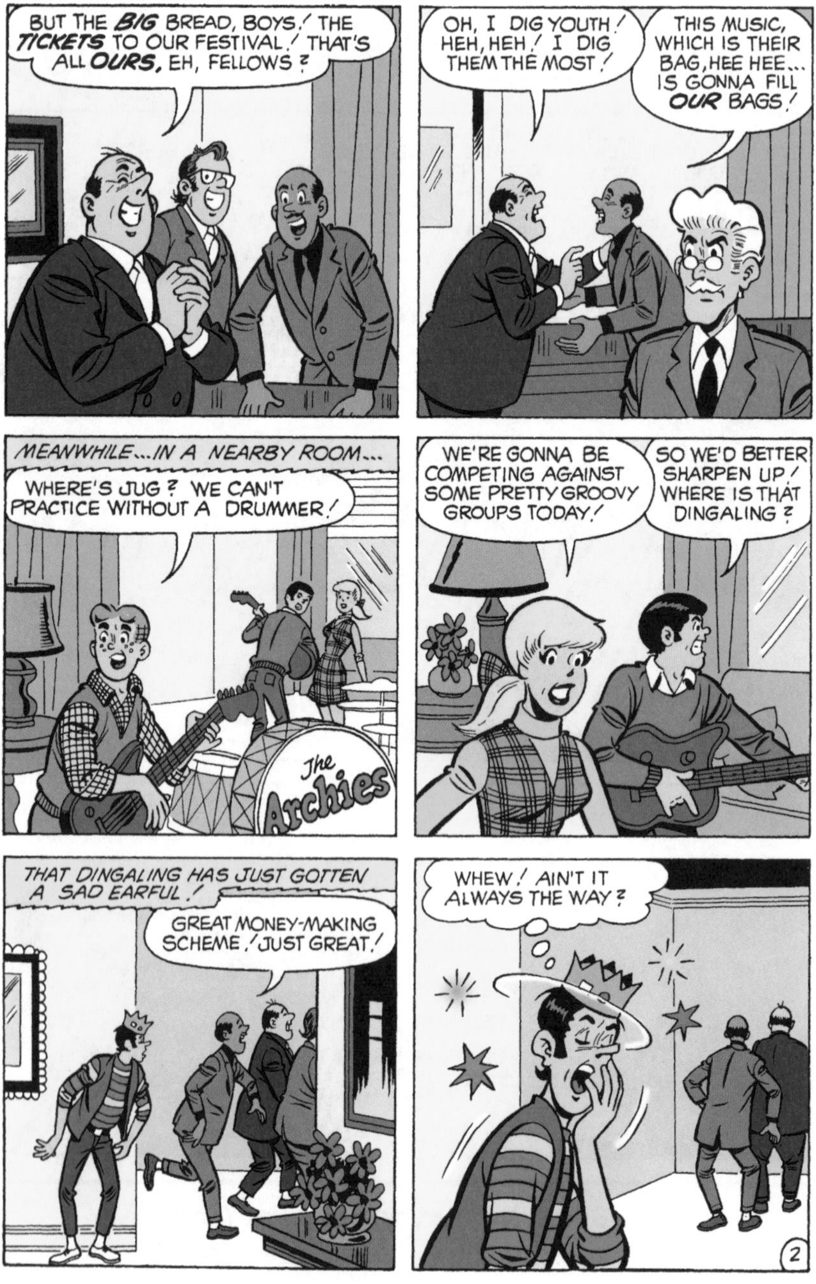
BUT THE BIG BREAD, BOYS! THE TICKETS TO OUR FESTIVAL! THAT'S ALL OURS, EH, FELLOWS?
OH, I DIG YOUTH! HEH, HEH! I DIG THEM THE MOST!
THIS MUSIC, WHICH IS THEIR BAG, HEE HEE... IS GONNA FILL OUR BAGS!
MEANWHILE...IN A NEARBY ROOM...
WHERE'S JUG? WE CAN'T PRACTICE WITHOUT A DRUMMER!
The Archies
WE'RE GONNA BE COMPETING AGAINST SOME PRETTY GROOVY GROUPS TODAY!
SO WE'D BETTER SHARPEN UP! WHERE IS THAT DINGALING?
THAT DINGALING HAS JUST GOTTEN A SAD EARFUL!
GREAT MONEY-MAKING SCHEME! JUST GREAT!
WHEW! AIN'T IT ALWAYS THE WAY?
2

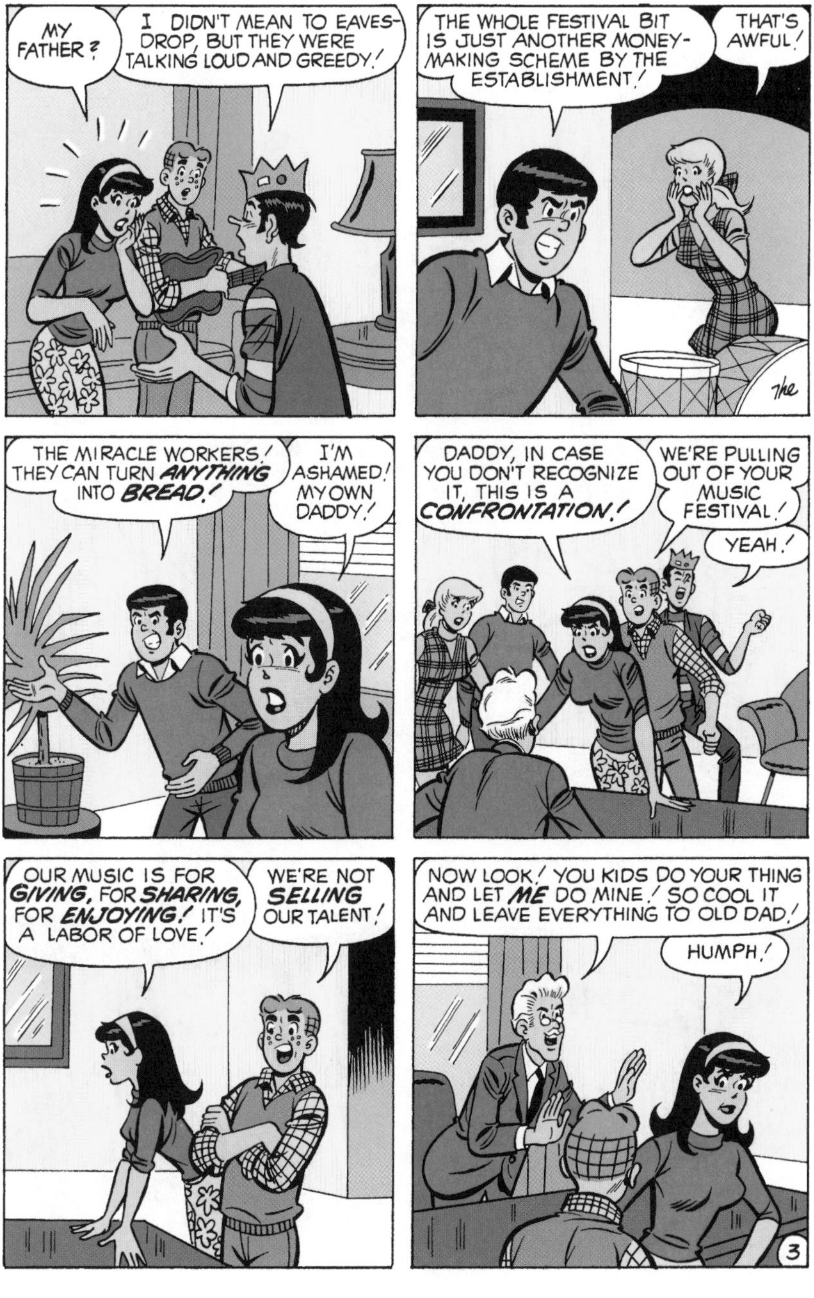
MY FATHER?
I DIDN'T MEAN TO EAVES-DROP, BUT THEY WERE TALKING LOUD AND GREEDY!
THE WHOLE FESTIVAL BIT IS JUST ANOTHER MONEY-MAKING SCHEME BY THE ESTABLISHMENT!
THAT'S AWFUL!
THE MIRACLE WORKERS! THEY CAN TURN ANYTHING INTO BREAD!
I'M ASHAMED! MY OWN DADDY!
DADDY, IN CASE YOU DON'T RECOGNIZE IT, THIS IS A CONFRONTATION!
WE'RE PULLING OUT OF YOUR MUSIC FESTIVAL!
YEAH!
OUR MUSIC IS FOR GIVING, FOR SHARING, FOR ENJOYING! IT'S A LABOR OF LOVE!
WE'RE NOT SELLING OUR TALENT!
NOW LOOK! YOU KIDS DO YOUR THING AND LET ME DO MINE! SO COOL IT AND LEAVE EVERYTHING TO OLD DAD!
HUMPH!
3

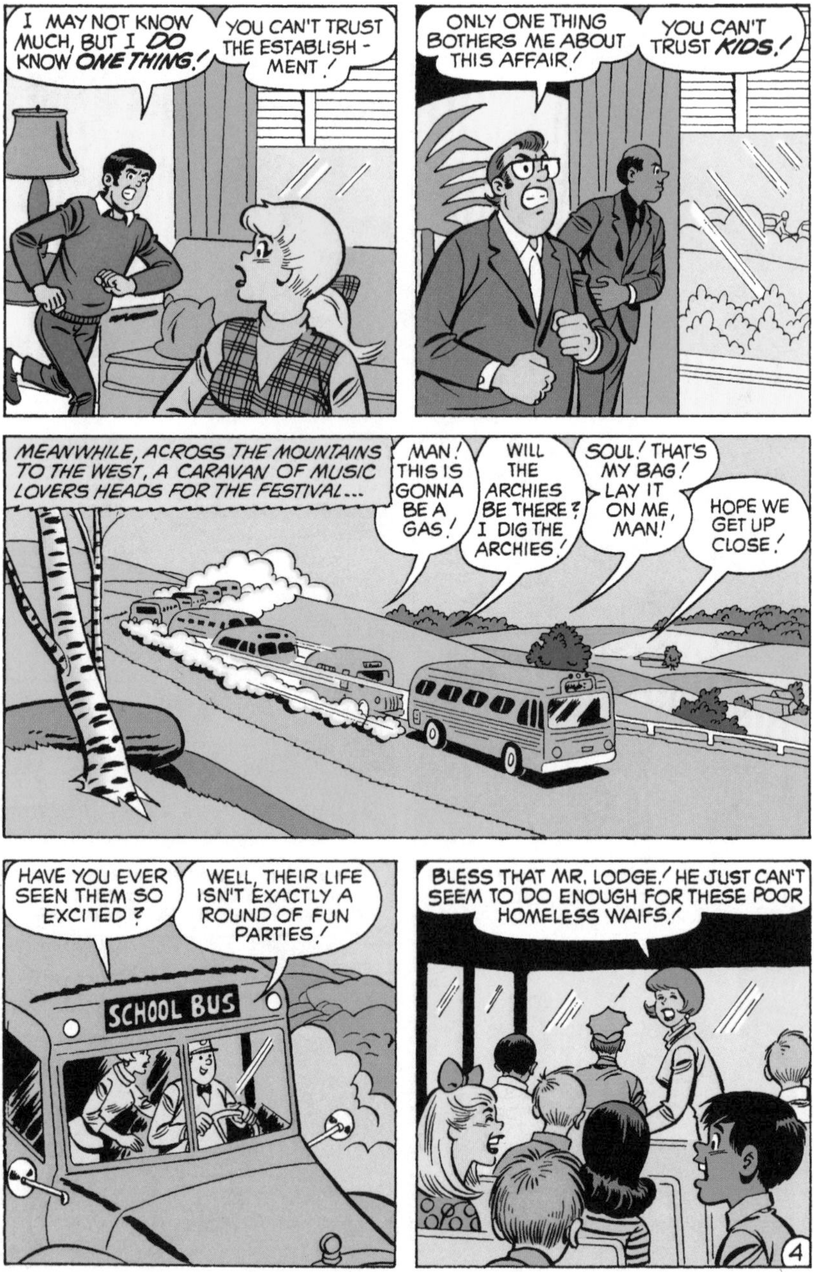
I MAY NOT KNOW MUCH, BUT I DO KNOW ONE THING!
YOU CAN'T TRUST THE ESTABLISH-MENT!
ONLY ONE THING BOTHERS ME ABOUT THIS AFFAIR!
YOU CAN'T TRUST KIDS!
MEANWHILE, ACROSS THE MOUNTAINS TO THE WEST, A CARAVAN OF MUSIC LOVERS HEADS FOR THE FESTIVAL...
MAN! THIS IS GONNA BE A GAS!
WILL THE ARCHIES BE THERE? I DIG THE ARCHIES!
SOUL! THAT'S MY BAG! LAY IT ON ME, MAN!
HOPE WE GET UP CLOSE!
HAVE YOU EVER SEEN THEM SO EXCITED?
WELL, THEIR LIFE ISN'T EXACTLY A ROUND OF FUN PARTIES!
SCHOOL BUS
BLESS THAT MR. LODGE! HE JUST CAN'T SEEM TO DO ENOUGH FOR THESE POOR HOMELESS WAIFS!
4

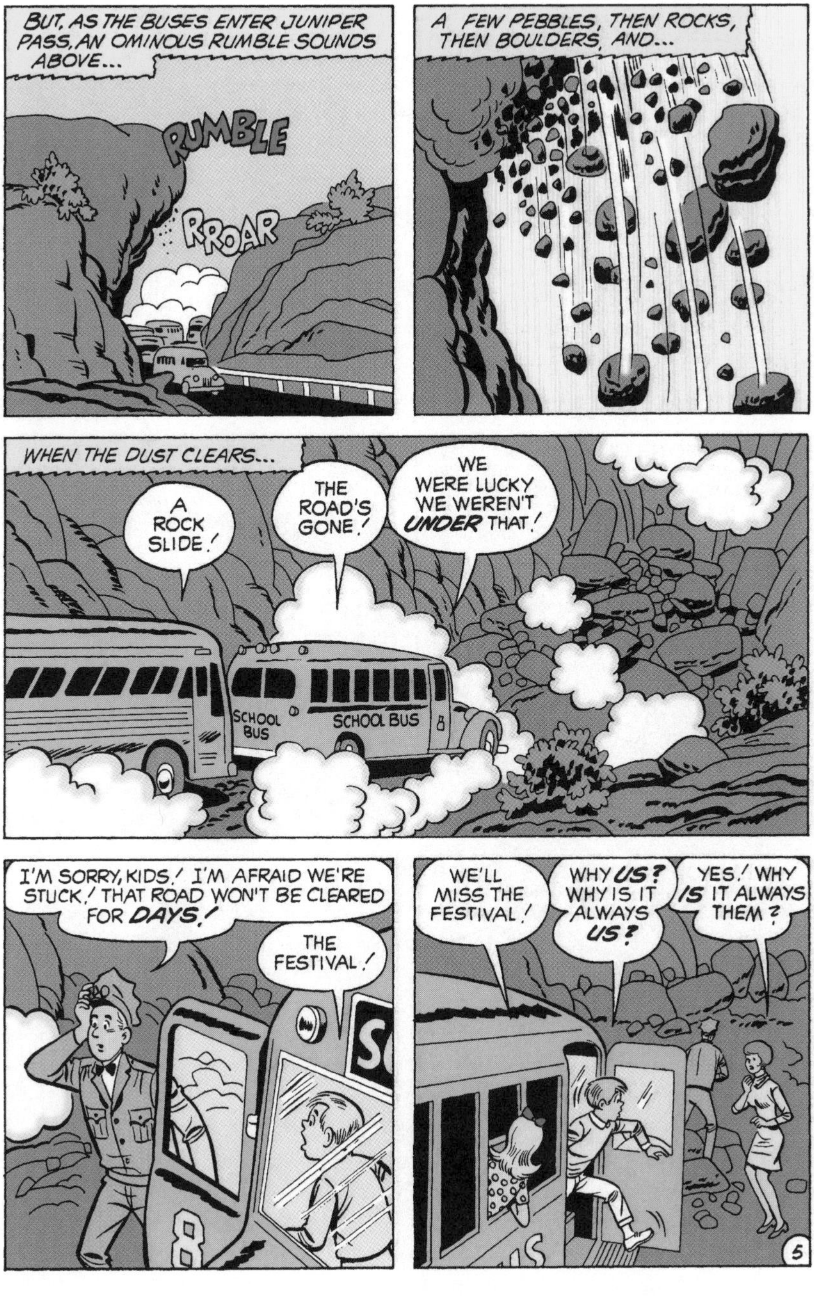
BUT, AS THE BUSES ENTER JUNIPER PASS, AN OMINOUS RUMBLE SOUNDS ABOVE...
RUMBLE
RROAR
A FEW PEBBLES, THEN ROCKS, THEN BOULDERS, AND...
WHEN THE DUST CLEARS...
A ROCK SLIDE!
THE ROAD'S GONE!
WE WERE LUCKY WE WEREN'T UNDER THAT!
SCHOOL BUS
SCHOOL BUS
I'M SORRY, KIDS! I'M AFRAID WE'RE STUCK! THAT ROAD WON'T BE CLEARED FOR DAYS!
THE FESTIVAL!
WE'LL MISS THE FESTIVAL!
WHY US? WHY IS IT ALWAYS US?
YES! WHY IS IT ALWAYS THEM?
5

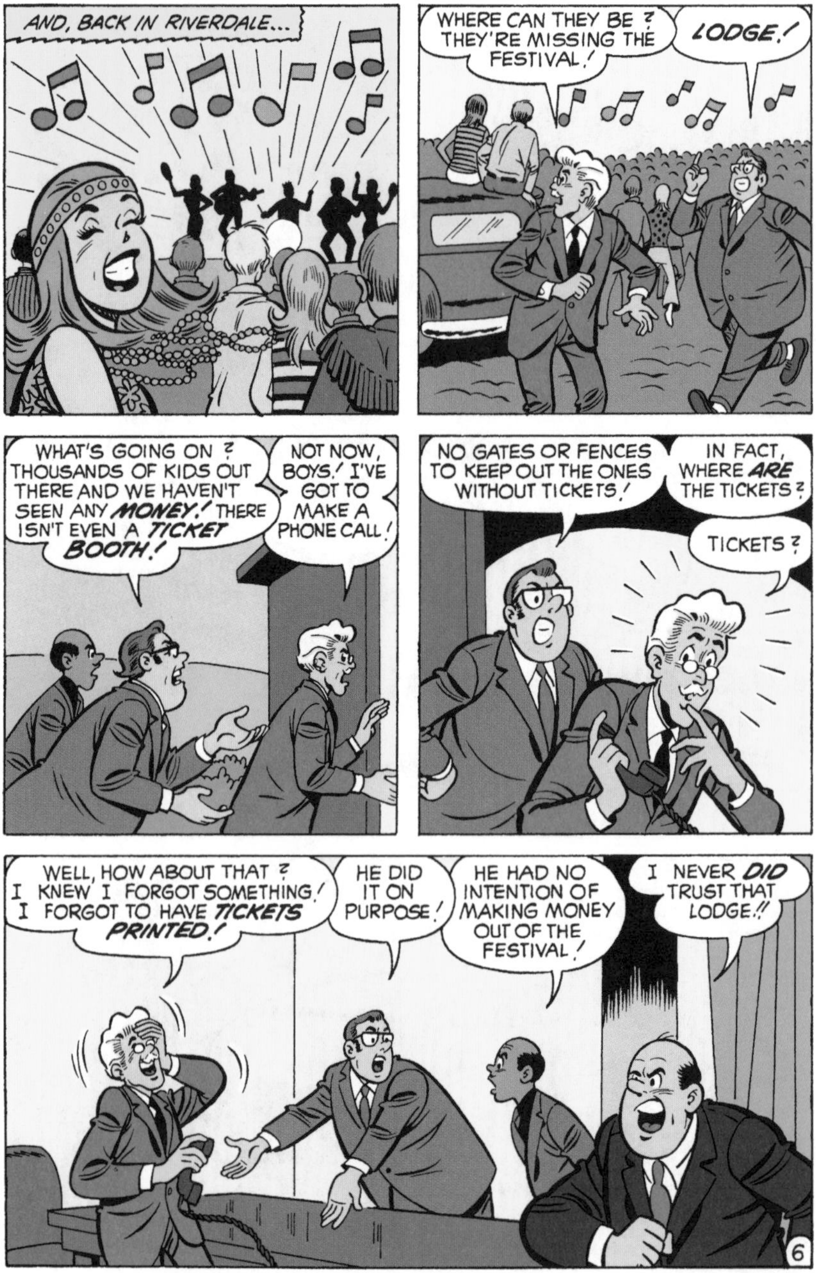
AND, BACK IN RIVERDALE...
WHERE CAN THEY BE ? THEY'RE MISSING THE FESTIVAL!
LODGE!
WHAT'S GOING ON ? THOUSANDS OF KIDS OUT THERE AND WE HAVEN'T SEEN ANY MONEY! THERE ISN'T EVEN A TICKET BOOTH!
NOT NOW, BOYS! I'VE GOT TO MAKE A PHONE CALL!
NO GATES OR FENCES TO KEEP OUT THE ONES WITHOUT TICKETS!
IN FACT, WHERE ARE THE TICKETS ?
TICKETS ?
WELL, HOW ABOUT THAT ? I KNEW I FORGOT SOMETHING! I FORGOT TO HAVE TICKETS PRINTED!
HE DID IT ON PURPOSE!
HE HAD NO INTENTION OF MAKING MONEY OUT OF THE FESTIVAL!
I NEVER DID TRUST THAT LODGE!!
6

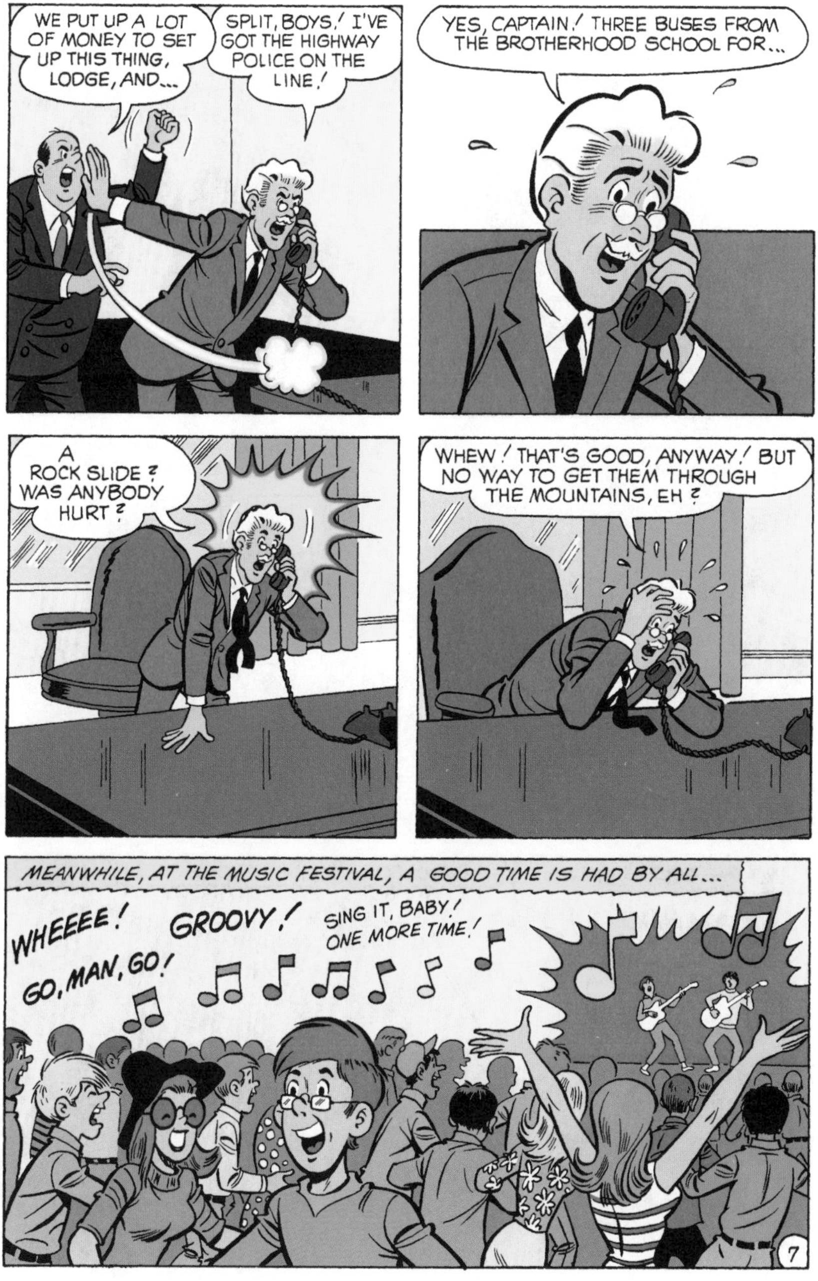
WE PUT UP A LOT OF MONEY TO SET UP THIS THING, LODGE, AND...
SPLIT, BOYS! I'VE GOT THE HIGHWAY POLICE ON THE LINE!
YES, CAPTAIN! THREE BUSES FROM THE BROTHERHOOD SCHOOL FOR...
A ROCK SLIDE? WAS ANYBODY HURT?
WHEW! THAT'S GOOD, ANYWAY! BUT NO WAY TO GET THEM THROUGH THE MOUNTAINS, EH?
MEANWHILE, AT THE MUSIC FESTIVAL, A GOOD TIME IS HAD BY ALL...
WHEEEE!
GROOVY!
SING IT, BABY! ONE MORE TIME!
GO, MAN, GO!
7

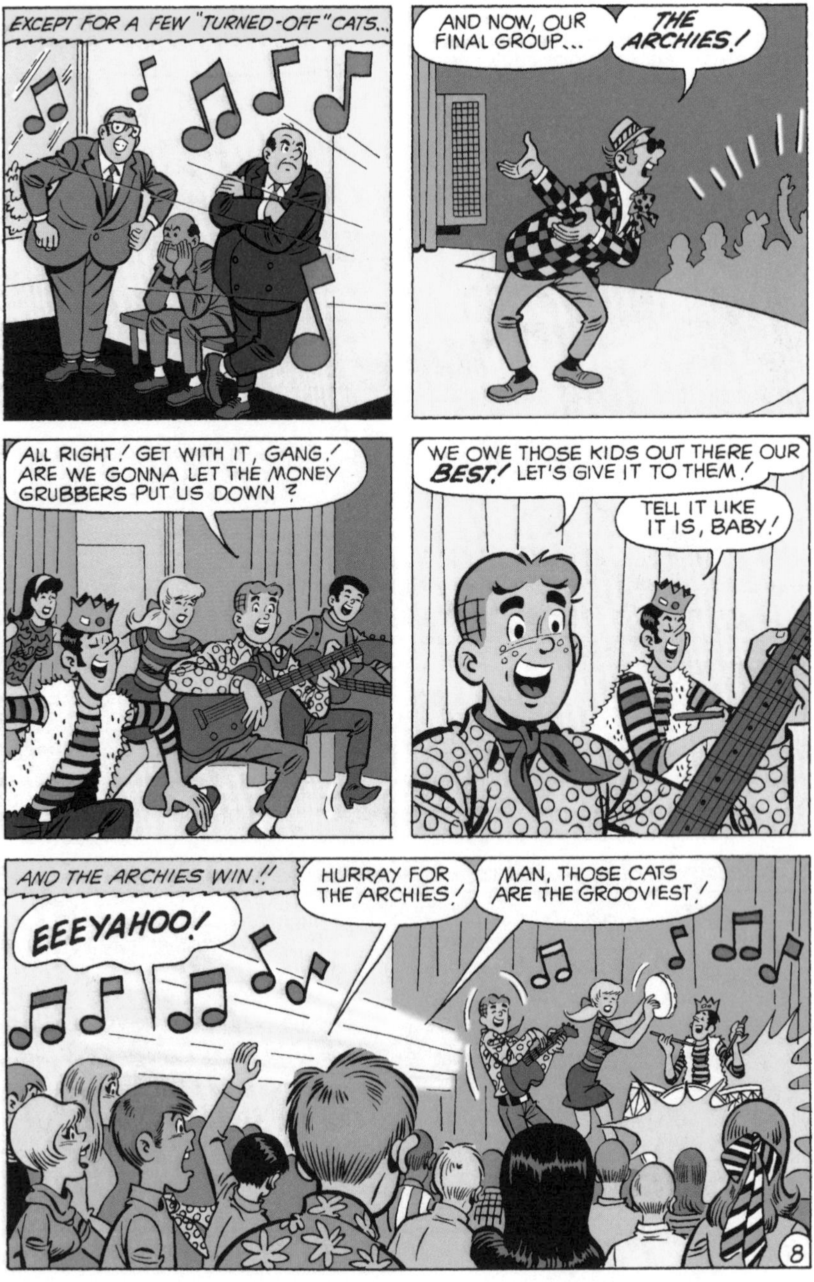
EXCEPT FOR A FEW "TURNED-OFF" CATS...
AND NOW, OUR FINAL GROUP...
THE ARCHIES!
ALL RIGHT! GET WITH IT, GANG! ARE WE GONNA LET THE MONEY GRUBBERS PUT US DOWN ?
WE OWE THOSE KIDS OUT THERE OUR BEST! LET'S GIVE IT TO THEM!
TELL IT LIKE IT IS, BABY!
AND THE ARCHIES WIN!!
HURRAY FOR THE ARCHIES!
MAN, THOSE CATS ARE THE GROOVIEST!
EEEYAHOO!
8

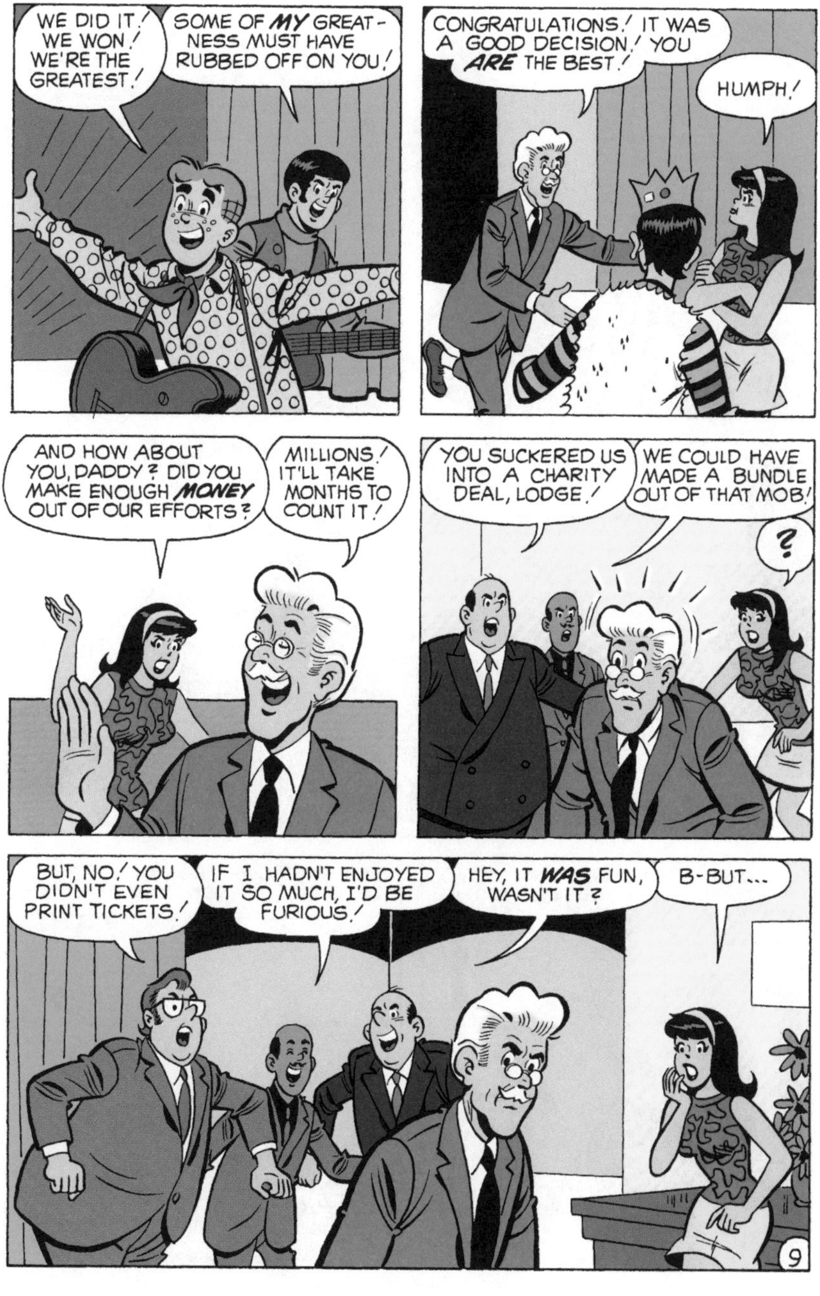
WE DID IT! WE WON! WE'RE THE GREATEST!
SOME OF MY GREAT-NESS MUST HAVE RUBBED OFF ON YOU!
CONGRATULATIONS! IT WAS A GOOD DECISION! YOU ARE THE BEST!
HUMPH!
AND HOW ABOUT YOU, DADDY? DID YOU MAKE ENOUGH MONEY OUT OF OUR EFFORTS?
MILLIONS! IT'LL TAKE MONTHS TO COUNT IT!
YOU SUCKERED US INTO A CHARITY DEAL, LODGE!
WE COULD HAVE MADE A BUNDLE OUT OF THAT MOB!
?
BUT, NO! YOU DIDN'T EVEN PRINT TICKETS!
IF I HADN'T ENJOYED IT SO MUCH, I'D BE FURIOUS!
HEY, IT WAS FUN, WASN'T IT?
B-BUT...
9

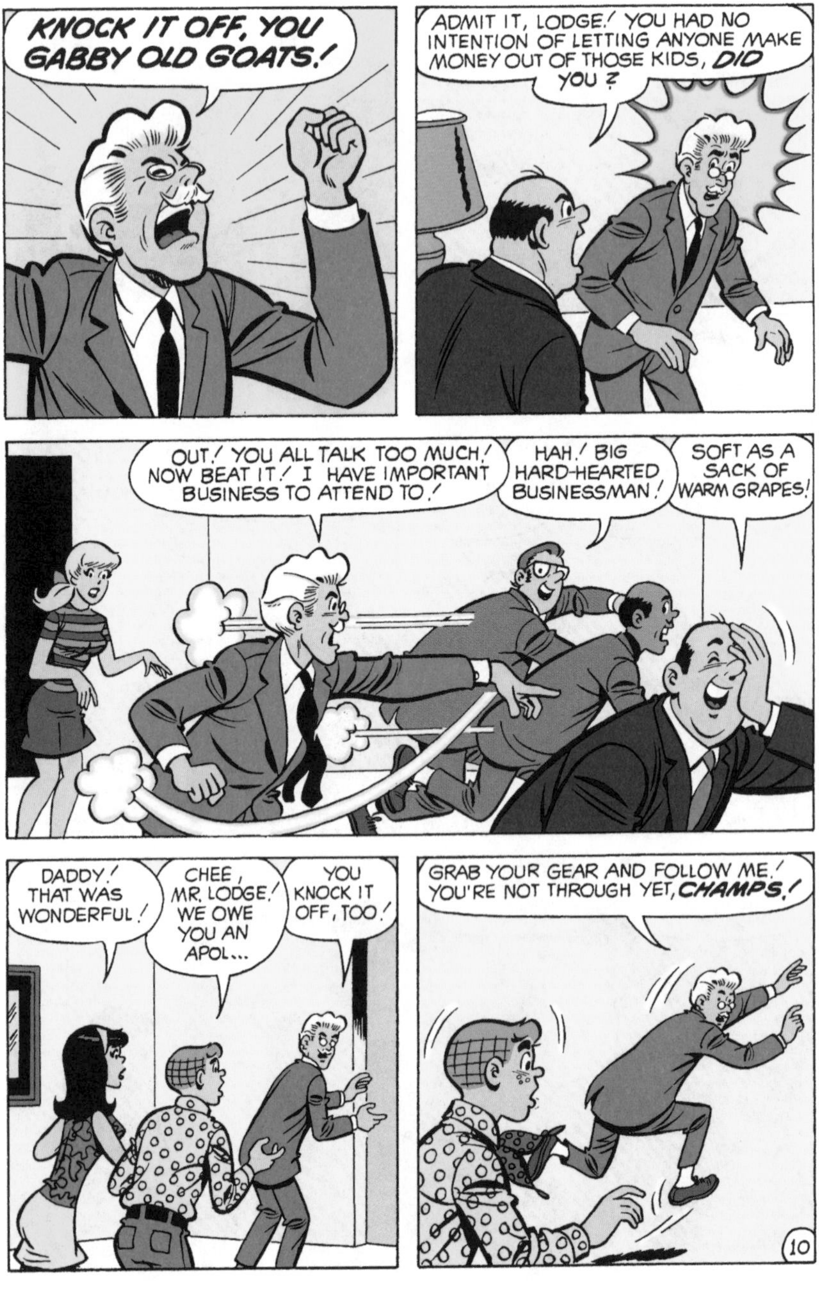
KNOCK IT OFF, YOU GABBY OLD GOATS!
ADMIT IT, LODGE! YOU HAD NO INTENTION OF LETTING ANYONE MAKE MONEY OUT OF THOSE KIDS, DID YOU?
OUT! YOU ALL TALK TOO MUCH! NOW BEAT IT! I HAVE IMPORTANT BUSINESS TO ATTEND TO!
HAH! BIG HARD-HEARTED BUSINESSMAN!
SOFT AS A SACK OF WARM GRAPES!
DADDY! THAT WAS WONDERFUL!
CHEE, MR. LODGE! WE OWE YOU AN APOL...
YOU KNOCK IT OFF, TOO!
GRAB YOUR GEAR AND FOLLOW ME! YOU'RE NOT THROUGH YET, CHAMPS!
10

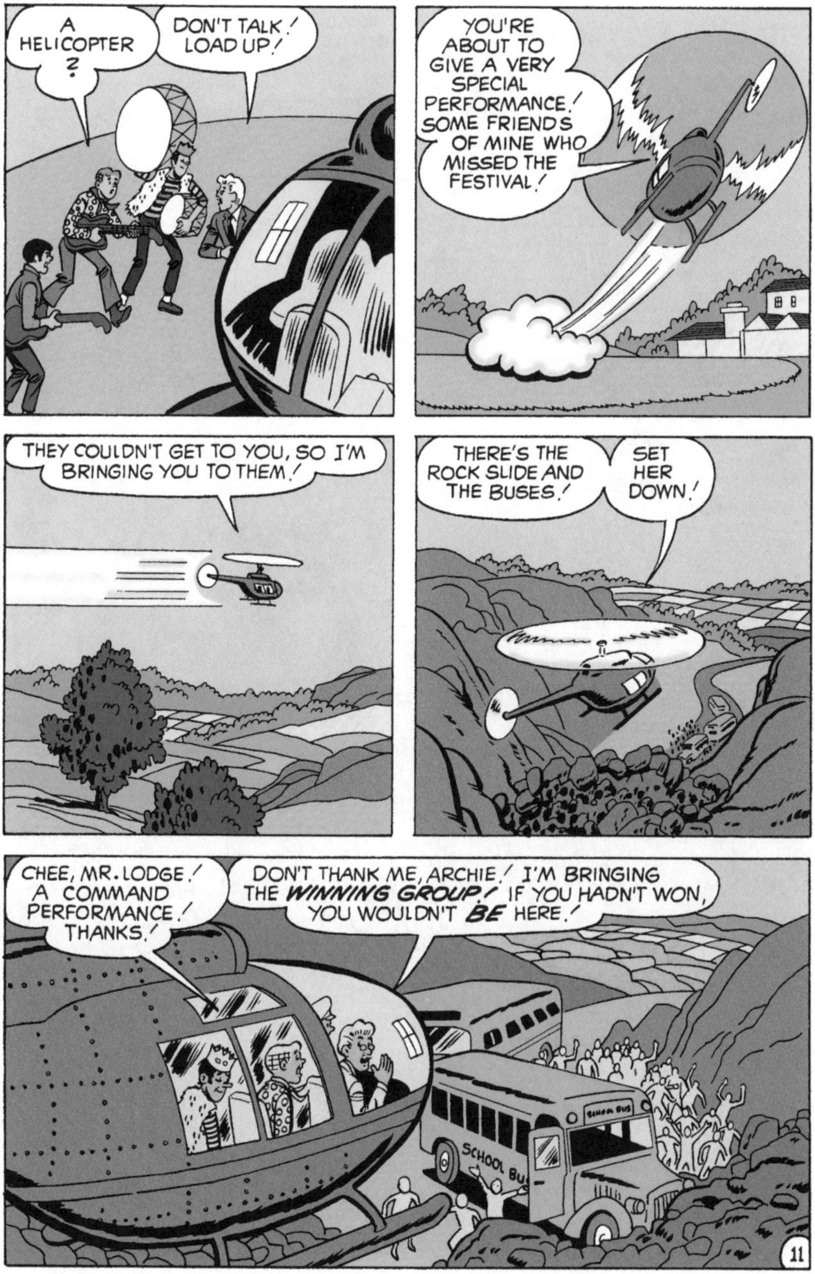
A HELICOPTER ?
DON'T TALK! LOAD UP!
YOU'RE ABOUT TO GIVE A VERY SPECIAL PERFORMANCE! SOME FRIENDS OF MINE WHO MISSED THE FESTIVAL!
THEY COULDN'T GET TO YOU, SO I'M BRINGING YOU TO THEM!
THERE'S THE ROCK SLIDE AND THE BUSES!
SET HER DOWN!
CHEE, MR. LODGE! A COMMAND PERFORMANCE! THANKS!
DON'T THANK ME, ARCHIE! I'M BRINGING THE WINNING GROUP! IF YOU HADN'T WON, YOU WOULDN'T BE HERE!
SCHOOL BUS
11

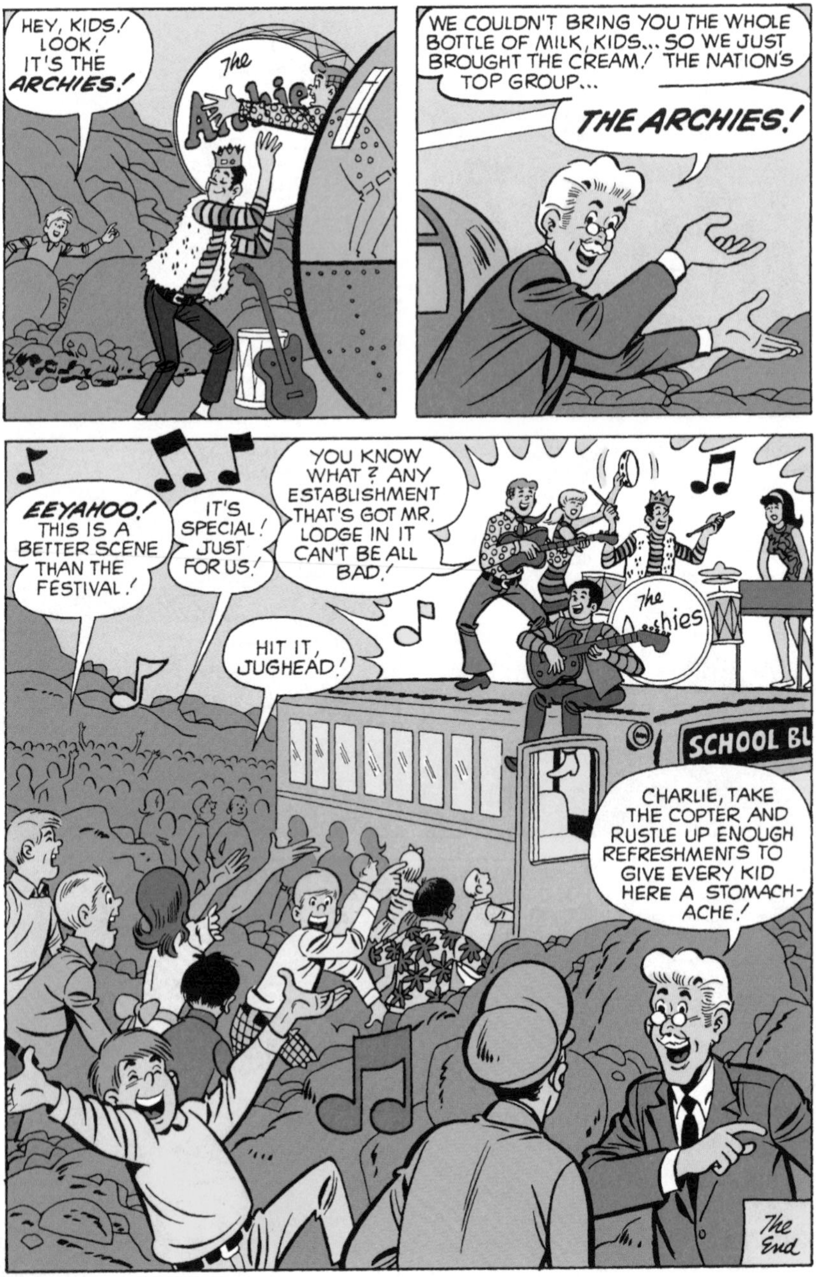
HEY, KIDS! LOOK! IT'S THE ARCHIES!
The Archies
WE COULDN'T BRING YOU THE WHOLE BOTTLE OF MILK, KIDS... SO WE JUST BROUGHT THE CREAM! THE NATION'S TOP GROUP...
THE ARCHIES!
EEYAHOO! THIS IS A BETTER SCENE THAN THE FESTIVAL!
IT'S SPECIAL! JUST FOR US!
YOU KNOW WHAT? ANY ESTABLISHMENT THAT'S GOT MR. LODGE IN IT CAN'T BE ALL BAD!
HIT IT, JUGHEAD!
SCHOOL BU
CHARLIE, TAKE THE COPTER AND RUSTLE UP ENOUGH REFRESHMENTS TO GIVE EVERY KID HERE A STOMACH-ACHE!
The End

Archie in "A MYNAH INCIDENT"

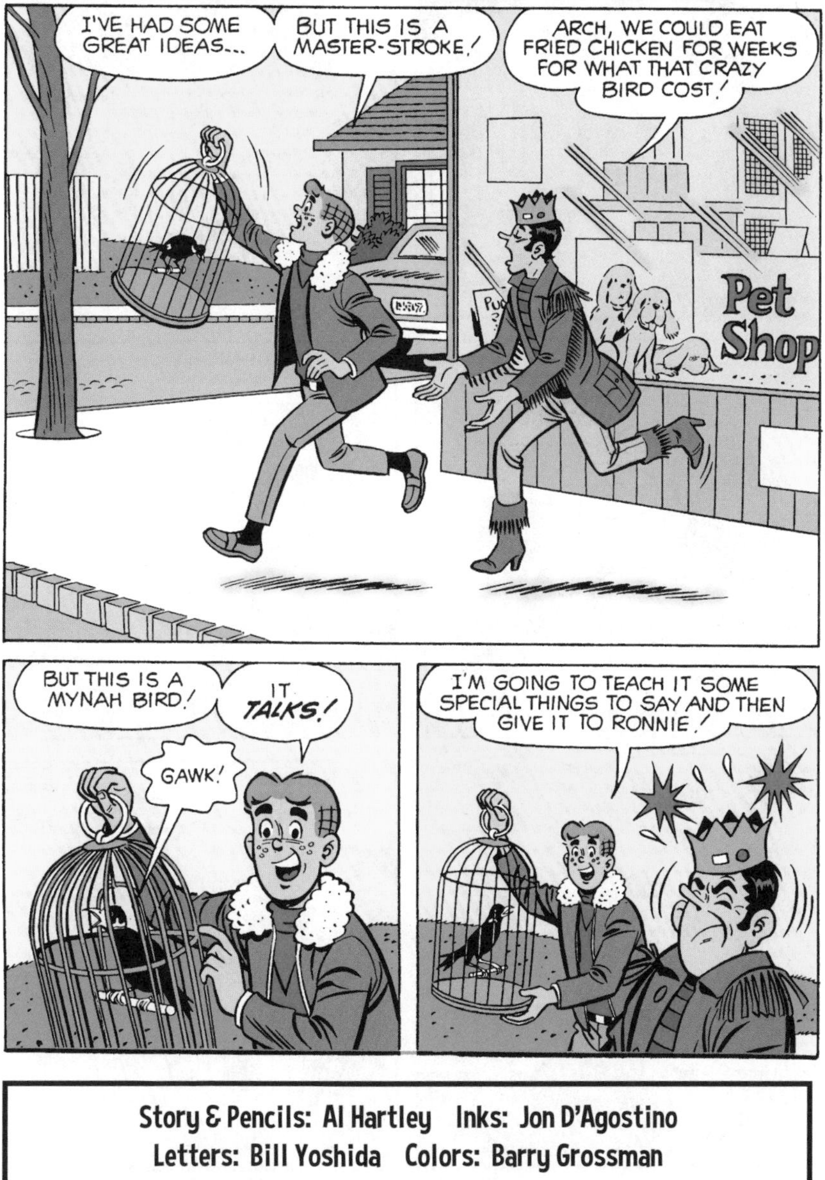
I'VE HAD SOME GREAT IDEAS...
BUT THIS IS A MASTER-STROKE!
ARCH, WE COULD EAT FRIED CHICKEN FOR WEEKS FOR WHAT THAT CRAZY BIRD COST!
Pet Shop
BUT THIS IS A MYNAH BIRD!
IT *TALKS!*
GAWK!
I'M GOING TO TEACH IT SOME SPECIAL THINGS TO SAY AND THEN GIVE IT TO RONNIE!

Story & Pencils: Al Hartley Inks: Jon D'Agostino
Letters: Bill Yoshida Colors: Barry Grossman

Originally printed in EVERYTHING'S ARCHIE #7, APRIL 1970

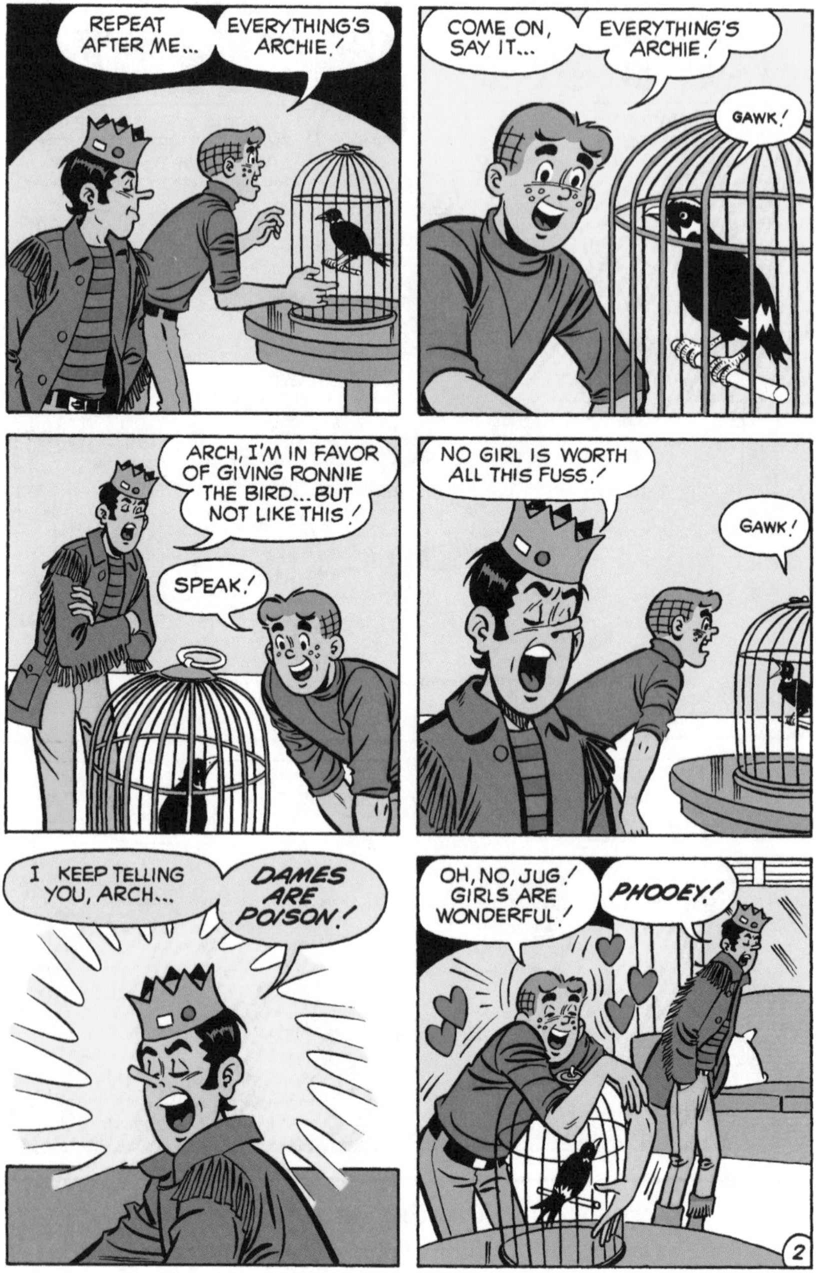
REPEAT AFTER ME...
EVERYTHING'S ARCHIE!
COME ON, SAY IT...
EVERYTHING'S ARCHIE!
GAWK!
ARCH, I'M IN FAVOR OF GIVING RONNIE THE BIRD... BUT NOT LIKE THIS!
SPEAK!
NO GIRL IS WORTH ALL THIS FUSS!
GAWK!
I KEEP TELLING YOU, ARCH...
DAMES ARE POISON!
OH, NO, JUG! GIRLS ARE WONDERFUL!
PHOOEY!
2

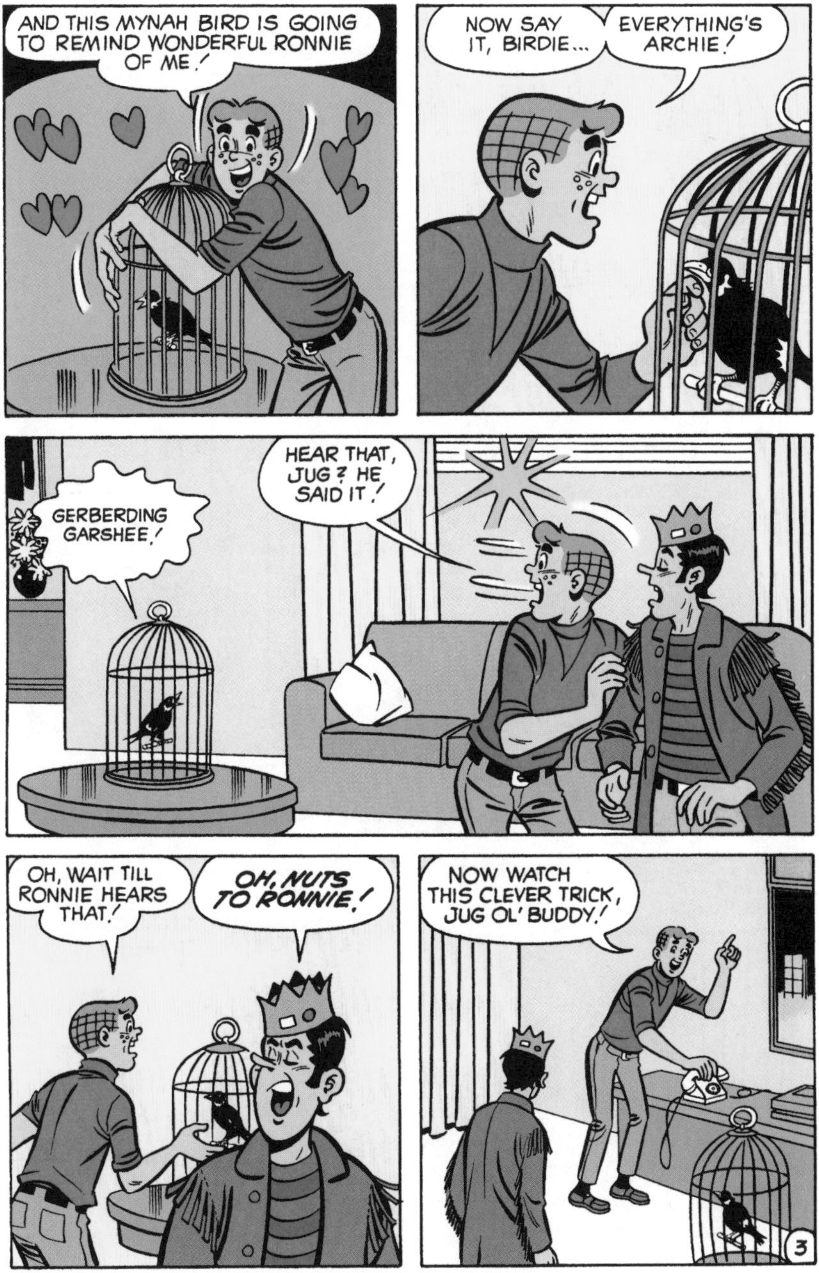
AND THIS MYNAH BIRD IS GOING TO REMIND WONDERFUL RONNIE OF ME!
NOW SAY IT, BIRDIE...
EVERYTHING'S ARCHIE!
GERBERDING GARSHEE!
HEAR THAT, JUG? HE SAID IT!
OH, WAIT TILL RONNIE HEARS THAT!
OH, NUTS TO RONNIE!
NOW WATCH THIS CLEVER TRICK, JUG OL' BUDDY!
3

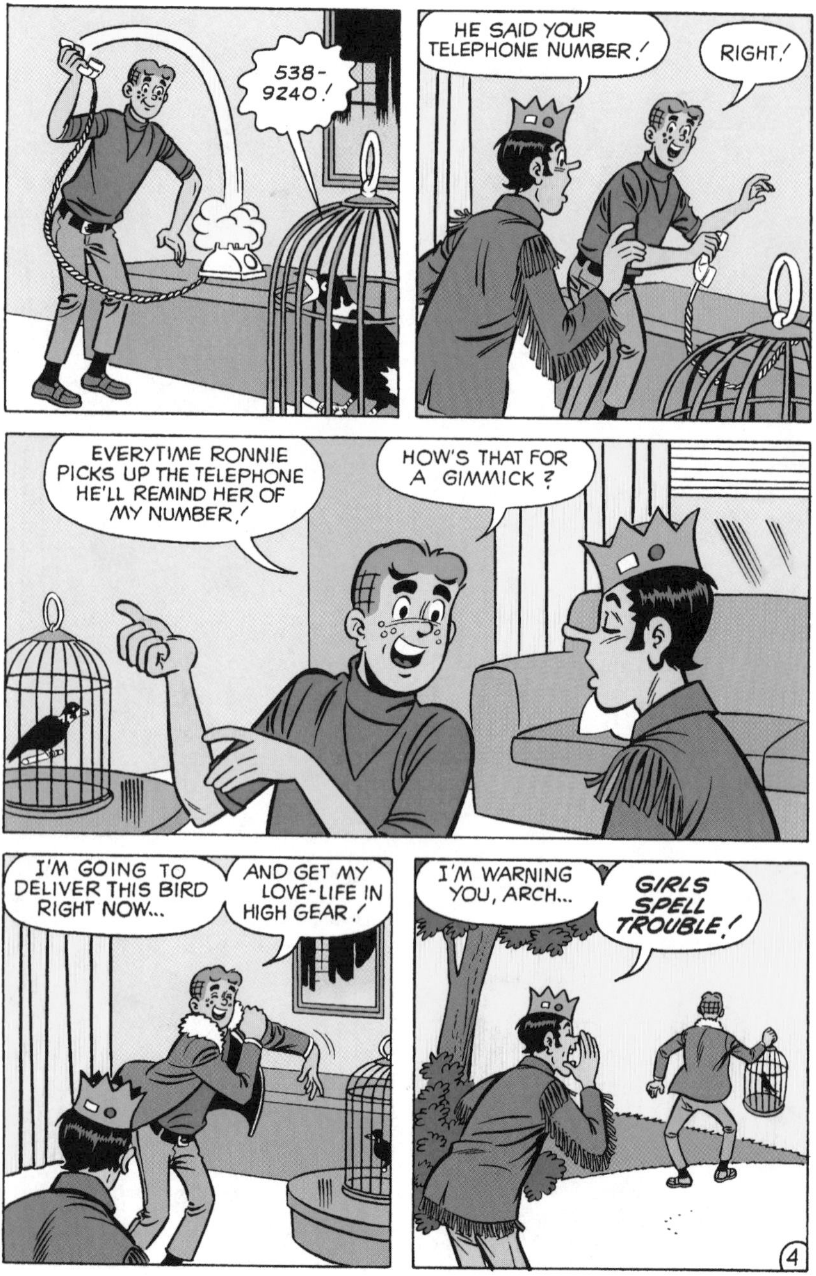
538-
9240!
HE SAID YOUR TELEPHONE NUMBER!
RIGHT!
EVERYTIME RONNIE PICKS UP THE TELEPHONE HE'LL REMIND HER OF MY NUMBER!
HOW'S THAT FOR A GIMMICK?
I'M GOING TO DELIVER THIS BIRD RIGHT NOW...
AND GET MY LOVE-LIFE IN HIGH GEAR!
I'M WARNING YOU, ARCH...
GIRLS SPELL TROUBLE!
4

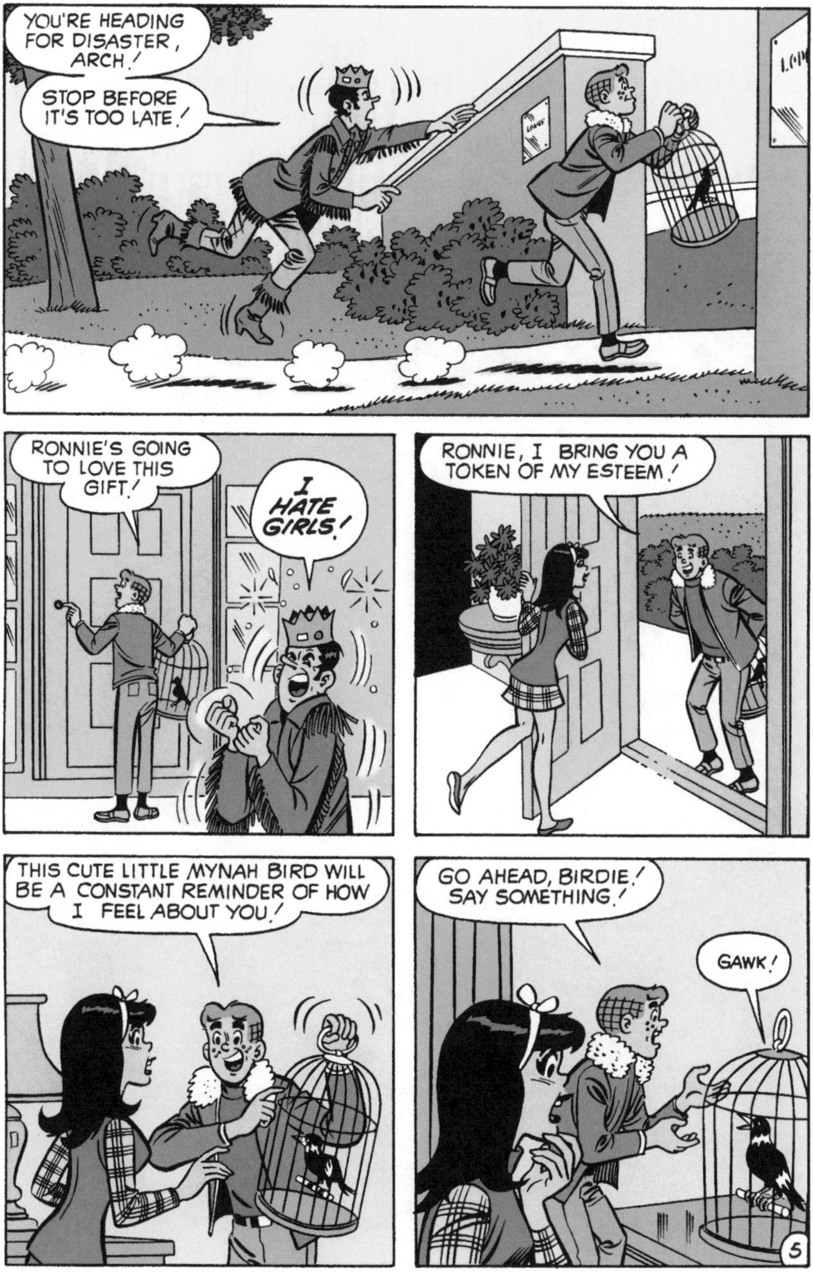
YOU'RE HEADING FOR DISASTER, ARCH!
STOP BEFORE IT'S TOO LATE!
RONNIE'S GOING TO LOVE THIS GIFT!
I HATE GIRLS!
RONNIE, I BRING YOU A TOKEN OF MY ESTEEM!
THIS CUTE LITTLE MYNAH BIRD WILL BE A CONSTANT REMINDER OF HOW I FEEL ABOUT YOU!
GO AHEAD, BIRDIE! SAY SOMETHING!
GAWK!
5

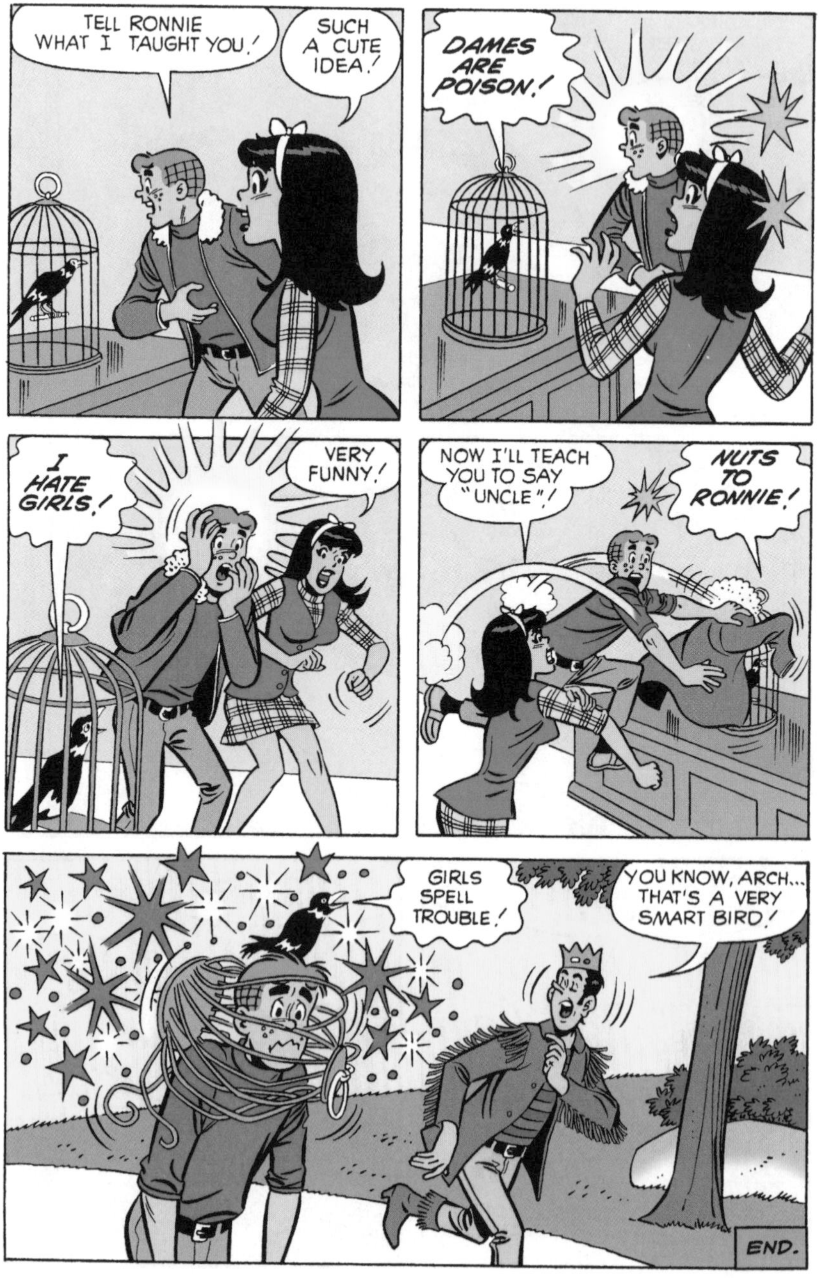
TELL RONNIE WHAT I TAUGHT YOU!
SUCH A CUTE IDEA!
DAMES ARE POISON!
I HATE GIRLS!
VERY FUNNY!
NOW I'LL TEACH YOU TO SAY "UNCLE"!
NUTS TO RONNIE!
GIRLS SPELL TROUBLE!
YOU KNOW, ARCH... THAT'S A VERY SMART BIRD!
END.

Story & Pencils: Al Hartley   Inks: Jon D'Agostino
Letters: Bill Yoshida   Colors: Barry Grossman

Originally printed in EVERYTHING'S ARCHIE #7, APRIL 1970

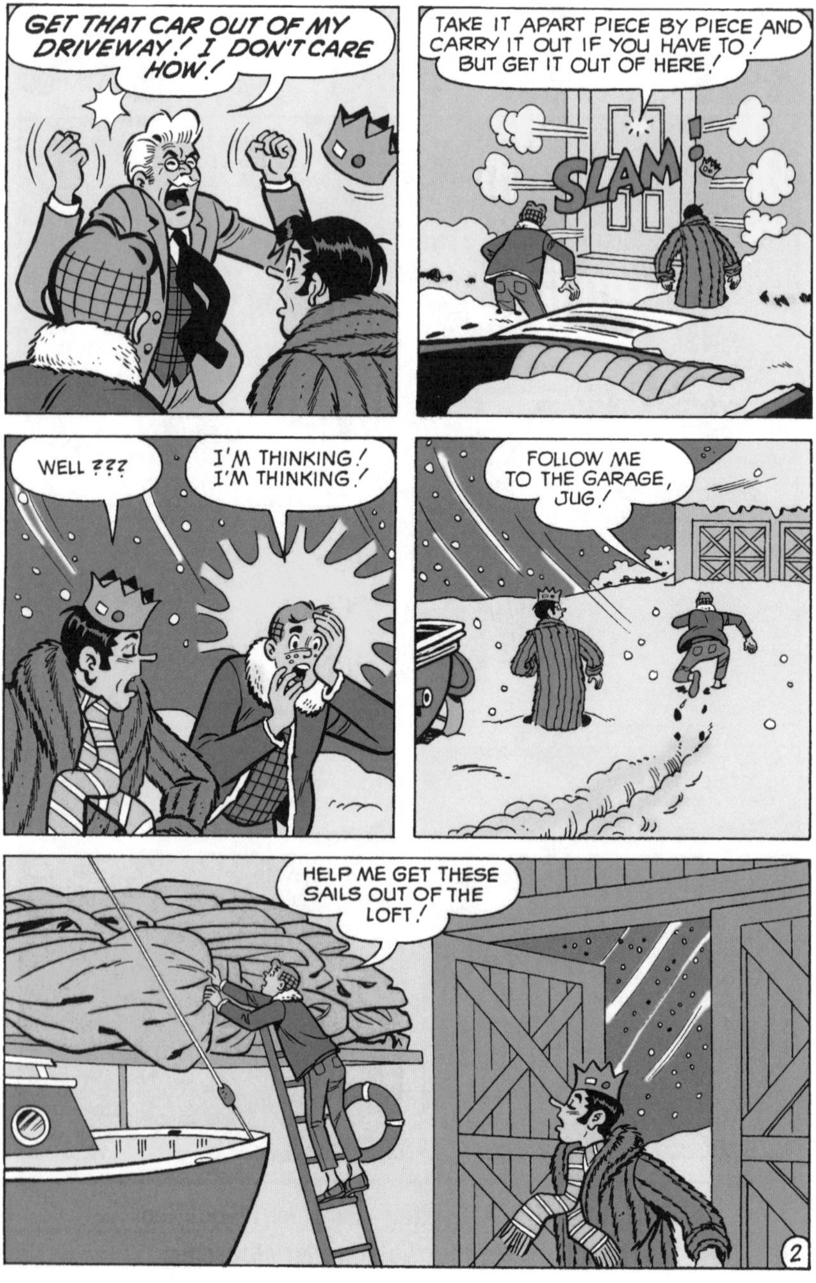
GET THAT CAR OUT OF MY DRIVEWAY! I DON'T CARE HOW!
TAKE IT APART PIECE BY PIECE AND CARRY IT OUT IF YOU HAVE TO! BUT GET IT OUT OF HERE!
SLAM!
WELL ???
I'M THINKING! I'M THINKING!
FOLLOW ME TO THE GARAGE, JUG!
HELP ME GET THESE SAILS OUT OF THE LOFT!
2

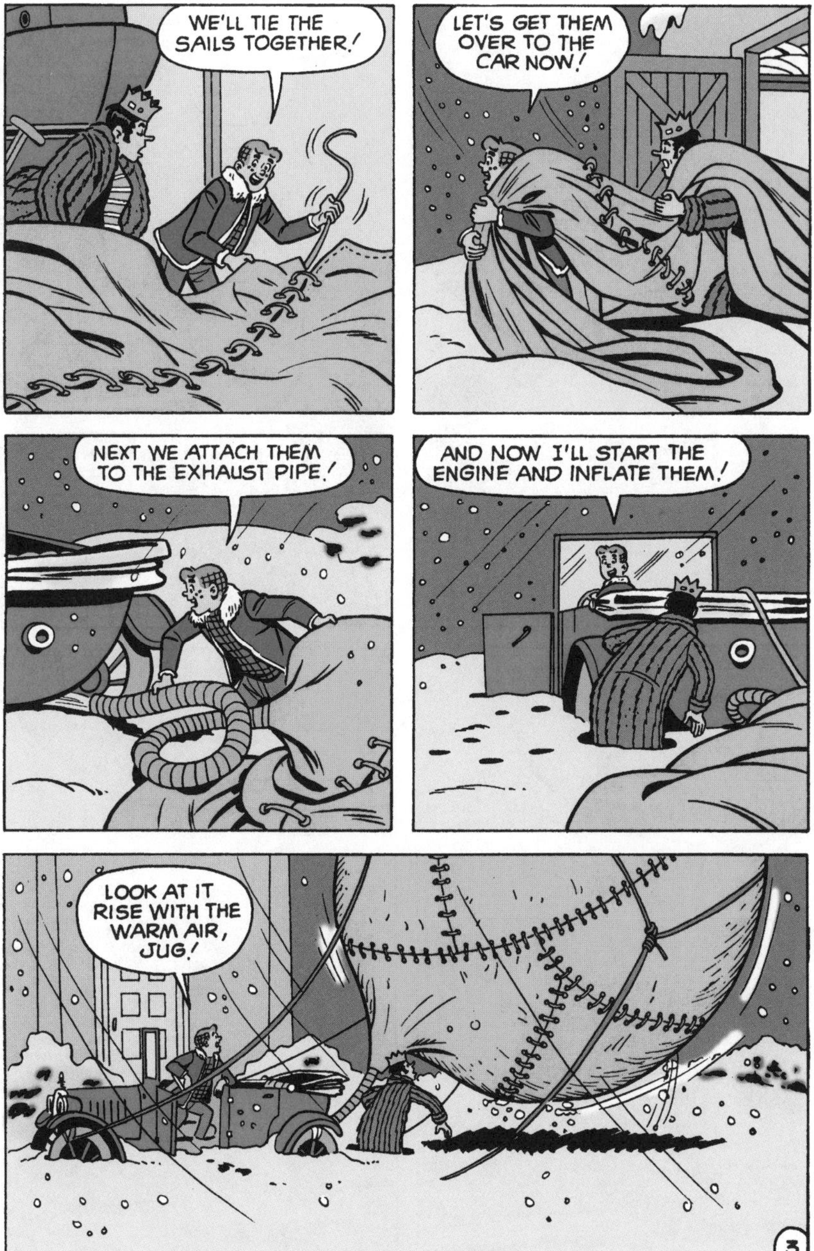
WE'LL TIE THE SAILS TOGETHER!
LET'S GET THEM OVER TO THE CAR NOW!
NEXT WE ATTACH THEM TO THE EXHAUST PIPE!
AND NOW I'LL START THE ENGINE AND INFLATE THEM!
LOOK AT IT RISE WITH THE WARM AIR, JUG!
3

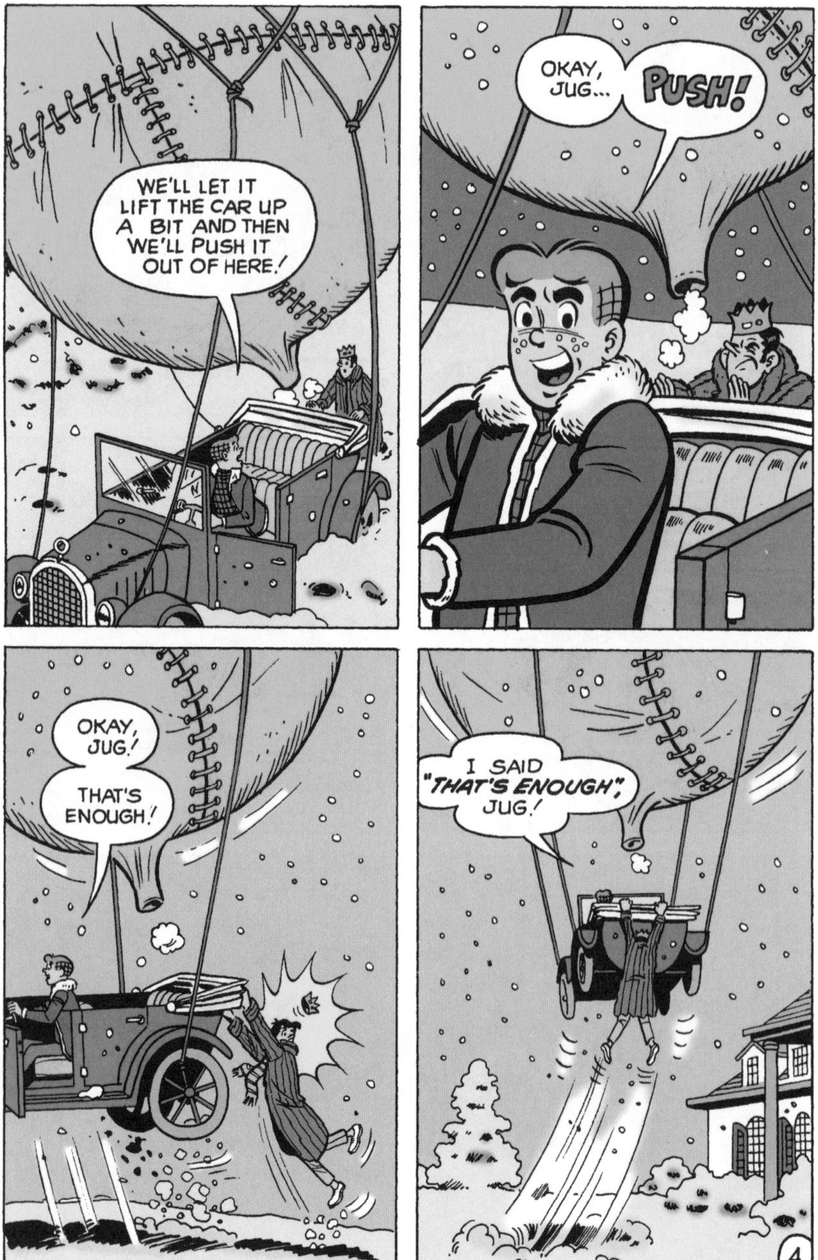
WE'LL LET IT LIFT THE CAR UP A BIT AND THEN WE'LL PUSH IT OUT OF HERE!
OKAY, JUG...
PUSH!
OKAY, JUG!
THAT'S ENOUGH!
I SAID "THAT'S ENOUGH", JUG!
4

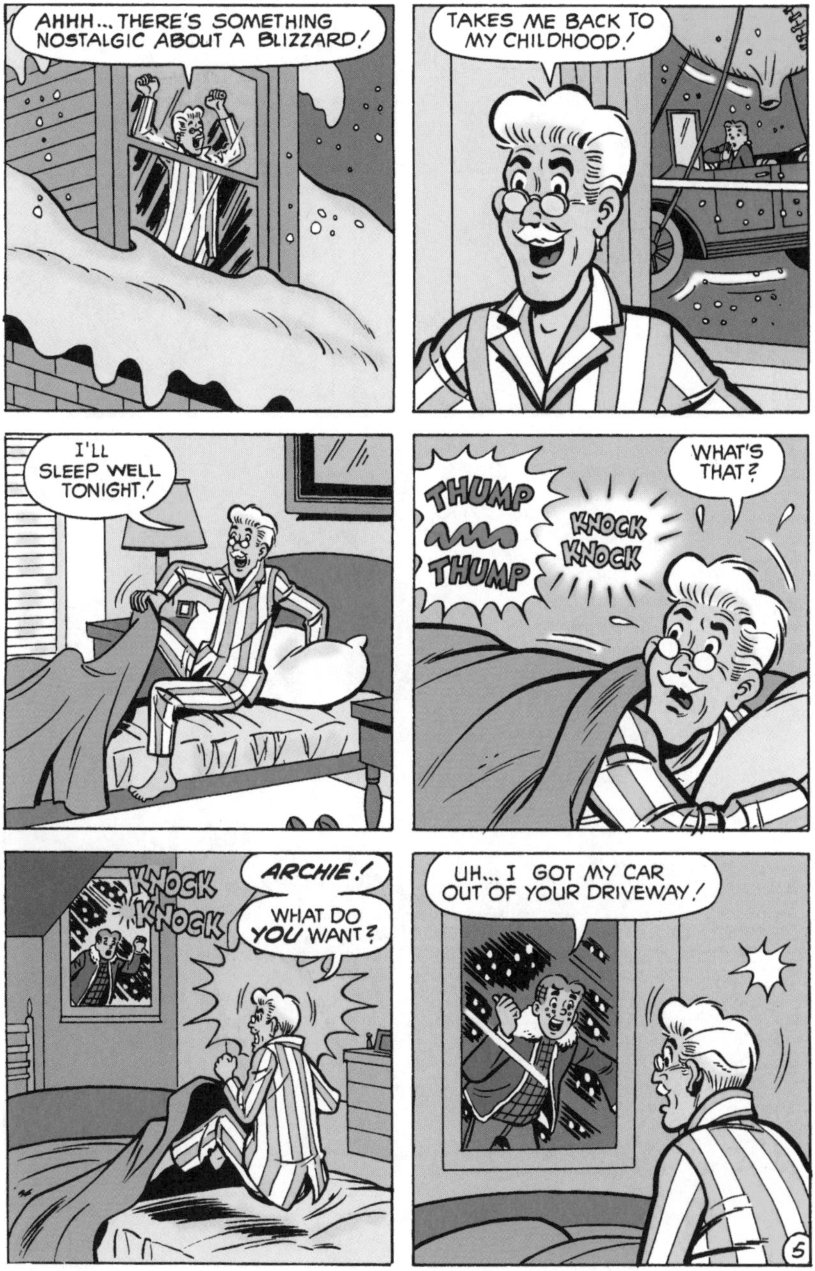
AHHH... THERE'S SOMETHING NOSTALGIC ABOUT A BLIZZARD!
TAKES ME BACK TO MY CHILDHOOD!
I'LL SLEEP WELL TONIGHT!
THUMP THUMP
KNOCK KNOCK
WHAT'S THAT?
KNOCK KNOCK
ARCHIE!
WHAT DO YOU WANT?
UH... I GOT MY CAR OUT OF YOUR DRIVEWAY!
5

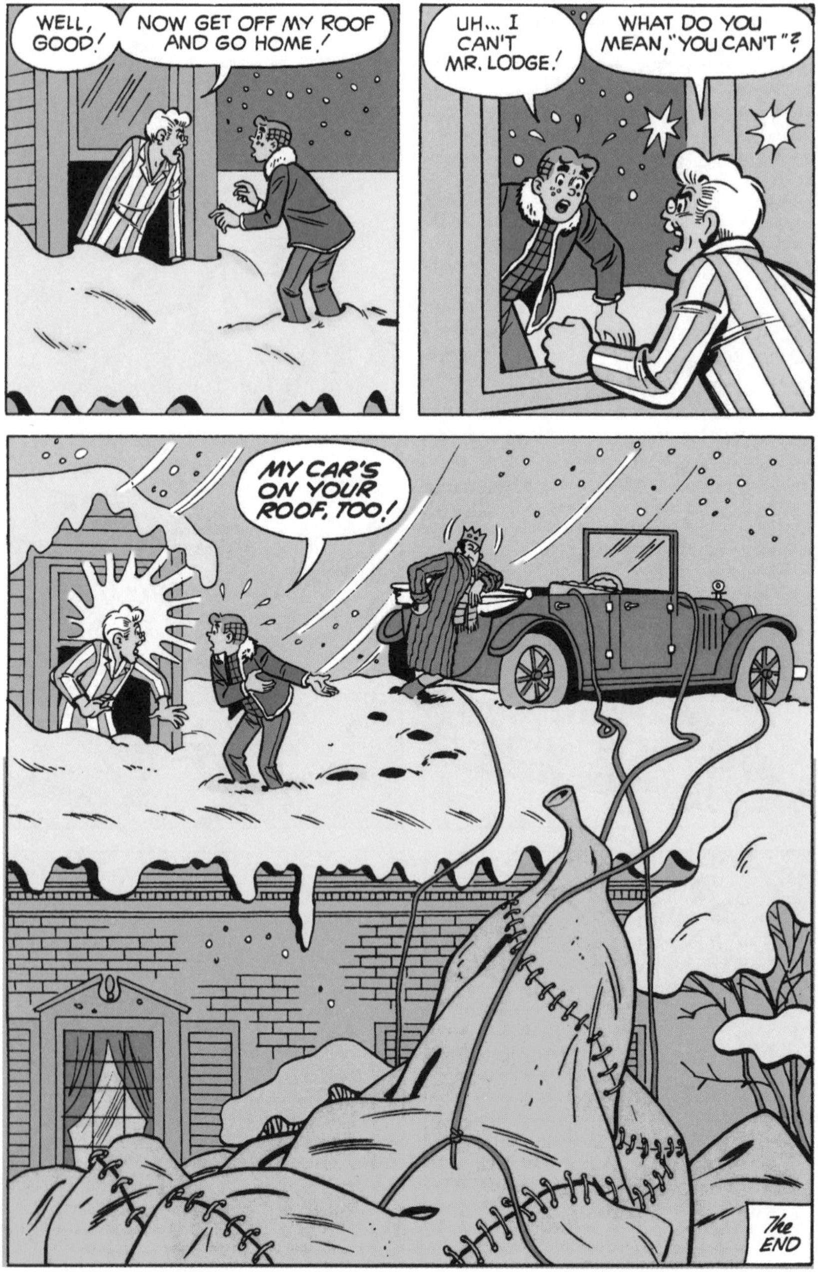
WELL, GOOD!
NOW GET OFF MY ROOF AND GO HOME!
UH... I CAN'T MR. LODGE!
WHAT DO YOU MEAN, "YOU CAN'T"?
MY CAR'S ON YOUR ROOF, TOO!
The END

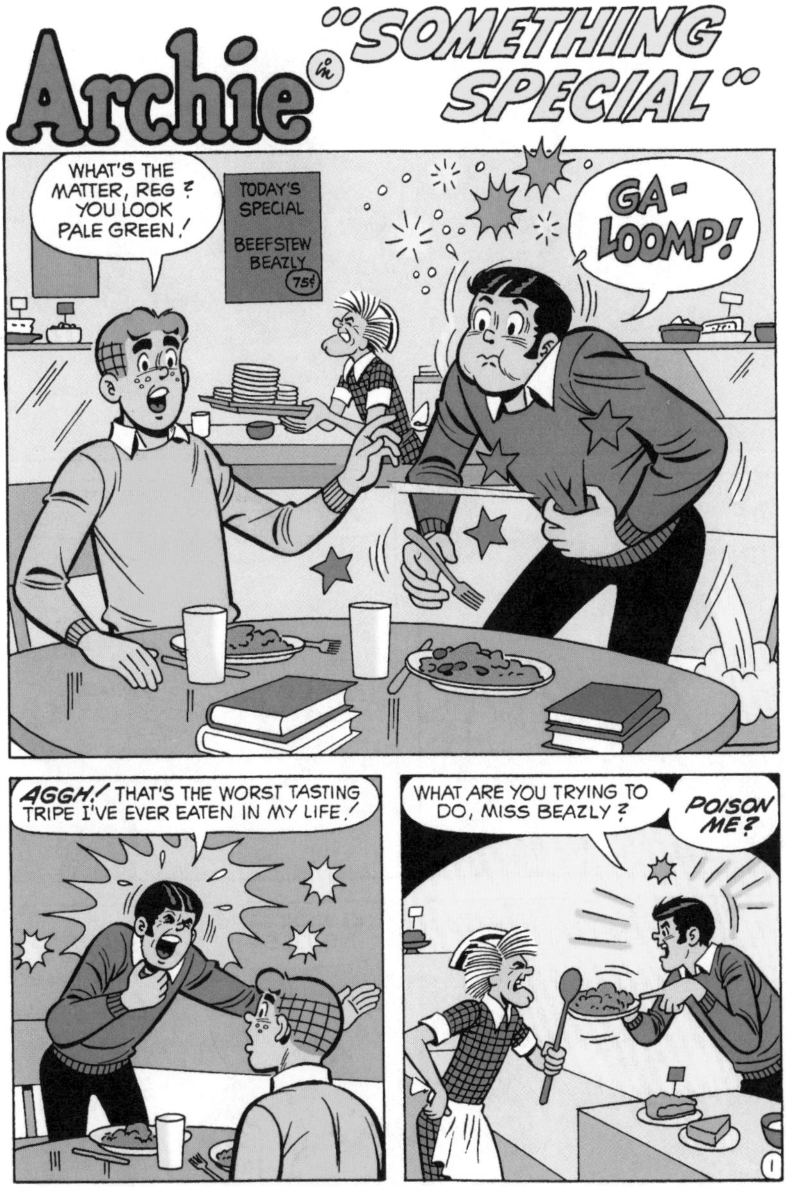
Archie
in
"SOMETHING SPECIAL"
WHAT'S THE MATTER, REG? YOU LOOK PALE GREEN!
TODAY'S SPECIAL
BEEFSTEW BEAZLY
75¢
GA-LOOMP!
AGGH! THAT'S THE WORST TASTING TRIPE I'VE EVER EATEN IN MY LIFE!
WHAT ARE YOU TRYING TO DO, MISS BEAZLY?
POISON ME?
1

Story & Pencils: Al Hartley Inks: Jon D'Agostino
Letters: Bill Yoshida Colors: Barry Grossman

Originally printed in EVERYTHING'S ARCHIE #7, APRIL 1970

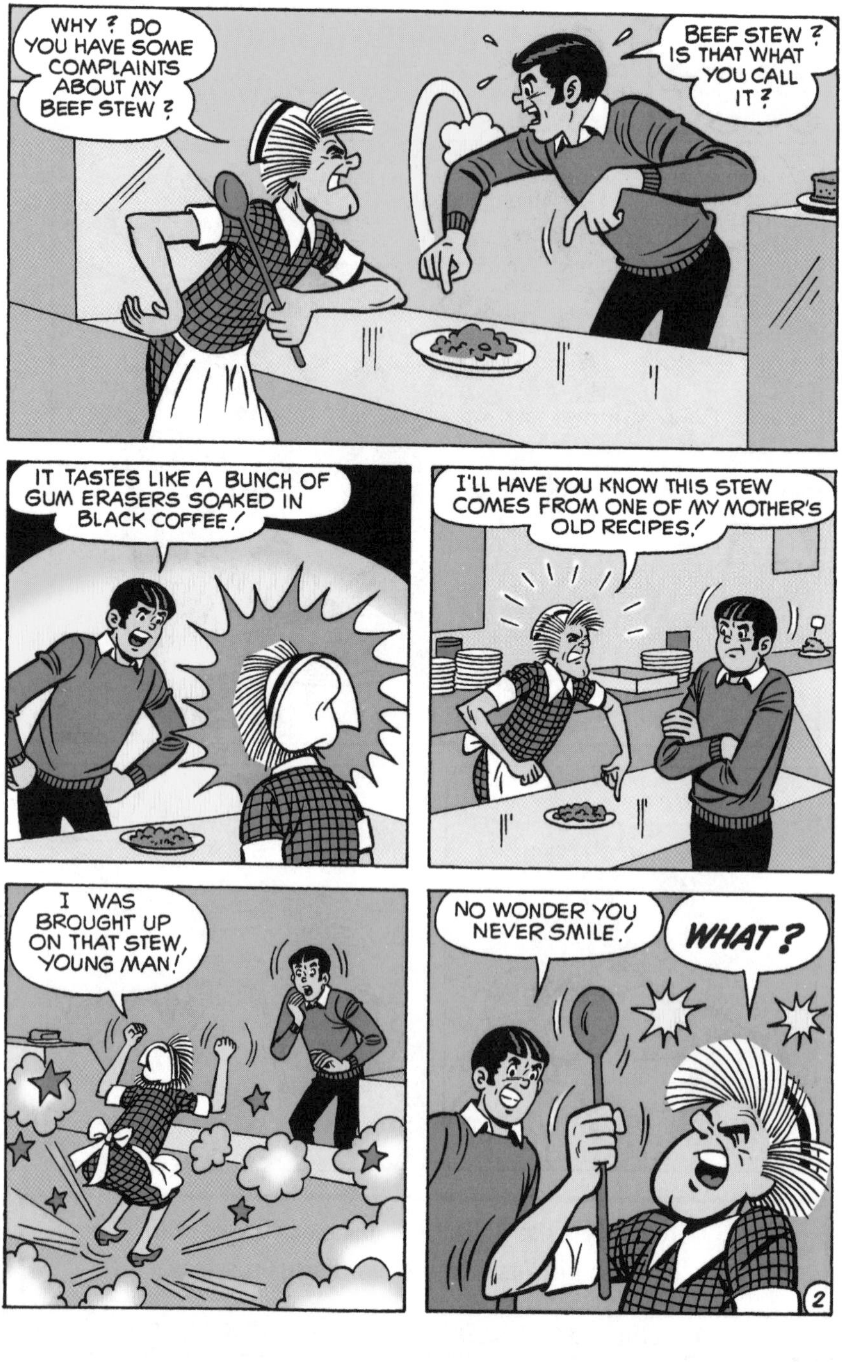
WHY ? DO YOU HAVE SOME COMPLAINTS ABOUT MY BEEF STEW ?
BEEF STEW ? IS THAT WHAT YOU CALL IT ?
IT TASTES LIKE A BUNCH OF GUM ERASERS SOAKED IN BLACK COFFEE!
I'LL HAVE YOU KNOW THIS STEW COMES FROM ONE OF MY MOTHER'S OLD RECIPES!
I WAS BROUGHT UP ON THAT STEW, YOUNG MAN!
NO WONDER YOU NEVER SMILE!
WHAT ?
2

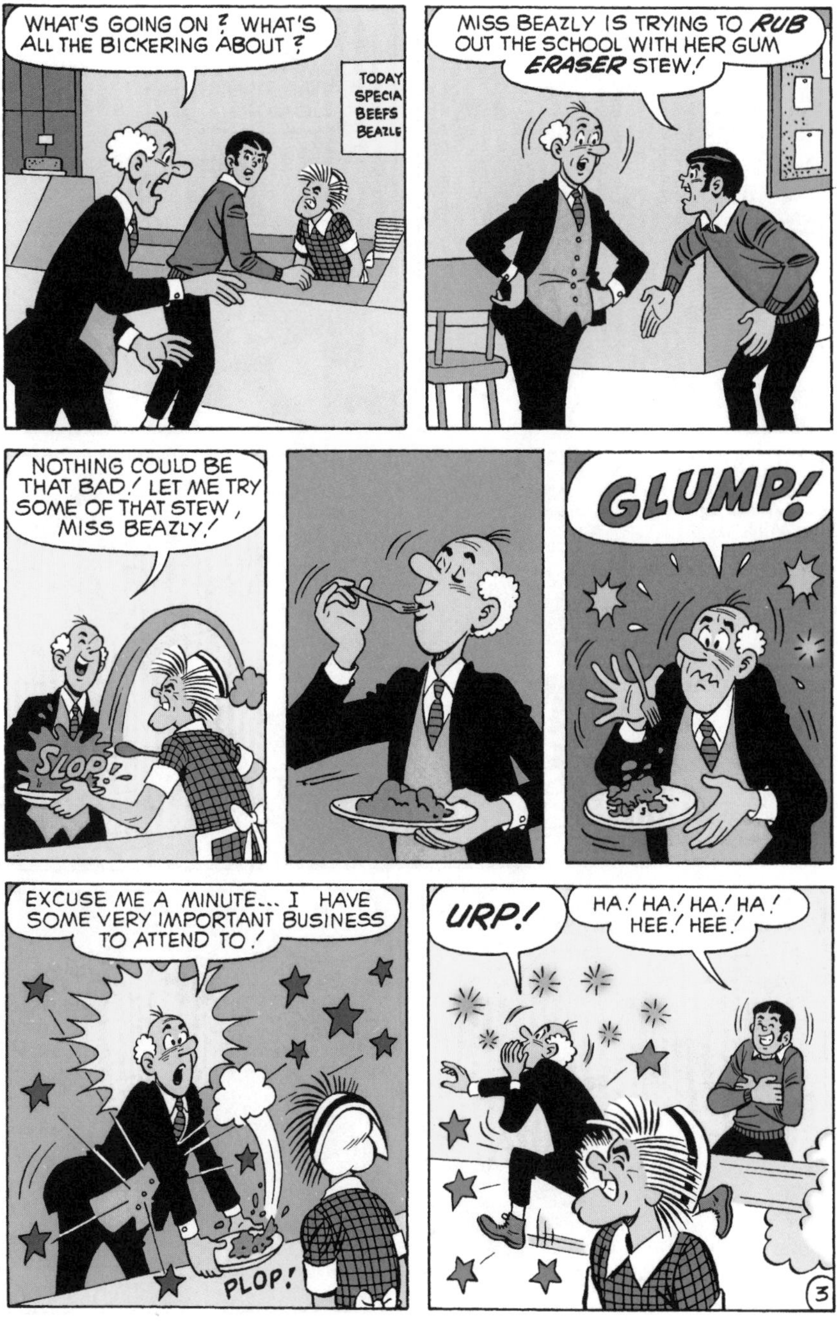
WHAT'S GOING ON ? WHAT'S ALL THE BICKERING ABOUT ?
TODAY SPECIA BEEFS BEAZLE
MISS BEAZLY IS TRYING TO RUB OUT THE SCHOOL WITH HER GUM ERASER STEW!
NOTHING COULD BE THAT BAD! LET ME TRY SOME OF THAT STEW, MISS BEAZLY!
SLOP!
GLUMP!
EXCUSE ME A MINUTE... I HAVE SOME VERY IMPORTANT BUSINESS TO ATTEND TO!
PLOP!
URP!
HA! HA! HA! HA! HEE! HEE!
3

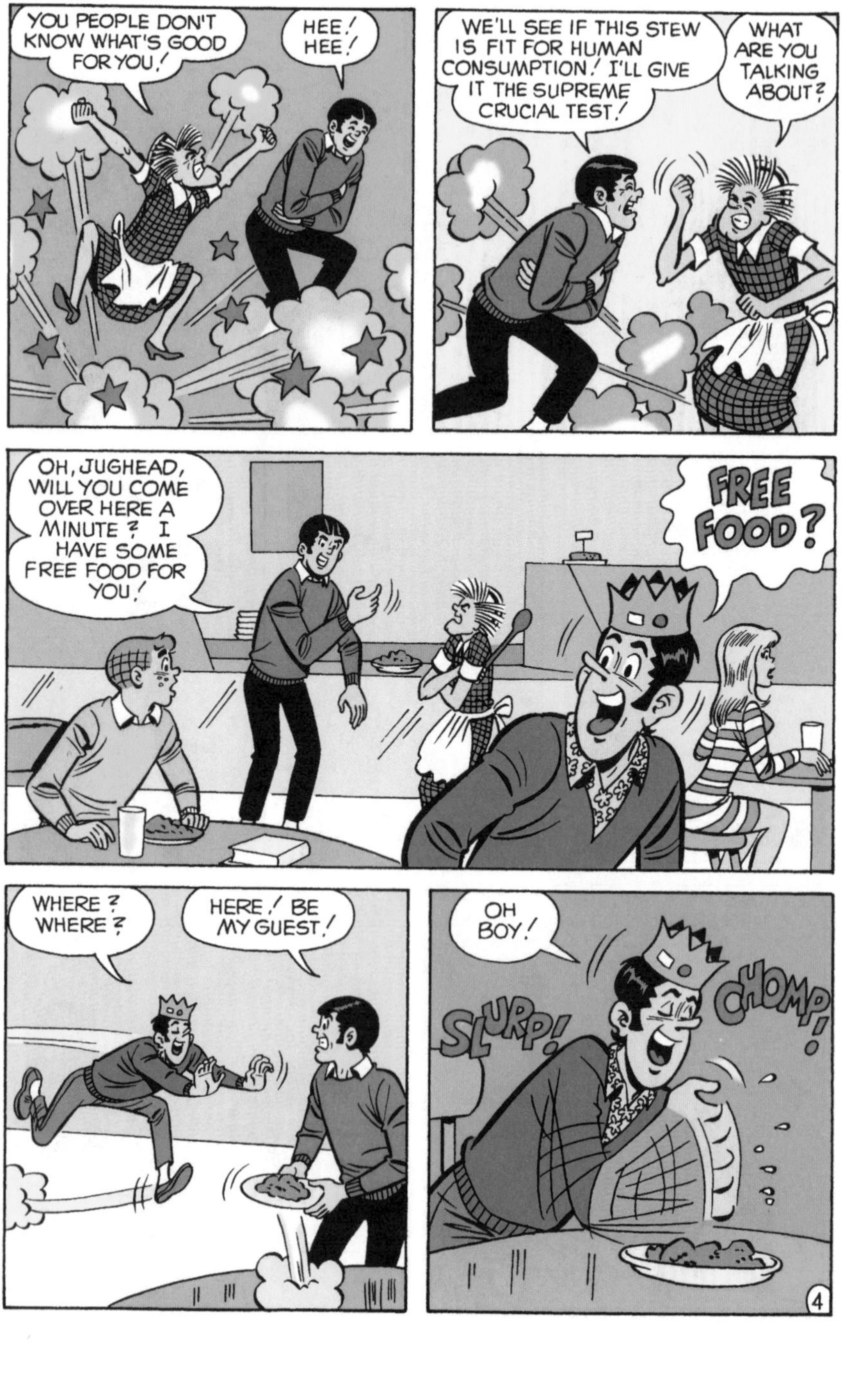
YOU PEOPLE DON'T KNOW WHAT'S GOOD FOR YOU!
HEE! HEE!
WE'LL SEE IF THIS STEW IS FIT FOR HUMAN CONSUMPTION! I'LL GIVE IT THE SUPREME CRUCIAL TEST!
WHAT ARE YOU TALKING ABOUT?
OH, JUGHEAD, WILL YOU COME OVER HERE A MINUTE? I HAVE SOME FREE FOOD FOR YOU!
FREE FOOD?
WHERE? WHERE?
HERE! BE MY GUEST!
OH BOY!
SLURP!
CHOMP!
4

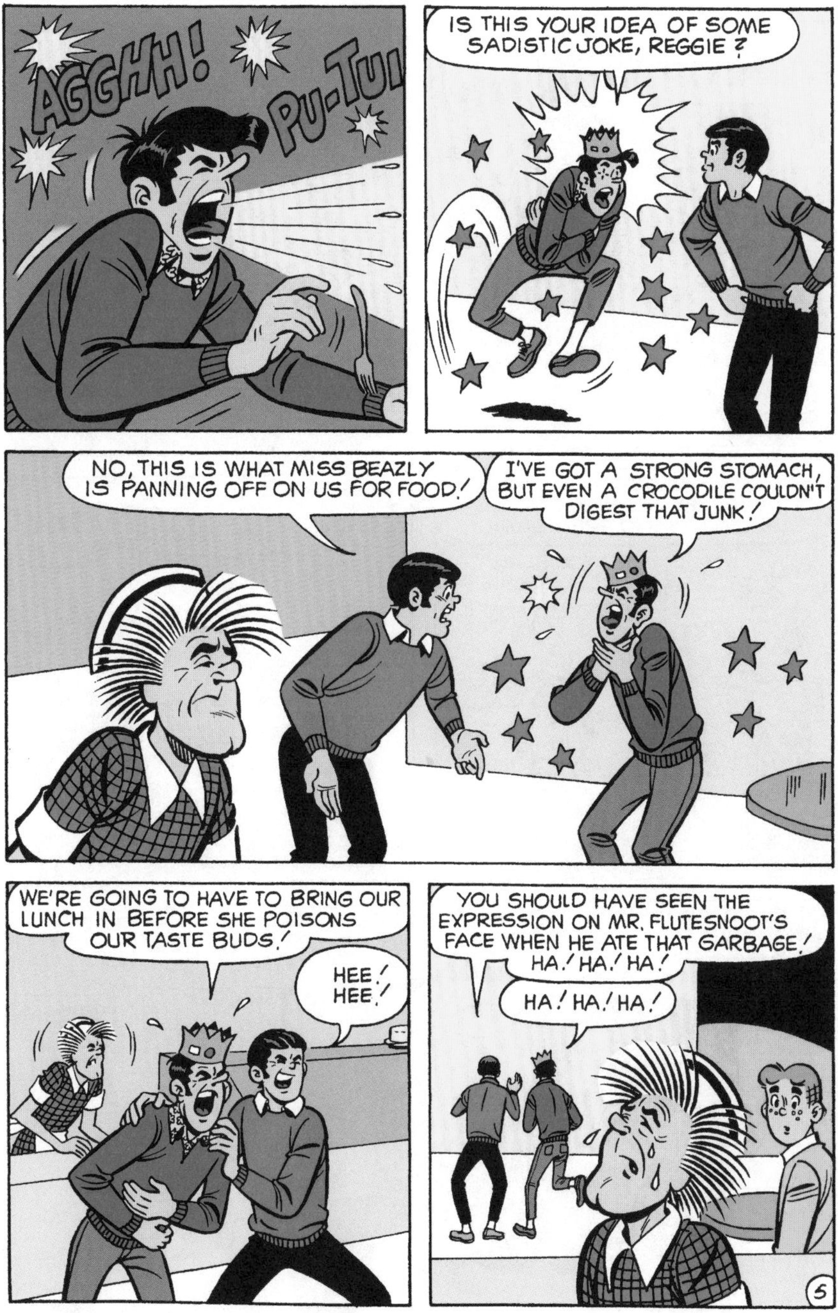
AGGHH!
PU-TUI
IS THIS YOUR IDEA OF SOME SADISTIC JOKE, REGGIE?
NO, THIS IS WHAT MISS BEAZLY IS PANNING OFF ON US FOR FOOD!
I'VE GOT A STRONG STOMACH, BUT EVEN A CROCODILE COULDN'T DIGEST THAT JUNK!
WE'RE GOING TO HAVE TO BRING OUR LUNCH IN BEFORE SHE POISONS OUR TASTE BUDS!
HEE! HEE!
YOU SHOULD HAVE SEEN THE EXPRESSION ON MR. FLUTESNOOT'S FACE WHEN HE ATE THAT GARBAGE! HA! HA! HA!
HA! HA! HA!
5

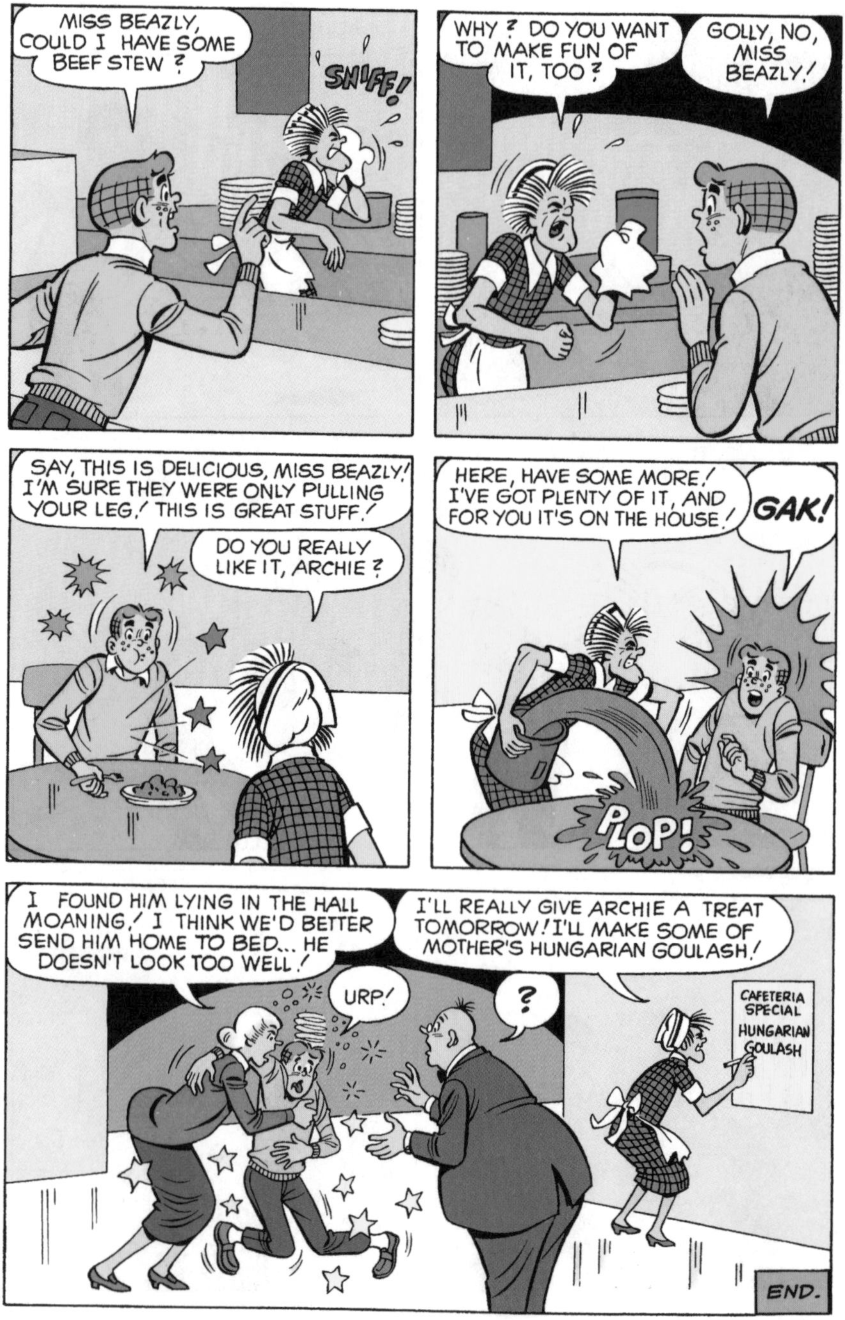
MISS BEAZLY, COULD I HAVE SOME BEEF STEW ?
SNIFF!
WHY ? DO YOU WANT TO MAKE FUN OF IT, TOO ?
GOLLY, NO, MISS BEAZLY!
SAY, THIS IS DELICIOUS, MISS BEAZLY! I'M SURE THEY WERE ONLY PULLING YOUR LEG! THIS IS GREAT STUFF!
DO YOU REALLY LIKE IT, ARCHIE ?
HERE, HAVE SOME MORE! I'VE GOT PLENTY OF IT, AND FOR YOU IT'S ON THE HOUSE!
GAK!
PLOP!
I FOUND HIM LYING IN THE HALL MOANING! I THINK WE'D BETTER SEND HIM HOME TO BED... HE DOESN'T LOOK TOO WELL!
URP!
?
I'LL REALLY GIVE ARCHIE A TREAT TOMORROW! I'LL MAKE SOME OF MOTHER'S HUNGARIAN GOULASH!
CAFETERIA SPECIAL
HUNGARIAN GOULASH
END.

Archie "A FRIEND IN NEED" (IS A PEST)

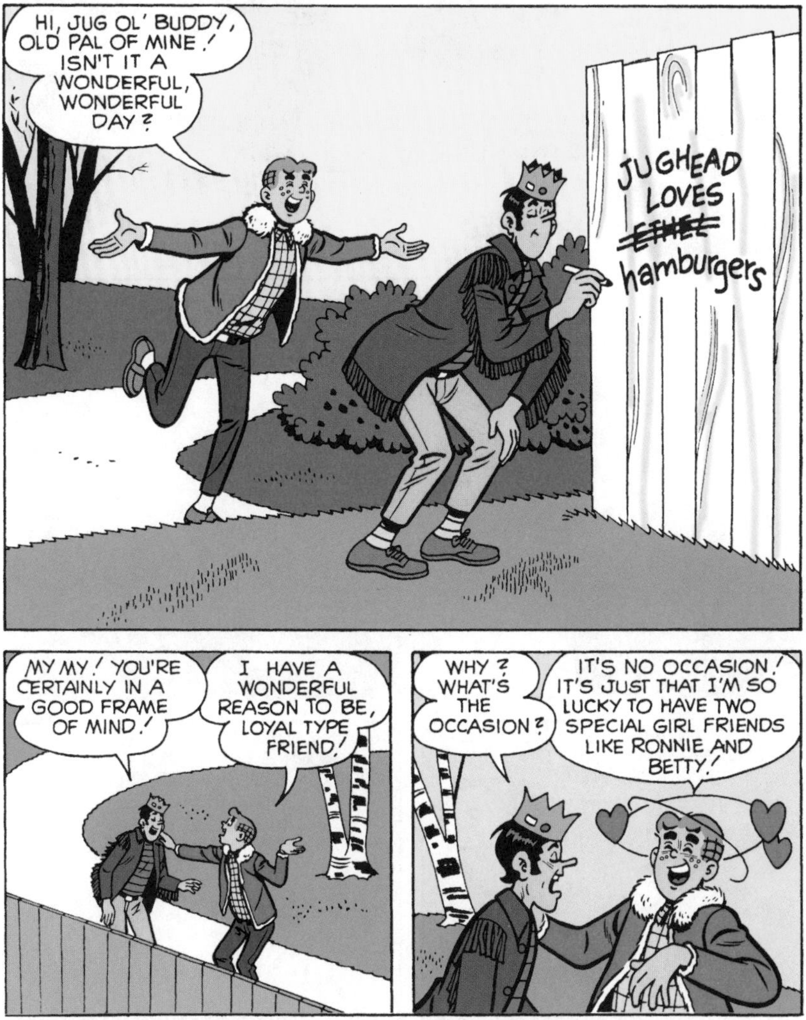
HI, JUG OL' BUDDY, OLD PAL OF MINE! ISN'T IT A WONDERFUL, WONDERFUL DAY?
JUGHEAD LOVES ETHEL hamburgers
MY MY! YOU'RE CERTAINLY IN A GOOD FRAME OF MIND!
I HAVE A WONDERFUL REASON TO BE, LOYAL TYPE FRIEND!
WHY? WHAT'S THE OCCASION?
IT'S NO OCCASION! IT'S JUST THAT I'M SO LUCKY TO HAVE TWO SPECIAL GIRL FRIENDS LIKE RONNIE AND BETTY!

Story & Pencils: Al Hartley Inks: Jon D'Agostino
Letters: Bill Yoshida Colors: Barry Grossman

Originally printed in EVERYTHING'S ARCHIE #7, APRIL 1970

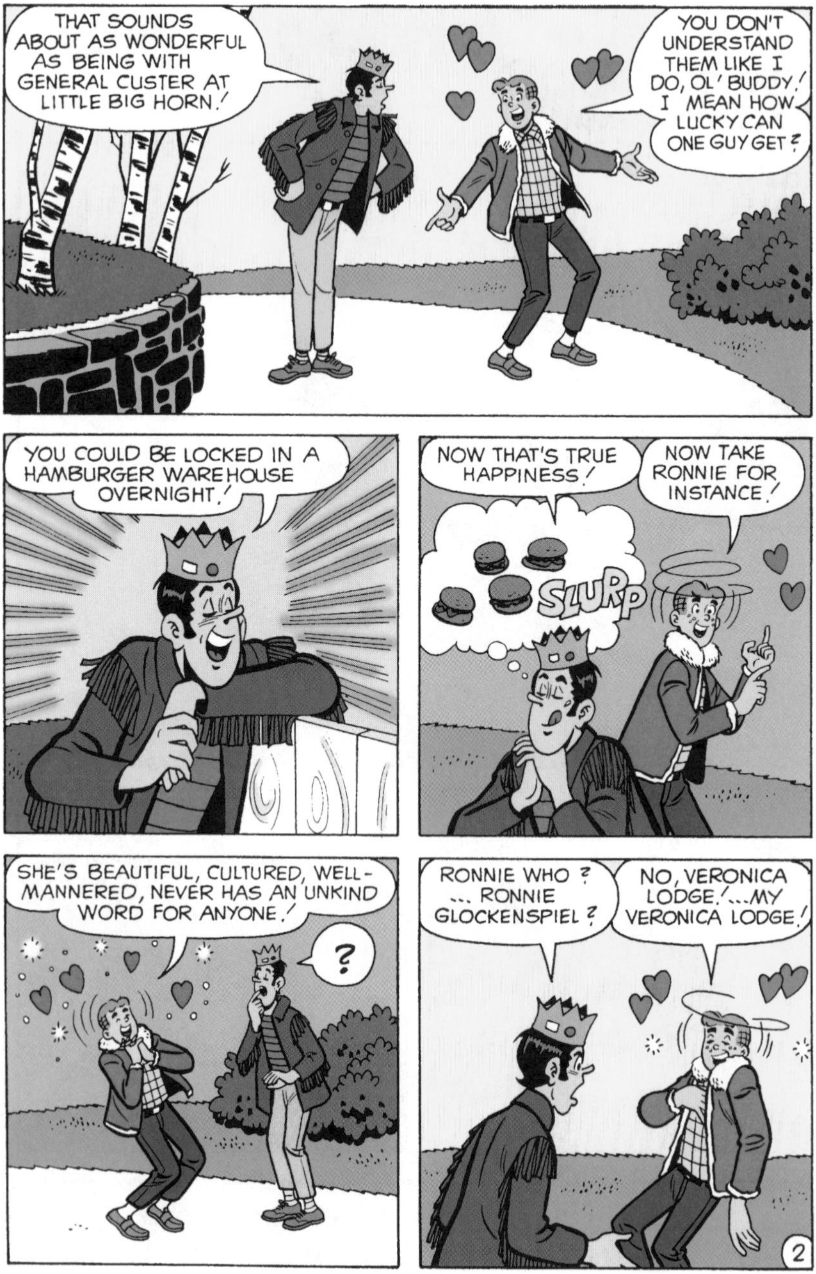
THAT SOUNDS ABOUT AS WONDERFUL AS BEING WITH GENERAL CUSTER AT LITTLE BIG HORN!
YOU DON'T UNDERSTAND THEM LIKE I DO, OL' BUDDY! I MEAN HOW LUCKY CAN ONE GUY GET?
YOU COULD BE LOCKED IN A HAMBURGER WAREHOUSE OVERNIGHT!
NOW THAT'S TRUE HAPPINESS!
SLURP
NOW TAKE RONNIE FOR INSTANCE!
SHE'S BEAUTIFUL, CULTURED, WELL-MANNERED, NEVER HAS AN UNKIND WORD FOR ANYONE!
?
RONNIE WHO? ... RONNIE GLOCKENSPIEL?
NO, VERONICA LODGE! ...MY VERONICA LODGE!
2

EVEN THE MERE MENTION OF HER NAME AND I BREAK OUT IN GOOSE PIMPLES!
THAT'S BECAUSE SHE'S ALWAYS COOKING YOUR GOOSE!
I'M GOING TO TAKE THAT WONDERFUL GIRL TO A MOVIE!
WHEN SHE LOOKS AT ME WITH THOSE BIG, SOULFUL, UNDERSTANDING, BEAUTIFUL, BROWN EYES I BECOME A PRISONER OF LOVE!
YEESH!
MAYBE IF YOU'RE LUCKY YOU'LL GET THE CHAIR!
BY NOW SHE'S PROBABLY ANXIOUSLY WAITING FOR ME TO CALL!
IT'S AWFULLY NICE OF REGGIE TO WAIT WITH HER!
3

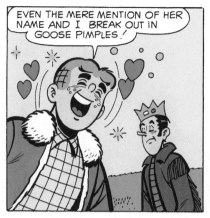

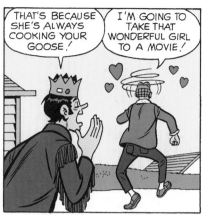

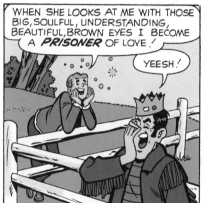

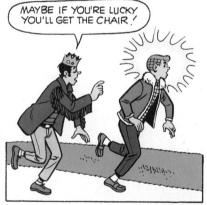

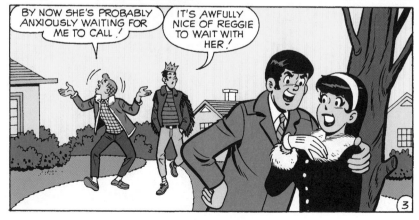

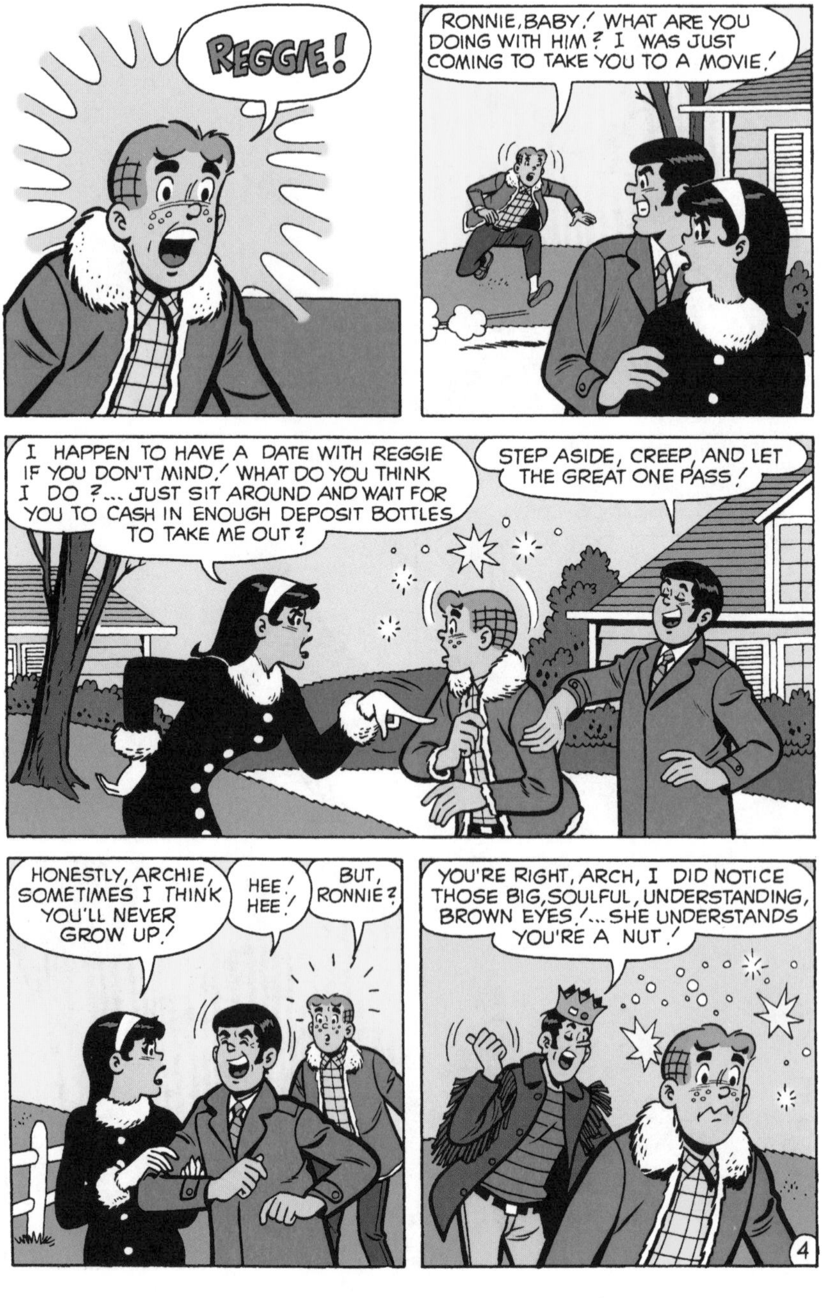
REGGIE!
RONNIE, BABY! WHAT ARE YOU DOING WITH HIM? I WAS JUST COMING TO TAKE YOU TO A MOVIE!
I HAPPEN TO HAVE A DATE WITH REGGIE IF YOU DON'T MIND! WHAT DO YOU THINK I DO ?... JUST SIT AROUND AND WAIT FOR YOU TO CASH IN ENOUGH DEPOSIT BOTTLES TO TAKE ME OUT?
STEP ASIDE, CREEP, AND LET THE GREAT ONE PASS!
HONESTLY, ARCHIE, SOMETIMES I THINK YOU'LL NEVER GROW UP!
HEE! HEE!
BUT, RONNIE?
YOU'RE RIGHT, ARCH, I DID NOTICE THOSE BIG, SOULFUL, UNDERSTANDING, BROWN EYES!... SHE UNDERSTANDS YOU'RE A NUT!
4

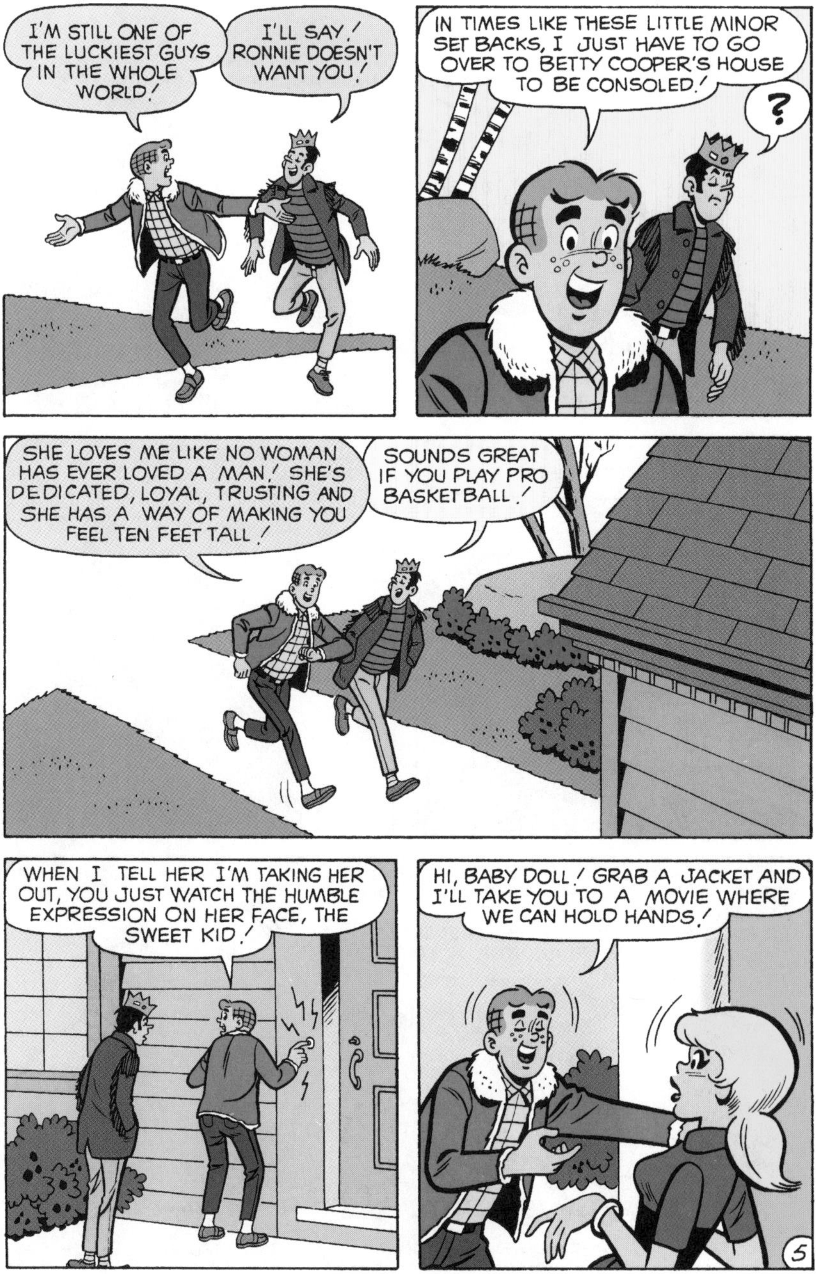
I'M STILL ONE OF THE LUCKIEST GUYS IN THE WHOLE WORLD!
I'LL SAY! RONNIE DOESN'T WANT YOU!
IN TIMES LIKE THESE LITTLE MINOR SET BACKS, I JUST HAVE TO GO OVER TO BETTY COOPER'S HOUSE TO BE CONSOLED!
?
SHE LOVES ME LIKE NO WOMAN HAS EVER LOVED A MAN! SHE'S DEDICATED, LOYAL, TRUSTING AND SHE HAS A WAY OF MAKING YOU FEEL TEN FEET TALL!
SOUNDS GREAT IF YOU PLAY PRO BASKETBALL!
WHEN I TELL HER I'M TAKING HER OUT, YOU JUST WATCH THE HUMBLE EXPRESSION ON HER FACE, THE SWEET KID!
HI, BABY DOLL! GRAB A JACKET AND I'LL TAKE YOU TO A MOVIE WHERE WE CAN HOLD HANDS!
5

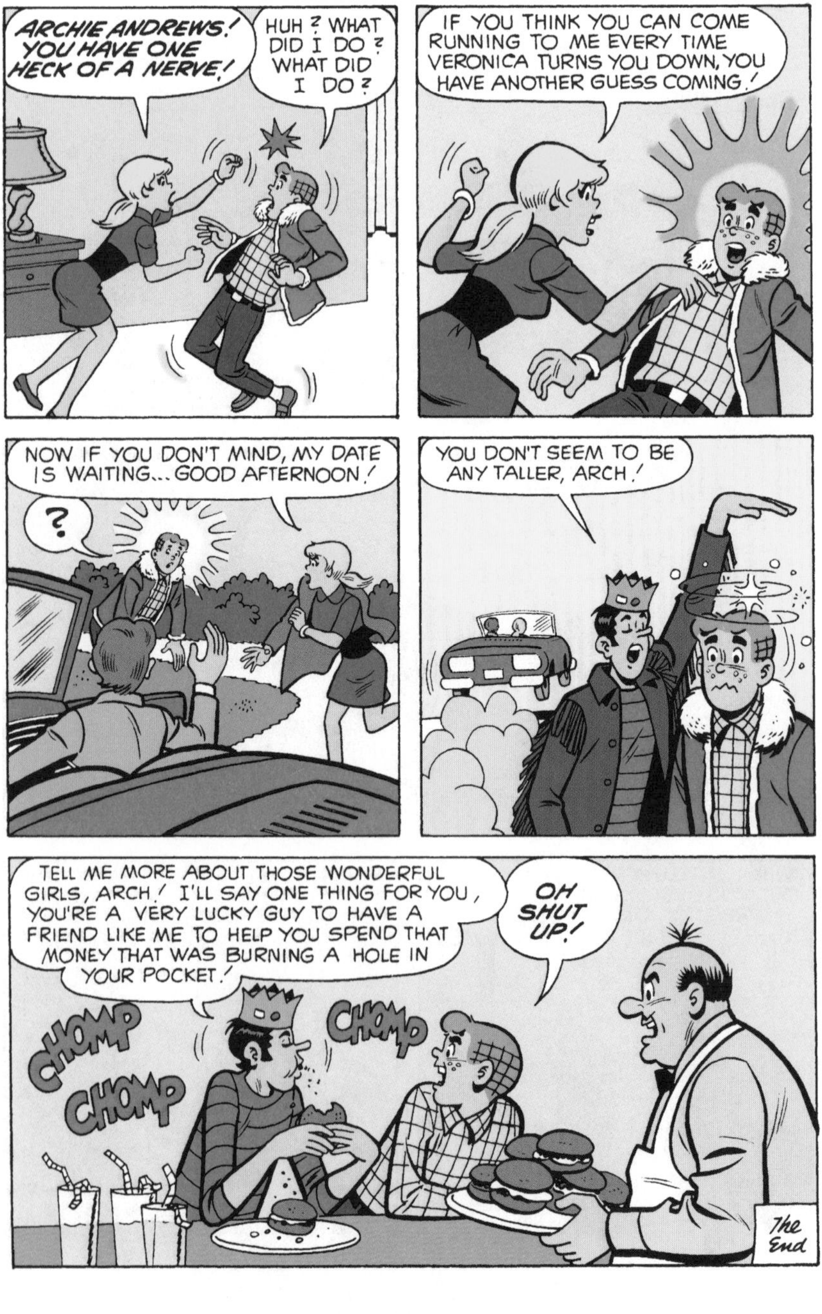
ARCHIE ANDREWS! YOU HAVE ONE HECK OF A NERVE!
HUH? WHAT DID I DO? WHAT DID I DO?
IF YOU THINK YOU CAN COME RUNNING TO ME EVERY TIME VERONICA TURNS YOU DOWN, YOU HAVE ANOTHER GUESS COMING!
NOW IF YOU DON'T MIND, MY DATE IS WAITING... GOOD AFTERNOON!
?
YOU DON'T SEEM TO BE ANY TALLER, ARCH!
TELL ME MORE ABOUT THOSE WONDERFUL GIRLS, ARCH! I'LL SAY ONE THING FOR YOU, YOU'RE A VERY LUCKY GUY TO HAVE A FRIEND LIKE ME TO HELP YOU SPEND THAT MONEY THAT WAS BURNING A HOLE IN YOUR POCKET!
OH SHUT UP!
CHOMP
CHOMP
CHOMP
The End

Everything's Archie "WINTER WONDERLAND"

NOTHING COULD BE KEENER THAN SLEIGH RIDING WITH SABRINA IN THE MORNING,
SPOUTING INCANTATIONS AND SUCH EERIE TYPE SENSATIONS WITHOUT WARNING,
HOKUS POKUS *TO* YOU,
PEOPLE SEE RIGHT *THROUGH* YOU,
YOU'LL BE ITCHY TO BE WITCHY AND WE PROMISE THAT YOU WON'T BE YAWNING!

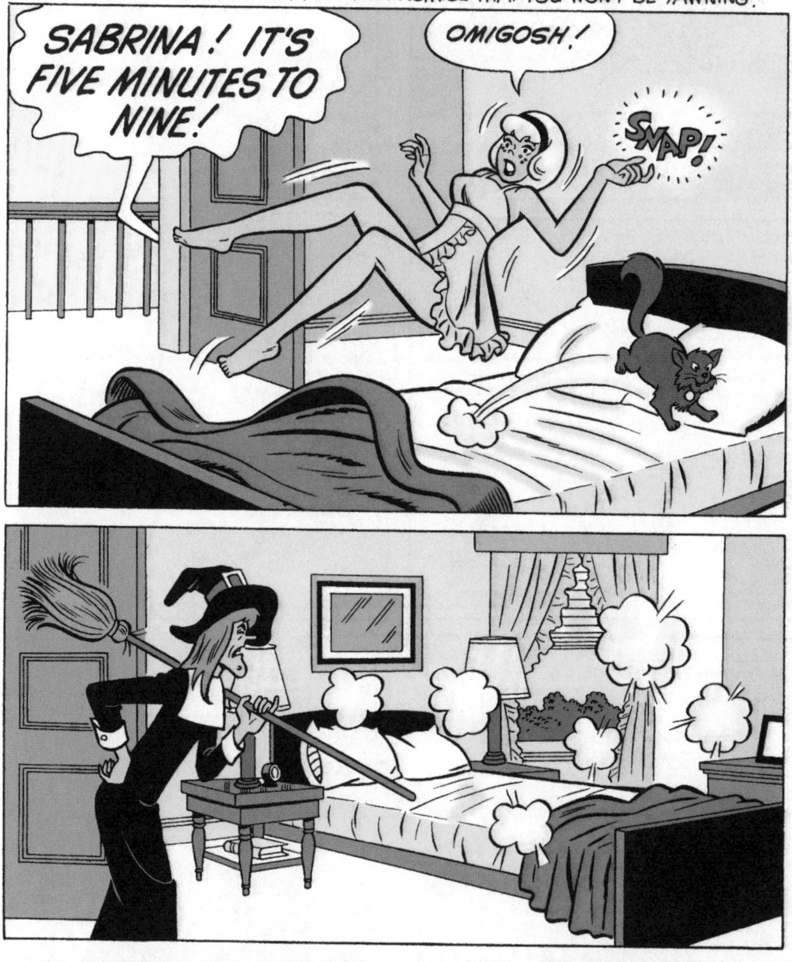
SABRINA! IT'S FIVE MINUTES TO NINE!
OMIGOSH!
SNAP!

Story & Pencils: Al Hartley Inks: Jon D'Agostino
Letters: Bill Yoshida Colors: Barry Grossman

Originally printed in EVERYTHING'S ARCHIE #7, APRIL 1970

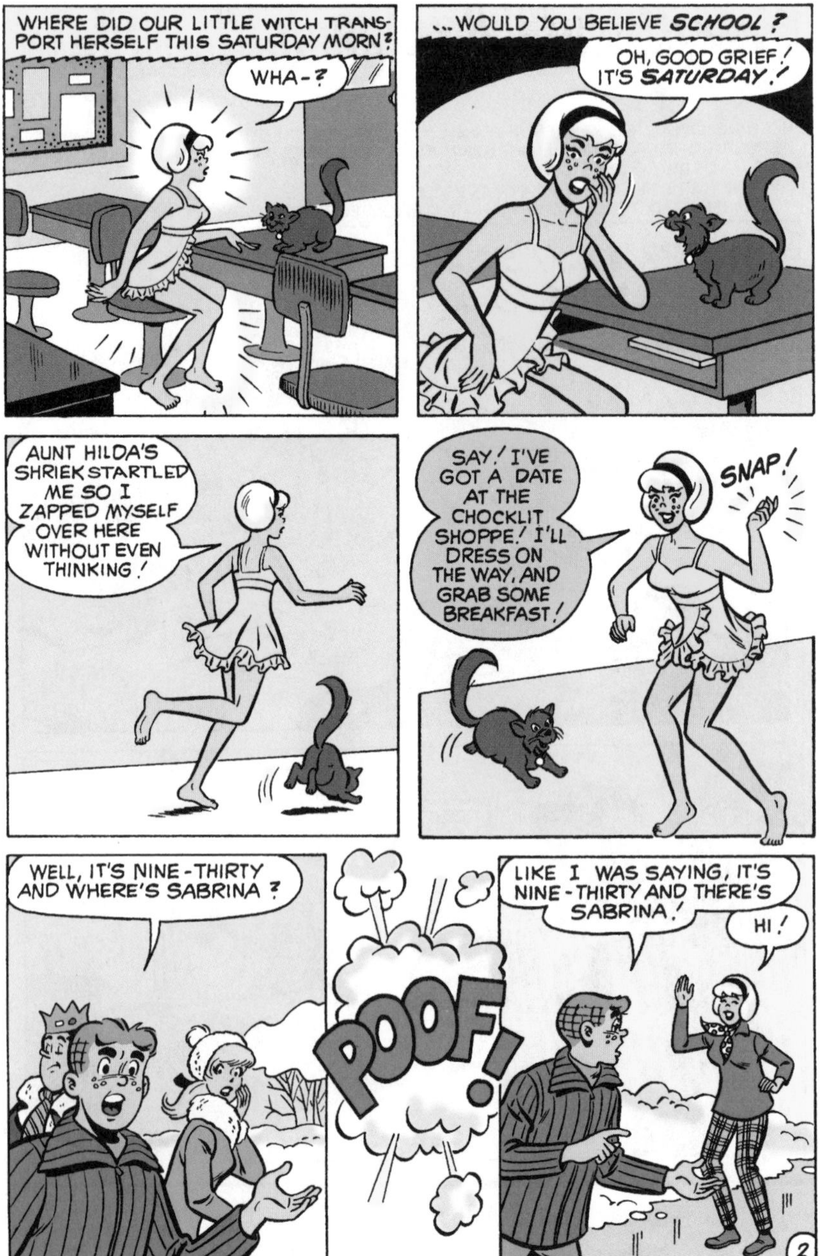
WHERE DID OUR LITTLE WITCH TRANSPORT HERSELF THIS SATURDAY MORN?
WHA-?
...WOULD YOU BELIEVE SCHOOL?
OH, GOOD GRIEF! IT'S SATURDAY!
AUNT HILDA'S SHRIEK STARTLED ME SO I ZAPPED MYSELF OVER HERE WITHOUT EVEN THINKING!
SAY! I'VE GOT A DATE AT THE CHOCKLIT SHOPPE! I'LL DRESS ON THE WAY, AND GRAB SOME BREAKFAST!
SNAP!
WELL, IT'S NINE-THIRTY AND WHERE'S SABRINA?
POOF!
LIKE I WAS SAYING, IT'S NINE-THIRTY AND THERE'S SABRINA!
HI!
2

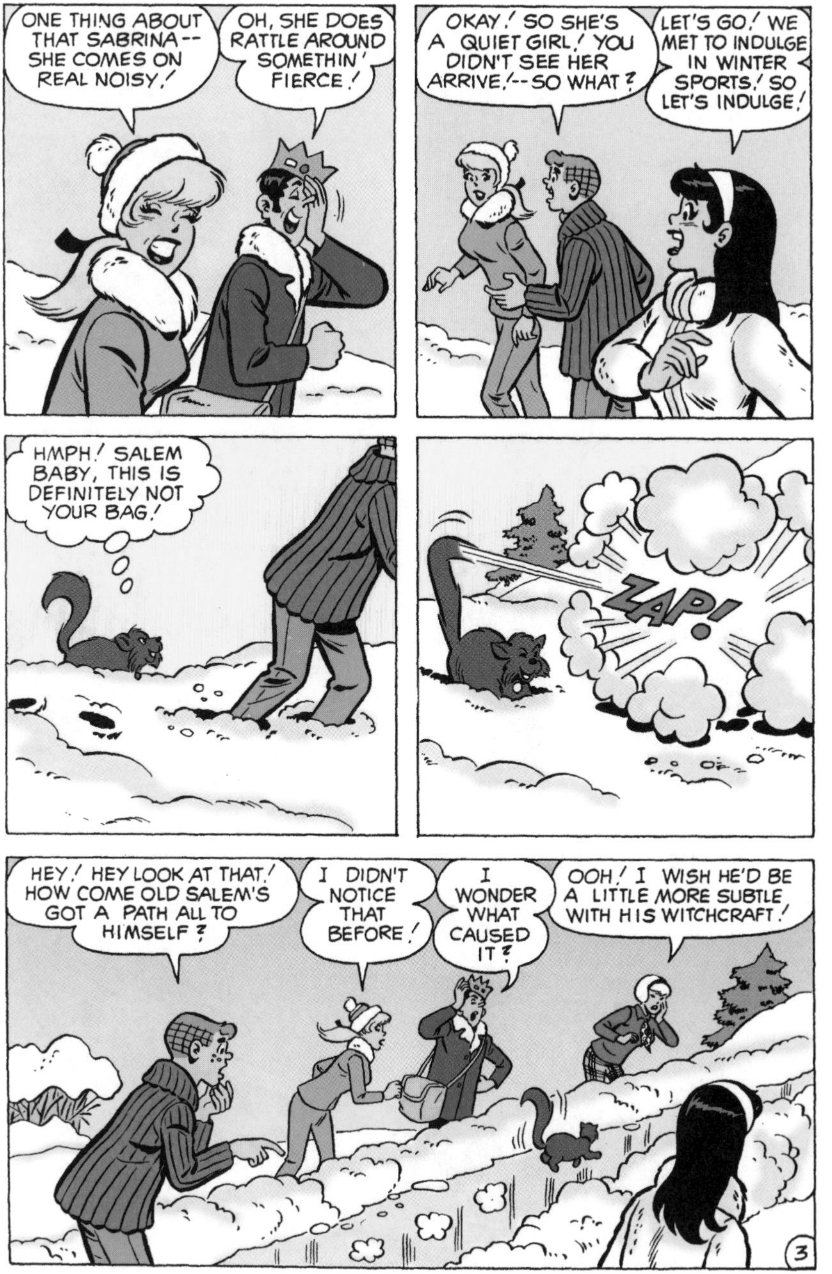
ONE THING ABOUT THAT SABRINA-- SHE COMES ON REAL NOISY!
OH, SHE DOES RATTLE AROUND SOMETHIN' FIERCE!
OKAY! SO SHE'S A QUIET GIRL! YOU DIDN'T SEE HER ARRIVE!--SO WHAT?
LET'S GO! WE MET TO INDULGE IN WINTER SPORTS! SO LET'S INDULGE!
HMPH! SALEM BABY, THIS IS DEFINITELY NOT YOUR BAG!
ZAP!
HEY! HEY LOOK AT THAT! HOW COME OLD SALEM'S GOT A PATH ALL TO HIMSELF?
I DIDN'T NOTICE THAT BEFORE!
I WONDER WHAT CAUSED IT?
OOH! I WISH HE'D BE A LITTLE MORE SUBTLE WITH HIS WITCHCRAFT!
3

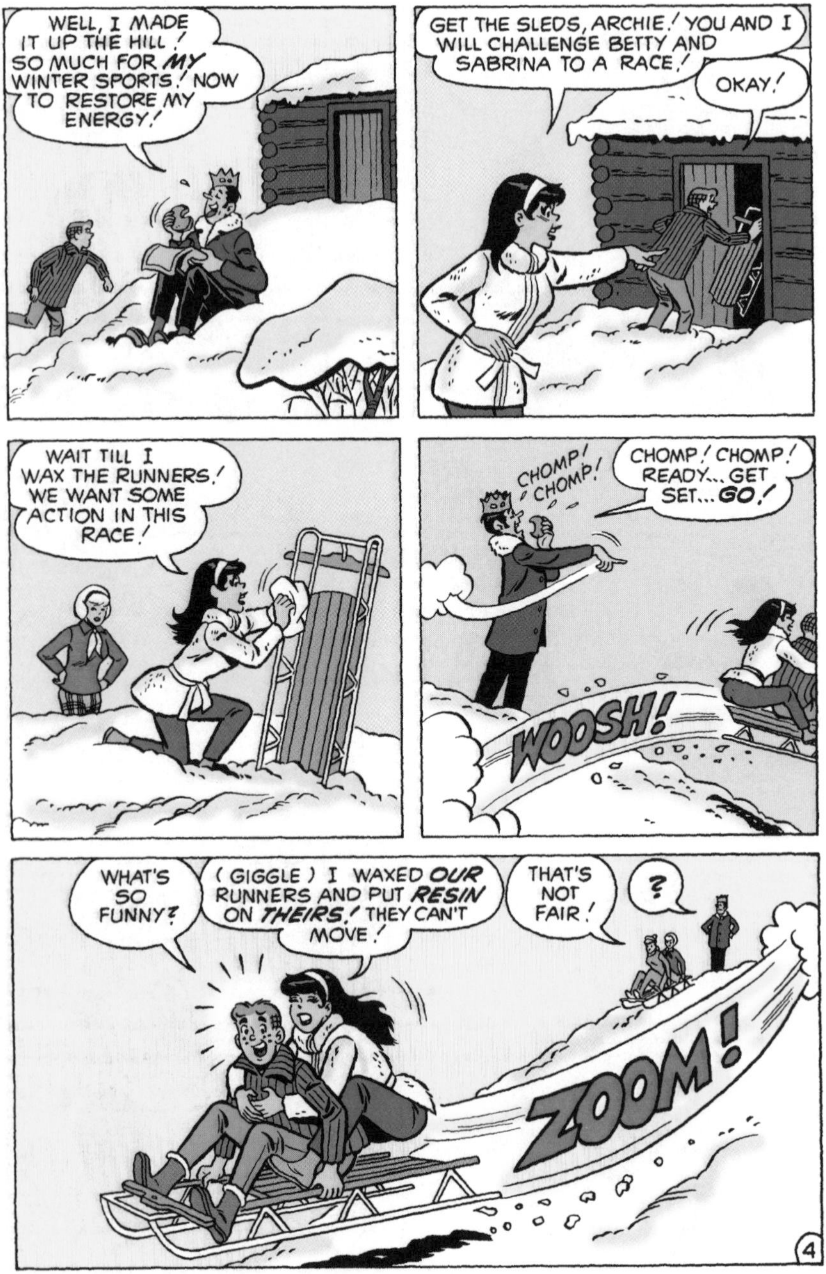
WELL, I MADE IT UP THE HILL! SO MUCH FOR MY WINTER SPORTS! NOW TO RESTORE MY ENERGY!
GET THE SLEDS, ARCHIE! YOU AND I WILL CHALLENGE BETTY AND SABRINA TO A RACE!
OKAY!
WAIT TILL I WAX THE RUNNERS! WE WANT SOME ACTION IN THIS RACE!
CHOMP! CHOMP!
CHOMP! CHOMP! READY... GET SET... GO!
WOOSH!
WHAT'S SO FUNNY?
(GIGGLE) I WAXED OUR RUNNERS AND PUT RESIN ON THEIRS! THEY CAN'T MOVE!
THAT'S NOT FAIR!
?
ZOOM!
4

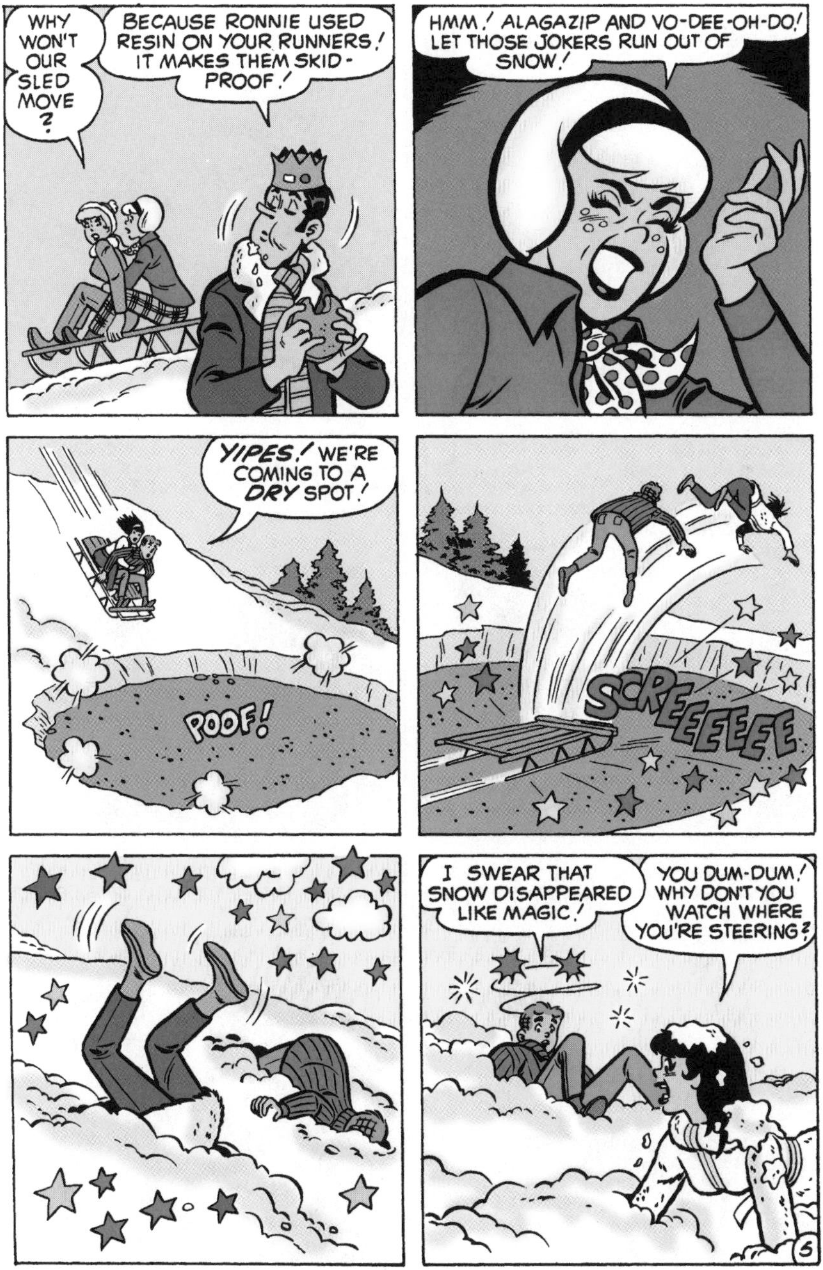
WHY WON'T OUR SLED MOVE?
BECAUSE RONNIE USED RESIN ON YOUR RUNNERS! IT MAKES THEM SKID-PROOF!
HMM! ALAGAZIP AND VO-DEE-OH-DO! LET THOSE JOKERS RUN OUT OF SNOW!
YIPES! WE'RE COMING TO A DRY SPOT!
POOF!
SCREEEEEEEE
I SWEAR THAT SNOW DISAPPEARED LIKE MAGIC!
YOU DUM-DUM! WHY DON'T YOU WATCH WHERE YOU'RE STEERING?
5

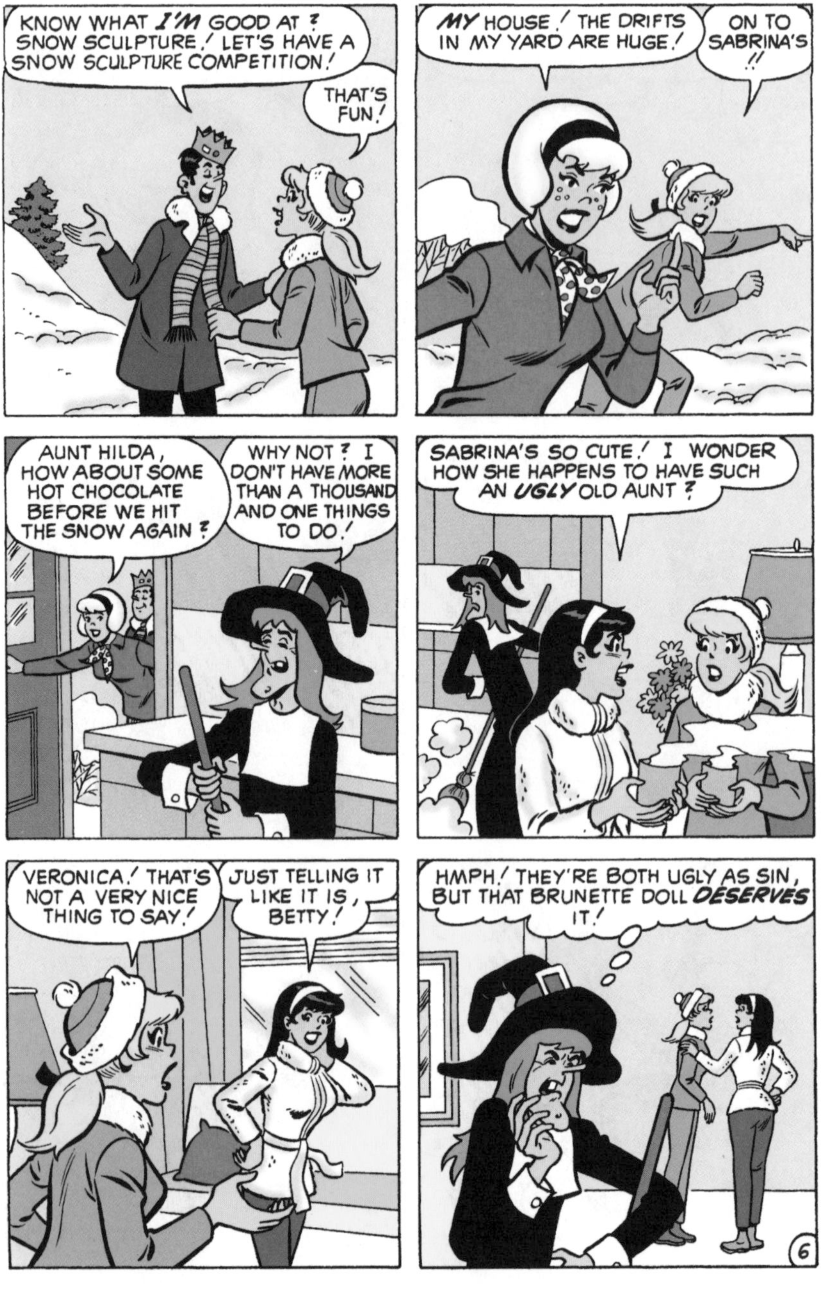
KNOW WHAT I'M GOOD AT ? SNOW SCULPTURE! LET'S HAVE A SNOW SCULPTURE COMPETITION!
THAT'S FUN!
MY HOUSE! THE DRIFTS IN MY YARD ARE HUGE!
ON TO SABRINA'S !!
AUNT HILDA, HOW ABOUT SOME HOT CHOCOLATE BEFORE WE HIT THE SNOW AGAIN ?
WHY NOT ? I DON'T HAVE MORE THAN A THOUSAND AND ONE THINGS TO DO!
SABRINA'S SO CUTE! I WONDER HOW SHE HAPPENS TO HAVE SUCH AN UGLY OLD AUNT ?
VERONICA! THAT'S NOT A VERY NICE THING TO SAY!
JUST TELLING IT LIKE IT IS, BETTY!
HMPH! THEY'RE BOTH UGLY AS SIN, BUT THAT BRUNETTE DOLL DESERVES IT!
6

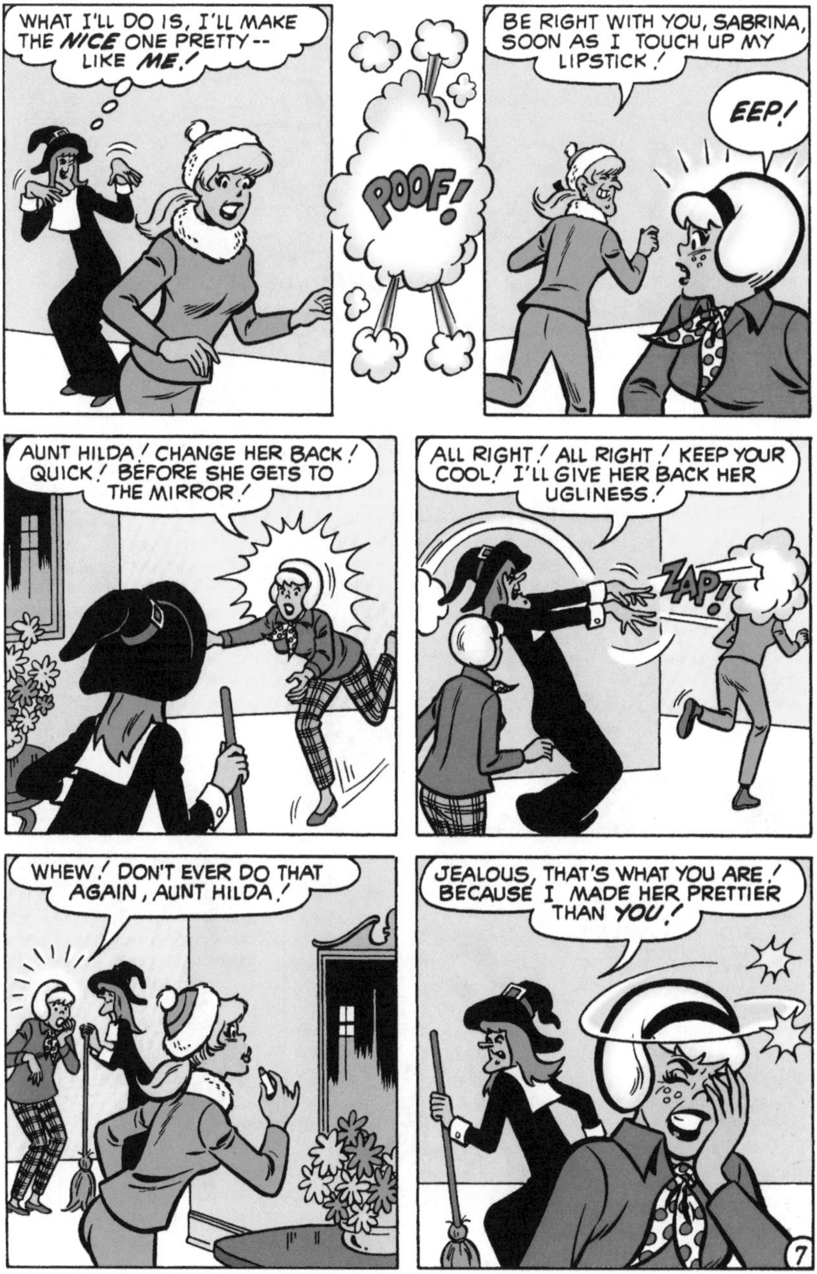
WHAT I'LL DO IS, I'LL MAKE THE NICE ONE PRETTY -- LIKE ME!
POOF!
BE RIGHT WITH YOU, SABRINA, SOON AS I TOUCH UP MY LIPSTICK!
EEP!
AUNT HILDA! CHANGE HER BACK! QUICK! BEFORE SHE GETS TO THE MIRROR!
ALL RIGHT! ALL RIGHT! KEEP YOUR COOL! I'LL GIVE HER BACK HER UGLINESS!
ZAP!
WHEW! DON'T EVER DO THAT AGAIN, AUNT HILDA!
JEALOUS, THAT'S WHAT YOU ARE! BECAUSE I MADE HER PRETTIER THAN YOU!
7

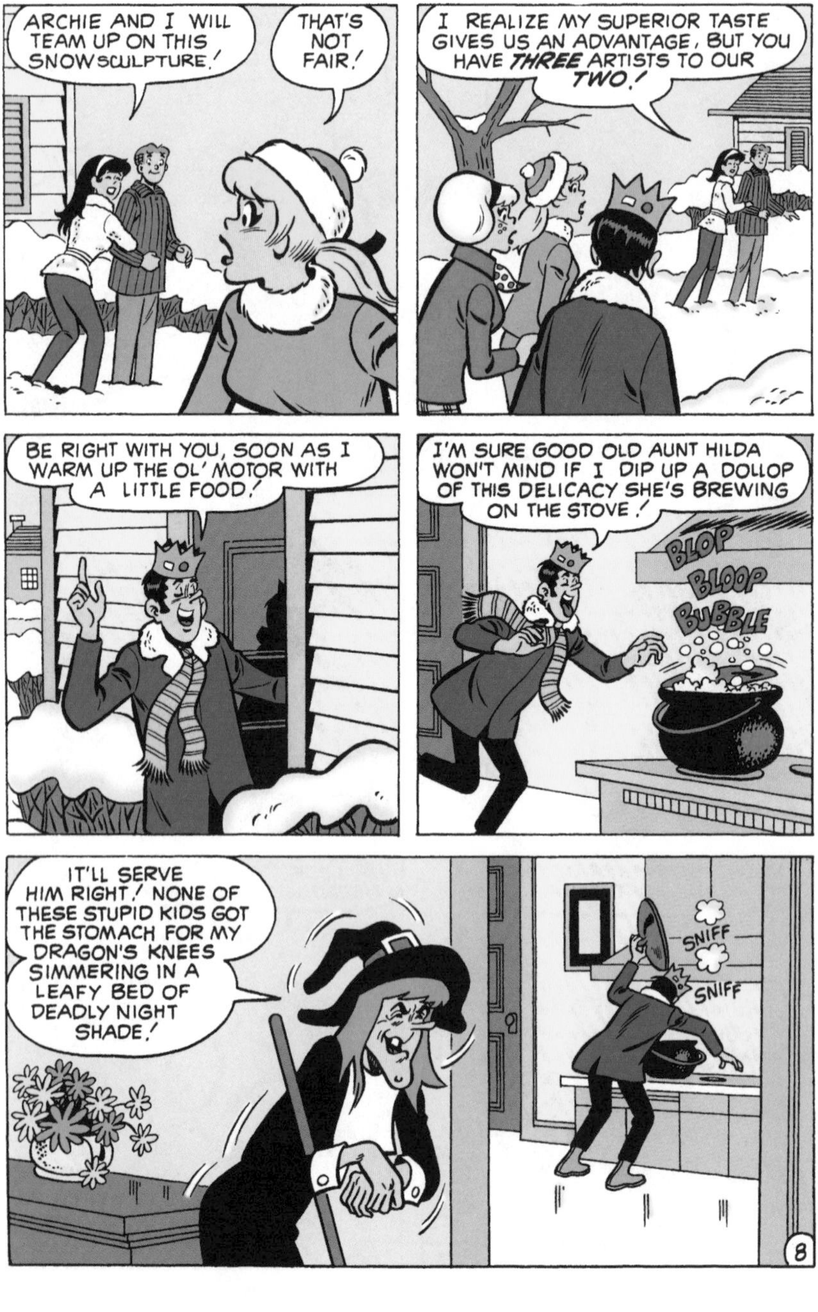
ARCHIE AND I WILL TEAM UP ON THIS SNOW SCULPTURE!
THAT'S NOT FAIR!
I REALIZE MY SUPERIOR TASTE GIVES US AN ADVANTAGE, BUT YOU HAVE THREE ARTISTS TO OUR TWO!
BE RIGHT WITH YOU, SOON AS I WARM UP THE OL' MOTOR WITH A LITTLE FOOD!
I'M SURE GOOD OLD AUNT HILDA WON'T MIND IF I DIP UP A DOLLOP OF THIS DELICACY SHE'S BREWING ON THE STOVE!
BLOP
BLOOP
BUBBLE
IT'LL SERVE HIM RIGHT! NONE OF THESE STUPID KIDS GOT THE STOMACH FOR MY DRAGON'S KNEES SIMMERING IN A LEAFY BED OF DEADLY NIGHT SHADE!
SNIFF
SNIFF
8

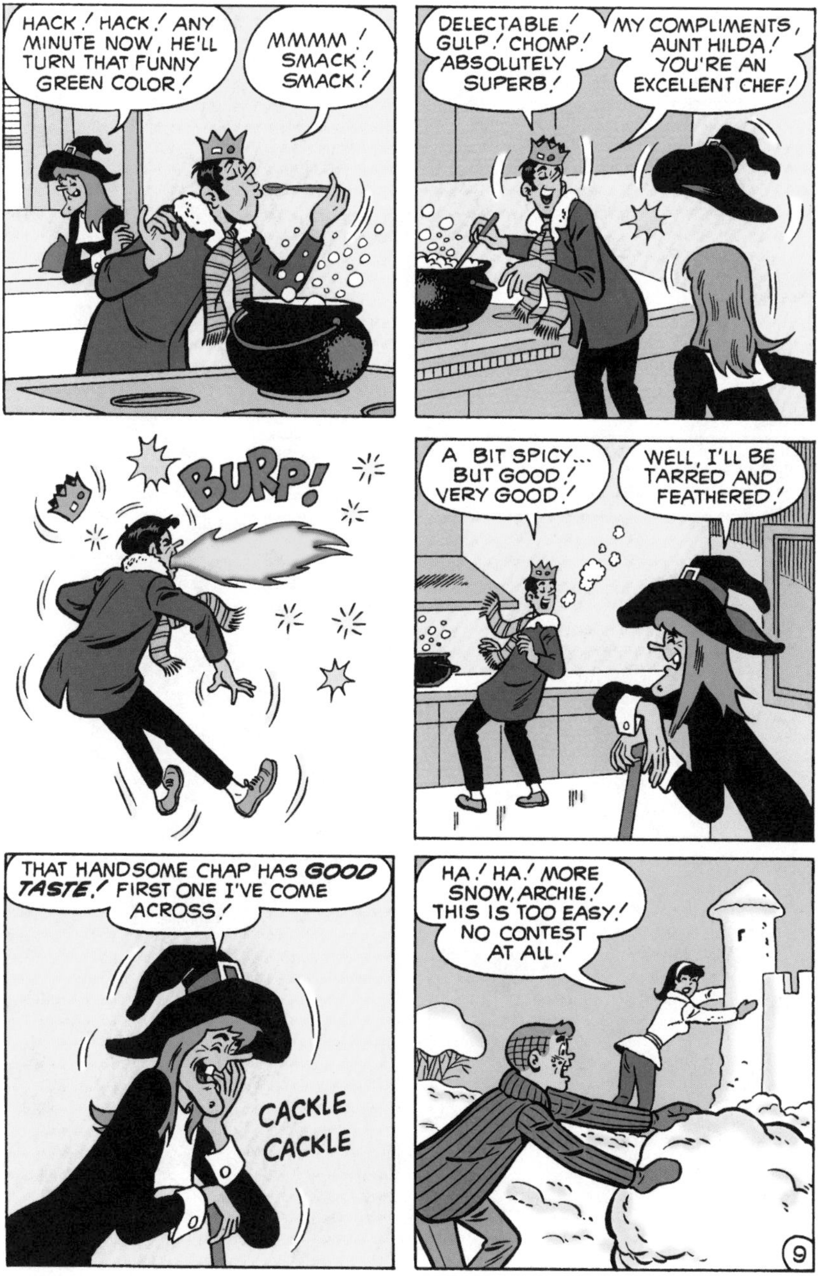
HACK! HACK! ANY MINUTE NOW, HE'LL TURN THAT FUNNY GREEN COLOR!
MMMM! SMACK! SMACK!
DELECTABLE! GULP! CHOMP! ABSOLUTELY SUPERB!
MY COMPLIMENTS, AUNT HILDA! YOU'RE AN EXCELLENT CHEF!
BURP!
A BIT SPICY... BUT GOOD! VERY GOOD!
WELL, I'LL BE TARRED AND FEATHERED!
THAT HANDSOME CHAP HAS GOOD TASTE! FIRST ONE I'VE COME ACROSS!
CACKLE CACKLE
HA! HA! MORE SNOW, ARCHIE! THIS IS TOO EASY! NO CONTEST AT ALL!
9

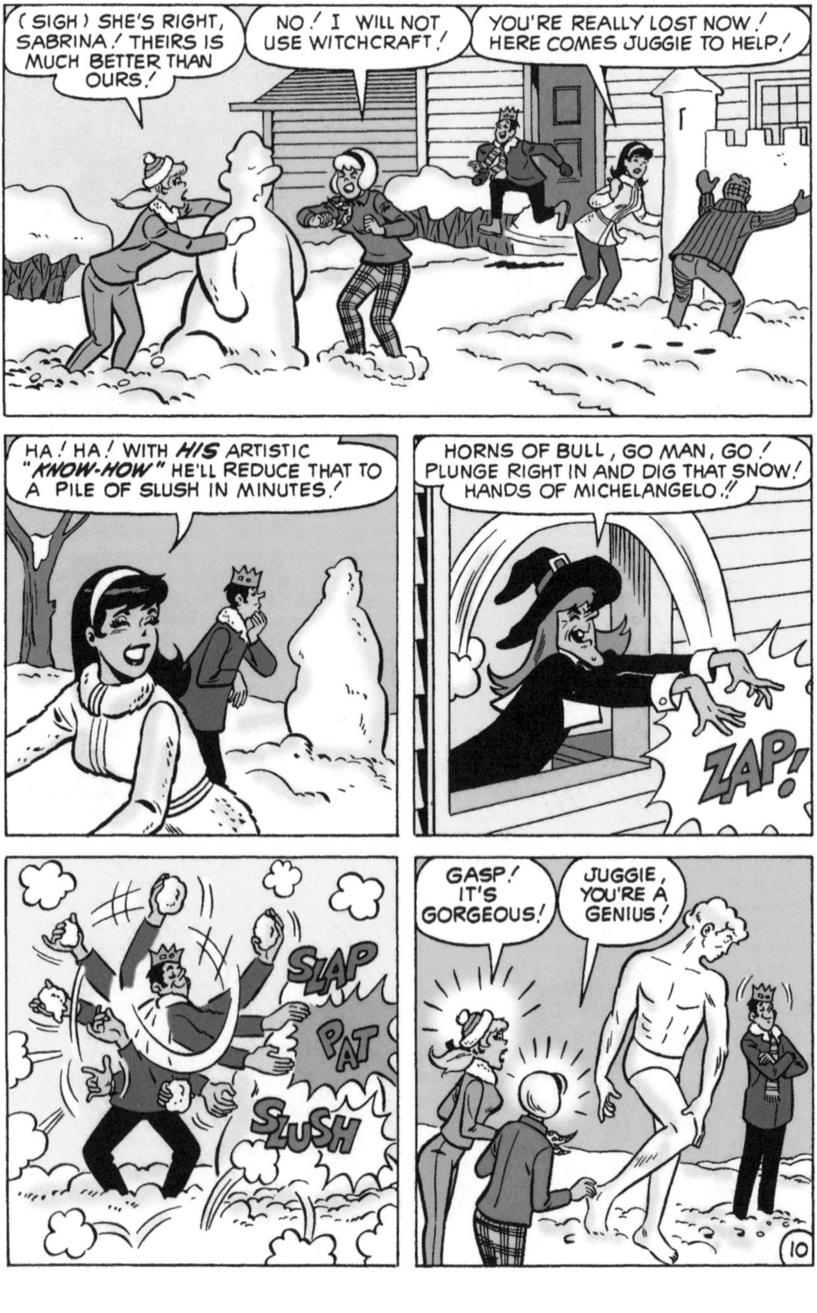
(SIGH) SHE'S RIGHT, SABRINA! THEIRS IS MUCH BETTER THAN OURS!
NO! I WILL NOT USE WITCHCRAFT!
YOU'RE REALLY LOST NOW! HERE COMES JUGGIE TO HELP!
HA! HA! WITH *HIS* ARTISTIC "*KNOW-HOW*" HE'LL REDUCE THAT TO A PILE OF SLUSH IN MINUTES!
HORNS OF BULL, GO MAN, GO! PLUNGE RIGHT IN AND DIG THAT SNOW! HANDS OF MICHELANGELO!!
ZAP!
SLAP
PAT
SLUSH
GASP! IT'S GORGEOUS!
JUGGIE, YOU'RE A GENIUS!
10

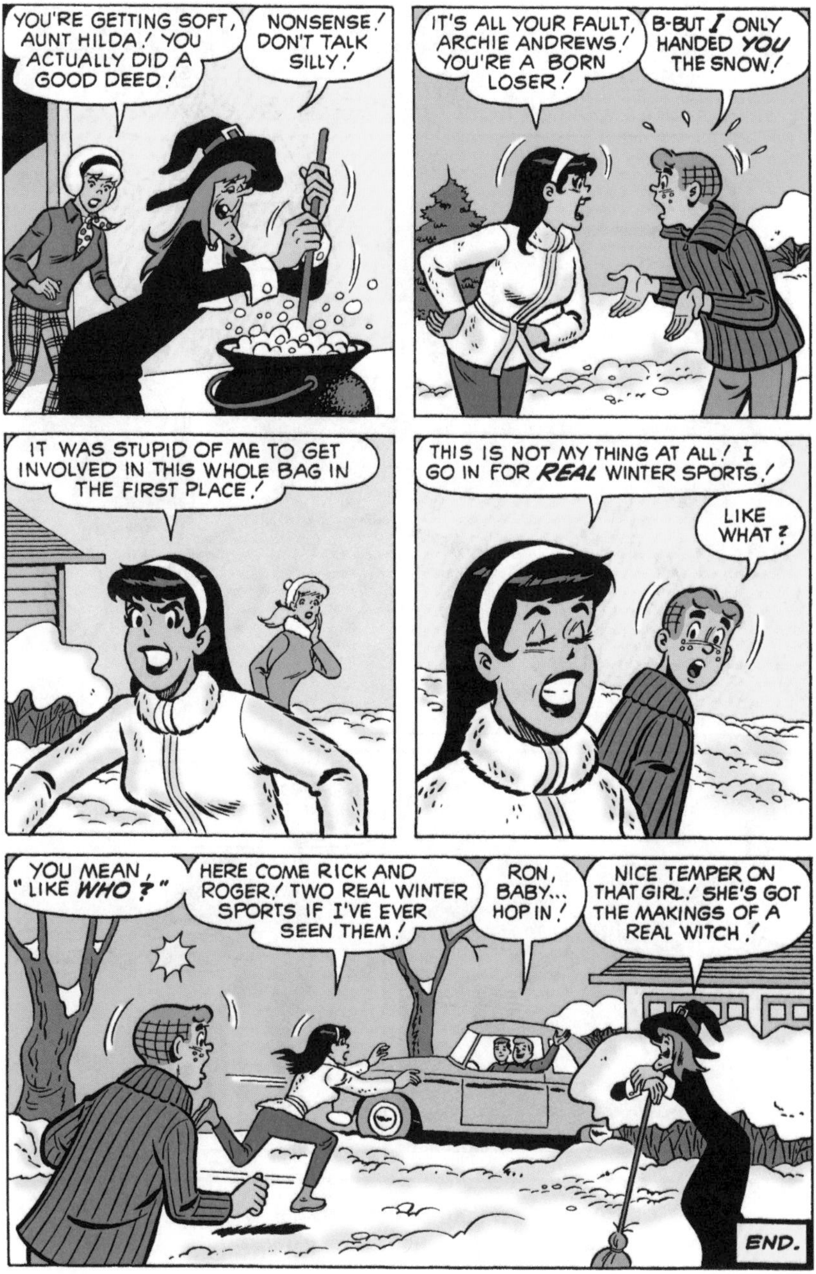
YOU'RE GETTING SOFT, AUNT HILDA! YOU ACTUALLY DID A GOOD DEED!
NONSENSE! DON'T TALK SILLY!
IT'S ALL YOUR FAULT, ARCHIE ANDREWS! YOU'RE A BORN LOSER!
B-BUT I ONLY HANDED YOU THE SNOW!
IT WAS STUPID OF ME TO GET INVOLVED IN THIS WHOLE BAG IN THE FIRST PLACE!
THIS IS NOT MY THING AT ALL! I GO IN FOR REAL WINTER SPORTS!
LIKE WHAT?
YOU MEAN, "LIKE WHO?"
HERE COME RICK AND ROGER! TWO REAL WINTER SPORTS IF I'VE EVER SEEN THEM!
RON, BABY... HOP IN!
NICE TEMPER ON THAT GIRL! SHE'S GOT THE MAKINGS OF A REAL WITCH!
END.

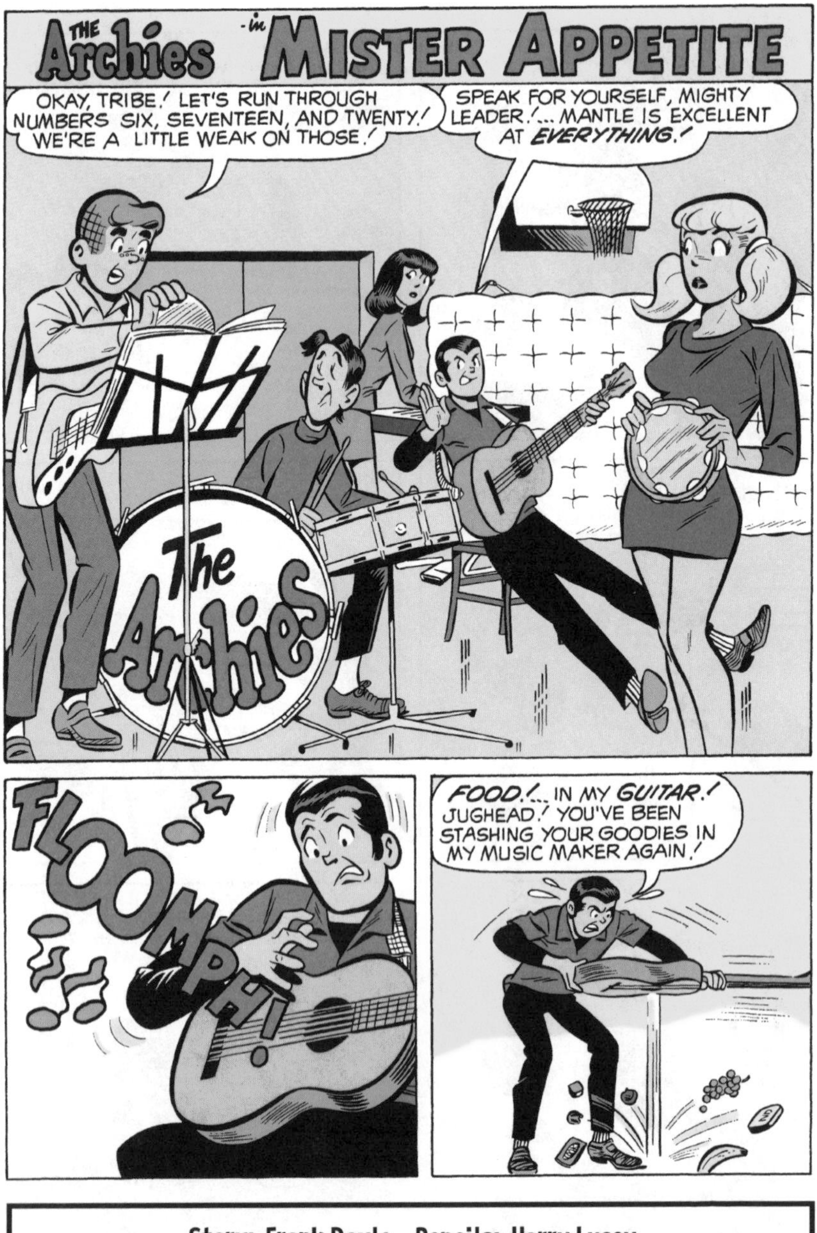
THE Archies -in- MISTER APPETITE
OKAY, TRIBE! LET'S RUN THROUGH NUMBERS SIX, SEVENTEEN, AND TWENTY! WE'RE A LITTLE WEAK ON THOSE!
SPEAK FOR YOURSELF, MIGHTY LEADER!... MANTLE IS EXCELLENT AT EVERYTHING!
The Archies
FLOOMPH!
FOOD!... IN MY GUITAR! JUGHEAD! YOU'VE BEEN STASHING YOUR GOODIES IN MY MUSIC MAKER AGAIN!

Story: Frank Doyle Pencils: Harry Lucey
Inks: Marty Epp Letters: Bill Yoshida

Originally printed in EVERYTHING'S ARCHIE #8, JUNE 1970

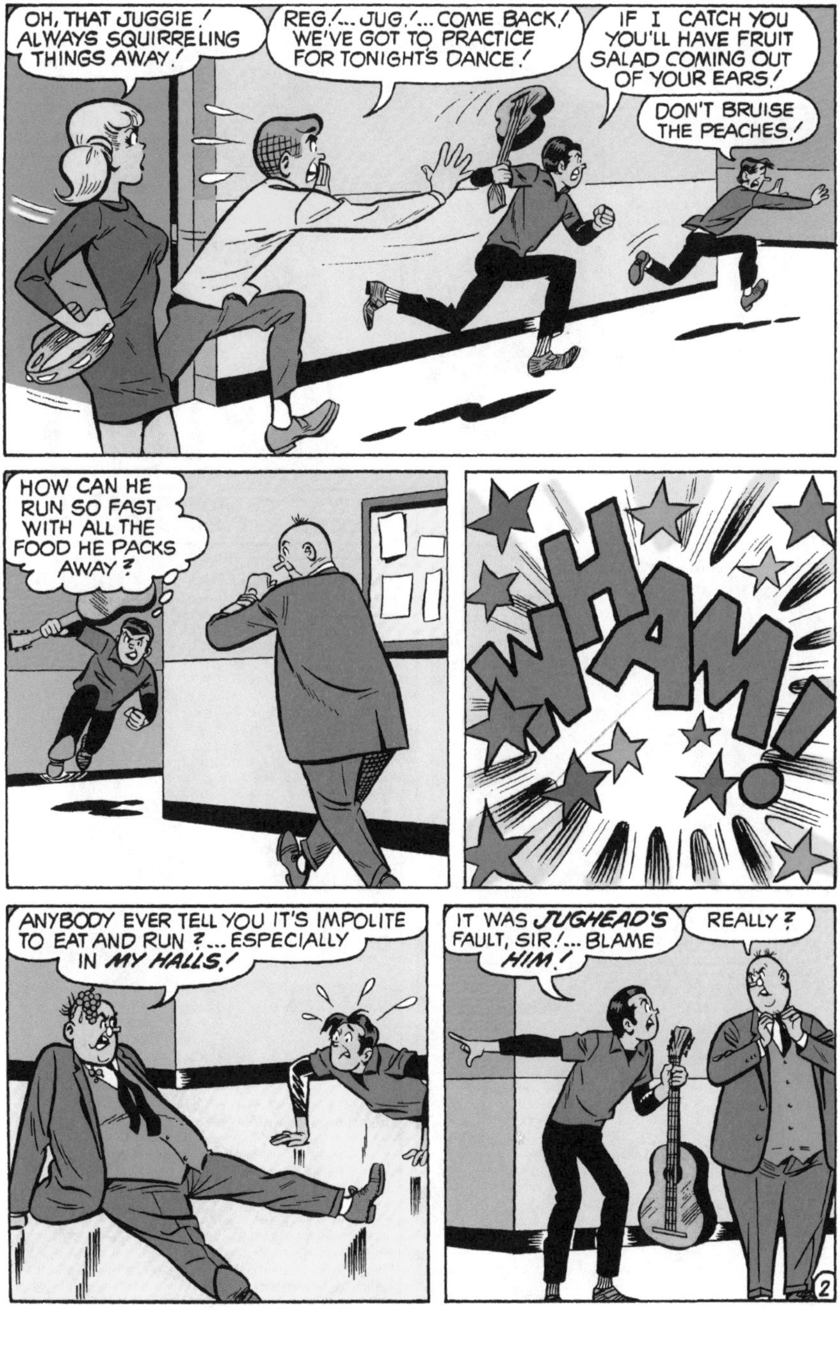
OH, THAT JUGGIE! ALWAYS SQUIRRELING THINGS AWAY!
REG.!... JUG.!... COME BACK! WE'VE GOT TO PRACTICE FOR TONIGHT'S DANCE!
IF I CATCH YOU YOU'LL HAVE FRUIT SALAD COMING OUT OF YOUR EARS!
DON'T BRUISE THE PEACHES!
HOW CAN HE RUN SO FAST WITH ALL THE FOOD HE PACKS AWAY?
WHAM!
ANYBODY EVER TELL YOU IT'S IMPOLITE TO EAT AND RUN?... ESPECIALLY IN MY HALLS!
IT WAS JUGHEAD'S FAULT, SIR!... BLAME HIM!
REALLY?
2

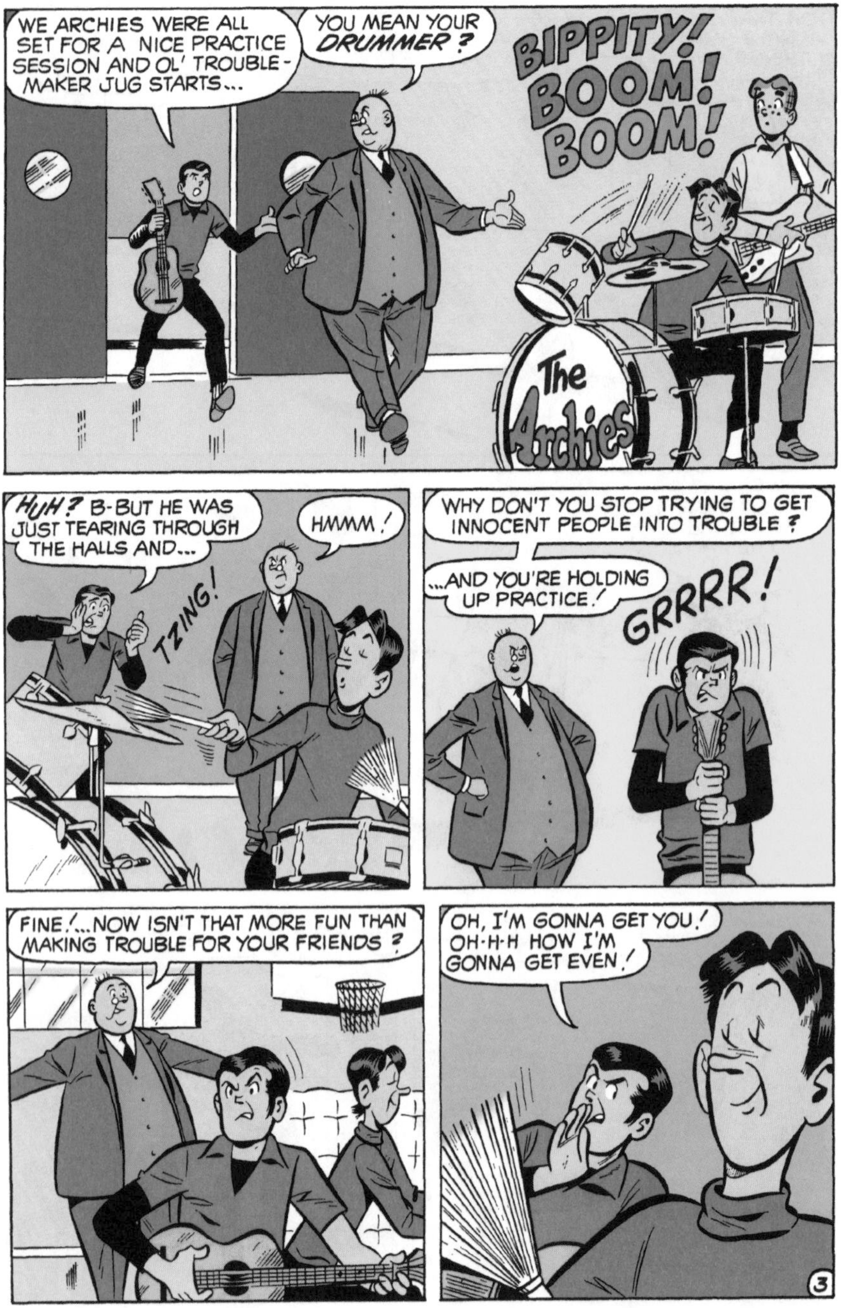
WE ARCHIES WERE ALL SET FOR A NICE PRACTICE SESSION AND OL' TROUBLE-MAKER JUG STARTS...
YOU MEAN YOUR DRUMMER?
BIPPITY! BOOM! BOOM!
The Archies
HUH? B-BUT HE WAS JUST TEARING THROUGH THE HALLS AND...
HMMM!
TZING!
WHY DON'T YOU STOP TRYING TO GET INNOCENT PEOPLE INTO TROUBLE?
...AND YOU'RE HOLDING UP PRACTICE!
GRRRR!
FINE!...NOW ISN'T THAT MORE FUN THAN MAKING TROUBLE FOR YOUR FRIENDS?
OH, I'M GONNA GET YOU! OH-H-H HOW I'M GONNA GET EVEN!
3

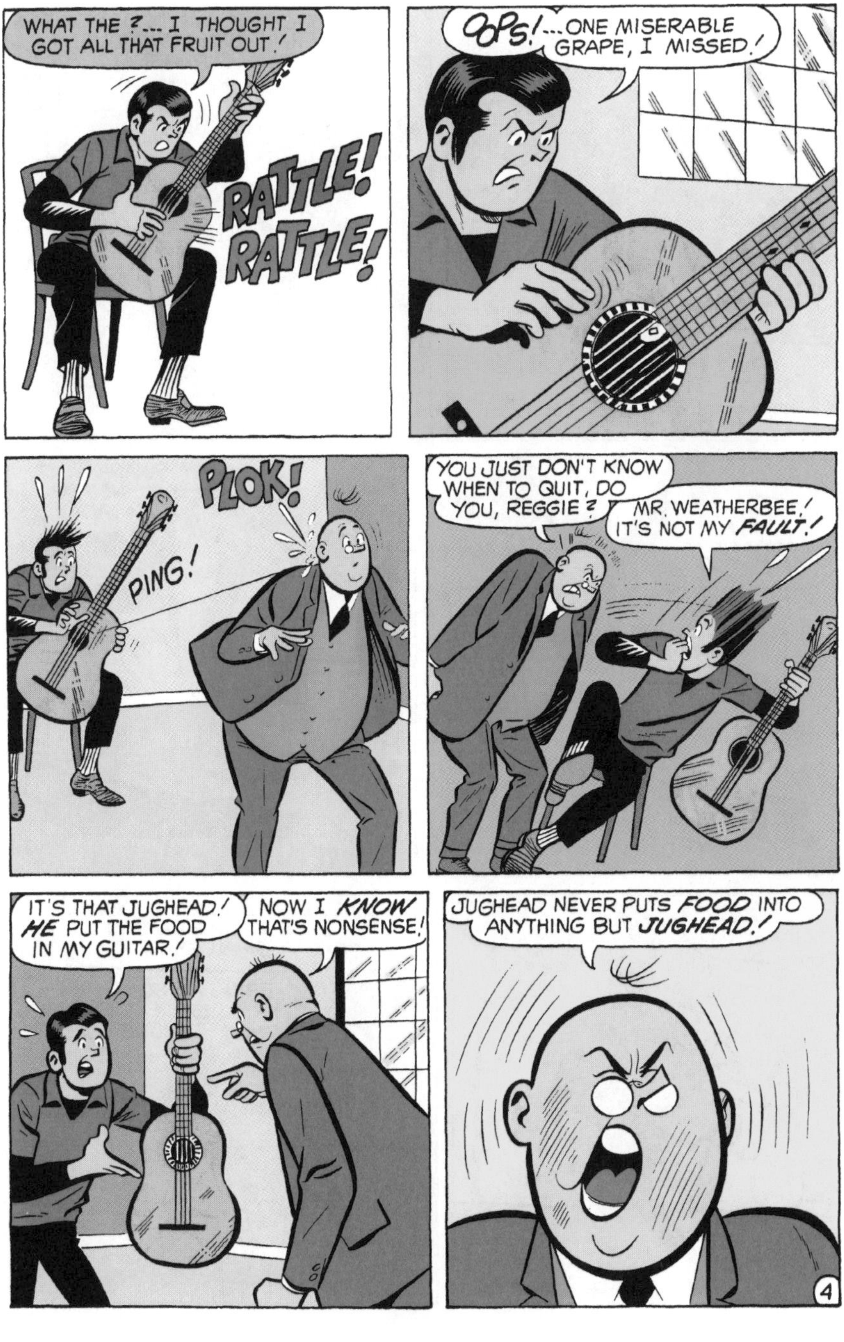
WHAT THE ?... I THOUGHT I GOT ALL THAT FRUIT OUT!
RATTLE! RATTLE!
OOPS! ...ONE MISERABLE GRAPE, I MISSED!
PLOK!
PING!
YOU JUST DON'T KNOW WHEN TO QUIT, DO YOU, REGGIE?
MR. WEATHERBEE! IT'S NOT MY FAULT!
IT'S THAT JUGHEAD! HE PUT THE FOOD IN MY GUITAR!
NOW I KNOW THAT'S NONSENSE!
JUGHEAD NEVER PUTS FOOD INTO ANYTHING BUT JUGHEAD!
4

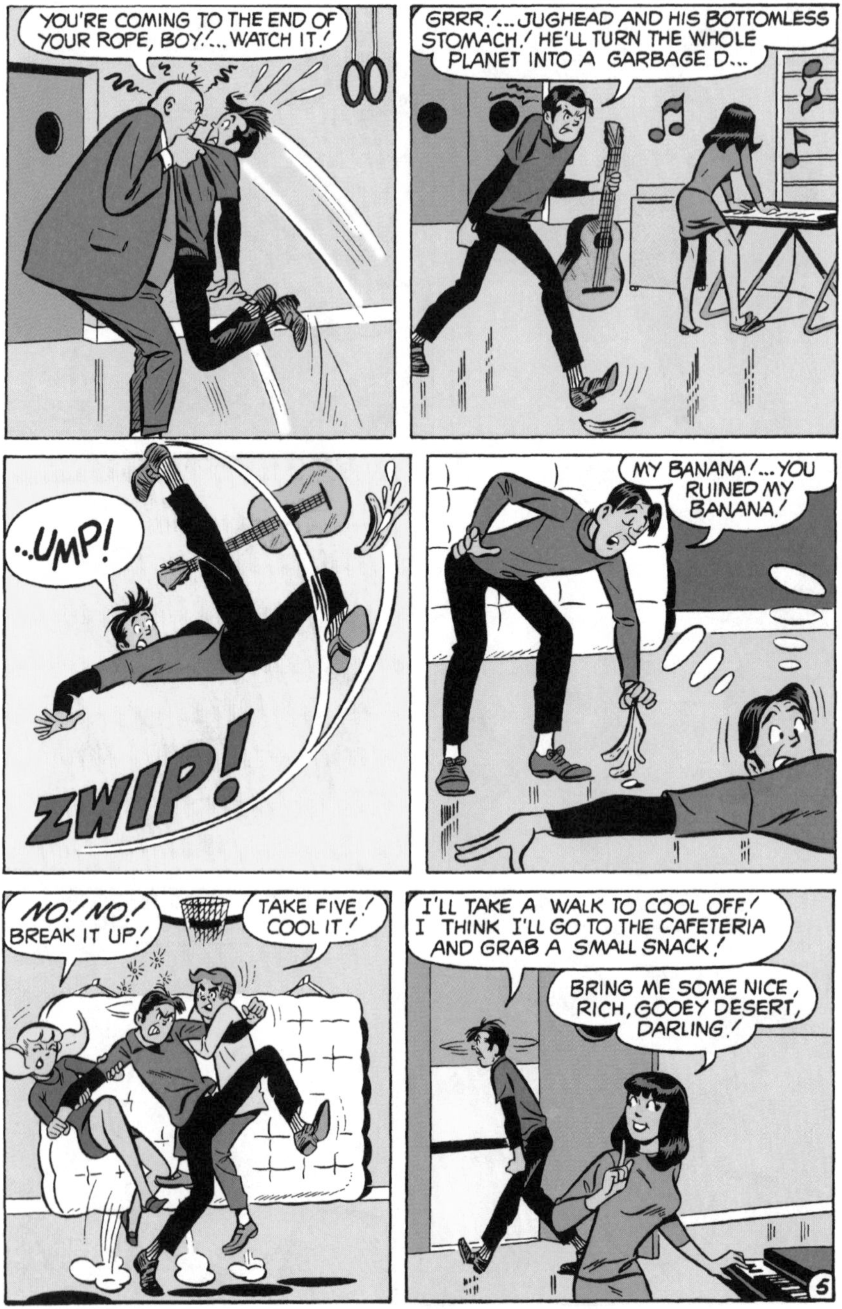
YOU'RE COMING TO THE END OF YOUR ROPE, BOY!... WATCH IT!
GRRR!... JUGHEAD AND HIS BOTTOMLESS STOMACH! HE'LL TURN THE WHOLE PLANET INTO A GARBAGE D...
..UMP!
ZWIP!
MY BANANA!... YOU RUINED MY BANANA!
NO! NO! BREAK IT UP!
TAKE FIVE! COOL IT!
I'LL TAKE A WALK TO COOL OFF! I THINK I'LL GO TO THE CAFETERIA AND GRAB A SMALL SNACK!
BRING ME SOME NICE, RICH, GOOEY DESERT, DARLING!
5

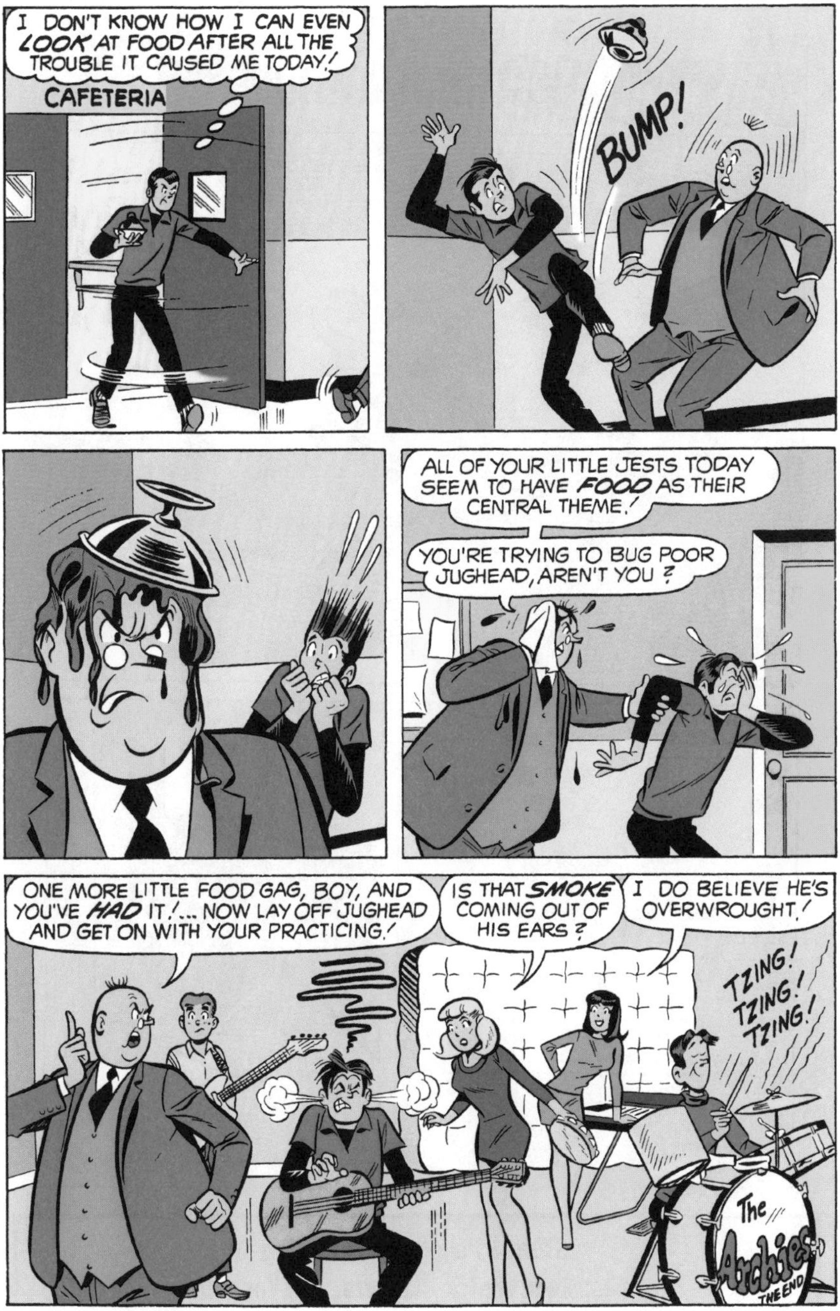
I DON'T KNOW HOW I CAN EVEN LOOK AT FOOD AFTER ALL THE TROUBLE IT CAUSED ME TODAY!
CAFETERIA
BUMP!
ALL OF YOUR LITTLE JESTS TODAY SEEM TO HAVE FOOD AS THEIR CENTRAL THEME.!
YOU'RE TRYING TO BUG POOR JUGHEAD, AREN'T YOU ?
ONE MORE LITTLE FOOD GAG, BOY, AND YOU'VE HAD IT.!... NOW LAY OFF JUGHEAD AND GET ON WITH YOUR PRACTICING.!
IS THAT SMOKE COMING OUT OF HIS EARS ?
I DO BELIEVE HE'S OVERWROUGHT.!
TZING! TZING! TZING!
The Archies
THE END

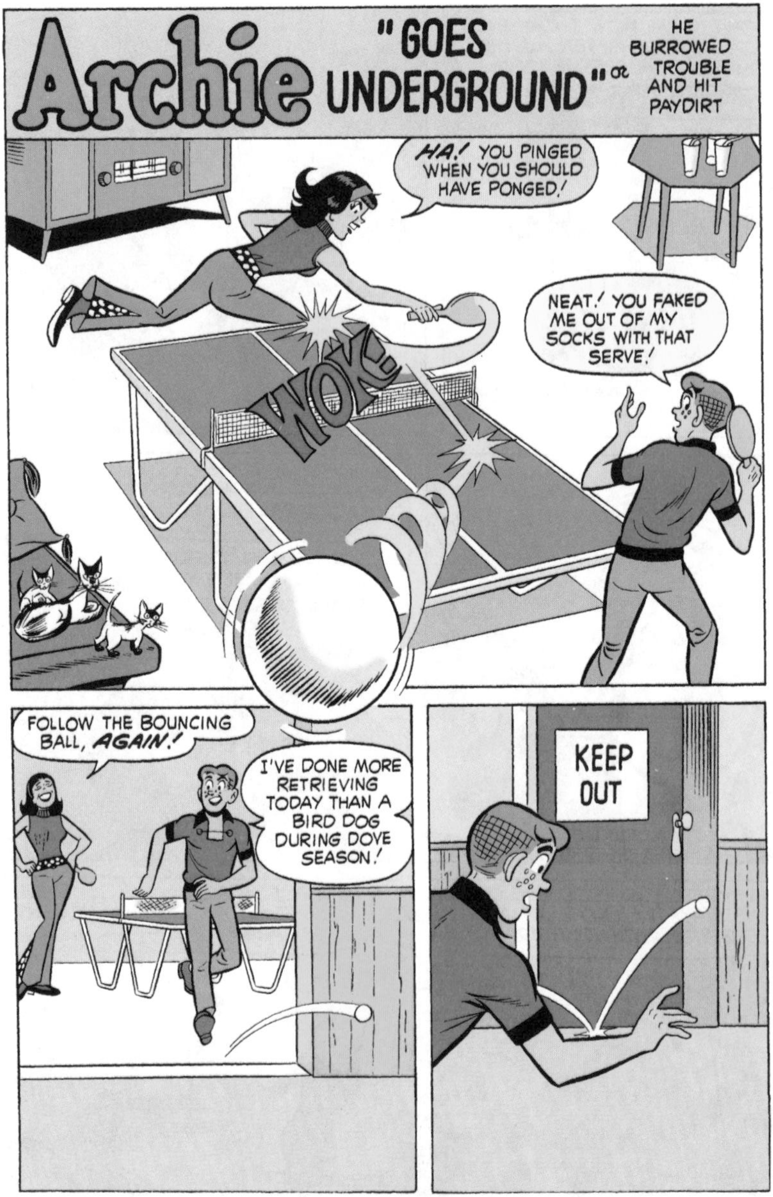
Archie
"GOES UNDERGROUND" or
HE BURROWED TROUBLE AND HIT PAYDIRT
HA! YOU PINGED WHEN YOU SHOULD HAVE PONGED!
WOK!
NEAT! YOU FAKED ME OUT OF MY SOCKS WITH THAT SERVE!
FOLLOW THE BOUNCING BALL, AGAIN!
I'VE DONE MORE RETRIEVING TODAY THAN A BIRD DOG DURING DOVE SEASON!
KEEP OUT

Story & Pencils: Bob Bolling

Inks: Rudy Lapick Letters: Bill Yoshida

Originally printed in EVERYTHING'S ARCHIE #8, JUNE 1970

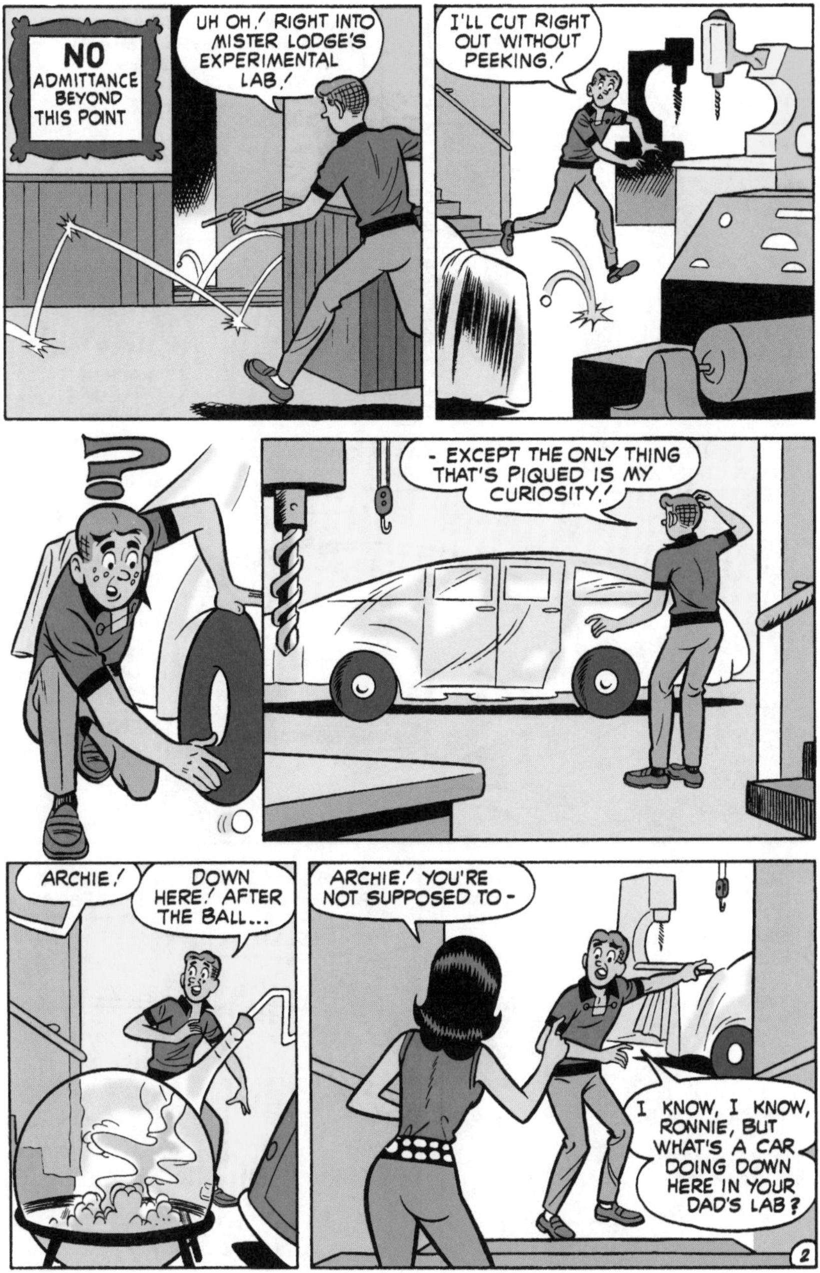
NO ADMITTANCE BEYOND THIS POINT
UH OH! RIGHT INTO MISTER LODGE'S EXPERIMENTAL LAB!
I'LL CUT RIGHT OUT WITHOUT PEEKING!
- EXCEPT THE ONLY THING THAT'S PIQUED IS MY CURIOSITY!
ARCHIE!
DOWN HERE! AFTER THE BALL...
ARCHIE! YOU'RE NOT SUPPOSED TO -
I KNOW, I KNOW, RONNIE, BUT WHAT'S A CAR DOING DOWN HERE IN YOUR DAD'S LAB?
2

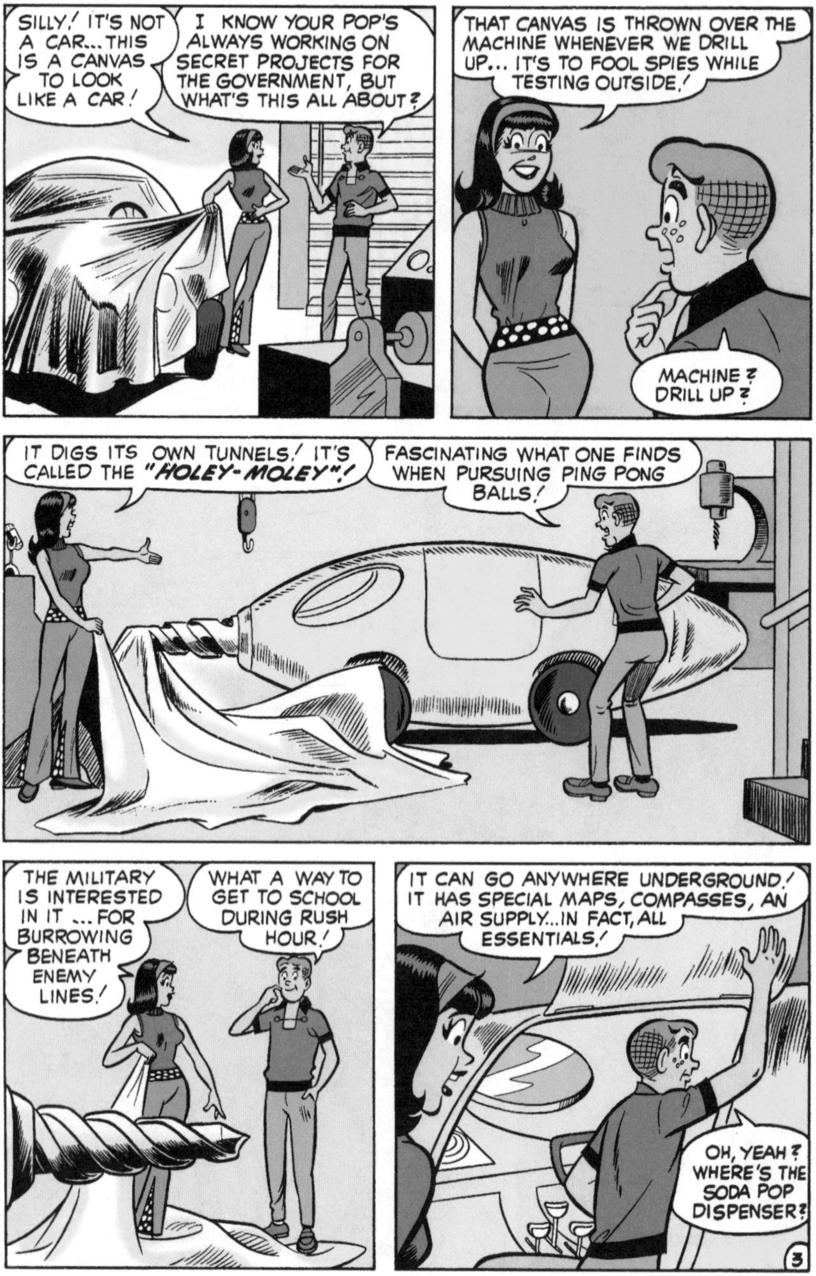
SILLY! IT'S NOT A CAR... THIS IS A CANVAS TO LOOK LIKE A CAR!
I KNOW YOUR POP'S ALWAYS WORKING ON SECRET PROJECTS FOR THE GOVERNMENT, BUT WHAT'S THIS ALL ABOUT?
THAT CANVAS IS THROWN OVER THE MACHINE WHENEVER WE DRILL UP... IT'S TO FOOL SPIES WHILE TESTING OUTSIDE!
MACHINE? DRILL UP?
IT DIGS ITS OWN TUNNELS! IT'S CALLED THE "HOLEY-MOLEY"!
FASCINATING WHAT ONE FINDS WHEN PURSUING PING PONG BALLS!
THE MILITARY IS INTERESTED IN IT ...FOR BURROWING BENEATH ENEMY LINES!
WHAT A WAY TO GET TO SCHOOL DURING RUSH HOUR!
IT CAN GO ANYWHERE UNDERGROUND! IT HAS SPECIAL MAPS, COMPASSES, AN AIR SUPPLY...IN FACT, ALL ESSENTIALS!
OH, YEAH? WHERE'S THE SODA POP DISPENSER?
3

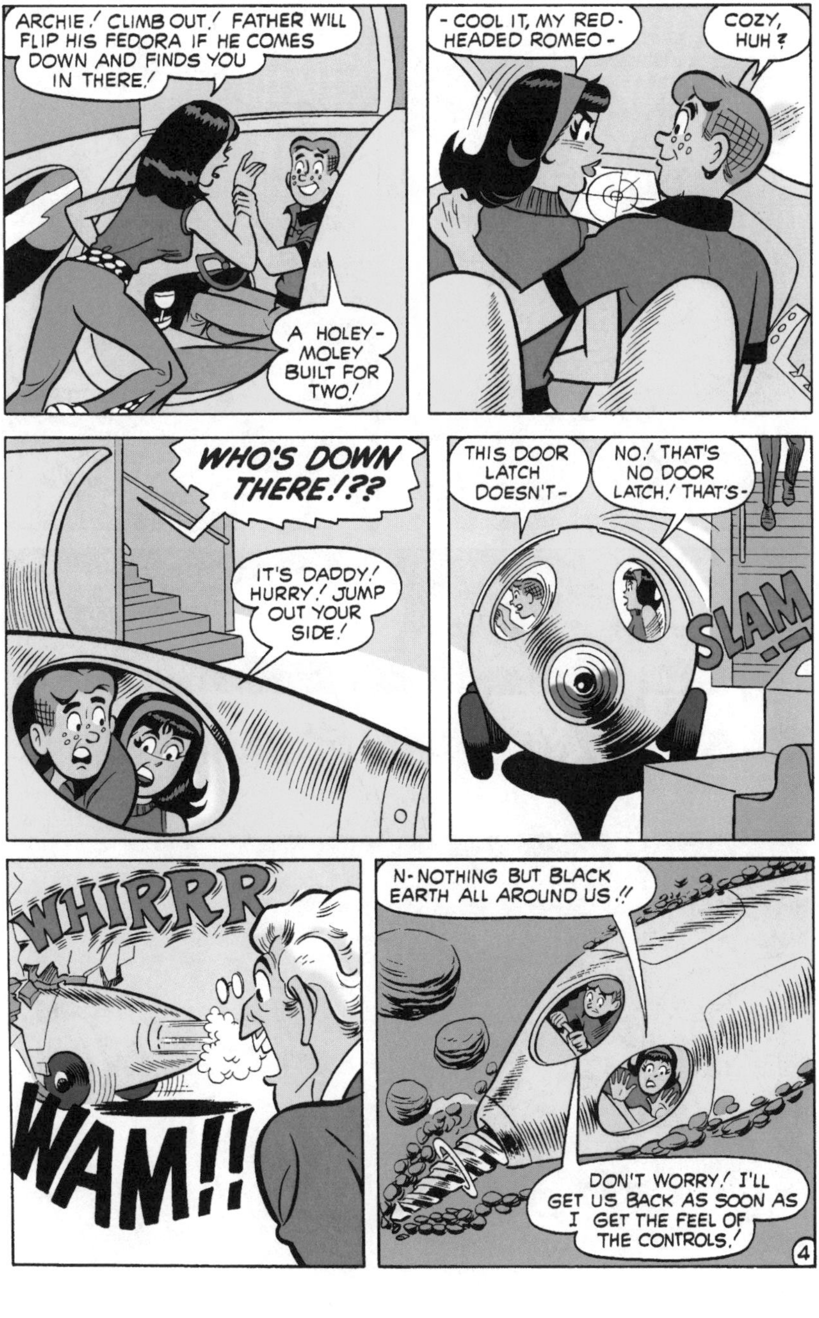
ARCHIE! CLIMB OUT! FATHER WILL FLIP HIS FEDORA IF HE COMES DOWN AND FINDS YOU IN THERE!
A HOLEY-MOLEY BUILT FOR TWO!
- COOL IT, MY RED-HEADED ROMEO -
COZY, HUH?
WHO'S DOWN THERE!??
IT'S DADDY! HURRY! JUMP OUT YOUR SIDE!
THIS DOOR LATCH DOESN'T-
NO! THAT'S NO DOOR LATCH! THAT'S-
SLAM
WHIRRR
WAM!!
N-NOTHING BUT BLACK EARTH ALL AROUND US!!
DON'T WORRY! I'LL GET US BACK AS SOON AS I GET THE FEEL OF THE CONTROLS!
4

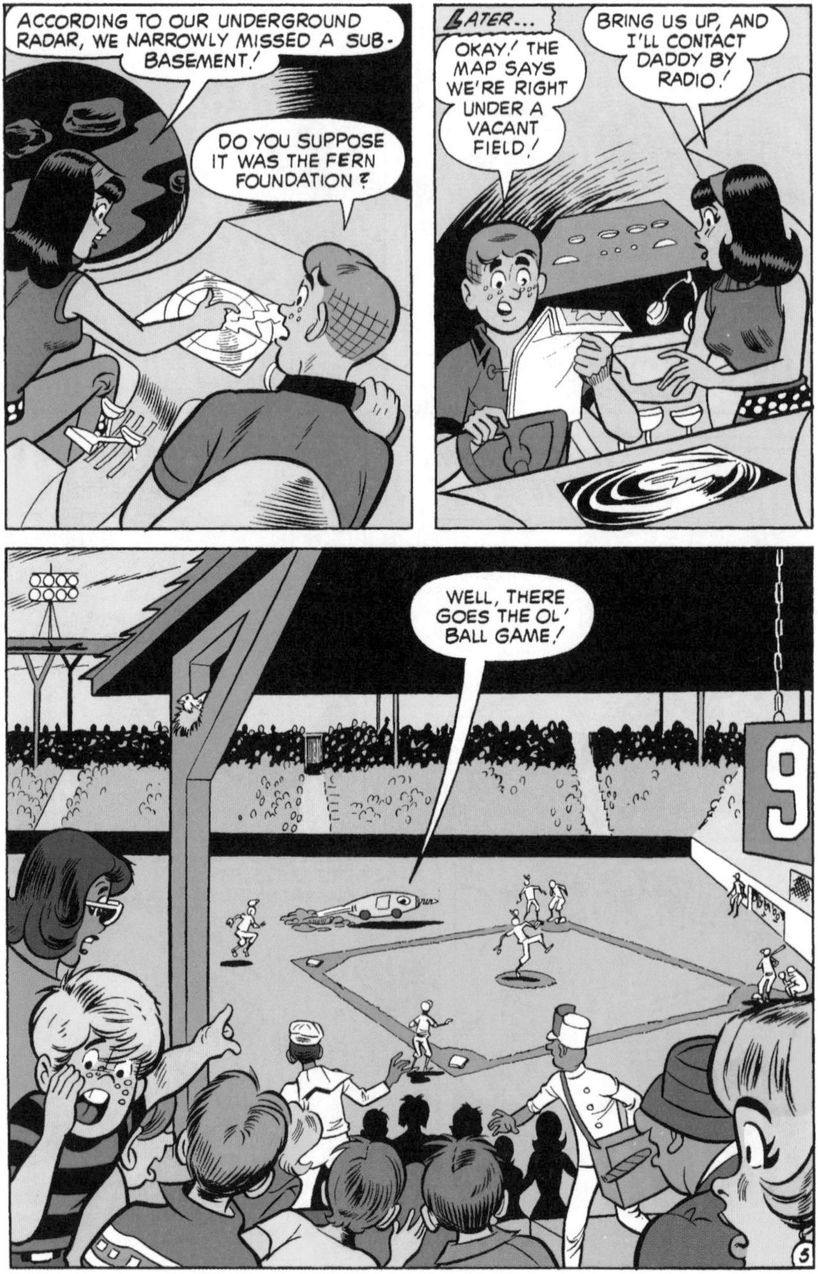
ACCORDING TO OUR UNDERGROUND RADAR, WE NARROWLY MISSED A SUB-BASEMENT!
DO YOU SUPPOSE IT WAS THE FERN FOUNDATION?
LATER...
OKAY! THE MAP SAYS WE'RE RIGHT UNDER A VACANT FIELD!
BRING US UP, AND I'LL CONTACT DADDY BY RADIO!
WELL, THERE GOES THE OL' BALL GAME!
9
5

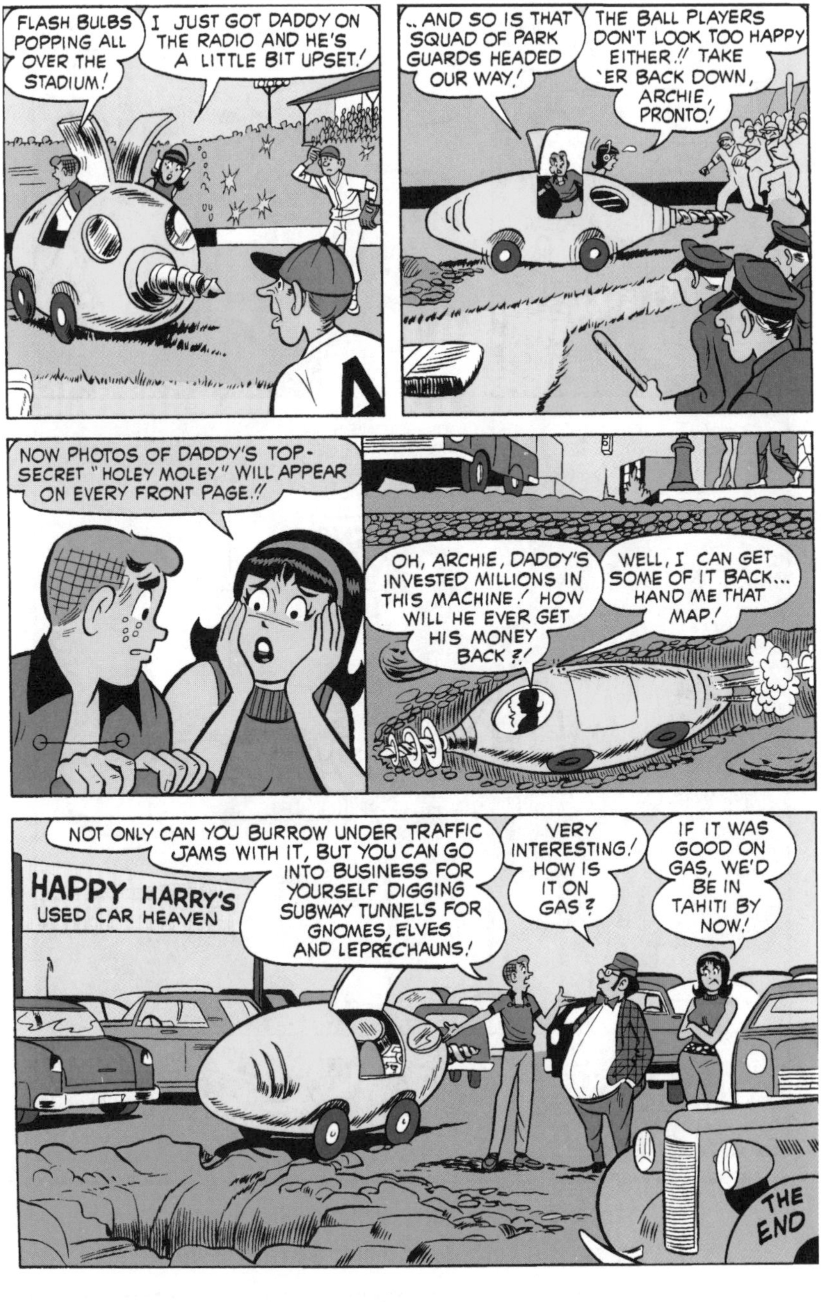
FLASH BULBS POPPING ALL OVER THE STADIUM!
I JUST GOT DADDY ON THE RADIO AND HE'S A LITTLE BIT UPSET!
.. AND SO IS THAT SQUAD OF PARK GUARDS HEADED OUR WAY!
THE BALL PLAYERS DON'T LOOK TOO HAPPY EITHER!! TAKE 'ER BACK DOWN, ARCHIE, PRONTO!
NOW PHOTOS OF DADDY'S TOP-SECRET "HOLEY MOLEY" WILL APPEAR ON EVERY FRONT PAGE!!
OH, ARCHIE, DADDY'S INVESTED MILLIONS IN THIS MACHINE! HOW WILL HE EVER GET HIS MONEY BACK?!
WELL, I CAN GET SOME OF IT BACK... HAND ME THAT MAP!
HAPPY HARRY'S
USED CAR HEAVEN
NOT ONLY CAN YOU BURROW UNDER TRAFFIC JAMS WITH IT, BUT YOU CAN GO INTO BUSINESS FOR YOURSELF DIGGING SUBWAY TUNNELS FOR GNOMES, ELVES AND LEPRÉCHAUNS!
VERY INTERESTING! HOW IS IT ON GAS?
IF IT WAS GOOD ON GAS, WE'D BE IN TAHITI BY NOW!
THE END

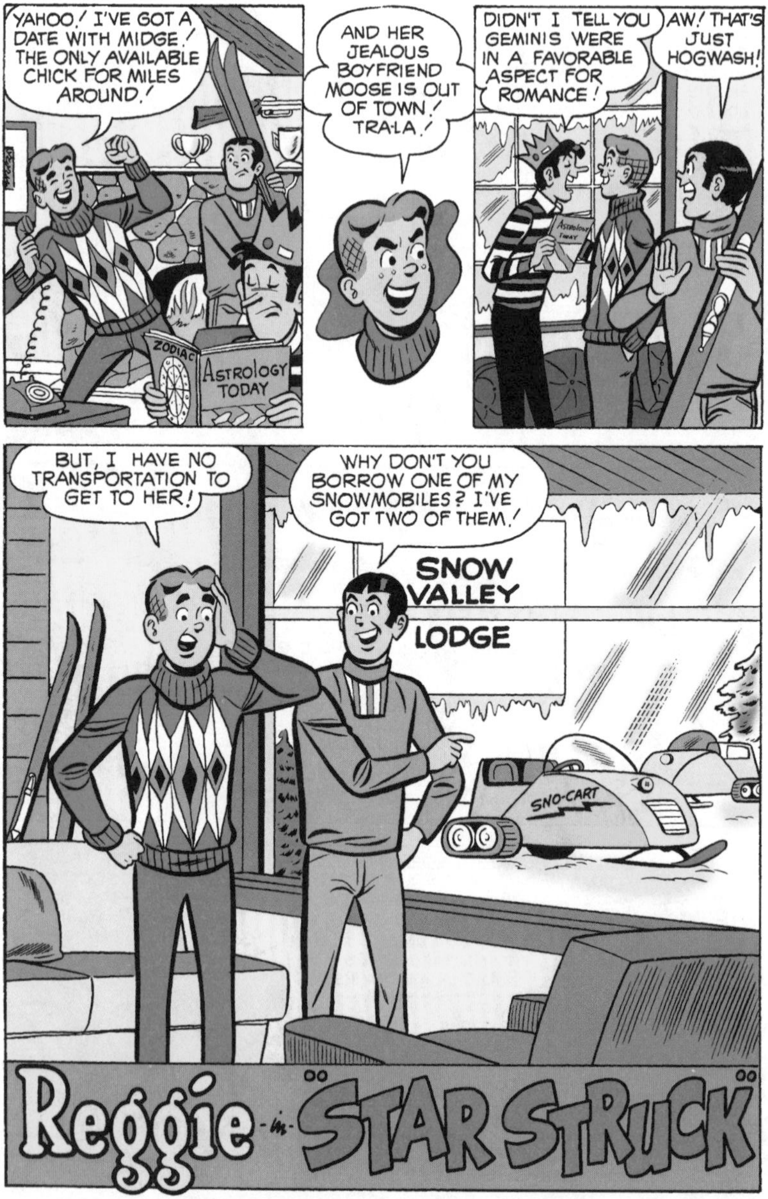
YAHOO! I'VE GOT A DATE WITH MIDGE! THE ONLY AVAILABLE CHICK FOR MILES AROUND!
ZODIAC
ASTROLOGY TODAY
AND HER JEALOUS BOYFRIEND MOOSE IS OUT OF TOWN! TRA-LA!
DIDN'T I TELL YOU GEMINIS WERE IN A FAVORABLE ASPECT FOR ROMANCE!
AW! THAT'S JUST HOGWASH!
BUT, I HAVE NO TRANSPORTATION TO GET TO HER!
WHY DON'T YOU BORROW ONE OF MY SNOWMOBILES? I'VE GOT TWO OF THEM!
SNOW VALLEY LODGE
SNO-CART
Reggie -in- STAR STRUCK

Story: George Gladir Pencils: Bill Vigoda
Letters: Bill Yoshida Colors: Barry Grossman

Originally printed in EVERYTHING'S ARCHIE #8, JUNE 1970

GEE, THANKS PAL! THIS MUST BE MORE OF MY GEMINI GOOD FORTUNE!

SNO-CART

SEE YOU LATER!

IT'LL BE SOONER THAN YOU THINK, CARROT-TOP!

VAROOM!

'CAUSE THE CRATE I LOANED HIM IS GOING TO RUN OUT OF GAS! HAR HAR!

AND I'LL STEP IN TO TAKE OVER ARCHIE'S DATE!

I'D BE CAREFUL IF I WERE YOU, REG!

SNOW VALLEY LODGE

ASTROLOGY TODAY

IT SAYS TODAY IS A DAY OF MISFORTUNE FOR YOU SCORPIOS!

ZODIAC

MORE HOGWASH! HA HA HA!

VAROOM!

ASTROLOGY TODAY

2

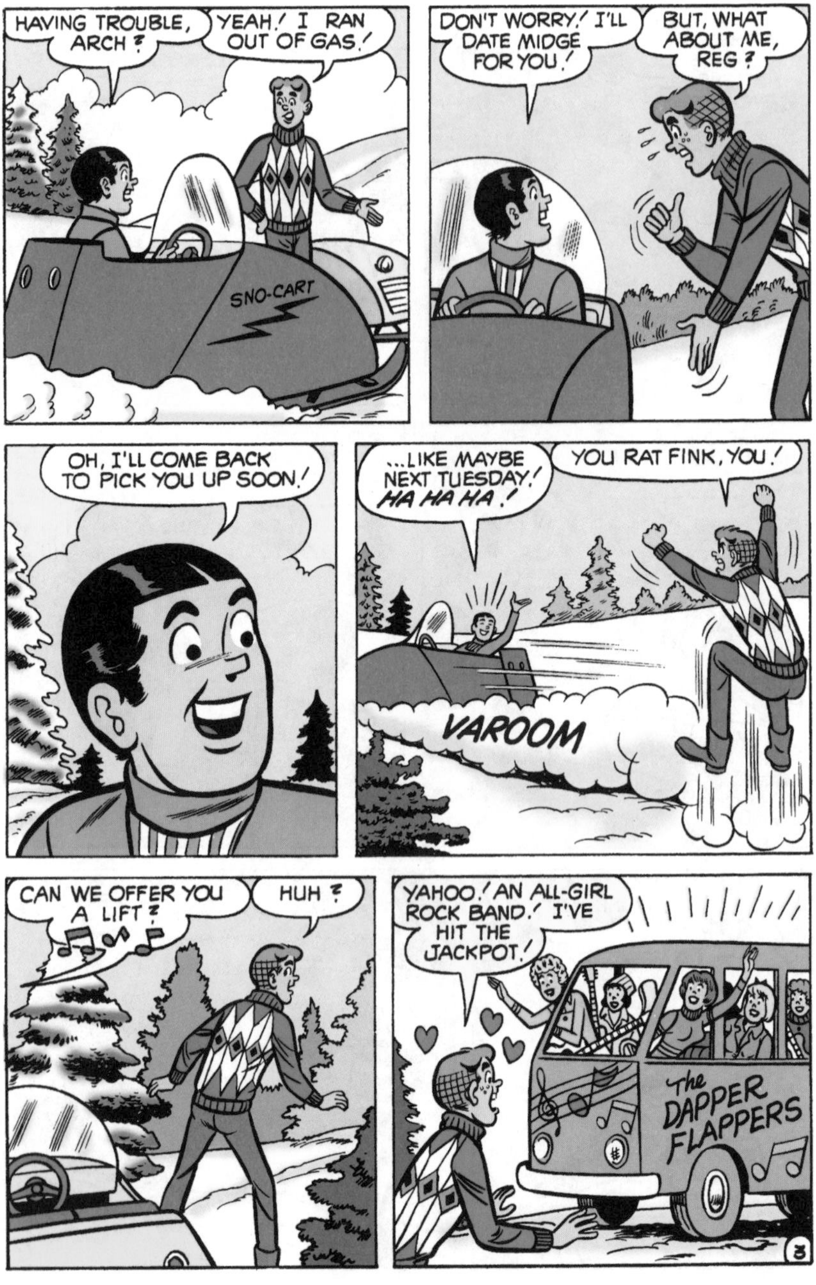
HAVING TROUBLE, ARCH?
YEAH! I RAN OUT OF GAS!
SNO-CART
DON'T WORRY! I'LL DATE MIDGE FOR YOU!
BUT, WHAT ABOUT ME, REG?
OH, I'LL COME BACK TO PICK YOU UP SOON!
...LIKE MAYBE NEXT TUESDAY! HA HA HA!
YOU RAT FINK, YOU!
VAROOM
CAN WE OFFER YOU A LIFT?
HUH?
YAHOO! AN ALL-GIRL ROCK BAND! I'VE HIT THE JACKPOT!
The DAPPER FLAPPERS
3

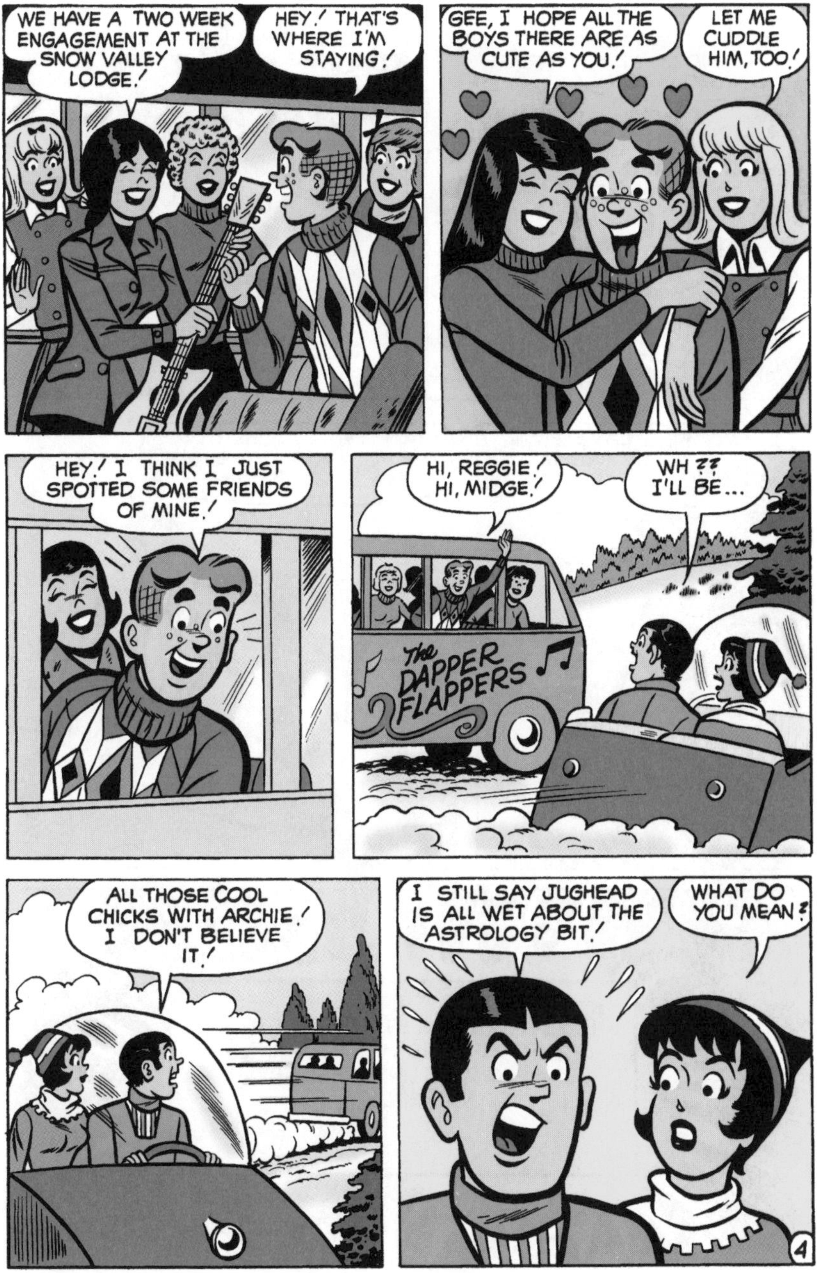
WE HAVE A TWO WEEK ENGAGEMENT AT THE SNOW VALLEY LODGE!
HEY! THAT'S WHERE I'M STAYING!
GEE, I HOPE ALL THE BOYS THERE ARE AS CUTE AS YOU!
LET ME CUDDLE HIM, TOO!
HEY! I THINK I JUST SPOTTED SOME FRIENDS OF MINE!
HI, REGGIE! HI, MIDGE!
WH ?? I'LL BE...
The DAPPER FLAPPERS
ALL THOSE COOL CHICKS WITH ARCHIE! I DON'T BELIEVE IT!
I STILL SAY JUGHEAD IS ALL WET ABOUT THE ASTROLOGY BIT!
WHAT DO YOU MEAN?
4

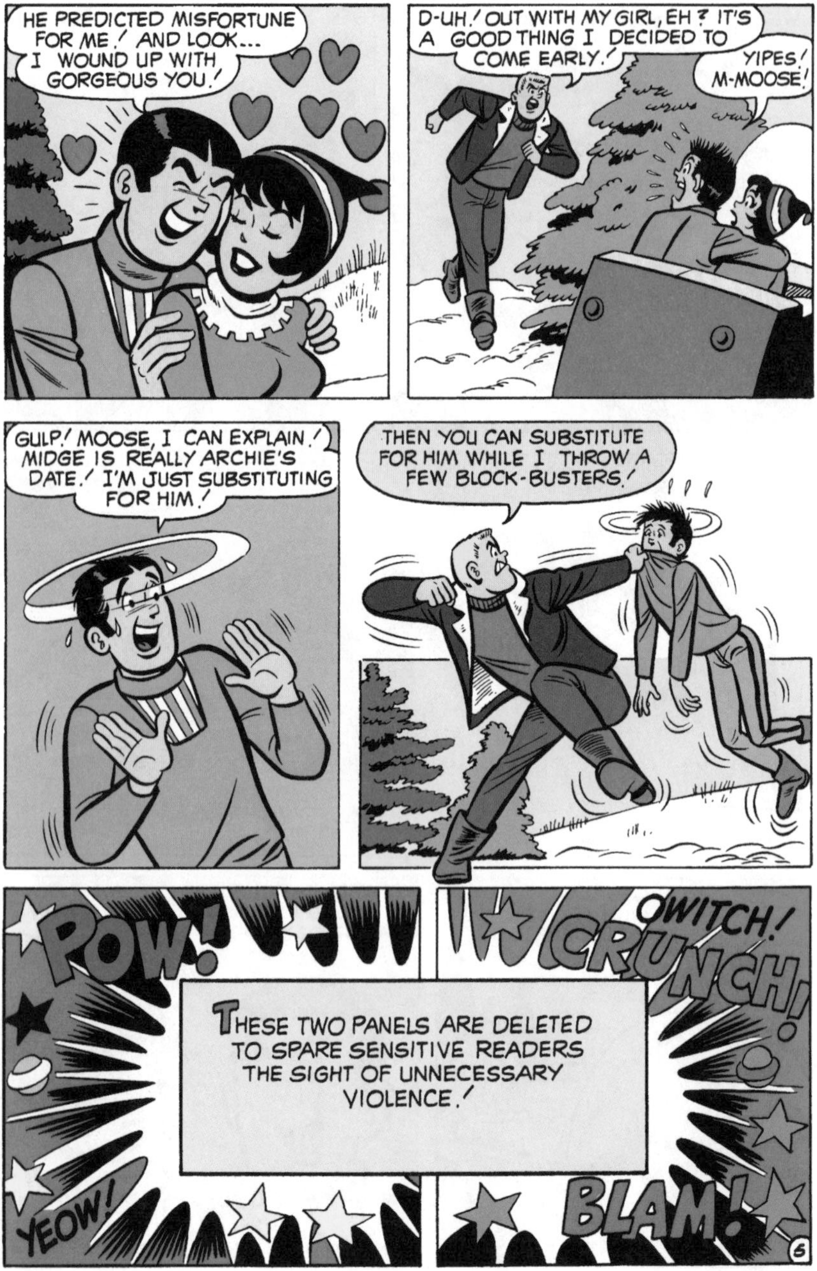
HE PREDICTED MISFORTUNE FOR ME! AND LOOK... I WOUND UP WITH GORGEOUS YOU!
D-UH! OUT WITH MY GIRL, EH? IT'S A GOOD THING I DECIDED TO COME EARLY!
YIPES! M-MOOSE!
GULP! MOOSE, I CAN EXPLAIN! MIDGE IS REALLY ARCHIE'S DATE! I'M JUST SUBSTITUTING FOR HIM!
THEN YOU CAN SUBSTITUTE FOR HIM WHILE I THROW A FEW BLOCK-BUSTERS!
POW!
OWITCH!
CRUNCH!
THESE TWO PANELS ARE DELETED TO SPARE SENSITIVE READERS THE SIGHT OF UNNECESSARY VIOLENCE!
YEOW!
BLAM!
6

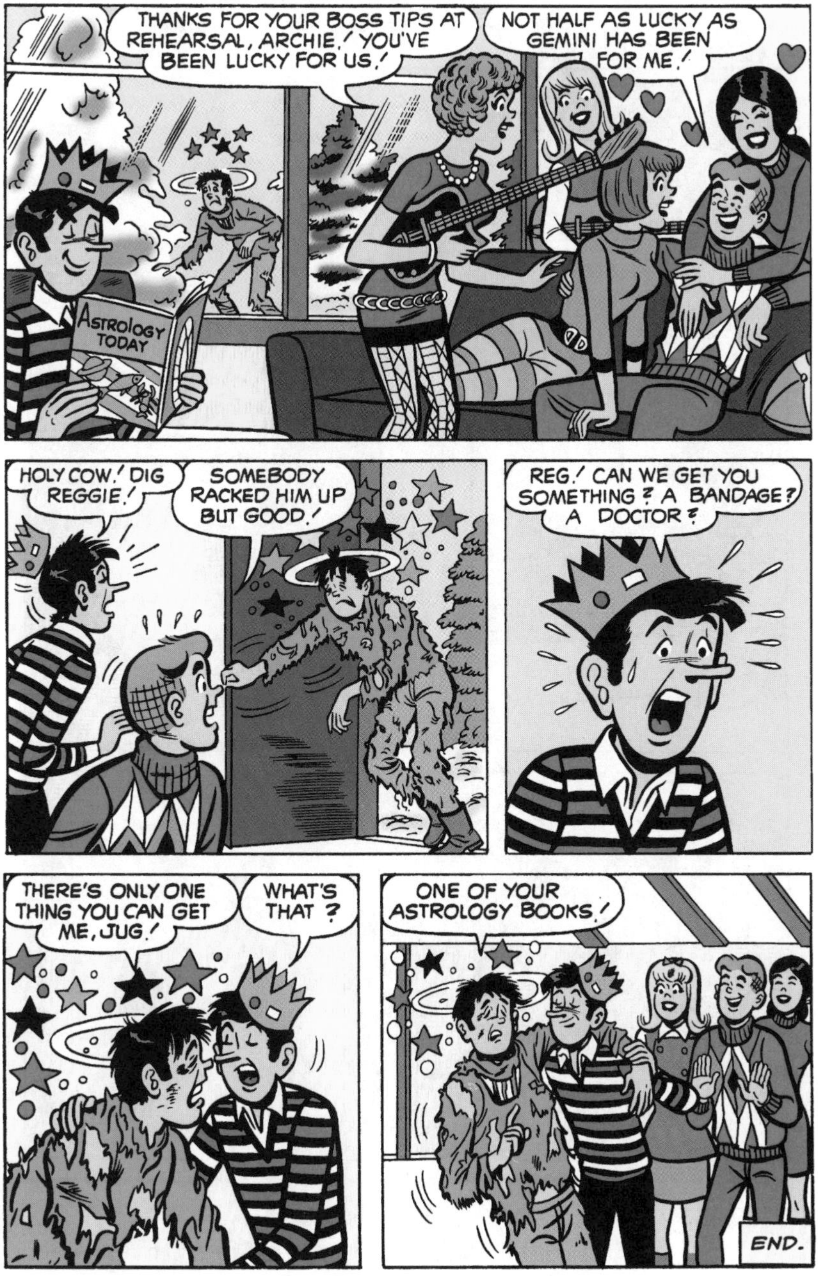
THANKS FOR YOUR BOSS TIPS AT REHEARSAL, ARCHIE! YOU'VE BEEN LUCKY FOR US!
NOT HALF AS LUCKY AS GEMINI HAS BEEN FOR ME!
ASTROLOGY TODAY
HOLY COW! DIG REGGIE!
SOMEBODY RACKED HIM UP BUT GOOD!
REG! CAN WE GET YOU SOMETHING? A BANDAGE? A DOCTOR?
THERE'S ONLY ONE THING YOU CAN GET ME, JUG!
WHAT'S THAT?
ONE OF YOUR ASTROLOGY BOOKS!
END.

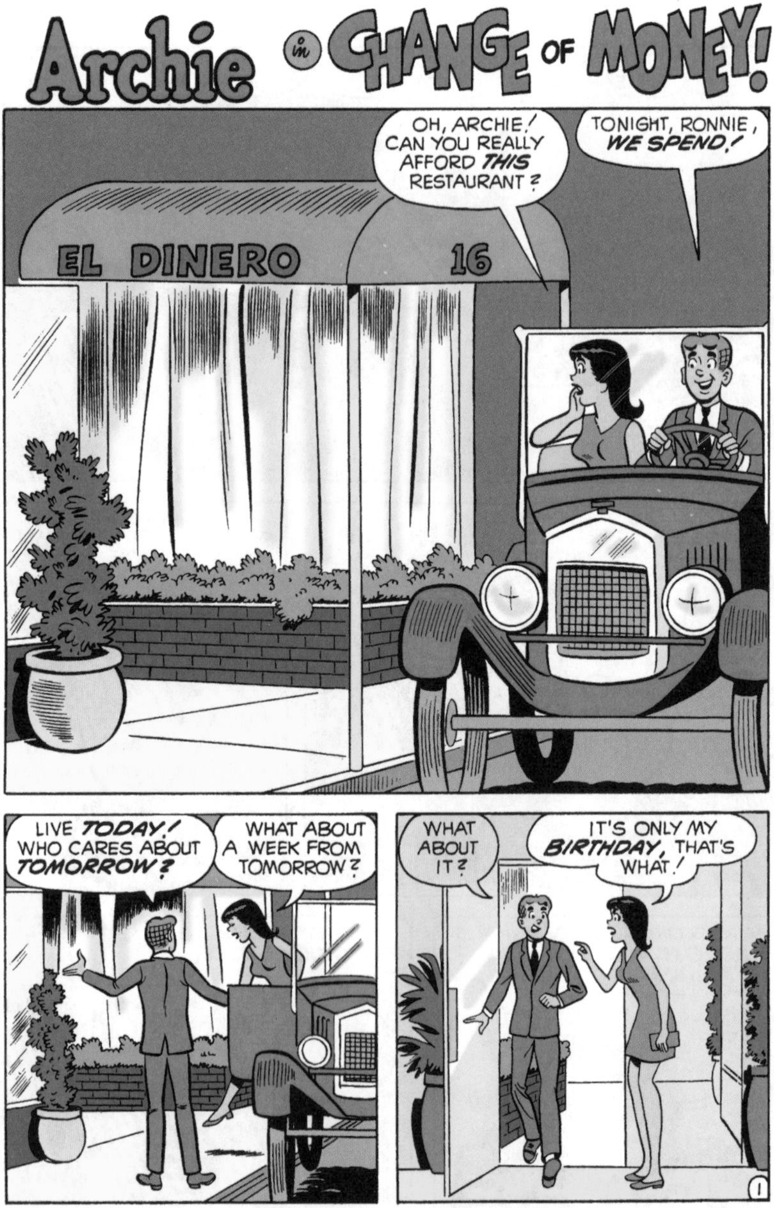
Archie in CHANGE OF MONEY!
EL DINERO 16
OH, ARCHIE! CAN YOU REALLY AFFORD THIS RESTAURANT?
TONIGHT, RONNIE, WE SPEND!
LIVE TODAY! WHO CARES ABOUT TOMORROW?
WHAT ABOUT A WEEK FROM TOMORROW?
WHAT ABOUT IT?
IT'S ONLY MY BIRTHDAY, THAT'S WHAT!
1

Story & Pencils: Bob White
Letters: Bill Yoshida Colors: Barry Grossman

Originally printed in EVERYTHING'S ARCHIE #8, JUNE 1970

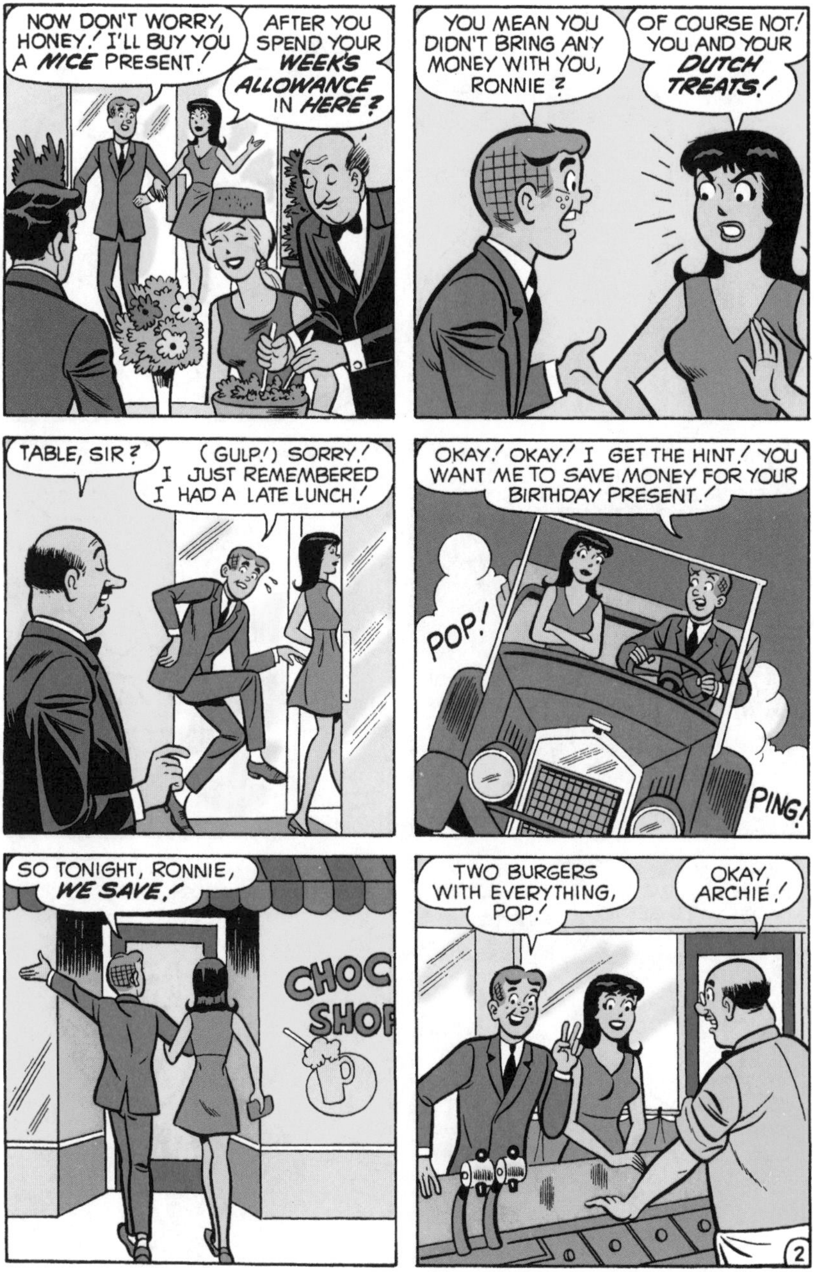
NOW DON'T WORRY, HONEY! I'LL BUY YOU A NICE PRESENT!
AFTER YOU SPEND YOUR WEEK'S ALLOWANCE IN HERE?
YOU MEAN YOU DIDN'T BRING ANY MONEY WITH YOU, RONNIE?
OF COURSE NOT! YOU AND YOUR DUTCH TREATS!
TABLE, SIR?
(GULP!) SORRY! I JUST REMEMBERED I HAD A LATE LUNCH!
OKAY! OKAY! I GET THE HINT! YOU WANT ME TO SAVE MONEY FOR YOUR BIRTHDAY PRESENT!
POP!
PING!
SO TONIGHT, RONNIE, WE SAVE!
CHOC
SHOP
TWO BURGERS WITH EVERYTHING, POP!
OKAY, ARCHIE!
2

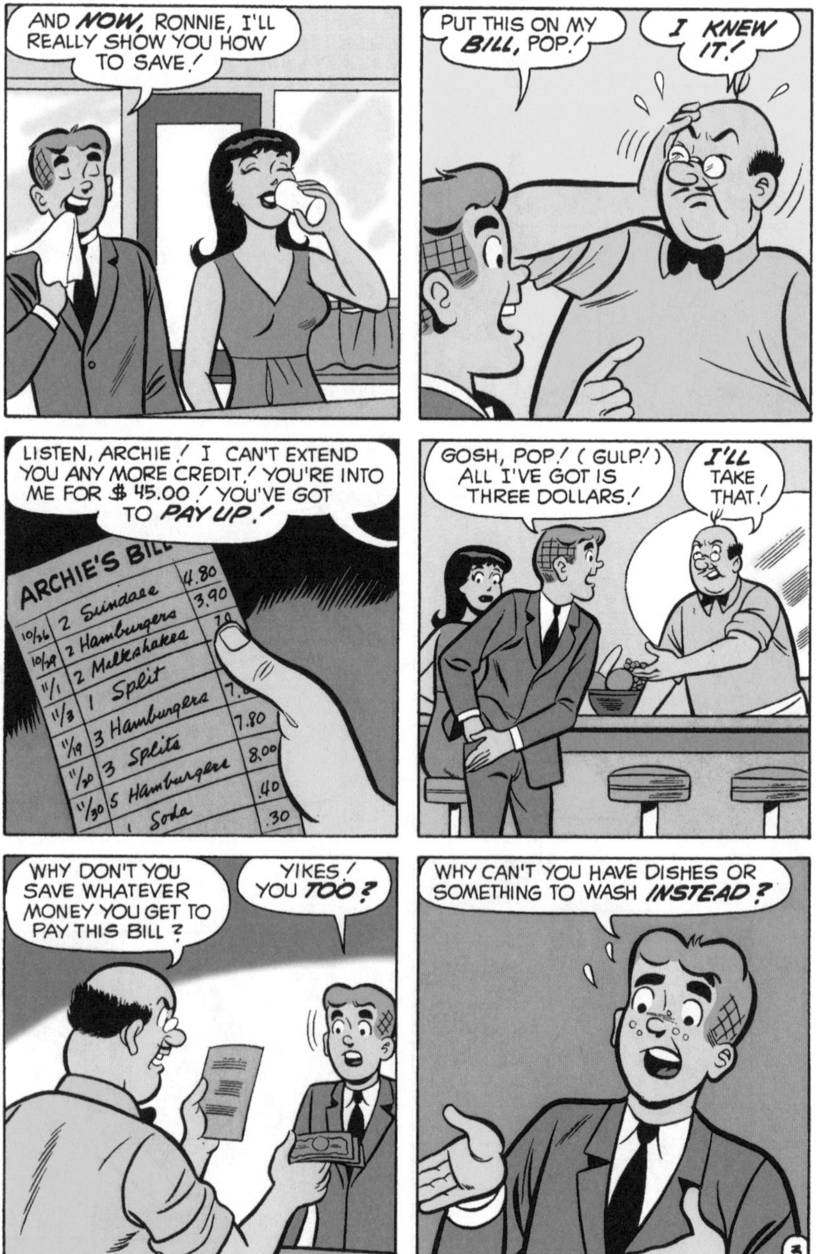
AND NOW, RONNIE, I'LL REALLY SHOW YOU HOW TO SAVE!
PUT THIS ON MY BILL, POP!
I KNEW IT!
LISTEN, ARCHIE! I CAN'T EXTEND YOU ANY MORE CREDIT! YOU'RE INTO ME FOR $ 45.00! YOU'VE GOT TO PAY UP!
ARCHIE'S
10/26 2 Sundaes 4.80
10/29 2 Hamburgers 3.90
2 Milkshakes
11/1 1 Split
11/3 3 Hamburgers
11/19 3 Splits 7.80
11/20 5 Hamburgers 8.00
11/30 1 Soda .40
.30
GOSH, POP! (GULP!) ALL I'VE GOT IS THREE DOLLARS!
I'LL TAKE THAT!
WHY DON'T YOU SAVE WHATEVER MONEY YOU GET TO PAY THIS BILL ?
YIKES! YOU TOO ?
WHY CAN'T YOU HAVE DISHES OR SOMETHING TO WASH INSTEAD ?
3

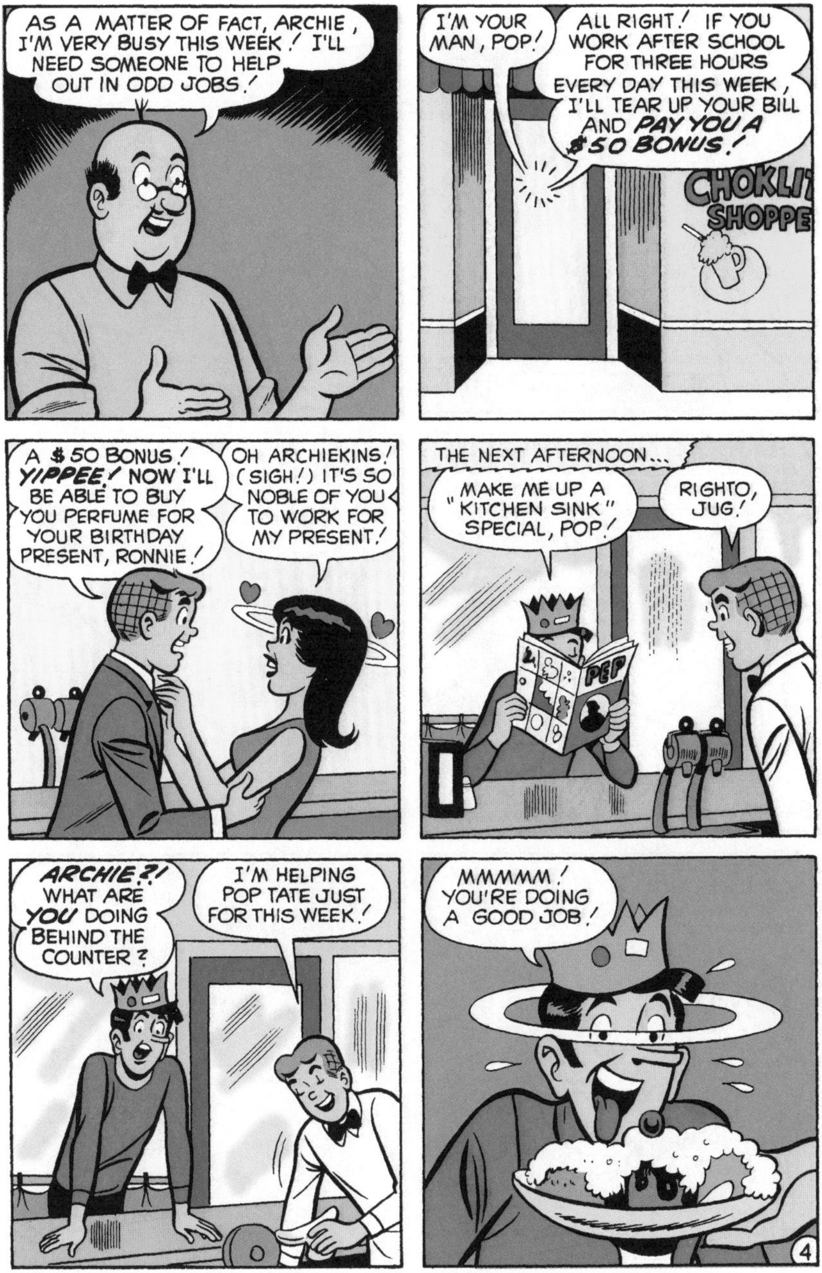
AS A MATTER OF FACT, ARCHIE, I'M VERY BUSY THIS WEEK! I'LL NEED SOMEONE TO HELP OUT IN ODD JOBS!
I'M YOUR MAN, POP!
ALL RIGHT! IF YOU WORK AFTER SCHOOL FOR THREE HOURS EVERY DAY THIS WEEK, I'LL TEAR UP YOUR BILL AND PAY YOU A $50 BONUS!
CHOKLIT SHOPPE
A $50 BONUS! YIPPEE! NOW I'LL BE ABLE TO BUY YOU PERFUME FOR YOUR BIRTHDAY PRESENT, RONNIE!
OH ARCHIEKINS! (SIGH!) IT'S SO NOBLE OF YOU TO WORK FOR MY PRESENT!
THE NEXT AFTERNOON...
"MAKE ME UP A "KITCHEN SINK" SPECIAL, POP!
RIGHTO, JUG!
PEP
ARCHIE?! WHAT ARE YOU DOING BEHIND THE COUNTER?
I'M HELPING POP TATE JUST FOR THIS WEEK!
MMMMM! YOU'RE DOING A GOOD JOB!
4

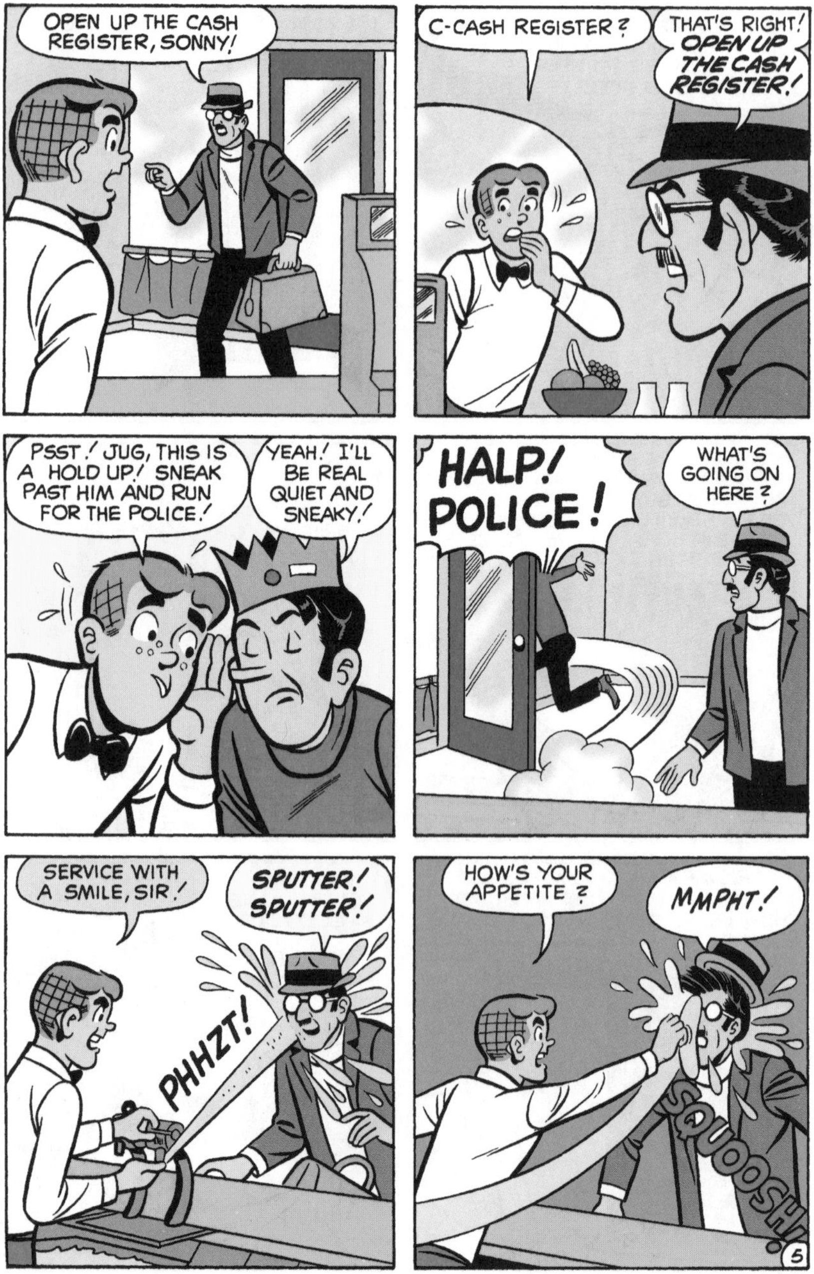
OPEN UP THE CASH REGISTER, SONNY!
C-CASH REGISTER?
THAT'S RIGHT! OPEN UP THE CASH REGISTER!
PSST! JUG, THIS IS A HOLD UP! SNEAK PAST HIM AND RUN FOR THE POLICE!
YEAH! I'LL BE REAL QUIET AND SNEAKY!
HALP! POLICE!
WHAT'S GOING ON HERE?
SERVICE WITH A SMILE, SIR!
SPUTTER! SPUTTER!
PHHZT!
HOW'S YOUR APPETITE?
MMPHT!
SQUOOSH!
5

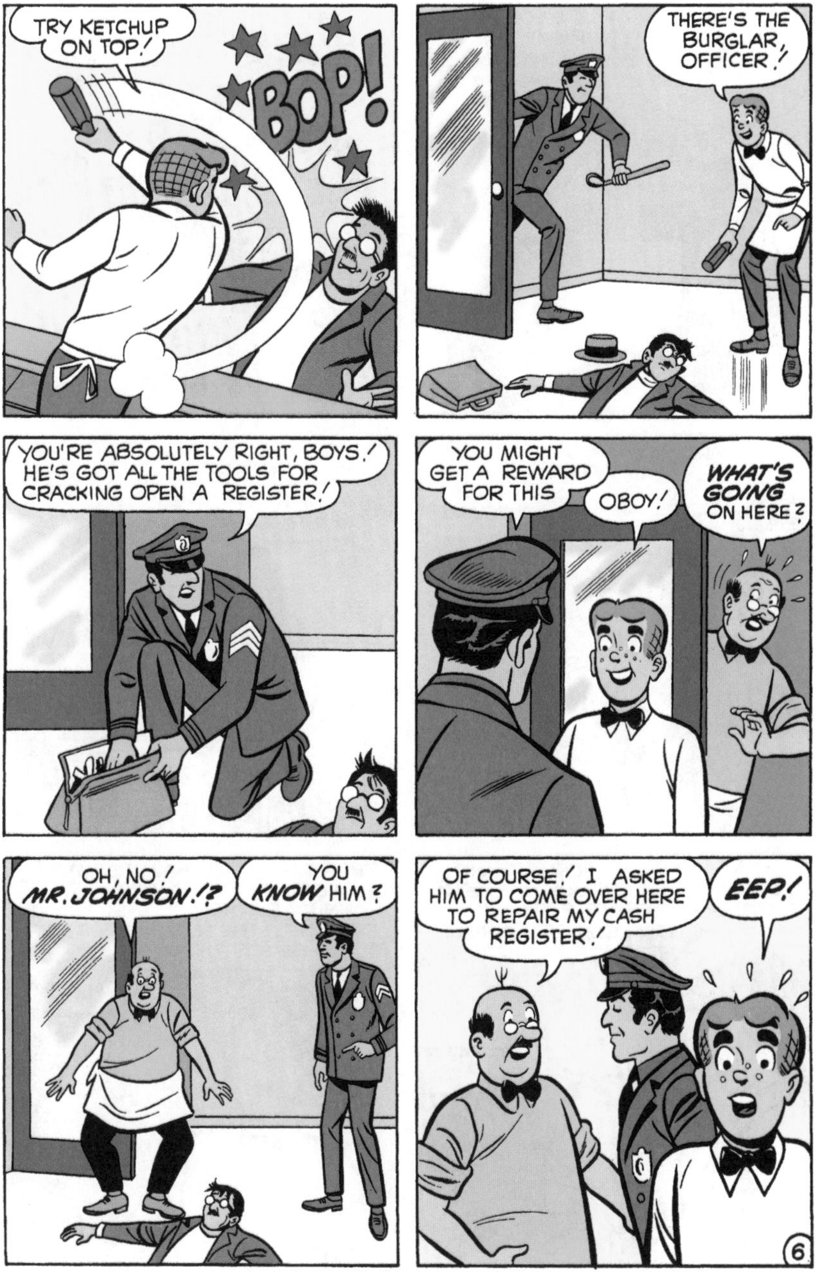
TRY KETCHUP ON TOP!
BOP!
THERE'S THE BURGLAR, OFFICER!
YOU'RE ABSOLUTELY RIGHT, BOYS! HE'S GOT ALL THE TOOLS FOR CRACKING OPEN A REGISTER!
YOU MIGHT GET A REWARD FOR THIS
OBOY!
WHAT'S GOING ON HERE?
OH, NO! MR. JOHNSON!?
YOU KNOW HIM?
OF COURSE! I ASKED HIM TO COME OVER HERE TO REPAIR MY CASH REGISTER!
EEP!
6

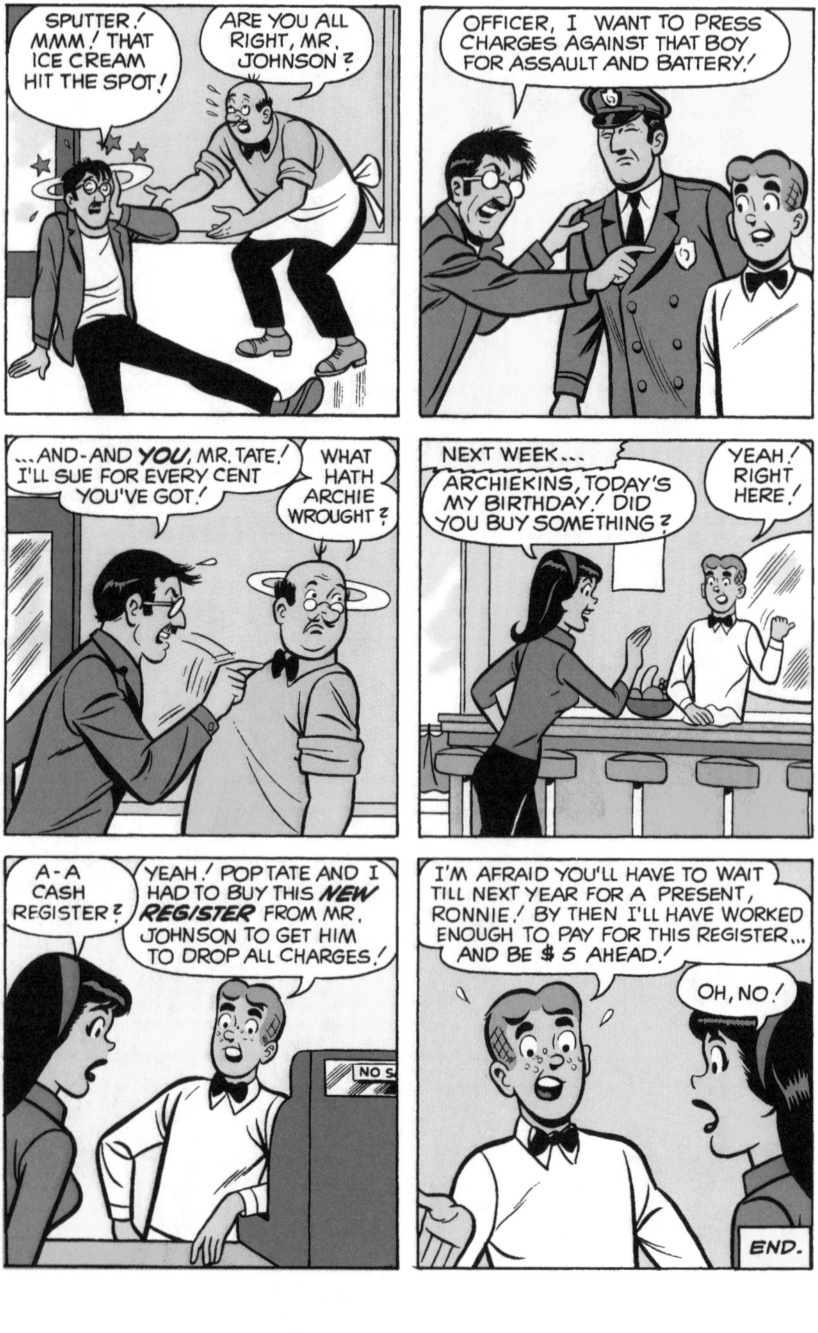
SPUTTER! MMM! THAT ICE CREAM HIT THE SPOT!
ARE YOU ALL RIGHT, MR. JOHNSON?
OFFICER, I WANT TO PRESS CHARGES AGAINST THAT BOY FOR ASSAULT AND BATTERY!
...AND-AND YOU, MR. TATE! I'LL SUE FOR EVERY CENT YOU'VE GOT!
WHAT HATH ARCHIE WROUGHT?
NEXT WEEK...
ARCHIEKINS, TODAY'S MY BIRTHDAY! DID YOU BUY SOMETHING?
YEAH! RIGHT HERE!
A-A CASH REGISTER?
YEAH! POP TATE AND I HAD TO BUY THIS NEW REGISTER FROM MR. JOHNSON TO GET HIM TO DROP ALL CHARGES!
NO S
I'M AFRAID YOU'LL HAVE TO WAIT TILL NEXT YEAR FOR A PRESENT, RONNIE! BY THEN I'LL HAVE WORKED ENOUGH TO PAY FOR THIS REGISTER... AND BE $ 5 AHEAD!
OH, NO!
END.

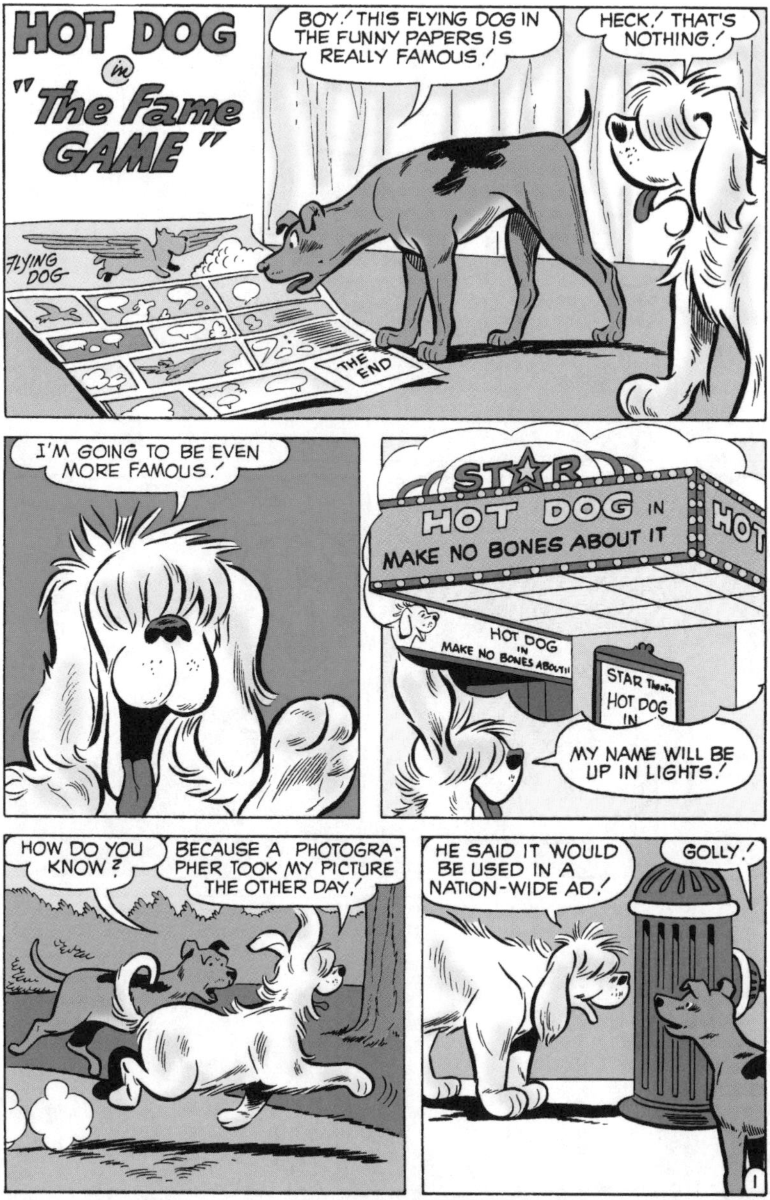
HOT DOG
in
"The Fame GAME"
BOY! THIS FLYING DOG IN THE FUNNY PAPERS IS REALLY FAMOUS!
HECK! THAT'S NOTHING!
FLYING DOG
THE END
I'M GOING TO BE EVEN MORE FAMOUS!
STAR
HOT DOG IN
MAKE NO BONES ABOUT IT
HOT
HOT DOG IN MAKE NO BONES ABOUT
STAR Theatre
HOT DOG IN
MY NAME WILL BE UP IN LIGHTS!
HOW DO YOU KNOW?
BECAUSE A PHOTOGRAPHER TOOK MY PICTURE THE OTHER DAY!
HE SAID IT WOULD BE USED IN A NATION-WIDE AD!
GOLLY!
1

Story: George Gladir Pencils: Bill Vigoda
Inks: Rudy Lapick Letters: Bill Yoshida Colors: Barry Grossman

Originally printed in EVERYTHING'S ARCHIE #8, JUNE 1970

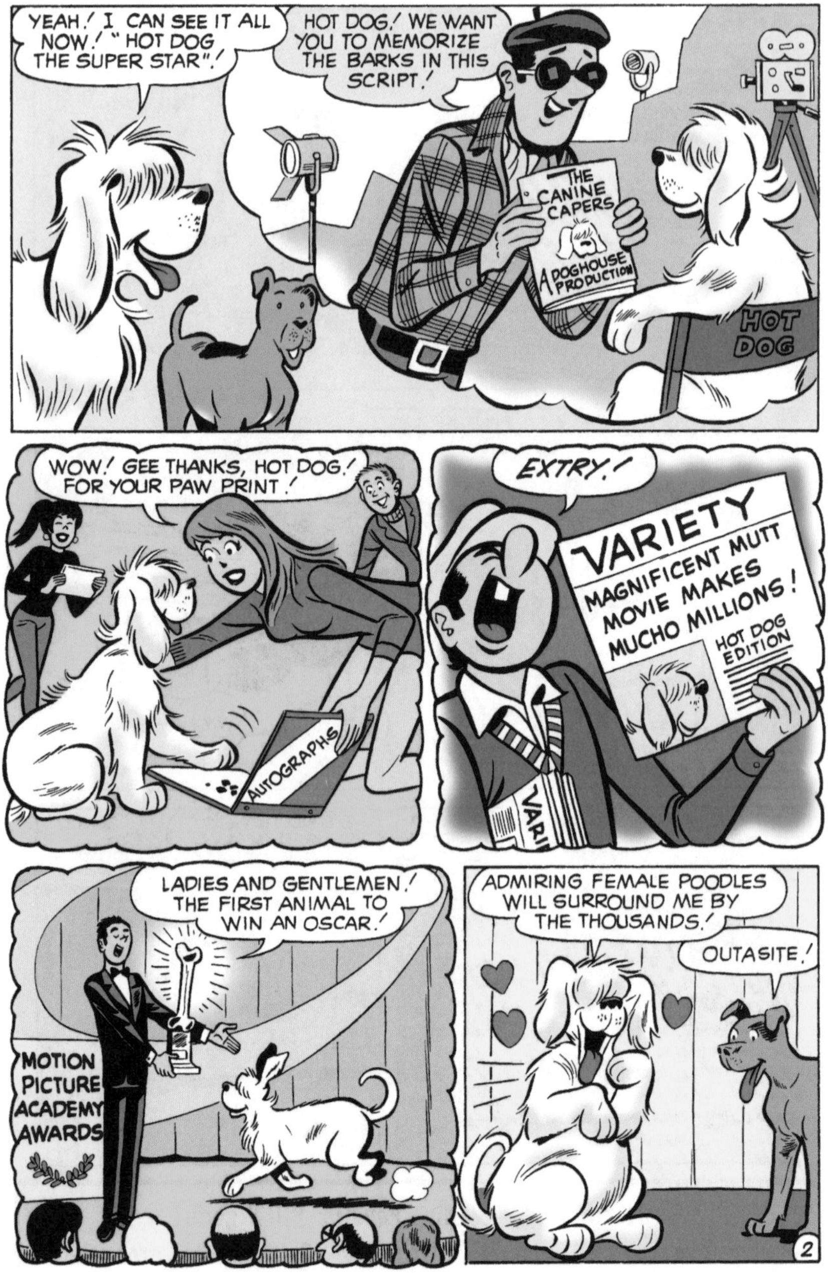
YEAH! I CAN SEE IT ALL NOW! "HOT DOG THE SUPER STAR"!
HOT DOG! WE WANT YOU TO MEMORIZE THE BARKS IN THIS SCRIPT!
THE CANINE CAPERS
A DOGHOUSE PRODUCTION
HOT DOG
WOW! GEE THANKS, HOT DOG! FOR YOUR PAW PRINT!
AUTOGRAPHS
EXTRY!
VARIETY
MAGNIFICENT MUTT MOVIE MAKES MUCHO MILLIONS!
HOT DOG EDITION
LADIES AND GENTLEMEN! THE FIRST ANIMAL TO WIN AN OSCAR!
MOTION PICTURE ACADEMY AWARDS
ADMIRING FEMALE POODLES WILL SURROUND ME BY THE THOUSANDS!
OUTASITE!
2

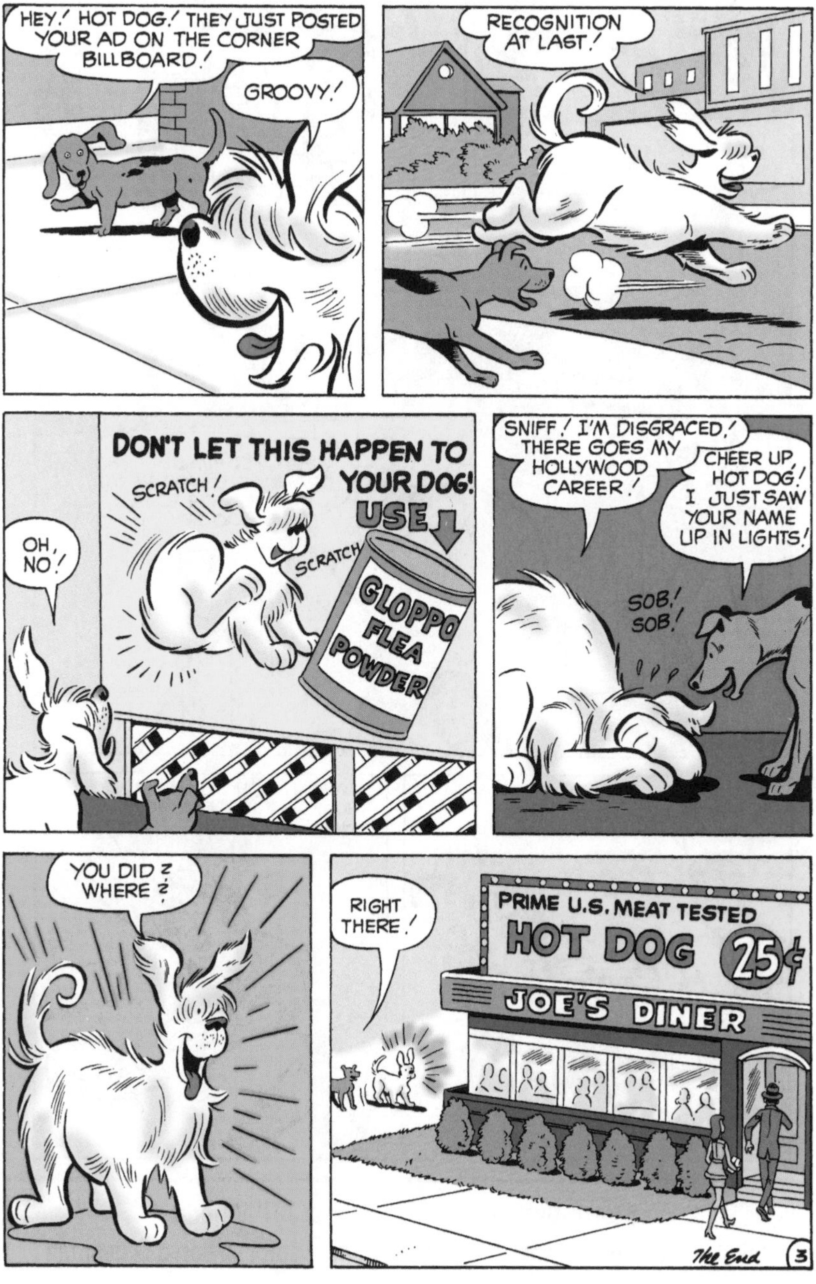
HEY! HOT DOG! THEY JUST POSTED YOUR AD ON THE CORNER BILLBOARD!
GROOVY!
RECOGNITION AT LAST!
OH, NO!
DON'T LET THIS HAPPEN TO YOUR DOG!
SCRATCH!
SCRATCH
USE
GLOPPO FLEA POWDER
SNIFF! I'M DISGRACED! THERE GOES MY HOLLYWOOD CAREER!
CHEER UP, HOT DOG! I JUST SAW YOUR NAME UP IN LIGHTS!
SOB! SOB!
YOU DID? WHERE?
RIGHT THERE!
PRIME U.S. MEAT TESTED
HOT DOG 25¢
JOE'S DINER
The End
3

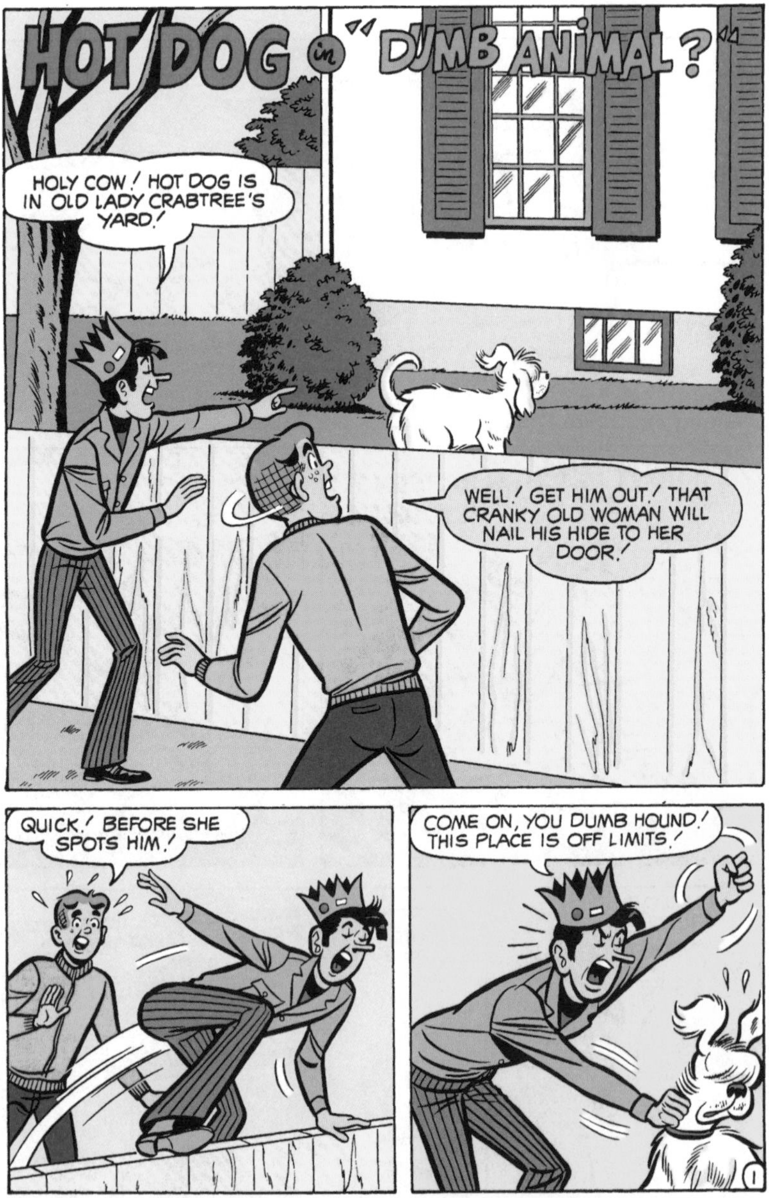
HOT DOG in "DUMB ANIMAL?"
HOLY COW! HOT DOG IS IN OLD LADY CRABTREE'S YARD!
WELL! GET HIM OUT! THAT CRANKY OLD WOMAN WILL NAIL HIS HIDE TO HER DOOR!
QUICK! BEFORE SHE SPOTS HIM!
COME ON, YOU DUMB HOUND! THIS PLACE IS OFF LIMITS!
1

Story: George Gladir **Pencils:** Bill Vigoda
Inks: Rudy Lapick **Letters:** Bill Yoshida **Colors:** Barry Grossman

Originally printed in EVERYTHING'S ARCHIE #8, JUNE 1970

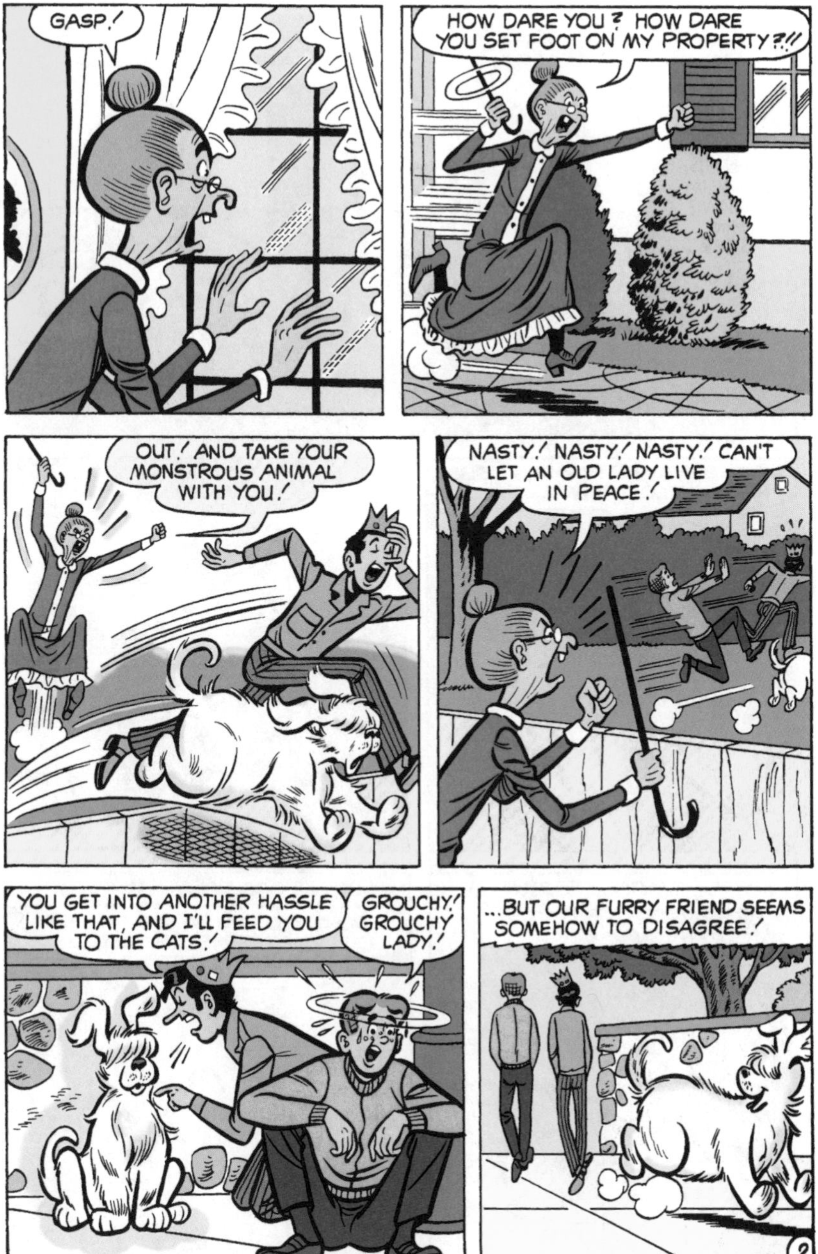
GASP!
HOW DARE YOU? HOW DARE YOU SET FOOT ON MY PROPERTY?!!
OUT! AND TAKE YOUR MONSTROUS ANIMAL WITH YOU!
NASTY! NASTY! NASTY! CAN'T LET AN OLD LADY LIVE IN PEACE!
YOU GET INTO ANOTHER HASSLE LIKE THAT, AND I'LL FEED YOU TO THE CATS!
GROUCHY! GROUCHY LADY!
...BUT OUR FURRY FRIEND SEEMS SOMEHOW TO DISAGREE!
2

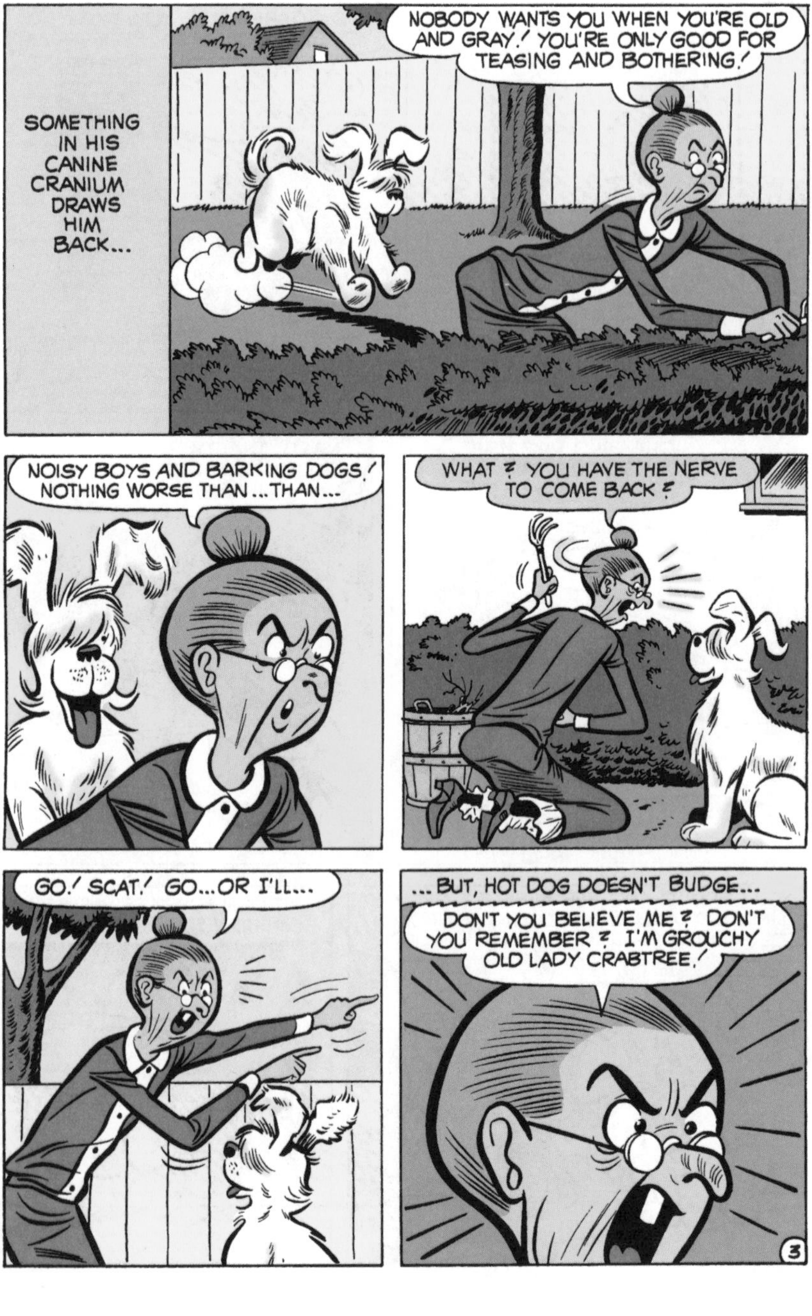
SOMETHING IN HIS CANINE CRANIUM DRAWS HIM BACK...
NOBODY WANTS YOU WHEN YOU'RE OLD AND GRAY! YOU'RE ONLY GOOD FOR TEASING AND BOTHERING!
NOISY BOYS AND BARKING DOGS! NOTHING WORSE THAN ... THAN...
WHAT ? YOU HAVE THE NERVE TO COME BACK ?
GO! SCAT! GO...OR I'LL...
... BUT, HOT DOG DOESN'T BUDGE...
DON'T YOU BELIEVE ME ? DON'T YOU REMEMBER ? I'M GROUCHY OLD LADY CRABTREE!
3

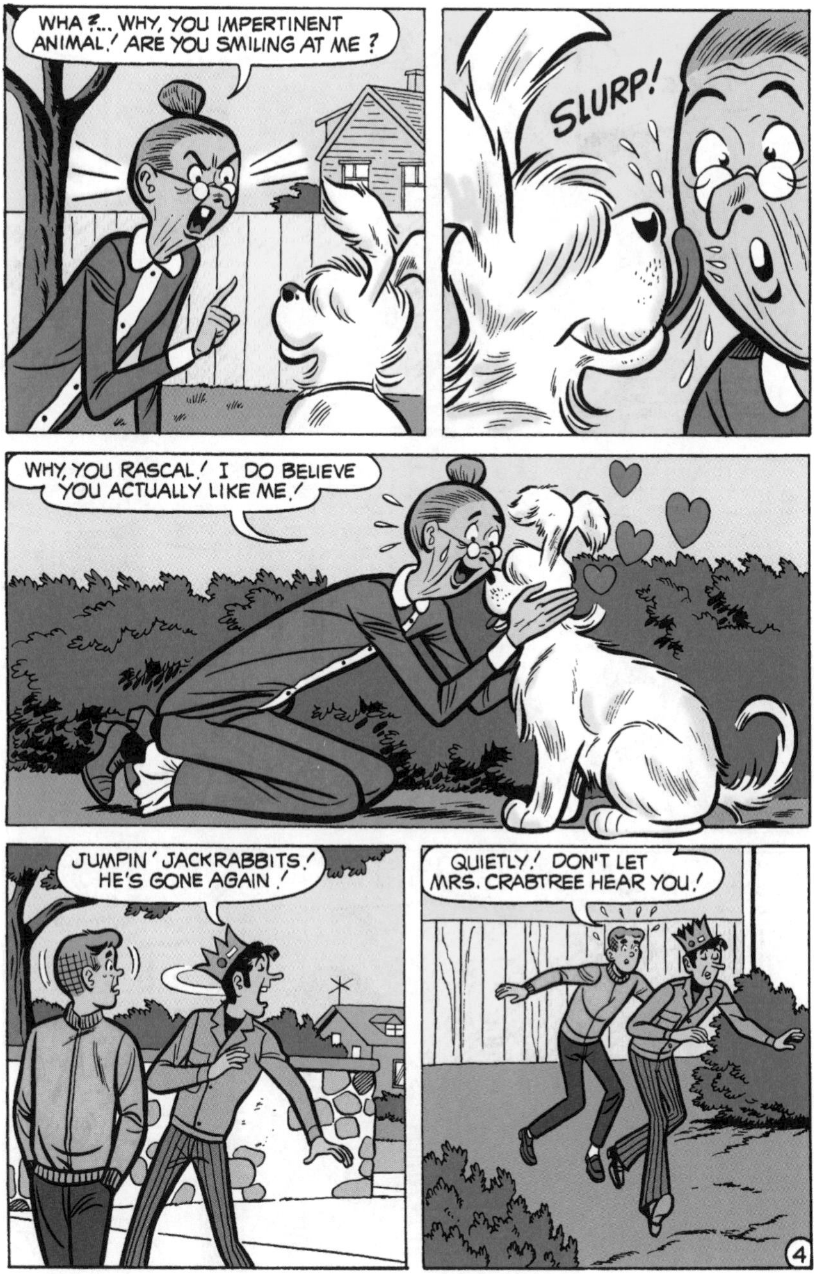
WHA ?... WHY, YOU IMPERTINENT ANIMAL! ARE YOU SMILING AT ME ?
SLURP!
WHY, YOU RASCAL! I DO BELIEVE YOU ACTUALLY LIKE ME!
JUMPIN' JACKRABBITS! HE'S GONE AGAIN!
QUIETLY! DON'T LET MRS. CRABTREE HEAR YOU!
4

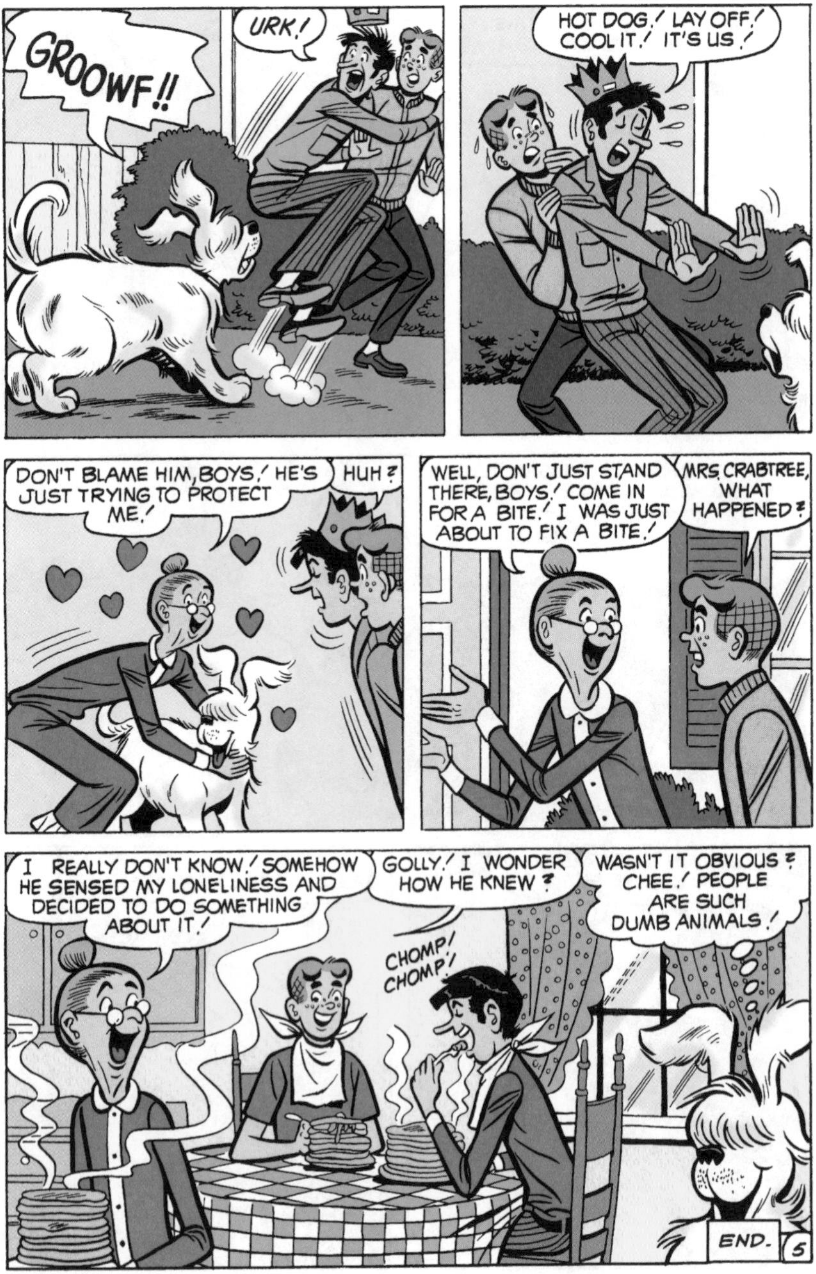
GROOWF!!
URK!
HOT DOG! LAY OFF! COOL IT! IT'S US!
DON'T BLAME HIM, BOYS! HE'S JUST TRYING TO PROTECT ME!
HUH?
WELL, DON'T JUST STAND THERE, BOYS! COME IN FOR A BITE! I WAS JUST ABOUT TO FIX A BITE!
MRS. CRABTREE, WHAT HAPPENED?
I REALLY DON'T KNOW! SOMEHOW HE SENSED MY LONELINESS AND DECIDED TO DO SOMETHING ABOUT IT!
GOLLY! I WONDER HOW HE KNEW?
CHOMP! CHOMP!
WASN'T IT OBVIOUS? CHEE! PEOPLE ARE SUCH DUMB ANIMALS!
END.
5

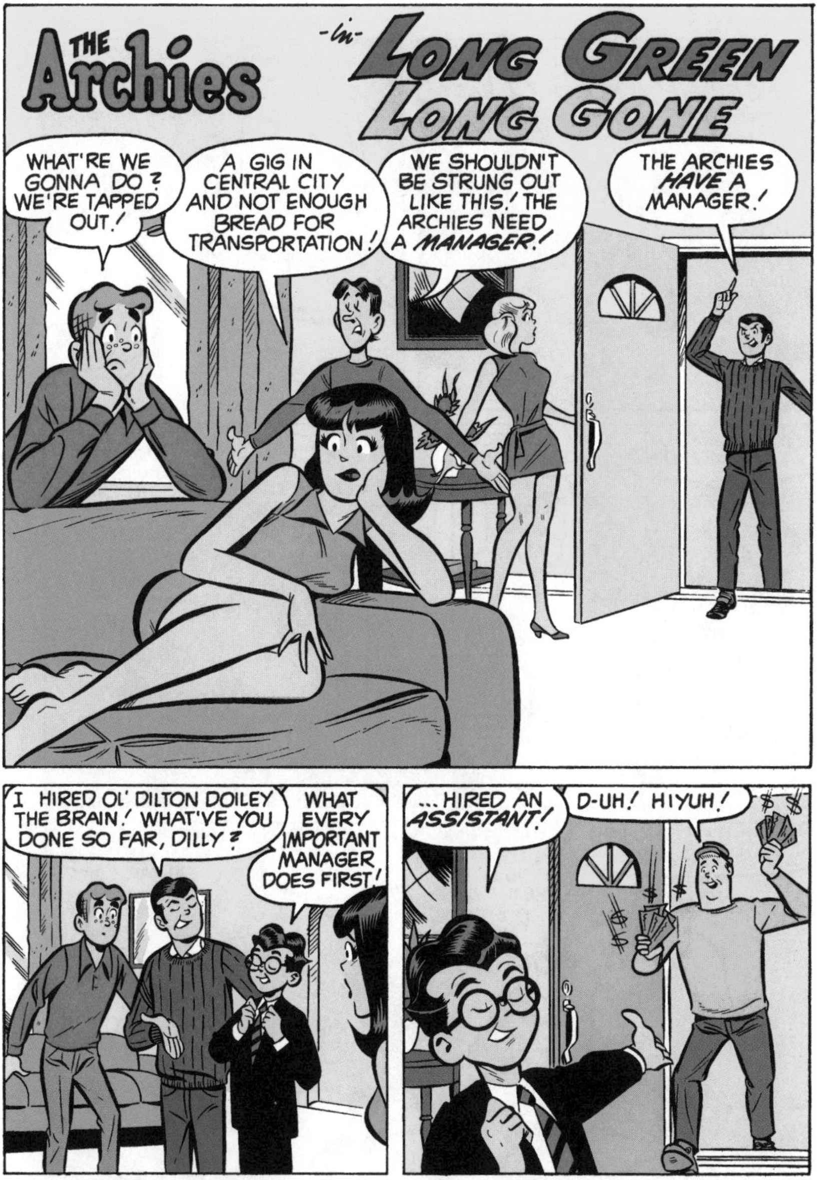
THE Archies
-in-
LONG GREEN LONG GONE
WHAT'RE WE GONNA DO? WE'RE TAPPED OUT!
A GIG IN CENTRAL CITY AND NOT ENOUGH BREAD FOR TRANSPORTATION!
WE SHOULDN'T BE STRUNG OUT LIKE THIS! THE ARCHIES NEED A MANAGER!
THE ARCHIES HAVE A MANAGER!
I HIRED OL' DILTON DOILEY THE BRAIN! WHAT'VE YOU DONE SO FAR, DILLY?
WHAT EVERY IMPORTANT MANAGER DOES FIRST!
...HIRED AN ASSISTANT!
D-UH! HIYUH!

Story: Frank Doyle Pencils: Harry Lucey
Inks: Chic Stone Letters: Bill Yoshida Colors: Barry Grossman

Originally printed in EVERYTHING'S ARCHIE #9, AUGUST 1970

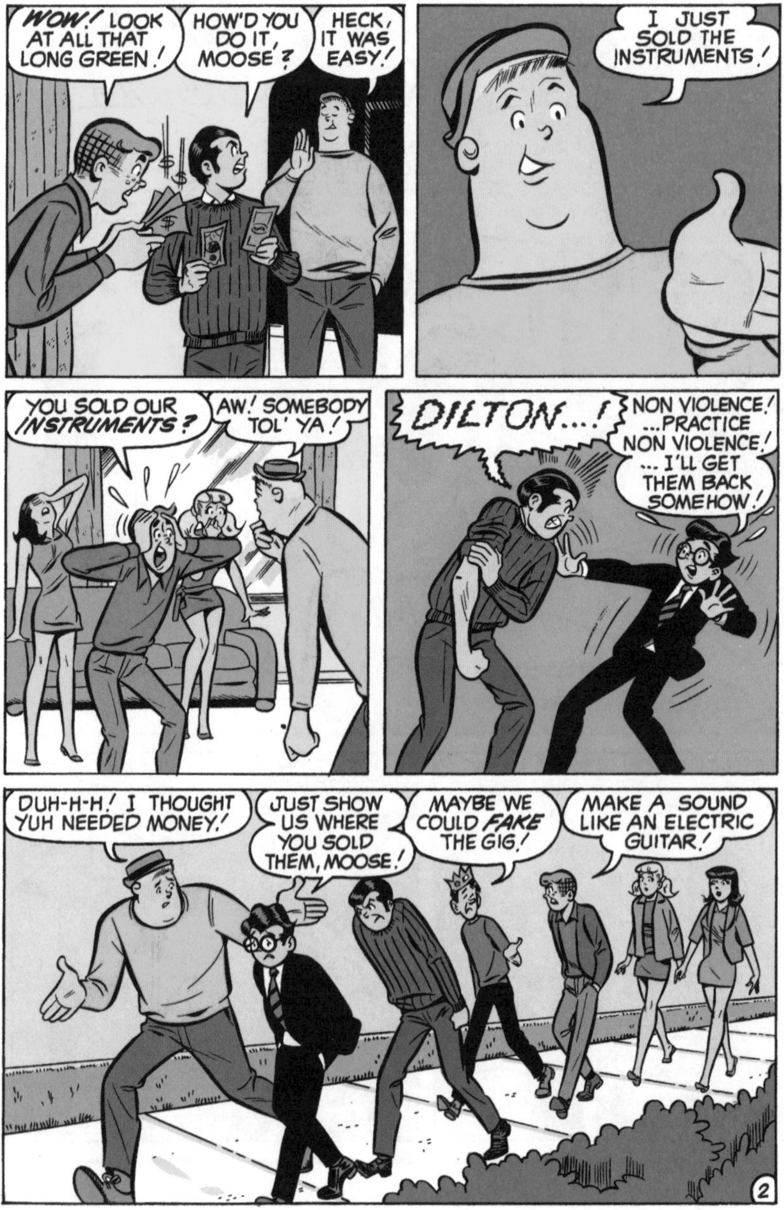
WOW! LOOK AT ALL THAT LONG GREEN!
HOW'D YOU DO IT, MOOSE?
HECK, IT WAS EASY!
I JUST SOLD THE INSTRUMENTS!
YOU SOLD OUR INSTRUMENTS?
AW! SOMEBODY TOL' YA!
DILTON...!
NON VIOLENCE! ...PRACTICE NON VIOLENCE! ... I'LL GET THEM BACK SOMEHOW!
DUH-H-H! I THOUGHT YUH NEEDED MONEY!
JUST SHOW US WHERE YOU SOLD THEM, MOOSE!
MAYBE WE COULD FAKE THE GIG!
MAKE A SOUND LIKE AN ELECTRIC GUITAR!
2

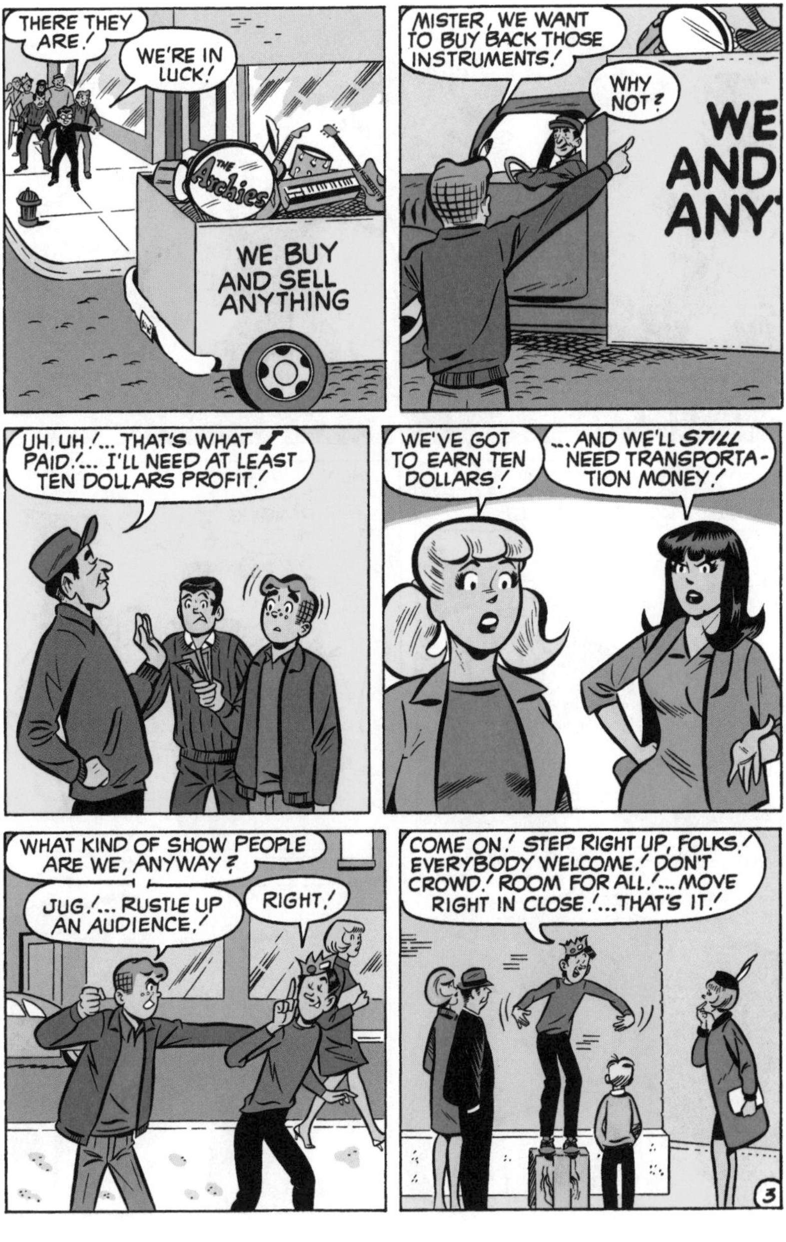
THERE THEY ARE!
WE'RE IN LUCK!
THE Archies
WE BUY AND SELL ANYTHING
MISTER, WE WANT TO BUY BACK THOSE INSTRUMENTS!
WHY NOT?
WE AND ANY
UH, UH!... THAT'S WHAT I PAID!... I'LL NEED AT LEAST TEN DOLLARS PROFIT!
WE'VE GOT TO EARN TEN DOLLARS!
...AND WE'LL STILL NEED TRANSPORTATION MONEY!
WHAT KIND OF SHOW PEOPLE ARE WE, ANYWAY?
JUG!... RUSTLE UP AN AUDIENCE!
RIGHT!
COME ON! STEP RIGHT UP, FOLKS! EVERYBODY WELCOME! DON'T CROWD! ROOM FOR ALL!... MOVE RIGHT IN CLOSE!...THAT'S IT!
3

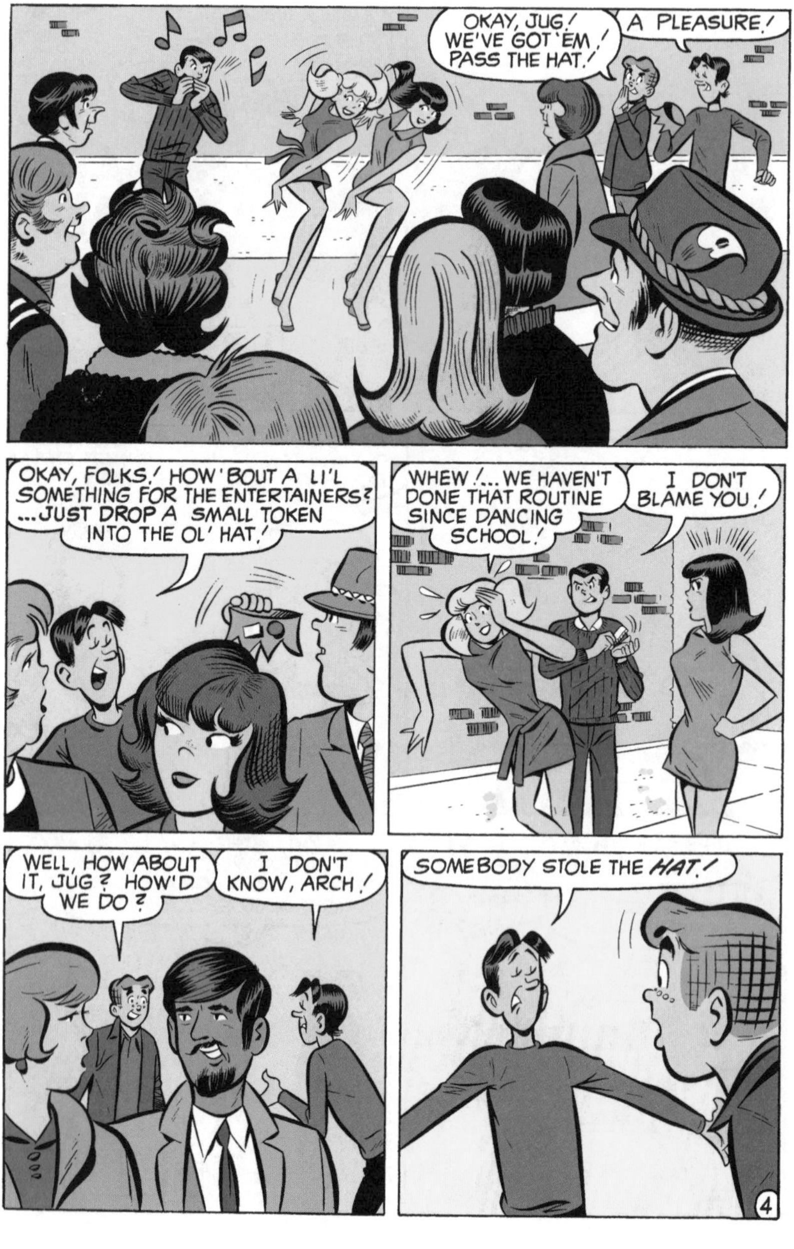
OKAY, JUG! WE'VE GOT 'EM! PASS THE HAT!
A PLEASURE!
OKAY, FOLKS! HOW 'BOUT A LI'L SOMETHING FOR THE ENTERTAINERS? ...JUST DROP A SMALL TOKEN INTO THE OL' HAT!
WHEW!... WE HAVEN'T DONE THAT ROUTINE SINCE DANCING SCHOOL!
I DON'T BLAME YOU!
WELL, HOW ABOUT IT, JUG? HOW'D WE DO?
I DON'T KNOW, ARCH!
SOMEBODY STOLE THE HAT!
4

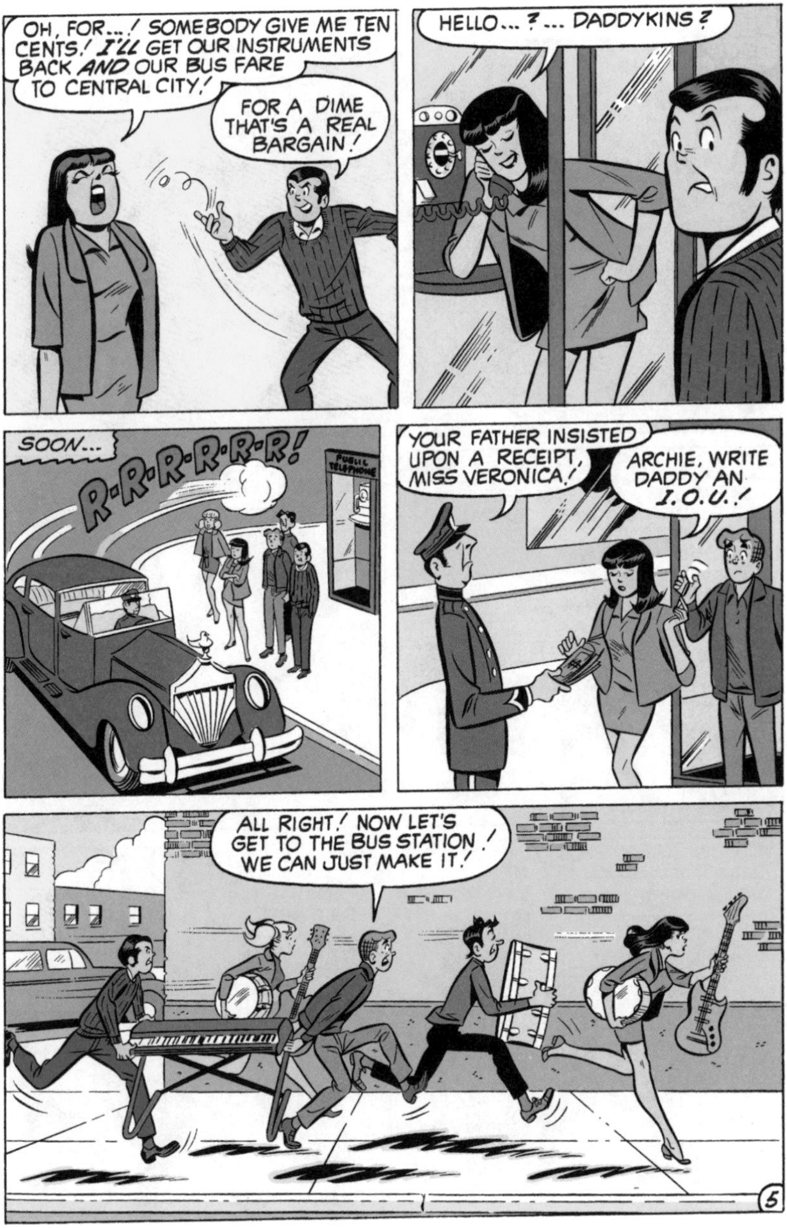
OH, FOR...! SOMEBODY GIVE ME TEN CENTS! I'LL GET OUR INSTRUMENTS BACK AND OUR BUS FARE TO CENTRAL CITY!
FOR A DIME THAT'S A REAL BARGAIN!
HELLO...?... DADDYKINS?
SOON...
R-R-R-R-R-R-R!
PUBLIC TELEPHONE
YOUR FATHER INSISTED UPON A RECEIPT, MISS VERONICA!
ARCHIE, WRITE DADDY AN I.O.U.!
ALL RIGHT! NOW LET'S GET TO THE BUS STATION! WE CAN JUST MAKE IT!
5

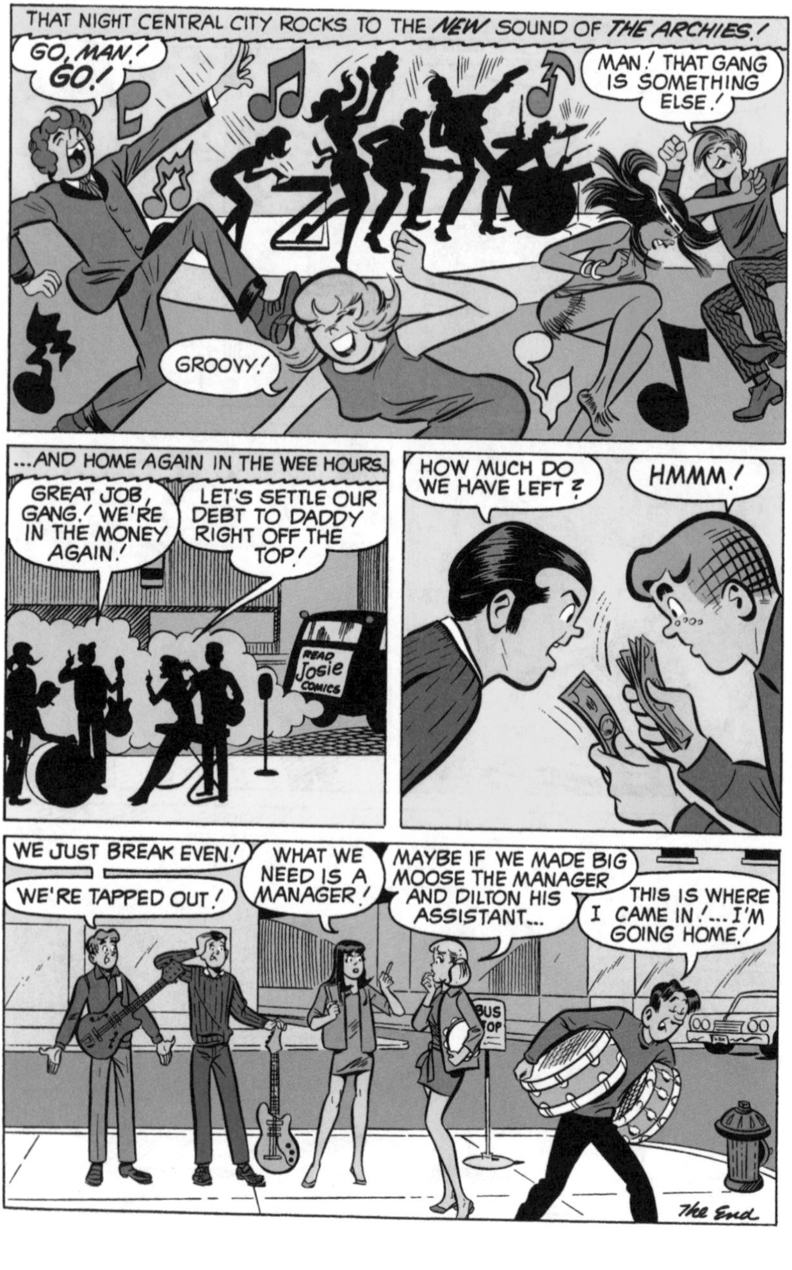
THAT NIGHT CENTRAL CITY ROCKS TO THE NEW SOUND OF THE ARCHIES!
GO, MAN! GO!
MAN! THAT GANG IS SOMETHING ELSE!
GROOVY!
...AND HOME AGAIN IN THE WEE HOURS.
GREAT JOB, GANG! WE'RE IN THE MONEY AGAIN!
LET'S SETTLE OUR DEBT TO DADDY RIGHT OFF THE TOP!
READ Josie COMICS
HOW MUCH DO WE HAVE LEFT?
HMMM!
WE JUST BREAK EVEN!
WE'RE TAPPED OUT!
WHAT WE NEED IS A MANAGER!
MAYBE IF WE MADE BIG MOOSE THE MANAGER AND DILTON HIS ASSISTANT...
THIS IS WHERE I CAME IN!... I'M GOING HOME!
BUS STOP
The End

Archie -in- "Droopy Sails"

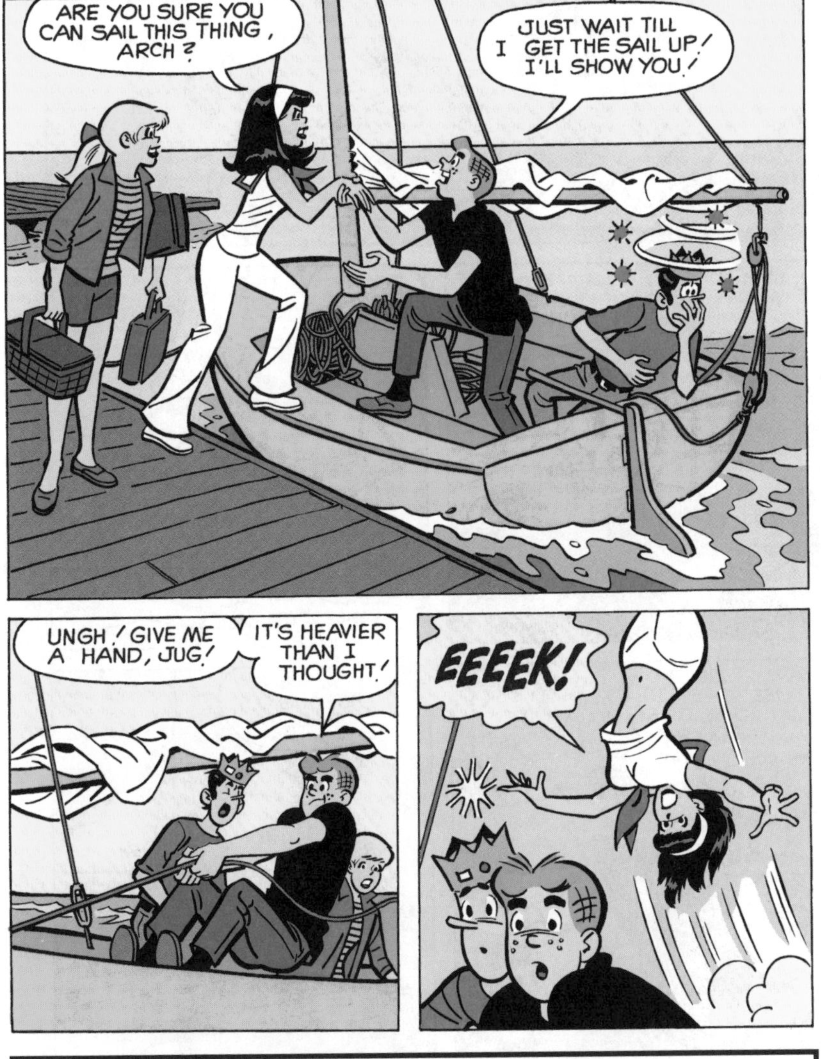
ARE YOU SURE YOU CAN SAIL THIS THING, ARCH?
JUST WAIT TILL I GET THE SAIL UP! I'LL SHOW YOU!
UNGH! GIVE ME A HAND, JUG!
IT'S HEAVIER THAN I THOUGHT!
EEEEK!

Story & Pencils: Al Hartley Letters: Bill Yoshida

Originally printed in EVERYTHING'S ARCHIE #10, OCTOBER 1970

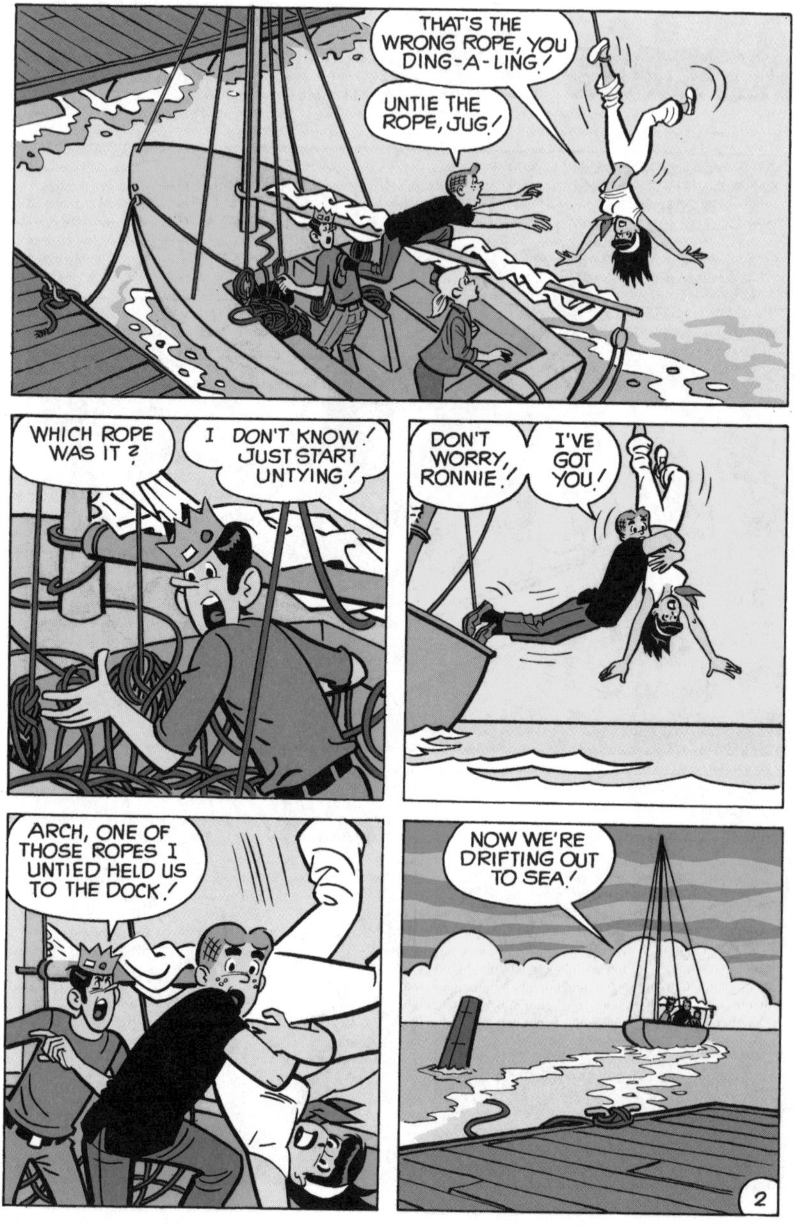
THAT'S THE WRONG ROPE, YOU DING-A-LING!
UNTIE THE ROPE, JUG!
WHICH ROPE WAS IT?
I DON'T KNOW! JUST START UNTYING!
DON'T WORRY, RONNIE!
I'VE GOT YOU!
ARCH, ONE OF THOSE ROPES I UNTIED HELD US TO THE DOCK!
NOW WE'RE DRIFTING OUT TO SEA!
2

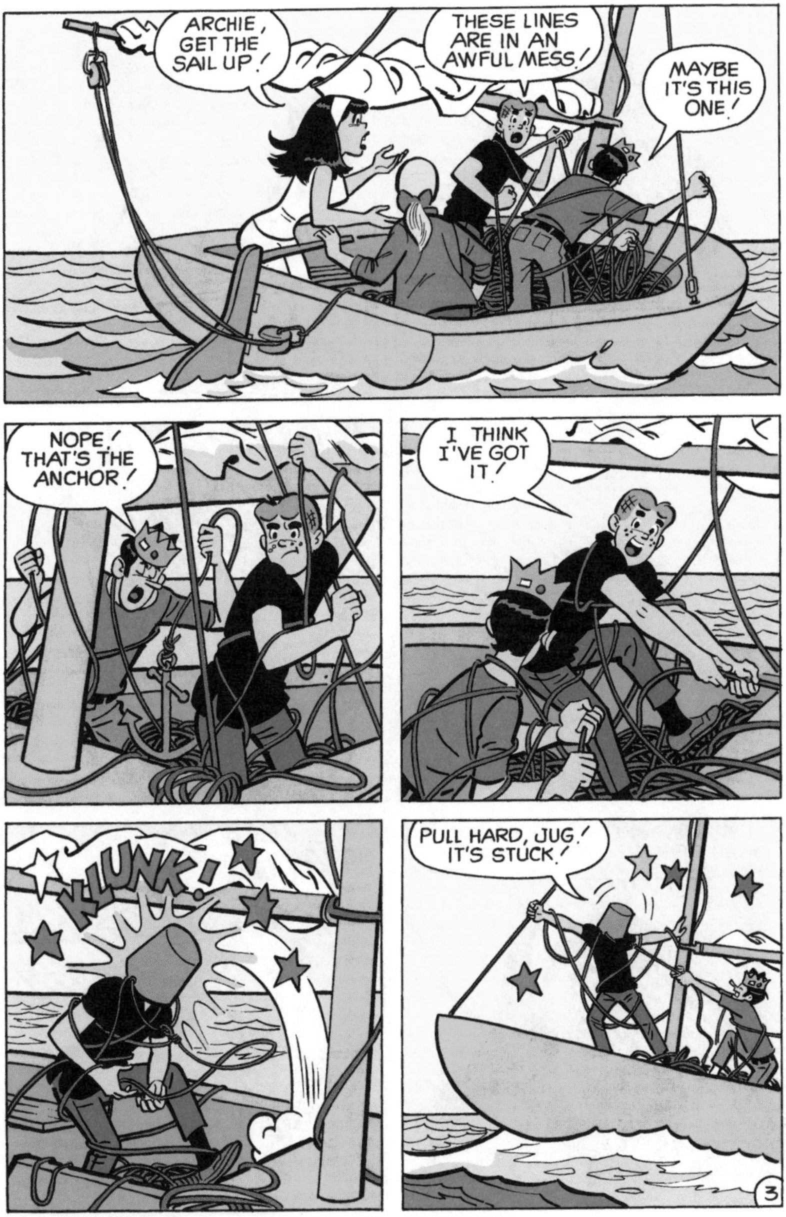
ARCHIE, GET THE SAIL UP!
THESE LINES ARE IN AN AWFUL MESS!
MAYBE IT'S THIS ONE!
NOPE! THAT'S THE ANCHOR!
I THINK I'VE GOT IT!
KLUNK!
PULL HARD, JUG! IT'S STUCK!
3

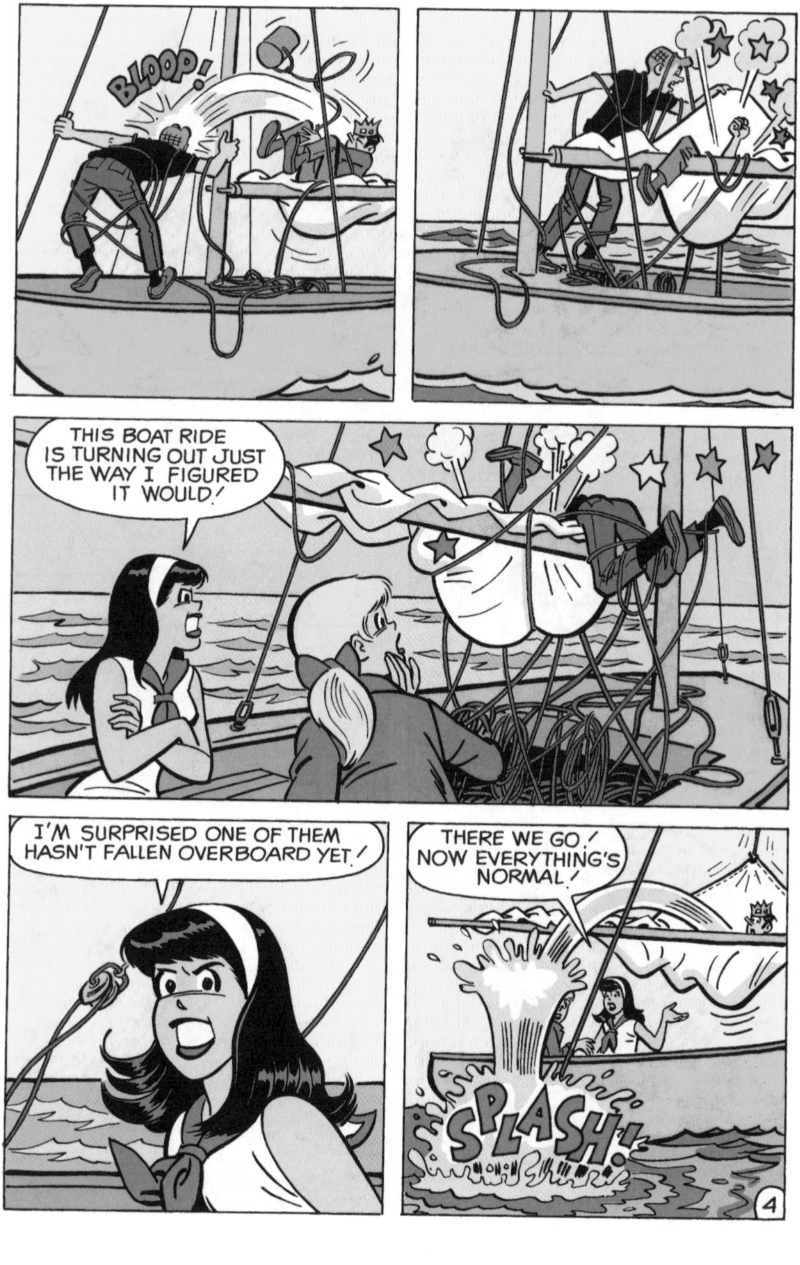
BLOOP!
THIS BOAT RIDE IS TURNING OUT JUST THE WAY I FIGURED IT WOULD!
I'M SURPRISED ONE OF THEM HASN'T FALLEN OVERBOARD YET!
THERE WE GO! NOW EVERYTHING'S NORMAL!
SPLASH!
4

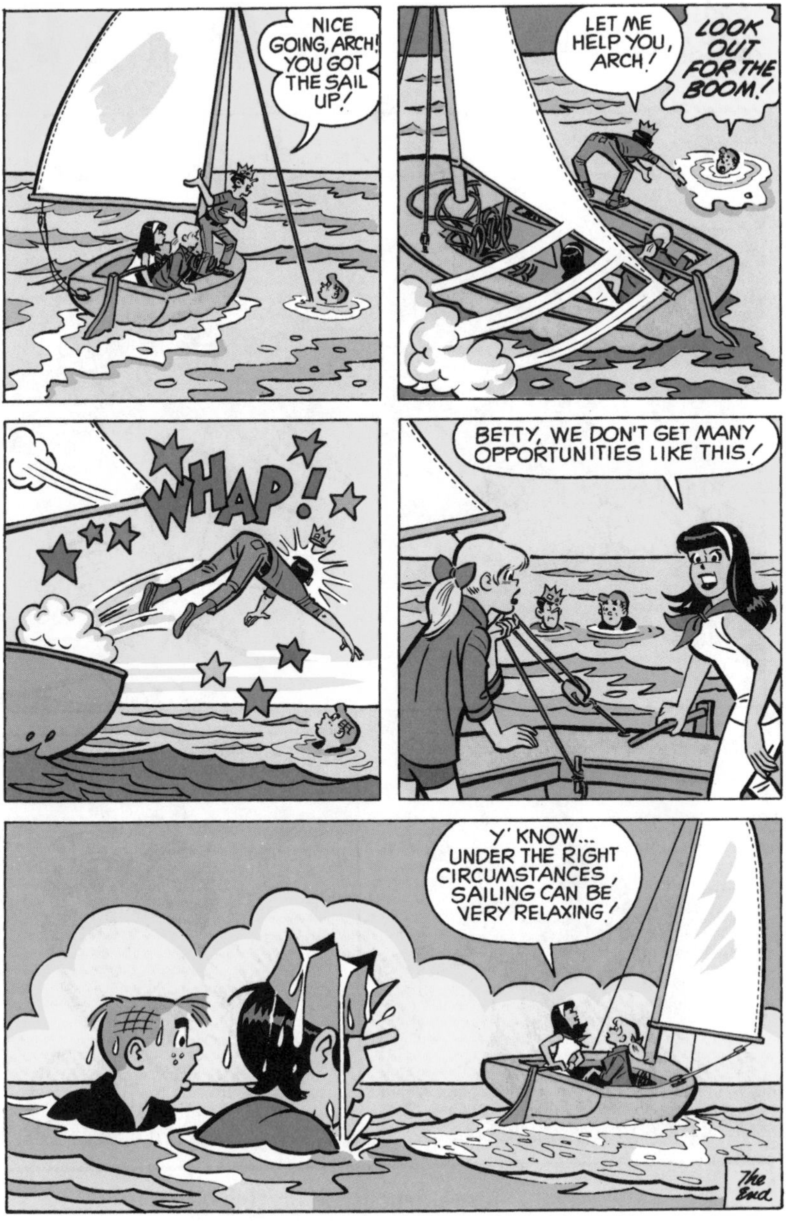
NICE GOING, ARCH! YOU GOT THE SAIL UP!
LET ME HELP YOU, ARCH!
LOOK OUT FOR THE BOOM!
WHAP!
BETTY, WE DON'T GET MANY OPPORTUNITIES LIKE THIS!
Y' KNOW... UNDER THE RIGHT CIRCUMSTANCES, SAILING CAN BE VERY RELAXING!
The End

Archie in "A Flip of the Lip"

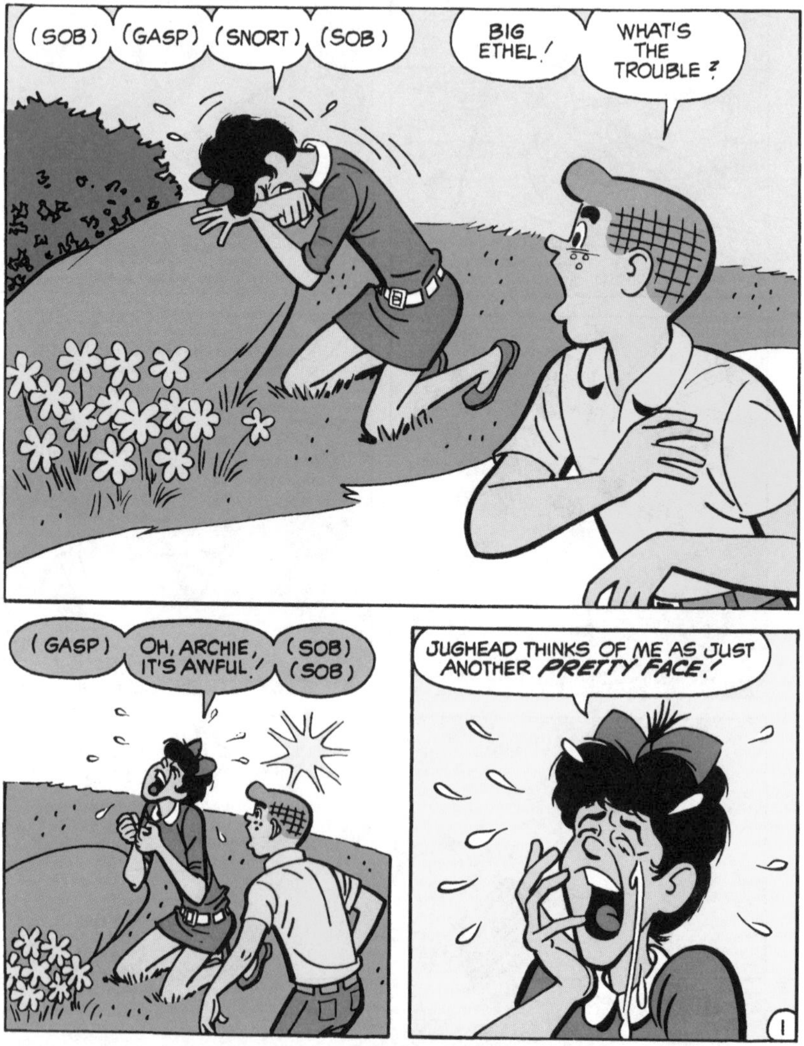
(SOB) (GASP) (SNORT) (SOB)
BIG ETHEL!
WHAT'S THE TROUBLE?
(GASP)
OH, ARCHIE, IT'S AWFUL!
(SOB) (SOB)
JUGHEAD THINKS OF ME AS JUST ANOTHER *PRETTY FACE!*
1

Story & Pencils: Al Hartley
Letters: Bill Yoshida Colors: Barry Grossman

Originally printed in EVERYTHING'S ARCHIE #11, DECEMBER 1970

I'VE TRIED EVERYTHING TO HOOK HIM!
BUT HE HARDLY KNOWS I'M ALIVE!
HAVE YOU TRIED MAKING HIM JEALOUS?
JEALOUS?
SURE! IF HE SAW THAT ANOTHER GUY WAS INTERESTED IN YOU...
THAT'S IT!
THAT'S A GREAT IDEA!
THANK YOU, ARCHIE!
THANK YOU!
WHAT TIME WILL YOU PICK ME UP TONIGHT?
I NEVER LEARN!
2

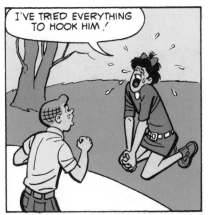

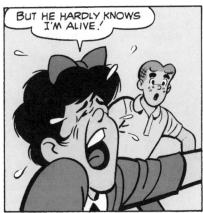

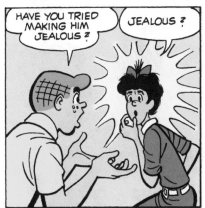

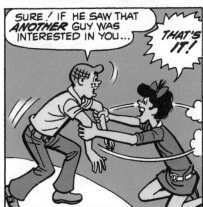

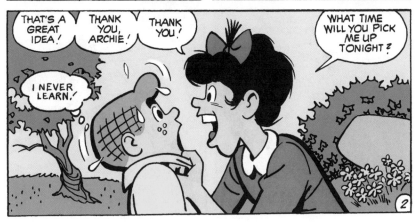

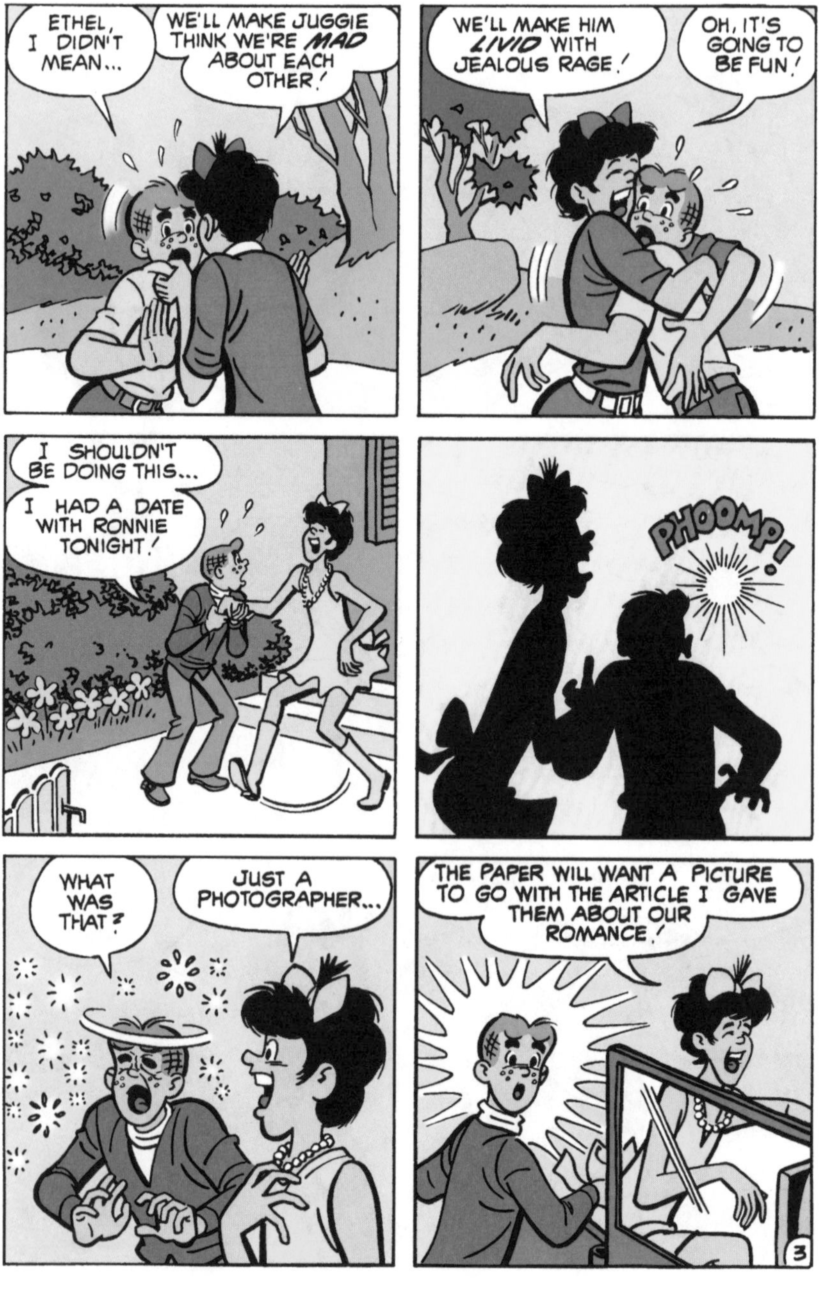
ETHEL, I DIDN'T MEAN...
WE'LL MAKE JUGGIE THINK WE'RE MAD ABOUT EACH OTHER!
WE'LL MAKE HIM LIVID WITH JEALOUS RAGE!
OH, IT'S GOING TO BE FUN!
I SHOULDN'T BE DOING THIS...
I HAD A DATE WITH RONNIE TONIGHT!
PHOOMP!
WHAT WAS THAT?
JUST A PHOTOGRAPHER...
THE PAPER WILL WANT A PICTURE TO GO WITH THE ARTICLE I GAVE THEM ABOUT OUR ROMANCE!
3

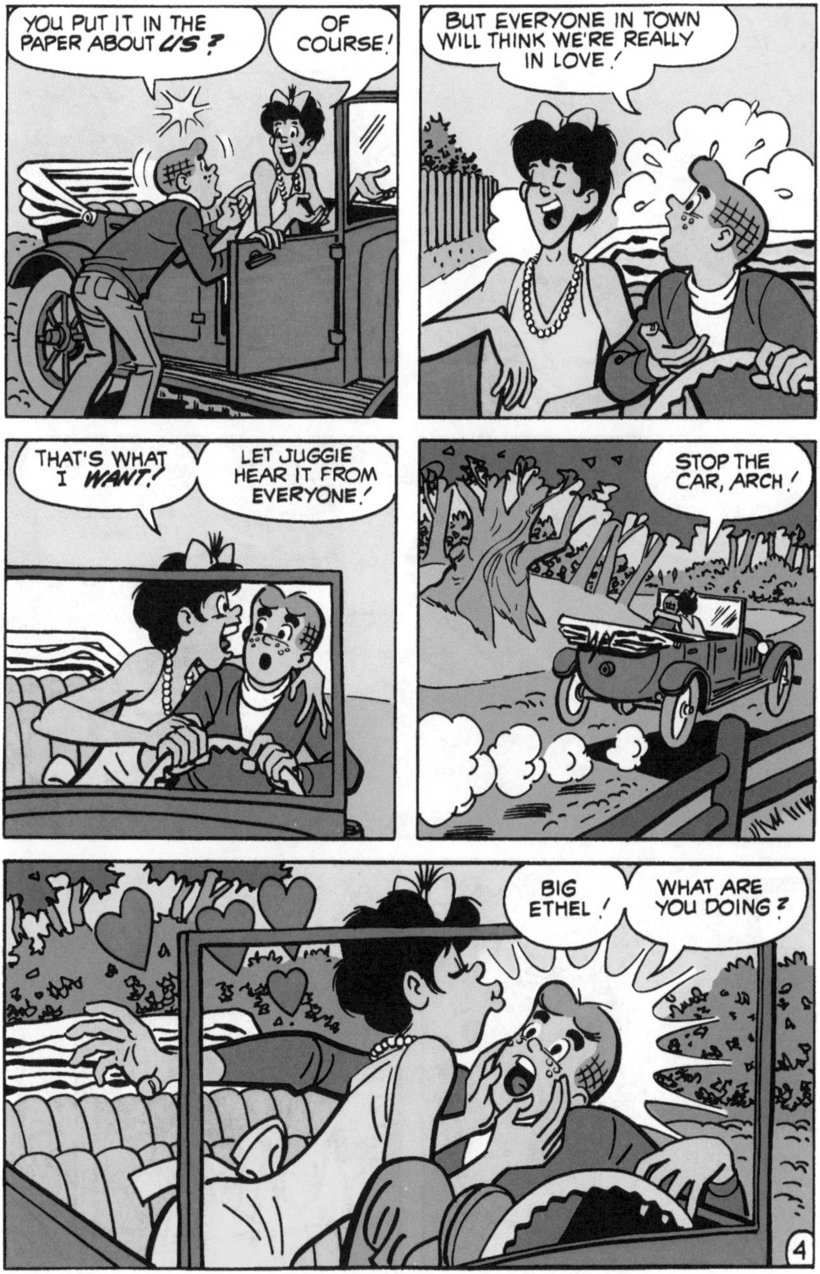
YOU PUT IT IN THE PAPER ABOUT US?
OF COURSE!
BUT EVERYONE IN TOWN WILL THINK WE'RE REALLY IN LOVE!
THAT'S WHAT I WANT!
LET JUGGIE HEAR IT FROM EVERYONE!
STOP THE CAR, ARCH!
BIG ETHEL!
WHAT ARE YOU DOING?
4

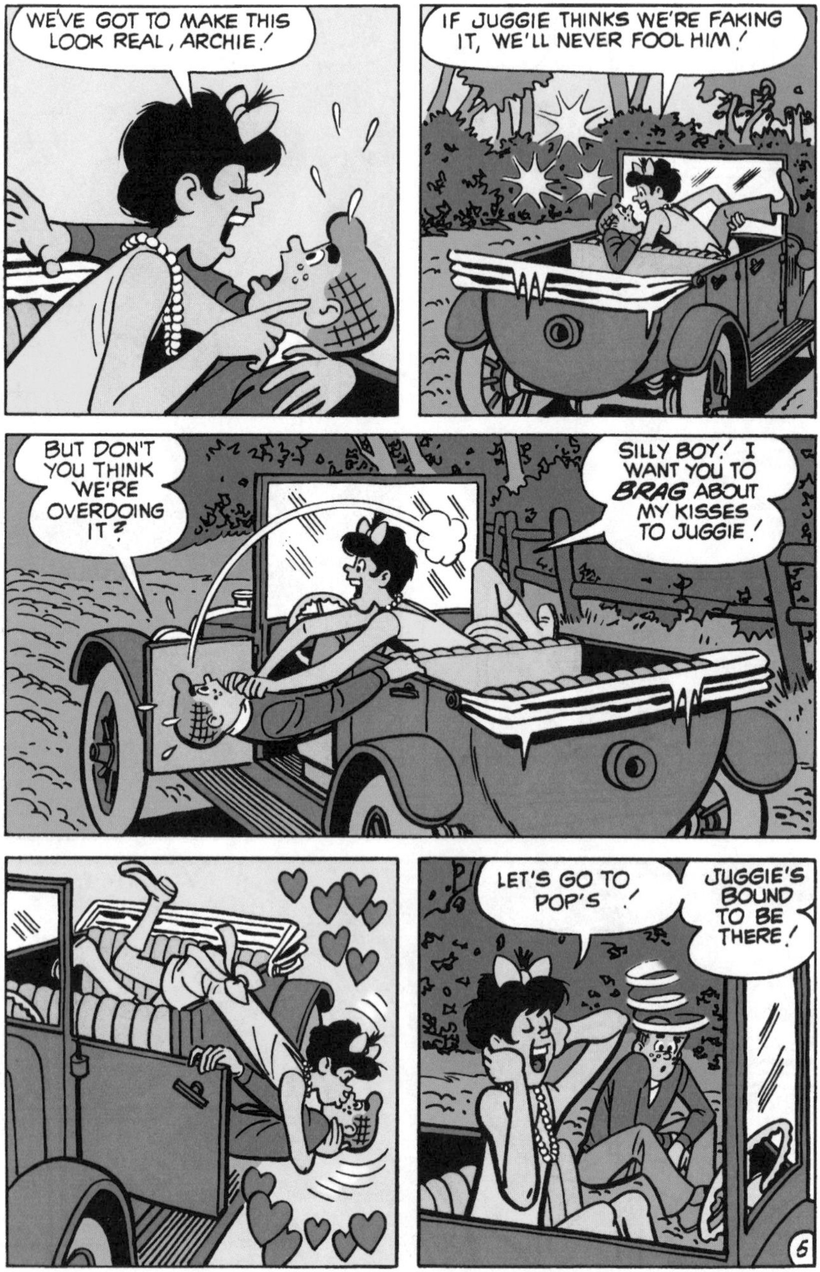
WE'VE GOT TO MAKE THIS LOOK REAL, ARCHIE!
IF JUGGIE THINKS WE'RE FAKING IT, WE'LL NEVER FOOL HIM!
BUT DON'T YOU THINK WE'RE OVERDOING IT?
SILLY BOY! I WANT YOU TO BRAG ABOUT MY KISSES TO JUGGIE!
LET'S GO TO POP'S!
JUGGIE'S BOUND TO BE THERE!
6

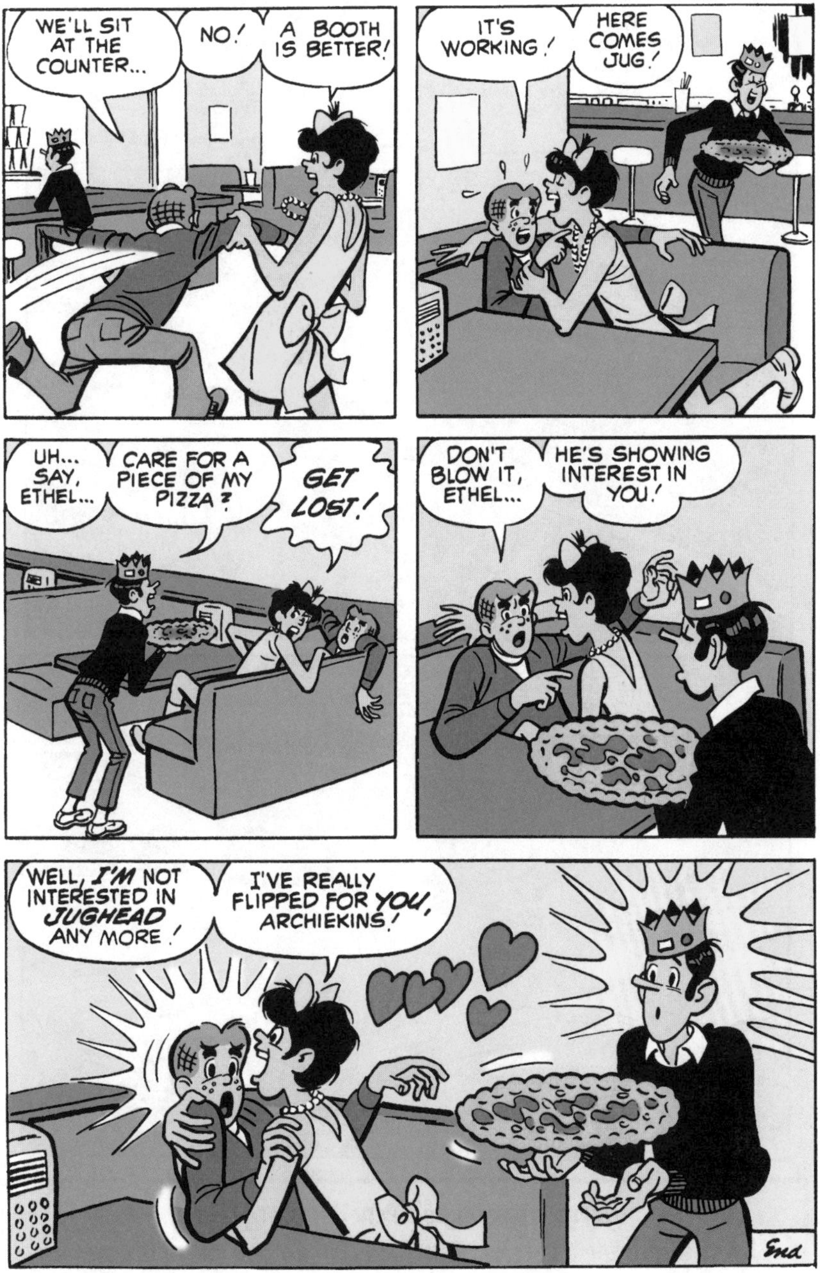
WE'LL SIT AT THE COUNTER...
NO!
A BOOTH IS BETTER!
IT'S WORKING!
HERE COMES JUG!
UH... SAY, ETHEL...
CARE FOR A PIECE OF MY PIZZA?
GET LOST!
DON'T BLOW IT, ETHEL...
HE'S SHOWING INTEREST IN YOU!
WELL, I'M NOT INTERESTED IN JUGHEAD ANY MORE!
I'VE REALLY FLIPPED FOR YOU, ARCHIEKINS!
End

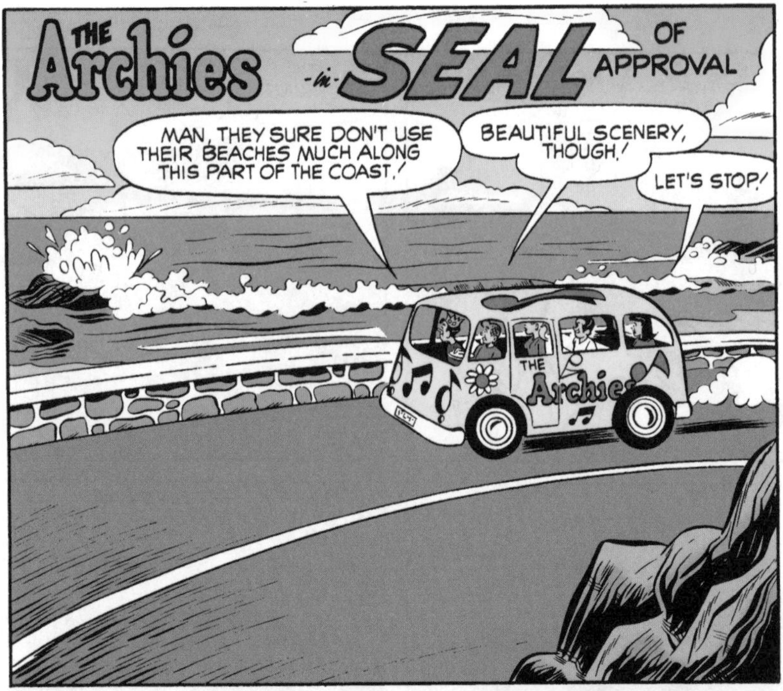
THE Archies
-in-
SEAL OF APPROVAL
MAN, THEY SURE DON'T USE THEIR BEACHES MUCH ALONG THIS PART OF THE COAST!
BEAUTIFUL SCENERY, THOUGH!
LET'S STOP!
THE Archies

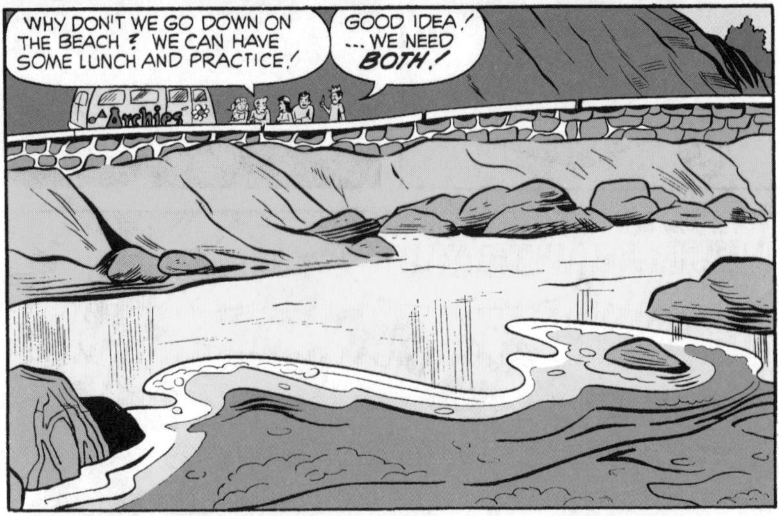
WHY DON'T WE GO DOWN ON THE BEACH ? WE CAN HAVE SOME LUNCH AND PRACTICE!
GOOD IDEA! ... WE NEED BOTH!
Archies

Story: Frank Doyle Pencils: Harry Lucey
Inks: Marty Epp Letters: Bill Yoshida Colors: Barry Grossman

Originally printed in EVERYTHING'S ARCHIE #11, DECEMBER 1970

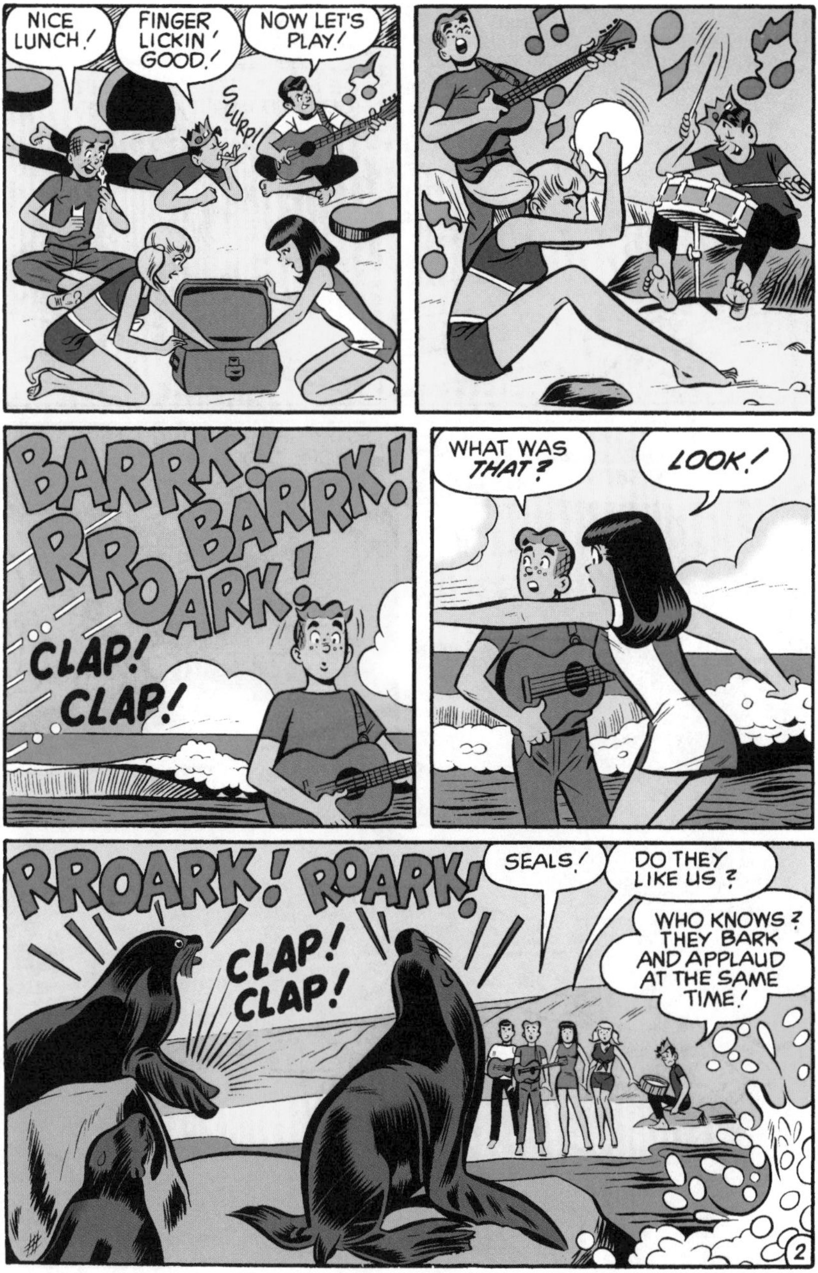
NICE LUNCH!
FINGER LICKIN' GOOD!
NOW LET'S PLAY!
SLURP!
BARRK! BARRK!
RROARK!
CLAP! CLAP!
WHAT WAS THAT?
LOOK!
RROARK! ROARK!
CLAP! CLAP!
SEALS!
DO THEY LIKE US?
WHO KNOWS? THEY BARK AND APPLAUD AT THE SAME TIME!
2

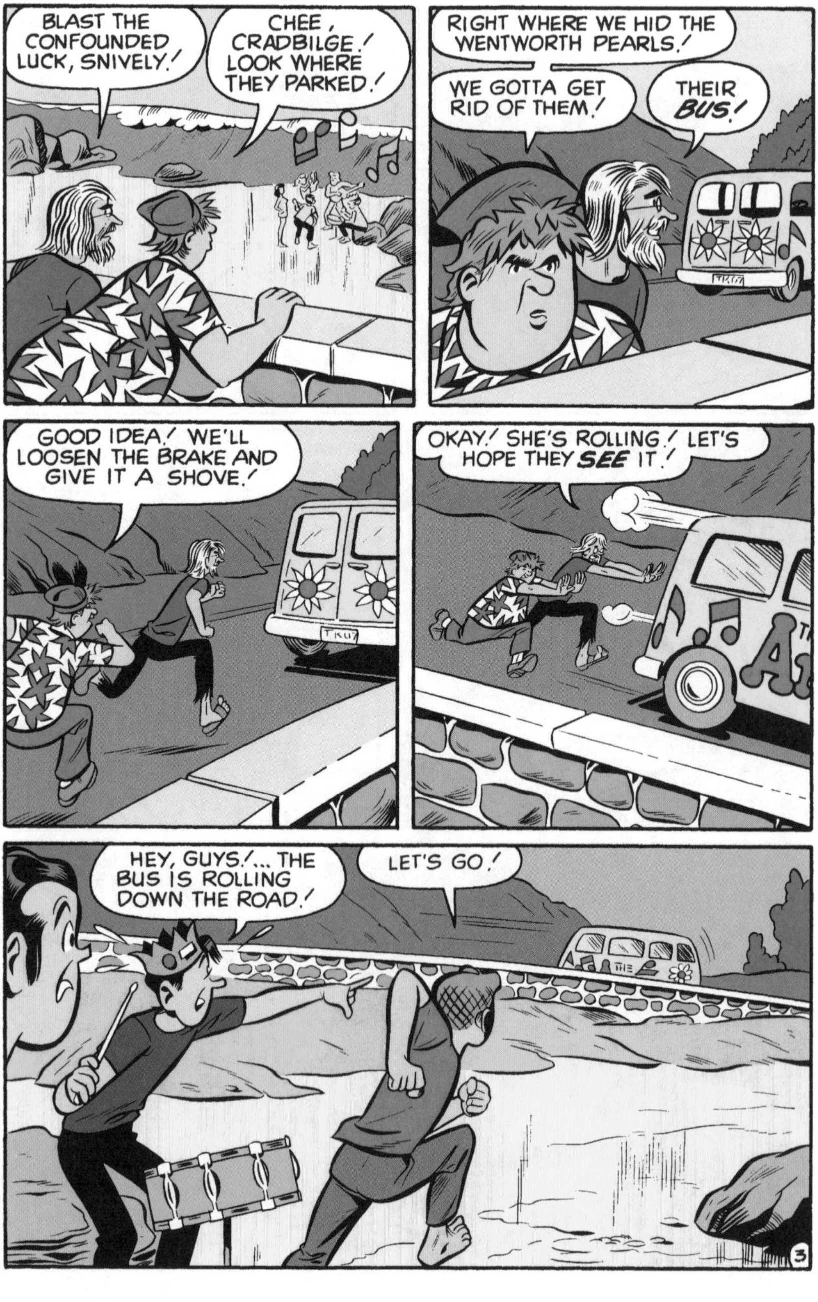
BLAST THE CONFOUNDED LUCK, SNIVELY!
CHEE, CRADBILGE! LOOK WHERE THEY PARKED!
RIGHT WHERE WE HID THE WENTWORTH PEARLS!
WE GOTTA GET RID OF THEM!
THEIR BUS!
GOOD IDEA! WE'LL LOOSEN THE BRAKE AND GIVE IT A SHOVE!
OKAY! SHE'S ROLLING! LET'S HOPE THEY SEE IT!
HEY, GUYS!... THE BUS IS ROLLING DOWN THE ROAD!
LET'S GO!
3

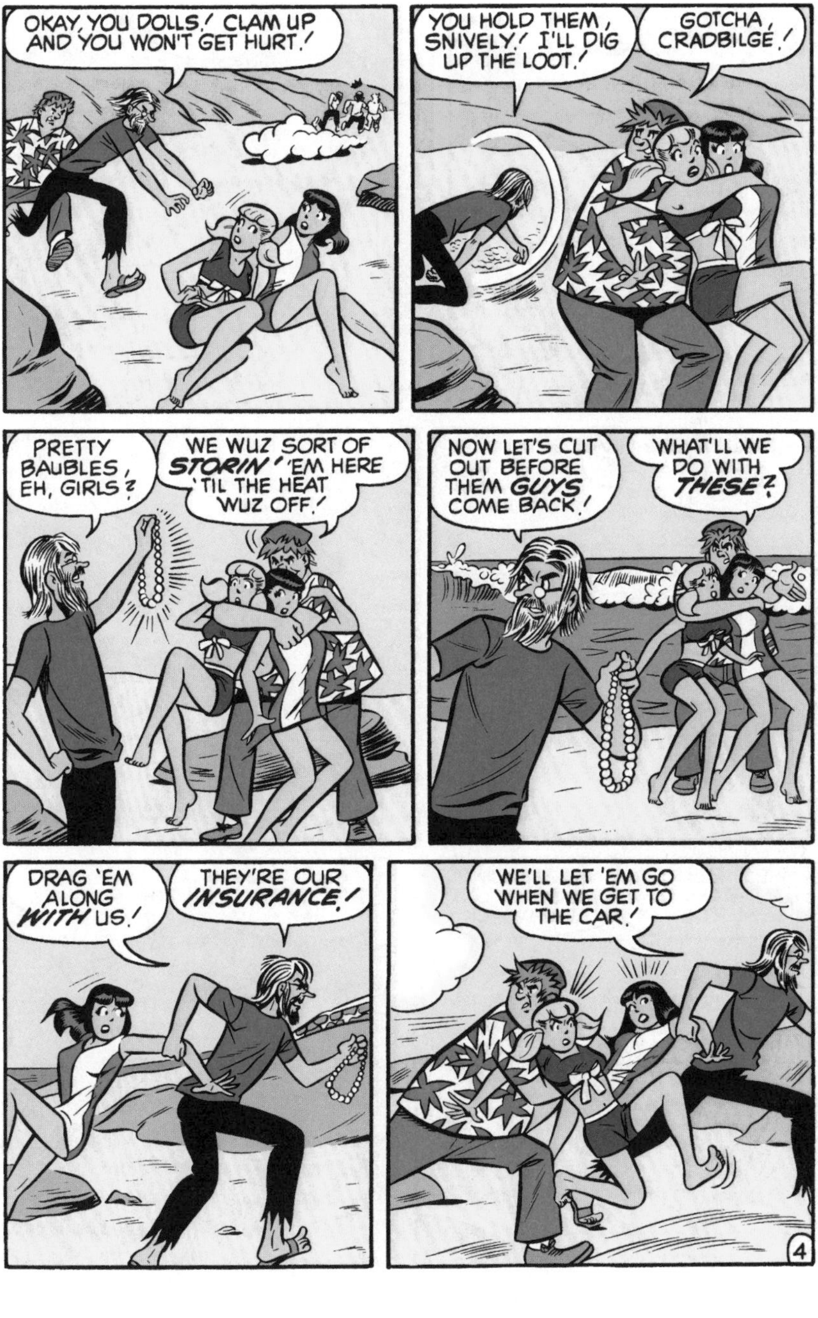
OKAY, YOU DOLLS! CLAM UP AND YOU WON'T GET HURT!
YOU HOLD THEM, SNIVELY! I'LL DIG UP THE LOOT!
GOTCHA, CRADBILGE!
PRETTY BAUBLES, EH, GIRLS?
WE WUZ SORT OF STORIN' 'EM HERE 'TIL THE HEAT WUZ OFF!
NOW LET'S CUT OUT BEFORE THEM GUYS COME BACK!
WHAT'LL WE DO WITH THESE?
DRAG 'EM ALONG WITH US!
THEY'RE OUR INSURANCE!
WE'LL LET 'EM GO WHEN WE GET TO THE CAR!
4

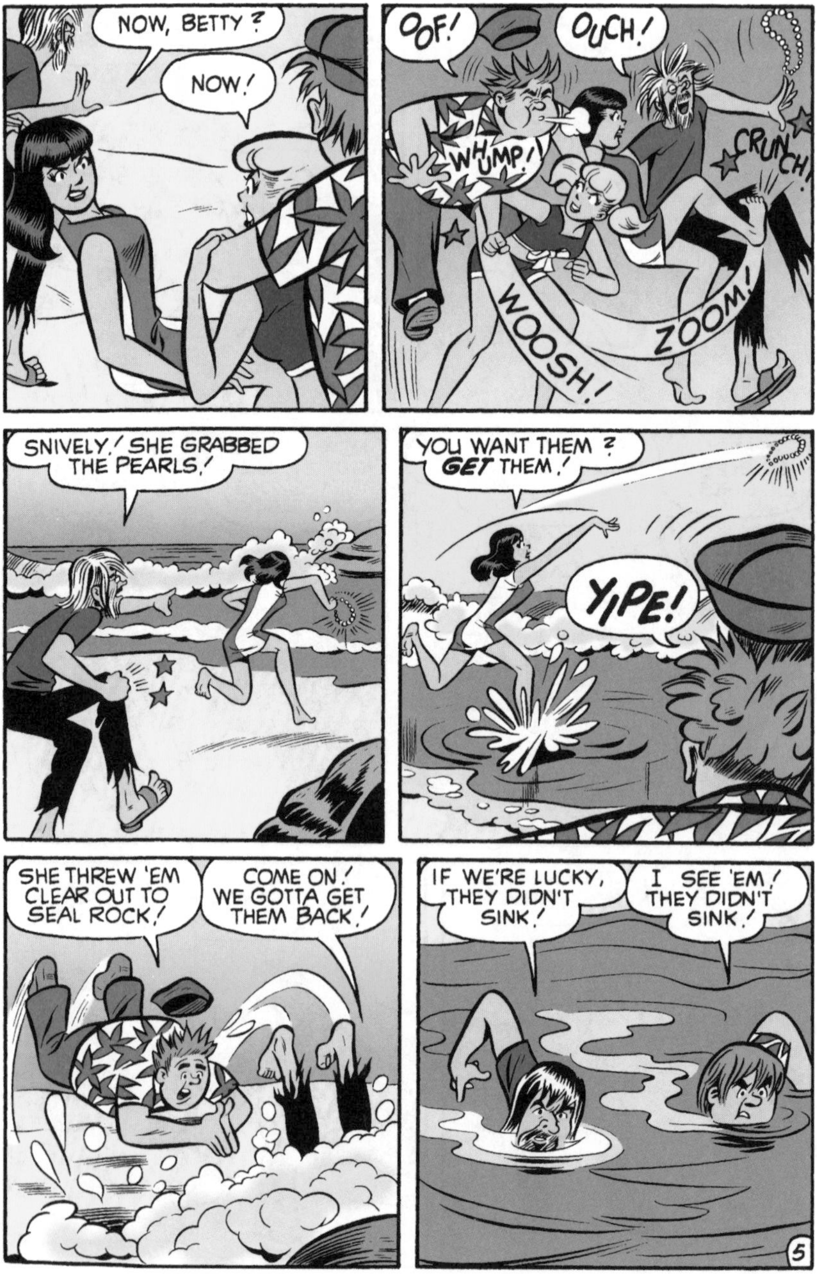
NOW, BETTY ?
NOW!
OOF!
OUCH!
WHUMP!
CRUNCH!
WOOSH!
ZOOM!
SNIVELY! SHE GRABBED THE PEARLS!
YOU WANT THEM ? GET THEM!
YIPE!
SHE THREW 'EM CLEAR OUT TO SEAL ROCK!
COME ON! WE GOTTA GET THEM BACK!
IF WE'RE LUCKY, THEY DIDN'T SINK!
I SEE 'EM! THEY DIDN'T SINK!
5

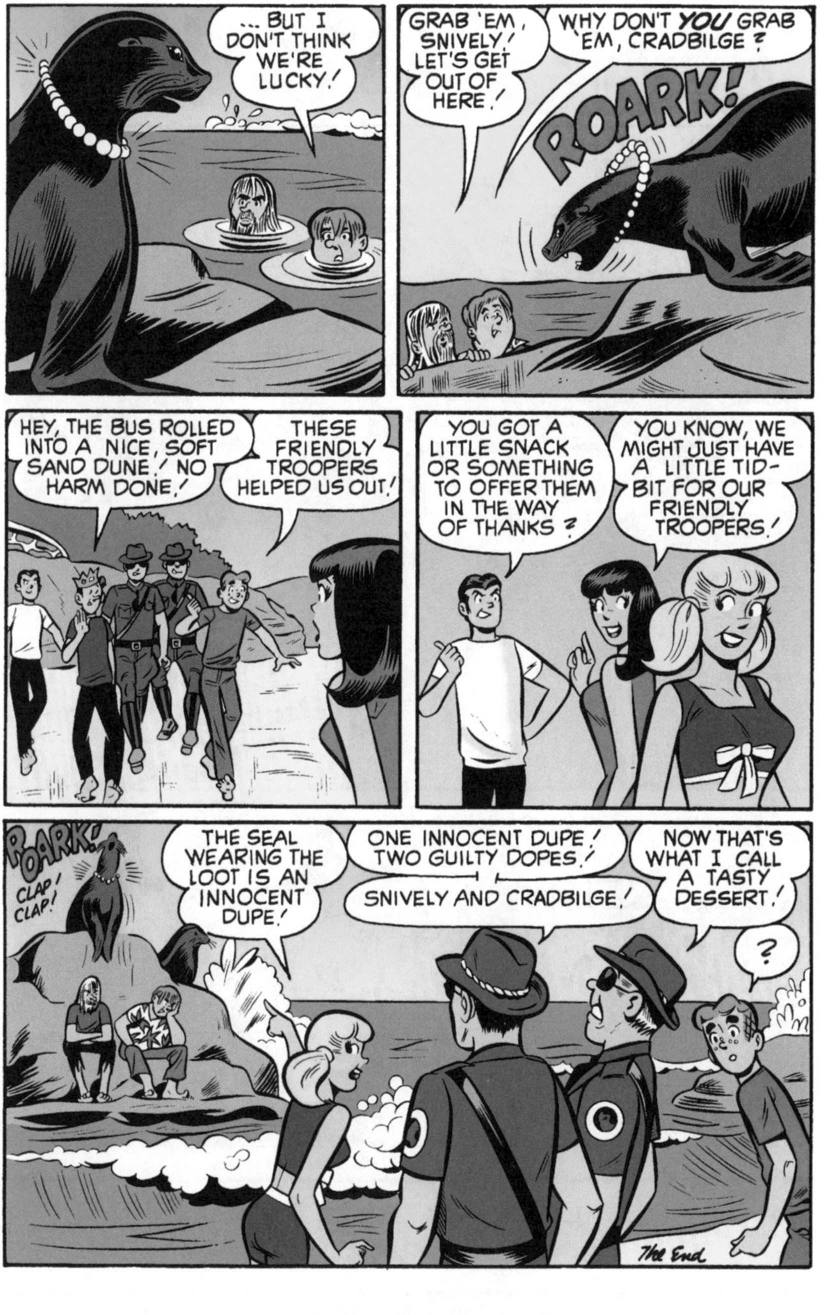
... BUT I DON'T THINK WE'RE LUCKY!
GRAB 'EM, SNIVELY! LET'S GET OUT OF HERE!
WHY DON'T YOU GRAB 'EM, CRADBILGE?
ROARK!
HEY, THE BUS ROLLED INTO A NICE, SOFT SAND DUNE! NO HARM DONE!
THESE FRIENDLY TROOPERS HELPED US OUT!
YOU GOT A LITTLE SNACK OR SOMETHING TO OFFER THEM IN THE WAY OF THANKS?
YOU KNOW, WE MIGHT JUST HAVE A LITTLE TID-BIT FOR OUR FRIENDLY TROOPERS!
ROARK!
CLAP! CLAP!
THE SEAL WEARING THE LOOT IS AN INNOCENT DUPE!
ONE INNOCENT DUPE! TWO GUILTY DOPES! SNIVELY AND CRADBILGE!
NOW THAT'S WHAT I CALL A TASTY DESSERT!
?
The End

THE Archies in "The Last Chord"

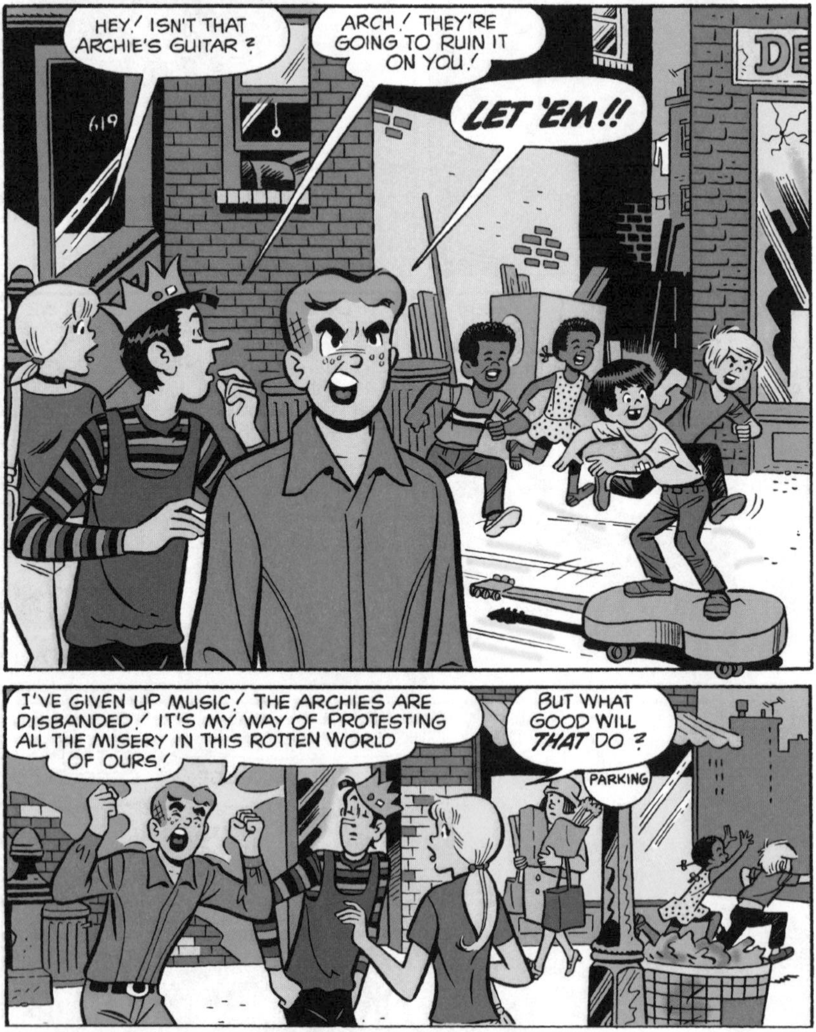
HEY! ISN'T THAT ARCHIE'S GUITAR?
ARCH! THEY'RE GOING TO RUIN IT ON YOU!
LET 'EM!!
619
DE
I'VE GIVEN UP MUSIC! THE ARCHIES ARE DISBANDED! IT'S MY WAY OF PROTESTING ALL THE MISERY IN THIS ROTTEN WORLD OF OURS!
BUT WHAT GOOD WILL *THAT* DO?
PARKING

Story: Frank Doyle   Pencils: Dan DeCarlo
Inks: Rudy Lapick   Letters: Bill Yoshida

Originally printed in EVERYTHING'S ARCHIE #12, FEBRUARY 1971

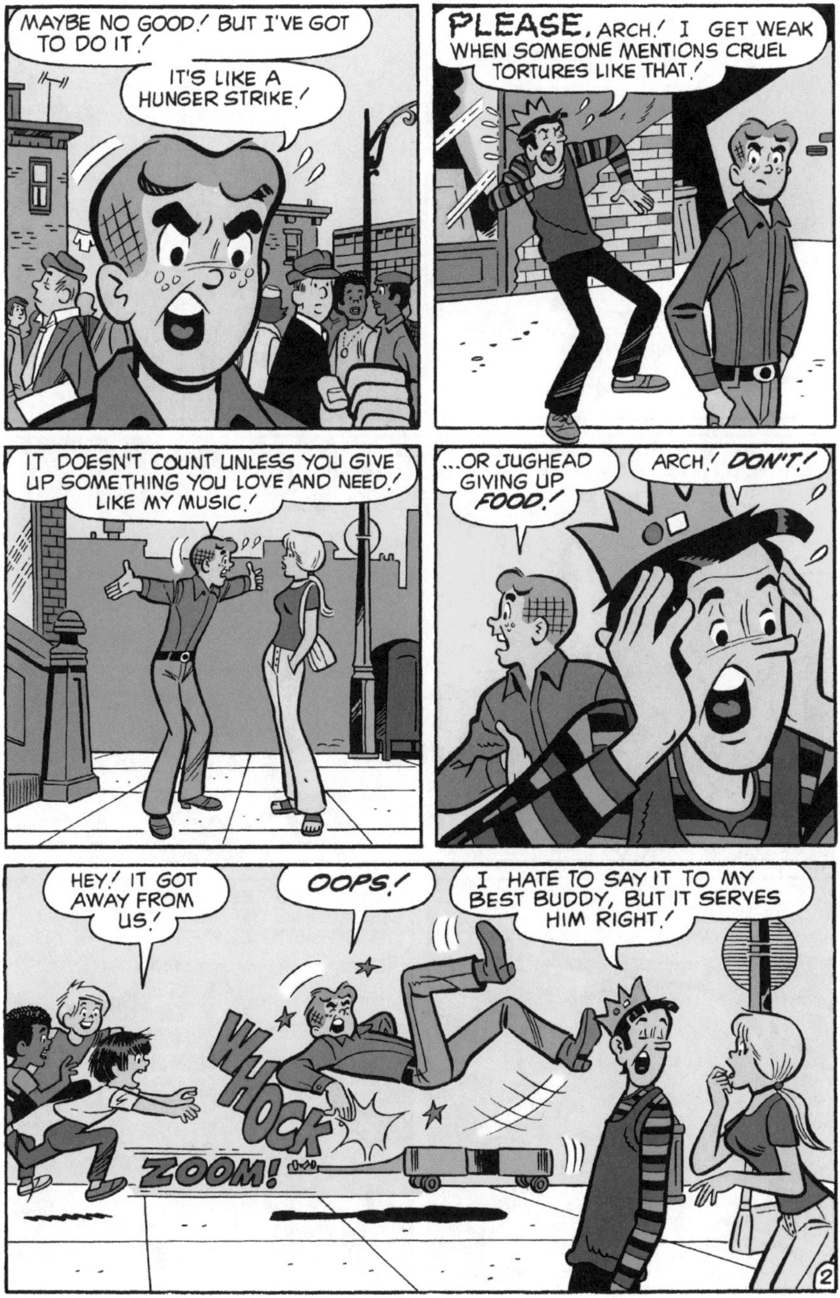
MAYBE NO GOOD! BUT I'VE GOT TO DO IT!
IT'S LIKE A HUNGER STRIKE!
PLEASE, ARCH! I GET WEAK WHEN SOMEONE MENTIONS CRUEL TORTURES LIKE THAT!
IT DOESN'T COUNT UNLESS YOU GIVE UP SOMETHING YOU LOVE AND NEED! LIKE MY MUSIC!
...OR JUGHEAD GIVING UP FOOD!
ARCH! DON'T!
HEY! IT GOT AWAY FROM US!
OOPS!
I HATE TO SAY IT TO MY BEST BUDDY, BUT IT SERVES HIM RIGHT!
WHOCK
ZOOM!
2

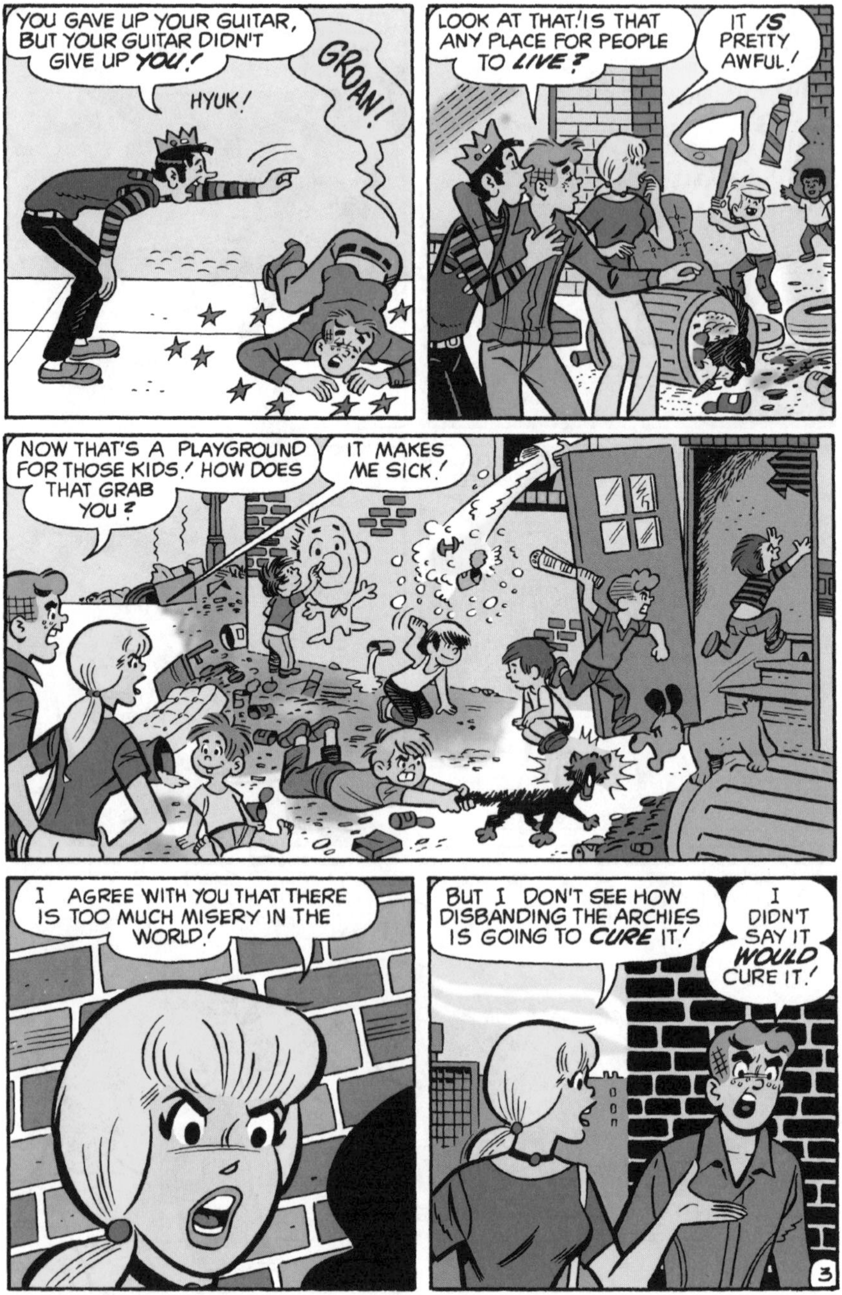
YOU GAVE UP YOUR GUITAR, BUT YOUR GUITAR DIDN'T GIVE UP *YOU!*
HYUK!
GROAN!
LOOK AT THAT! IS THAT ANY PLACE FOR PEOPLE TO *LIVE?*
IT *IS* PRETTY AWFUL!
NOW THAT'S A PLAYGROUND FOR THOSE KIDS! HOW DOES THAT GRAB YOU?
IT MAKES ME SICK!
I AGREE WITH YOU THAT THERE IS TOO MUCH MISERY IN THE WORLD!
BUT I DON'T SEE HOW DISBANDING THE ARCHIES IS GOING TO *CURE* IT!
I DIDN'T SAY IT *WOULD* CURE IT!
3

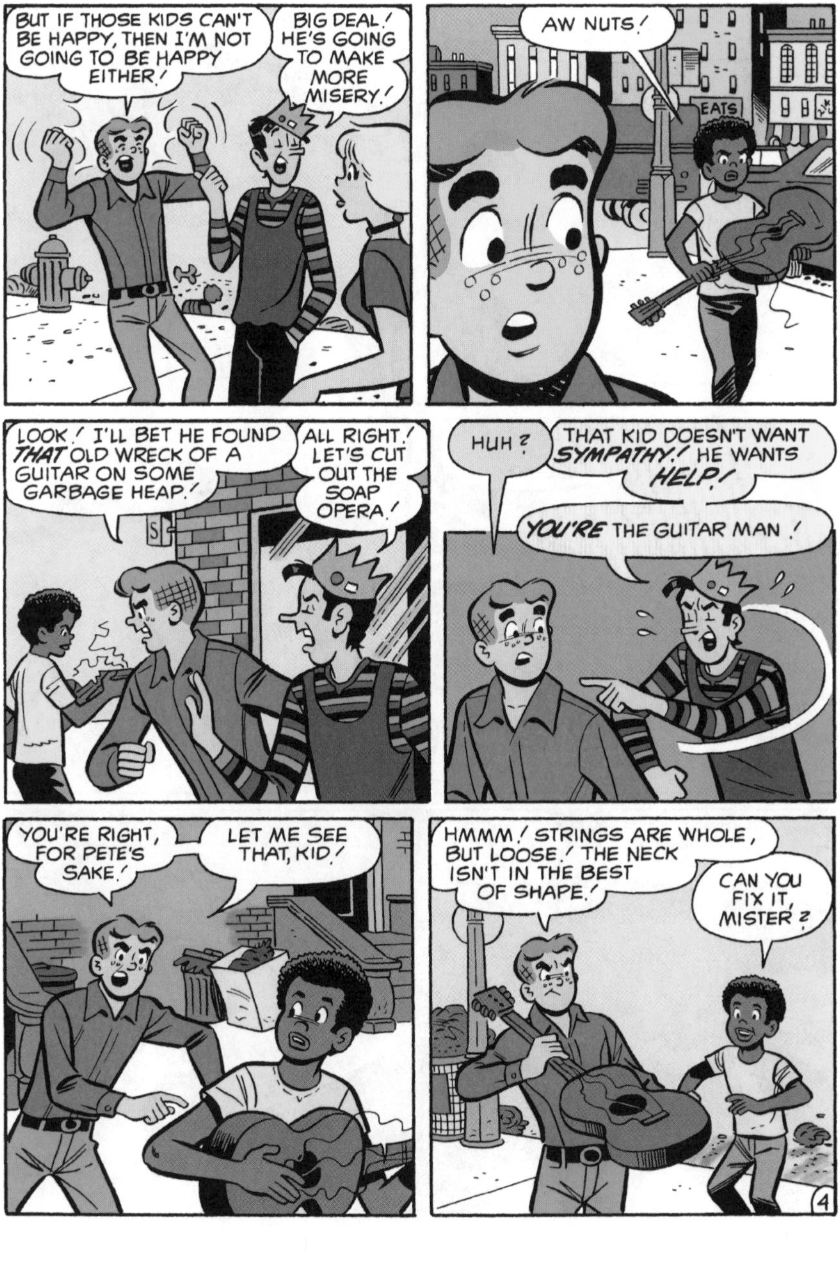
BUT IF THOSE KIDS CAN'T BE HAPPY, THEN I'M NOT GOING TO BE HAPPY EITHER!
BIG DEAL! HE'S GOING TO MAKE MORE MISERY!
AW NUTS!
EATS
LOOK! I'LL BET HE FOUND THAT OLD WRECK OF A GUITAR ON SOME GARBAGE HEAP!
ALL RIGHT! LET'S CUT OUT THE SOAP OPERA!
HUH?
THAT KID DOESN'T WANT SYMPATHY! HE WANTS HELP!
YOU'RE THE GUITAR MAN!
YOU'RE RIGHT, FOR PETE'S SAKE!
LET ME SEE THAT, KID!
HMMM! STRINGS ARE WHOLE, BUT LOOSE! THE NECK ISN'T IN THE BEST OF SHAPE!
CAN YOU FIX IT, MISTER?
4

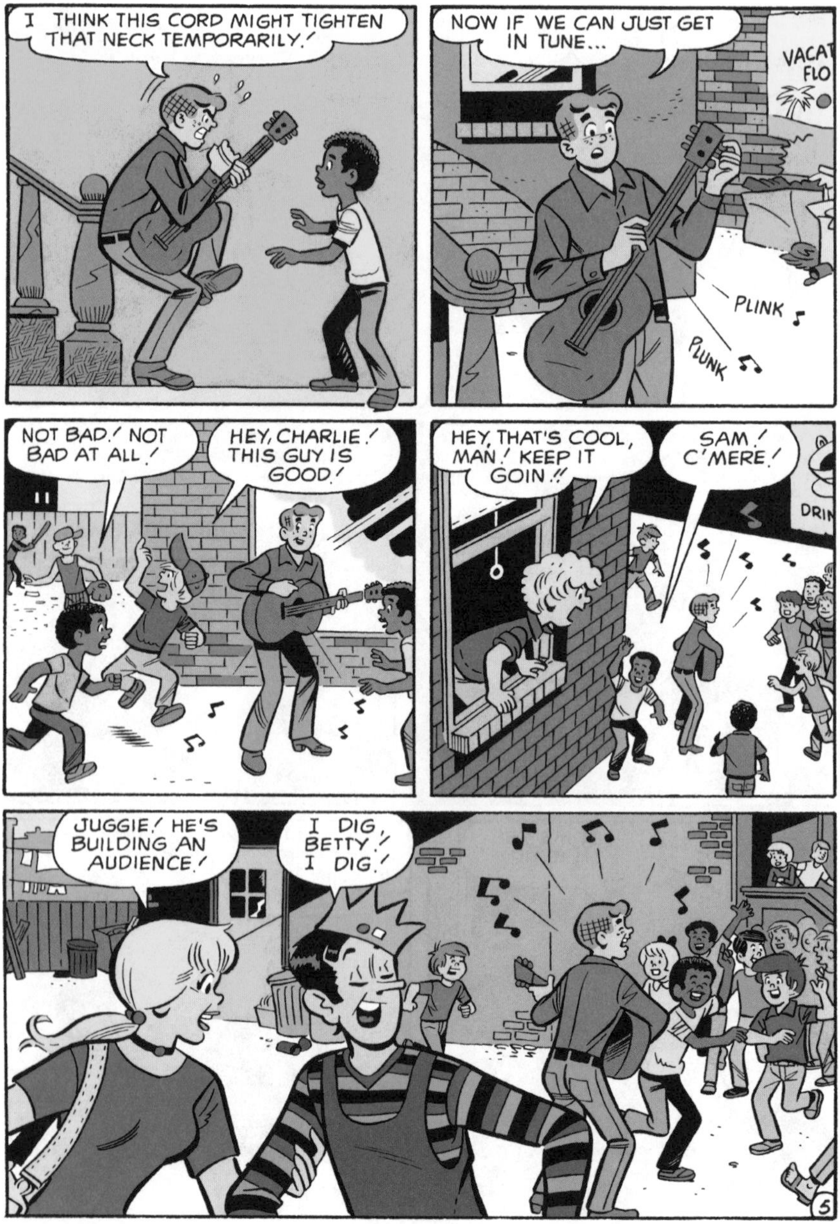
I THINK THIS CORD MIGHT TIGHTEN THAT NECK TEMPORARILY!
NOW IF WE CAN JUST GET IN TUNE...
VACAT FLO
PLINK
PLUNK
NOT BAD! NOT BAD AT ALL!
HEY, CHARLIE! THIS GUY IS GOOD!
HEY, THAT'S COOL, MAN! KEEP IT GOIN!!
SAM! C'MERE!
DRIN
JUGGIE! HE'S BUILDING AN AUDIENCE!
I DIG, BETTY! I DIG!
5

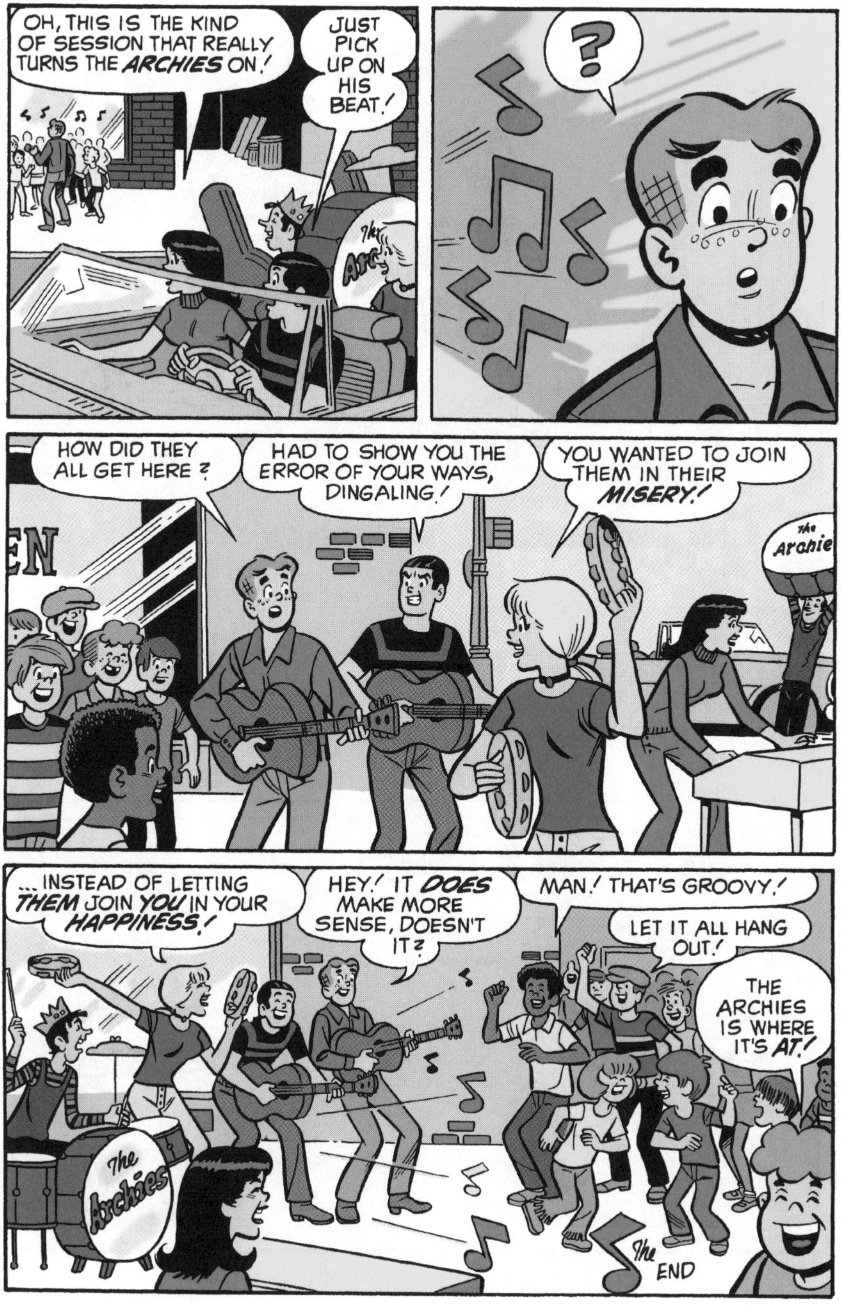
OH, THIS IS THE KIND OF SESSION THAT REALLY TURNS THE *ARCHIES* ON!
JUST PICK UP ON HIS BEAT!
?
HOW DID THEY ALL GET HERE?
HAD TO SHOW YOU THE ERROR OF YOUR WAYS, DINGALING!
YOU WANTED TO JOIN THEM IN THEIR *MISERY!*
...INSTEAD OF LETTING *THEM* JOIN *YOU* IN YOUR *HAPPINESS!*
HEY! IT *DOES* MAKE MORE SENSE, DOESN'T IT?
MAN! THAT'S GROOVY!
LET IT ALL HANG OUT!
THE ARCHIES IS WHERE IT'S *AT!*
The END

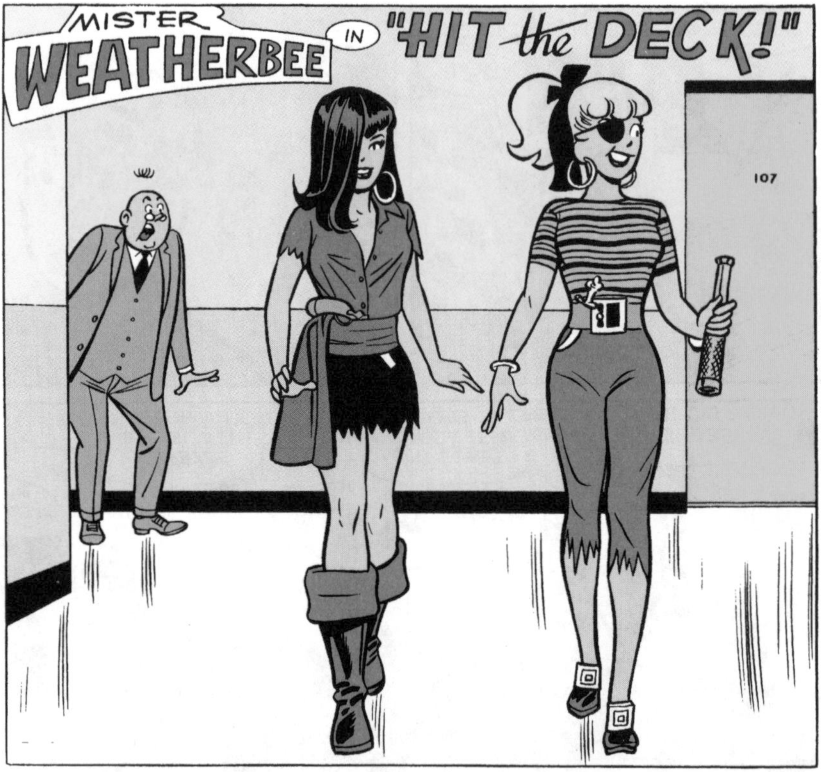
MISTER WEATHERBEE IN "HIT the DECK!"
107

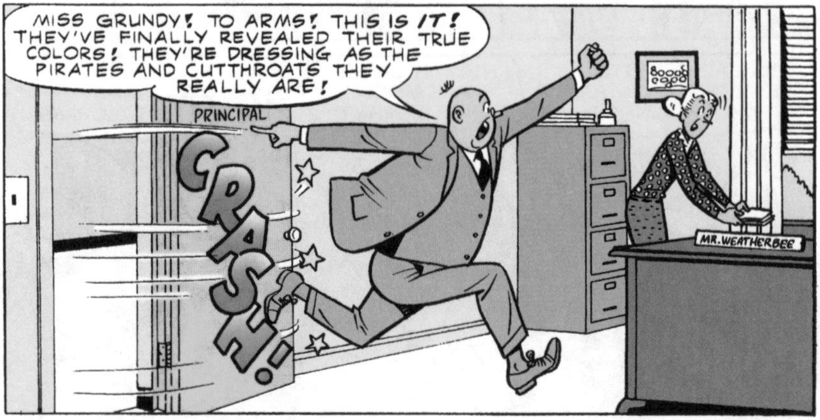
MISS GRUNDY! TO ARMS! THIS IS *IT*! THEY'VE FINALLY REVEALED THEIR TRUE COLORS! THEY'RE DRESSING AS THE PIRATES AND CUTTHROATS THEY REALLY ARE!
PRINCIPAL
CRASH!
MR. WEATHERBEE

Story: Frank Doyle Pencils: Harry Lucey

Originally printed in EVERYTHING'S ARCHIE #12, FEBRUARY 1971

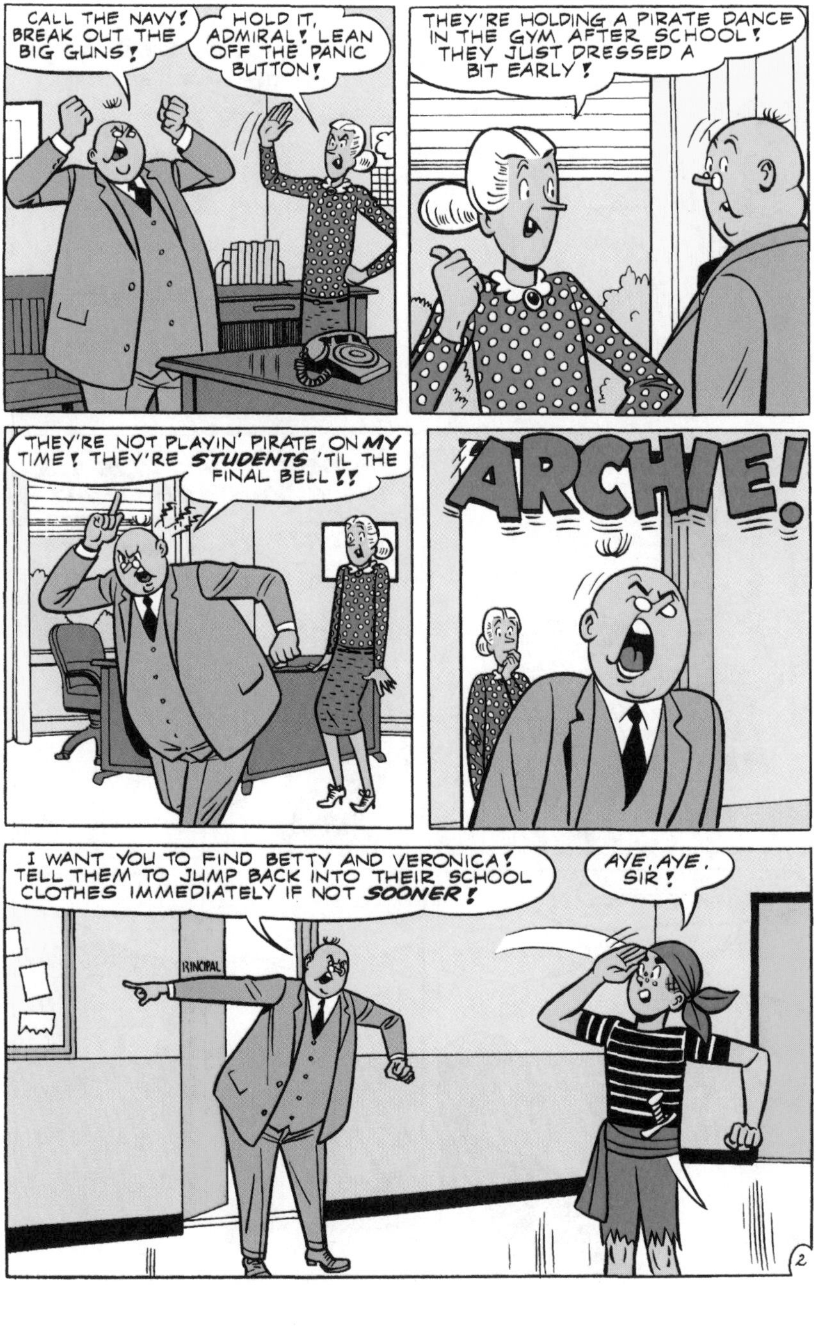
CALL THE NAVY! BREAK OUT THE BIG GUNS!
HOLD IT, ADMIRAL! LEAN OFF THE PANIC BUTTON!
THEY'RE HOLDING A PIRATE DANCE IN THE GYM AFTER SCHOOL! THEY JUST DRESSED A BIT EARLY!
THEY'RE NOT PLAYIN' PIRATE ON MY TIME! THEY'RE STUDENTS 'TIL THE FINAL BELL!!
ARCHIE!
I WANT YOU TO FIND BETTY AND VERONICA! TELL THEM TO JUMP BACK INTO THEIR SCHOOL CLOTHES IMMEDIATELY IF NOT SOONER!
AYE, AYE, SIR!
RINCIPAL
2

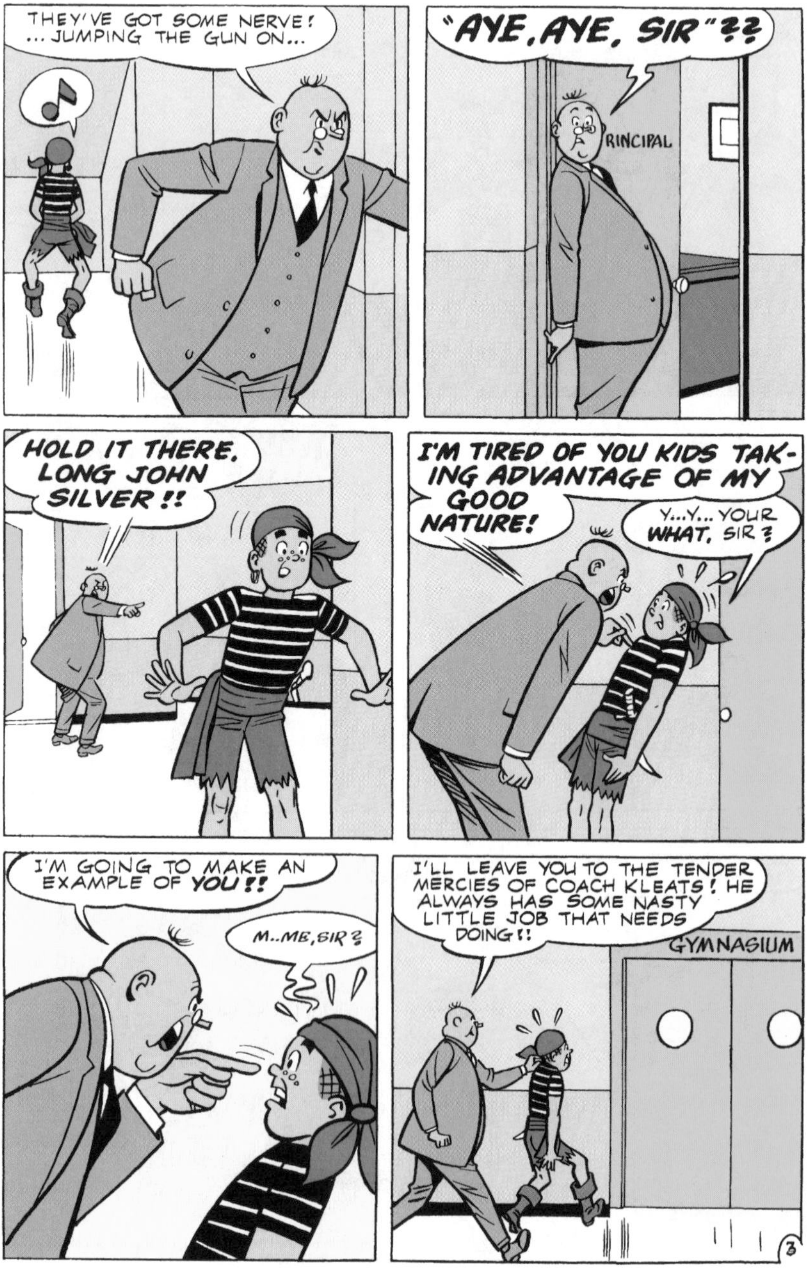
THEY'VE GOT SOME NERVE! ... JUMPING THE GUN ON...
"AYE, AYE, SIR"??
RINCIPAL
HOLD IT THERE, LONG JOHN SILVER!!
I'M TIRED OF YOU KIDS TAKING ADVANTAGE OF MY GOOD NATURE!
Y...Y... YOUR WHAT, SIR?
I'M GOING TO MAKE AN EXAMPLE OF YOU!!
M...ME, SIR?
I'LL LEAVE YOU TO THE TENDER MERCIES OF COACH KLEATS! HE ALWAYS HAS SOME NASTY LITTLE JOB THAT NEEDS DOING!!
GYMNASIUM
3

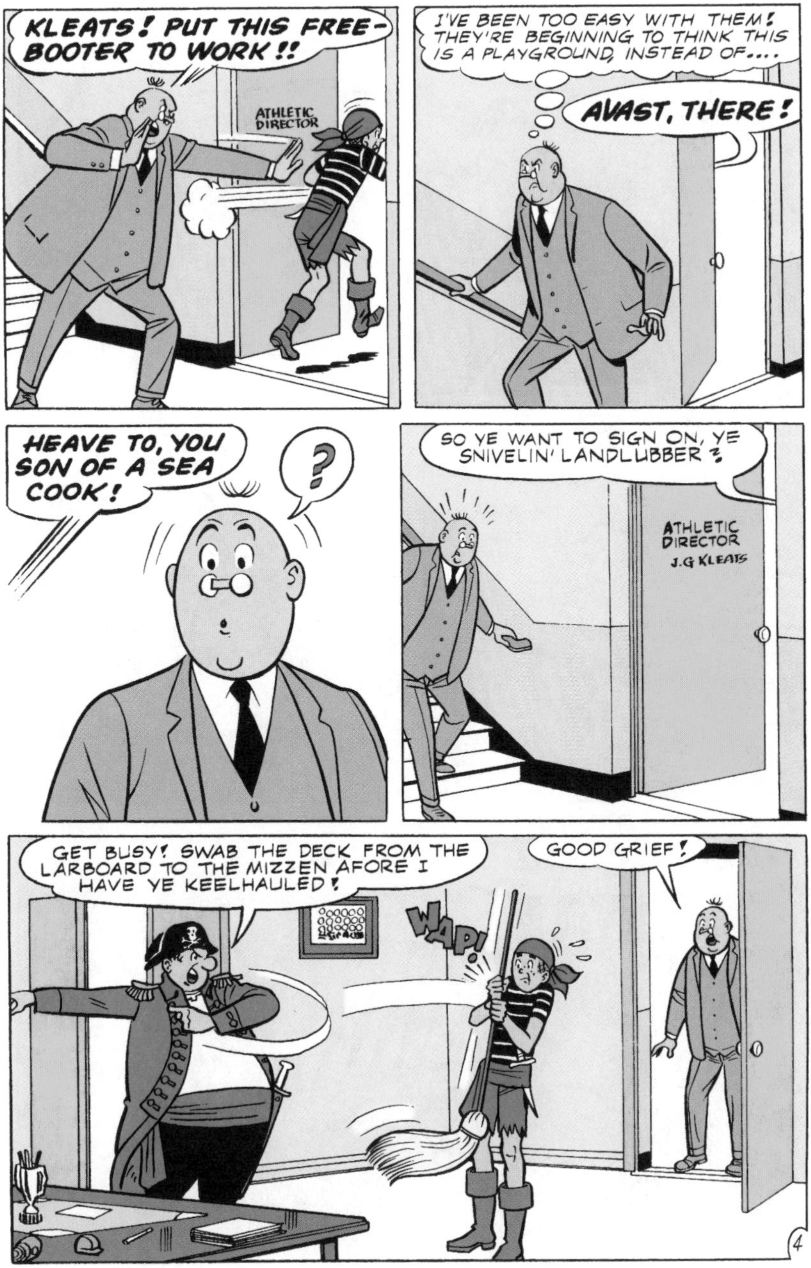
KLEATS! PUT THIS FREE-BOOTER TO WORK!!
ATHLETIC DIRECTOR
I'VE BEEN TOO EASY WITH THEM! THEY'RE BEGINNING TO THINK THIS IS A PLAYGROUND, INSTEAD OF....
AVAST, THERE!
HEAVE TO, YOU SON OF A SEA COOK!
?
SO YE WANT TO SIGN ON, YE SNIVELIN' LANDLUBBER?
ATHLETIC DIRECTOR
J.G KLEATS
GET BUSY! SWAB THE DECK FROM THE LARBOARD TO THE MIZZEN AFORE I HAVE YE KEELHAULED!
GOOD GRIEF!
WAP!
4

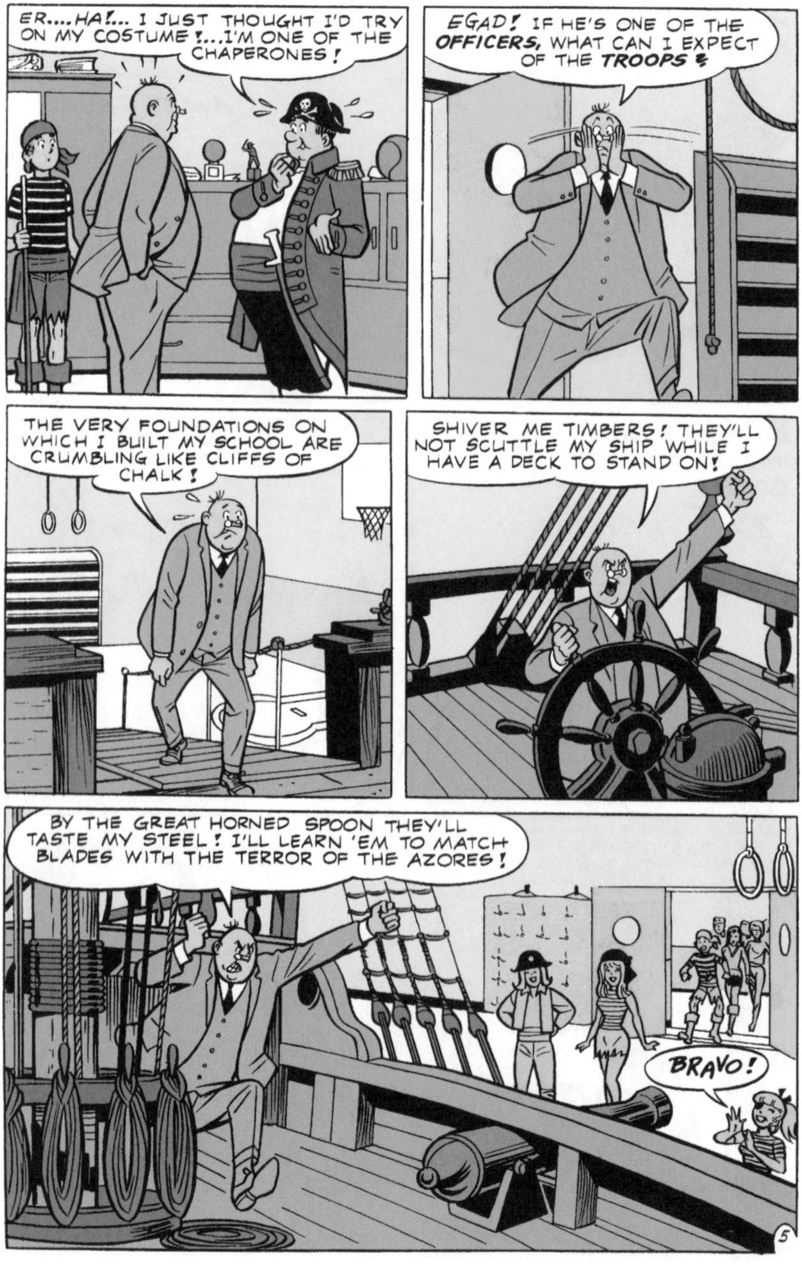
ER....HA!... I JUST THOUGHT I'D TRY ON MY COSTUME!...I'M ONE OF THE CHAPERONES!
EGAD! IF HE'S ONE OF THE OFFICERS, WHAT CAN I EXPECT OF THE TROOPS?
THE VERY FOUNDATIONS ON WHICH I BUILT MY SCHOOL ARE CRUMBLING LIKE CLIFFS OF CHALK!
SHIVER ME TIMBERS! THEY'LL NOT SCUTTLE MY SHIP WHILE I HAVE A DECK TO STAND ON!
BY THE GREAT HORNED SPOON THEY'LL TASTE MY STEEL! I'LL LEARN 'EM TO MATCH BLADES WITH THE TERROR OF THE AZORES!
BRAVO!
5

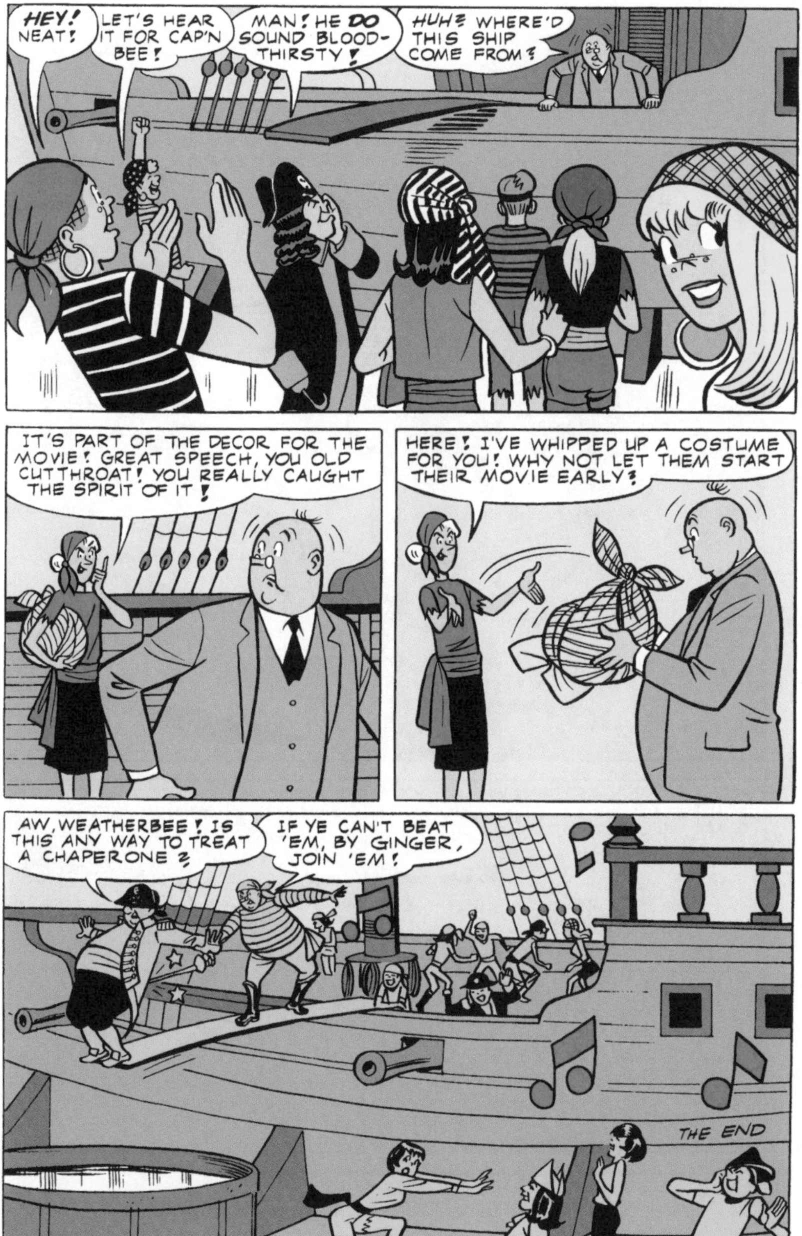
HEY! NEAT!
LET'S HEAR IT FOR CAP'N BEE!
MAN! HE DO SOUND BLOOD-THIRSTY!
HUH? WHERE'D THIS SHIP COME FROM?
IT'S PART OF THE DECOR FOR THE MOVIE! GREAT SPEECH, YOU OLD CUTTHROAT! YOU REALLY CAUGHT THE SPIRIT OF IT!
HERE! I'VE WHIPPED UP A COSTUME FOR YOU! WHY NOT LET THEM START THEIR MOVIE EARLY?
AW, WEATHERBEE! IS THIS ANY WAY TO TREAT A CHAPERONE?
IF YE CAN'T BEAT 'EM, BY GINGER, JOIN 'EM!
THE END

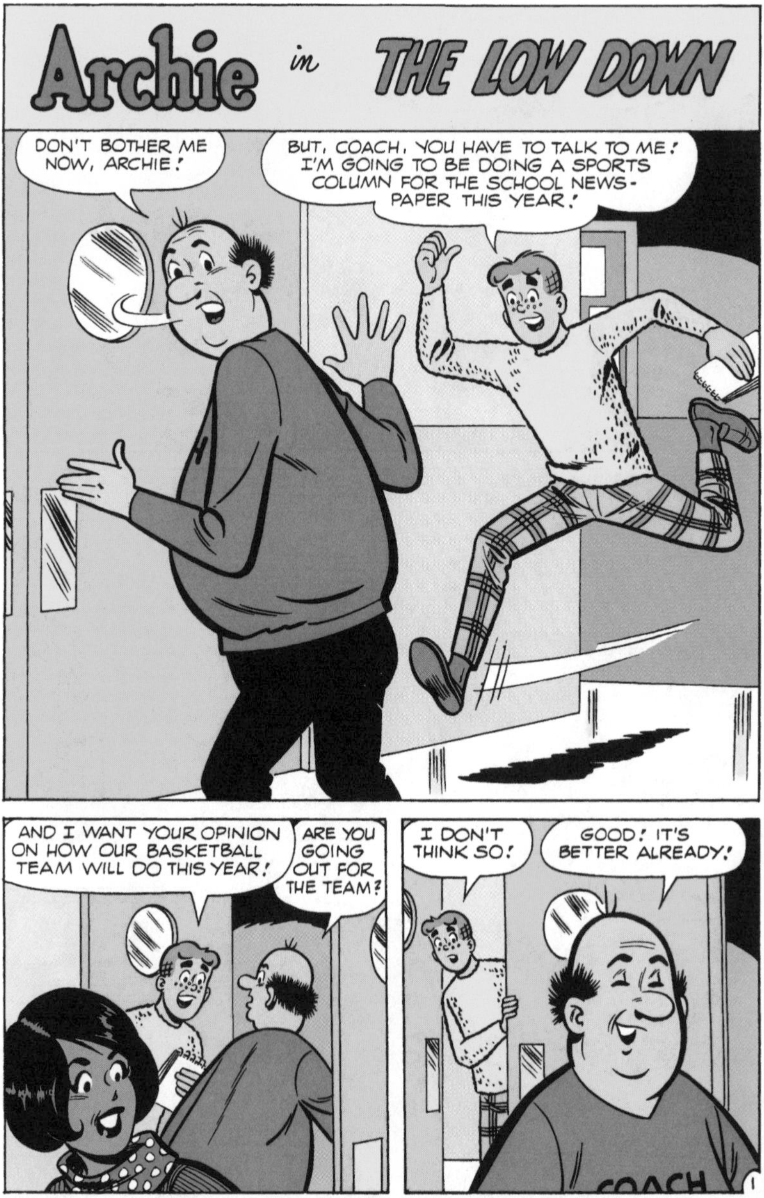
Archie in THE LOW DOWN
DON'T BOTHER ME NOW, ARCHIE!
BUT, COACH, YOU HAVE TO TALK TO ME! I'M GOING TO BE DOING A SPORTS COLUMN FOR THE SCHOOL NEWS-PAPER THIS YEAR!
AND I WANT YOUR OPINION ON HOW OUR BASKETBALL TEAM WILL DO THIS YEAR!
ARE YOU GOING OUT FOR THE TEAM?
I DON'T THINK SO!
GOOD! IT'S BETTER ALREADY!
COACH

Story: George Gladir Pencils: Gus Lemoine
Inks & Letters: Jon D'Agostino Colors: Barry Grossman

Originally printed in EVERYTHING'S ARCHIE #13, APRIL 1971

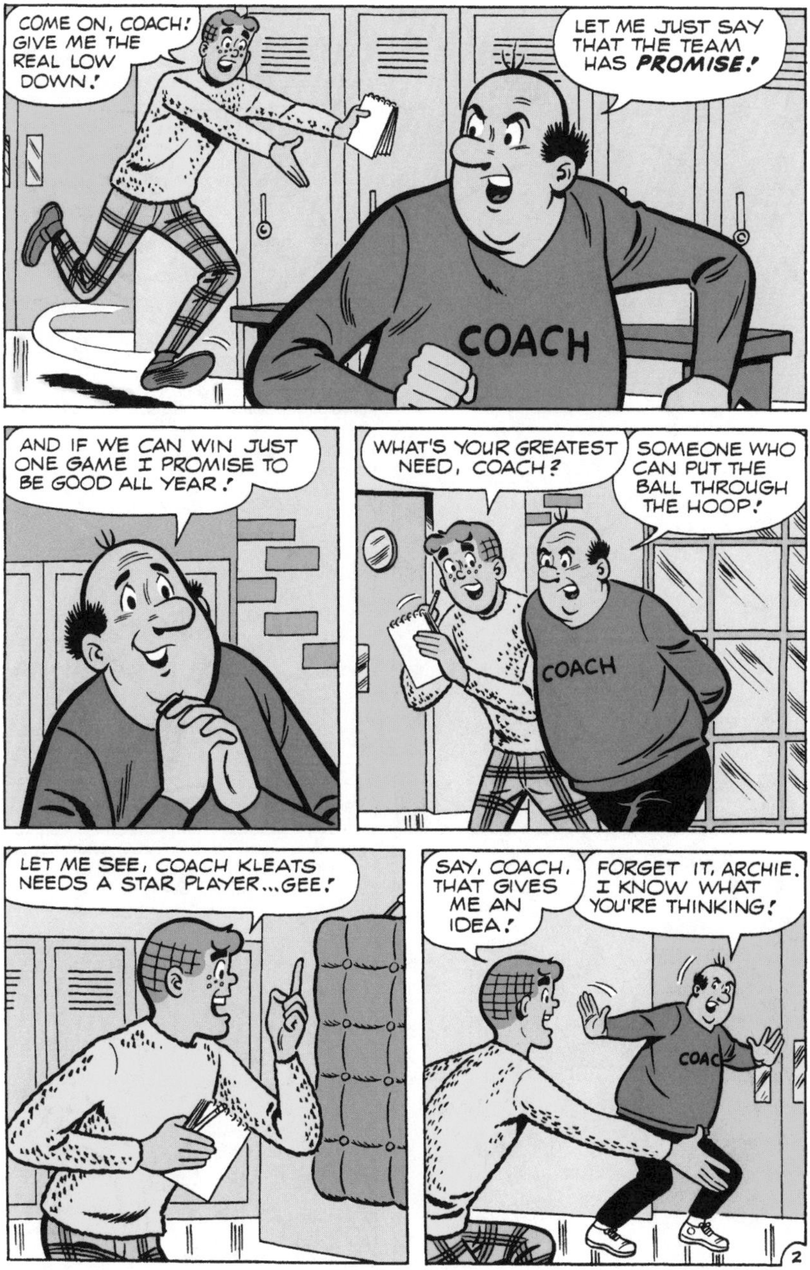
COME ON, COACH! GIVE ME THE REAL LOW DOWN!
LET ME JUST SAY THAT THE TEAM HAS **PROMISE!**
COACH
AND IF WE CAN WIN JUST ONE GAME I PROMISE TO BE GOOD ALL YEAR!
WHAT'S YOUR GREATEST NEED, COACH?
SOMEONE WHO CAN PUT THE BALL THROUGH THE HOOP!
COACH
LET ME SEE, COACH KLEATS NEEDS A STAR PLAYER...GEE!
SAY, COACH, THAT GIVES ME AN IDEA!
FORGET IT, ARCHIE. I KNOW WHAT YOU'RE THINKING!
COAC
2

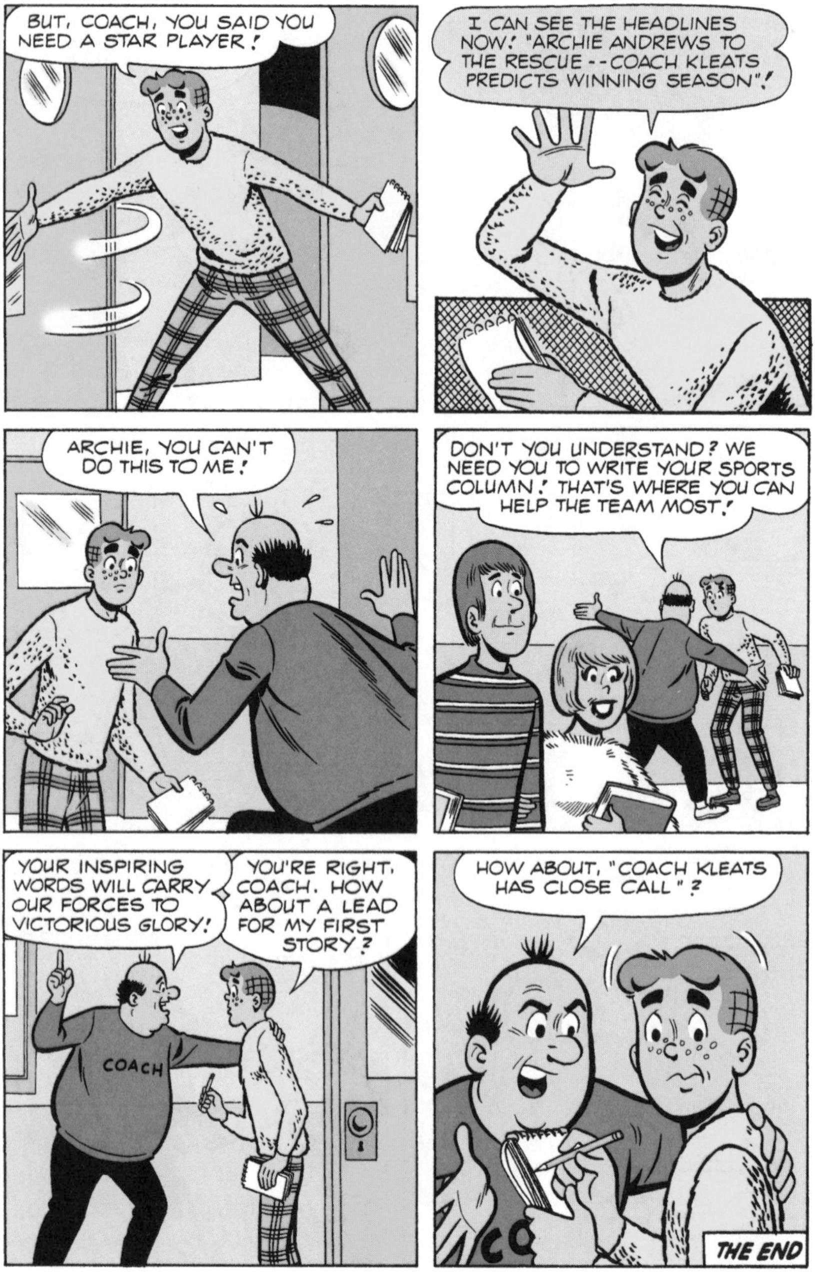
BUT, COACH, YOU SAID YOU NEED A STAR PLAYER!
I CAN SEE THE HEADLINES NOW! "ARCHIE ANDREWS TO THE RESCUE--COACH KLEATS PREDICTS WINNING SEASON"!
ARCHIE, YOU CAN'T DO THIS TO ME!
DON'T YOU UNDERSTAND? WE NEED YOU TO WRITE YOUR SPORTS COLUMN! THAT'S WHERE YOU CAN HELP THE TEAM MOST!
YOUR INSPIRING WORDS WILL CARRY OUR FORCES TO VICTORIOUS GLORY!
YOU'RE RIGHT, COACH. HOW ABOUT A LEAD FOR MY FIRST STORY?
COACH
HOW ABOUT, "COACH KLEATS HAS CLOSE CALL"?
THE END

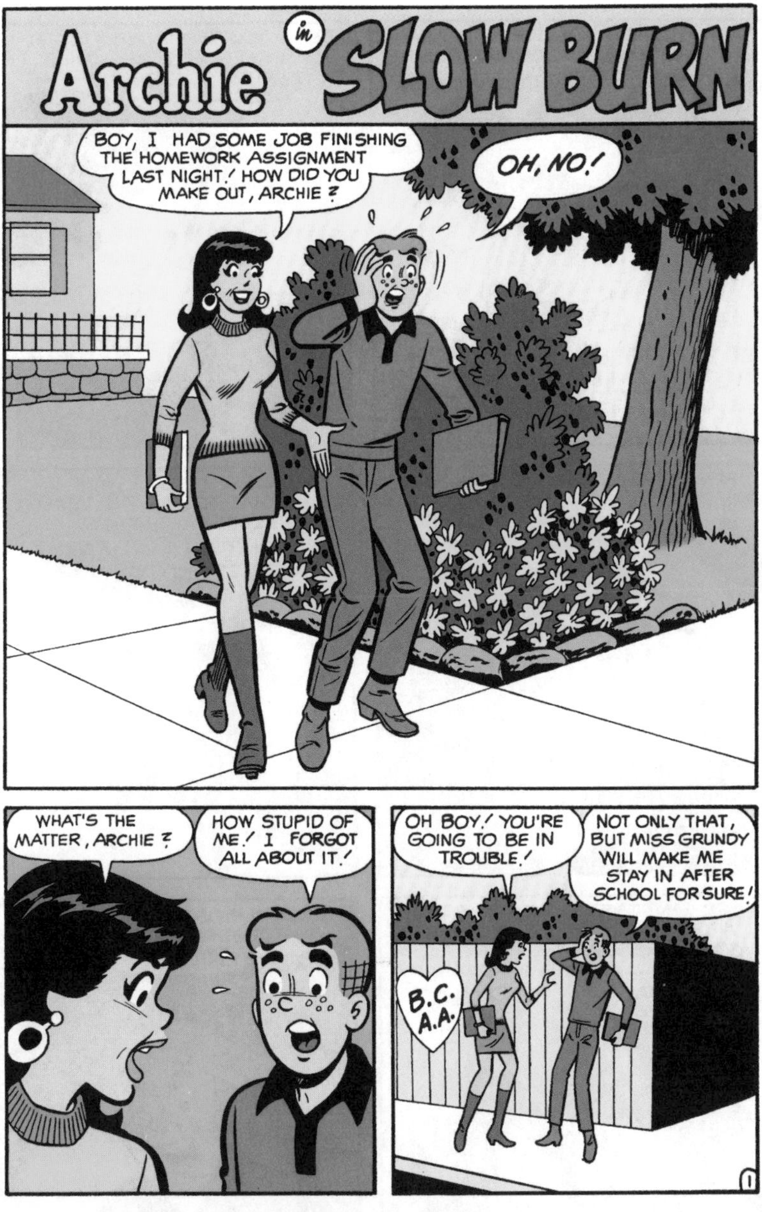
Archie in SLOW BURN
BOY, I HAD SOME JOB FINISHING THE HOMEWORK ASSIGNMENT LAST NIGHT! HOW DID YOU MAKE OUT, ARCHIE?
OH, NO!
WHAT'S THE MATTER, ARCHIE?
HOW STUPID OF ME! I FORGOT ALL ABOUT IT!
OH BOY! YOU'RE GOING TO BE IN TROUBLE!
NOT ONLY THAT, BUT MISS GRUNDY WILL MAKE ME STAY IN AFTER SCHOOL FOR SURE!
B.C. A.A.
1

Story: George Gladir **Pencils:** Bob White
Inks: Jon D'Agostino **Letters:** Bill Yoshida

Originally printed in EVERYTHING'S ARCHIE #13, APRIL 1971

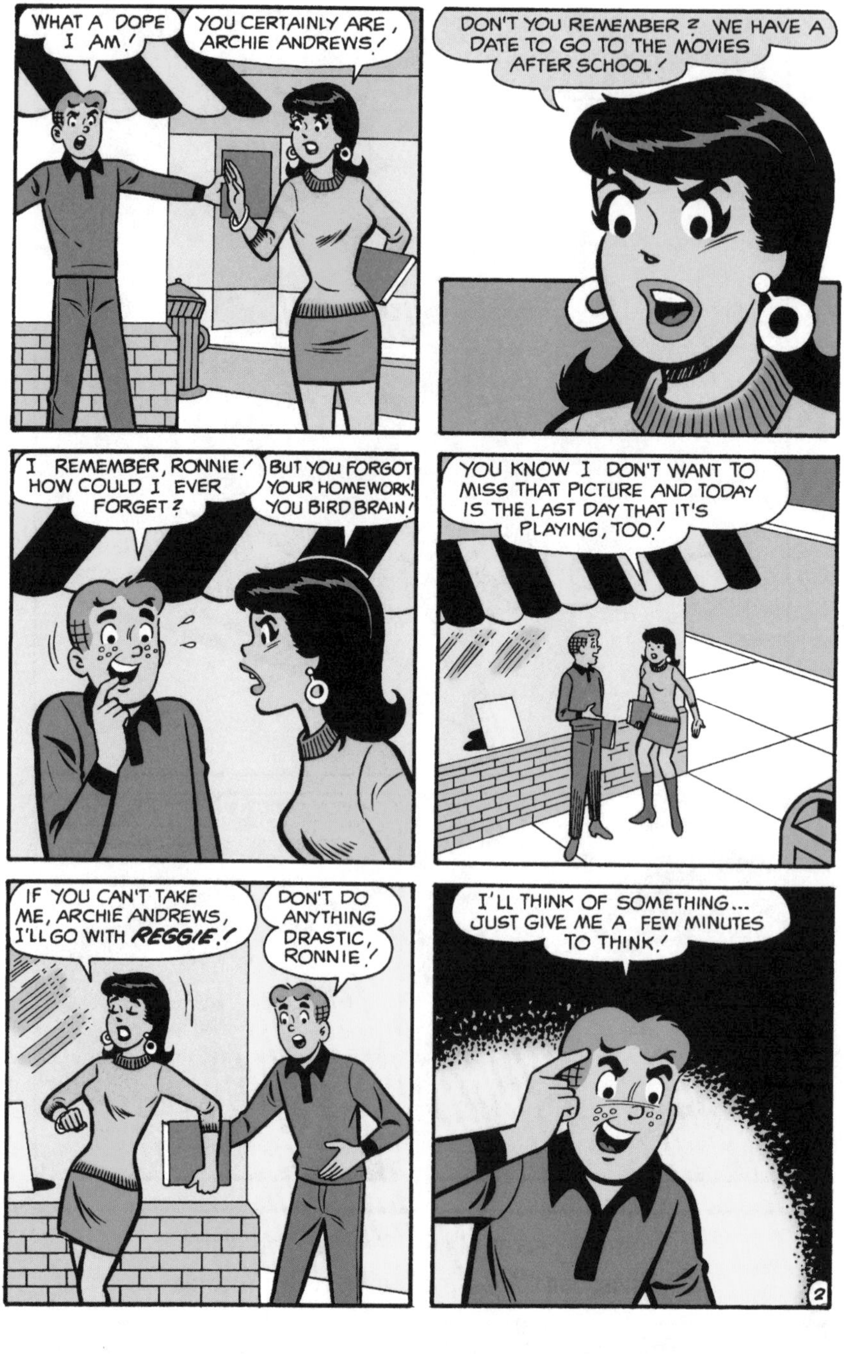
WHAT A DOPE I AM!
YOU CERTAINLY ARE, ARCHIE ANDREWS!
DON'T YOU REMEMBER? WE HAVE A DATE TO GO TO THE MOVIES AFTER SCHOOL!
I REMEMBER, RONNIE! HOW COULD I EVER FORGET?
BUT YOU FORGOT YOUR HOMEWORK! YOU BIRD BRAIN!
YOU KNOW I DON'T WANT TO MISS THAT PICTURE AND TODAY IS THE LAST DAY THAT IT'S PLAYING, TOO!
IF YOU CAN'T TAKE ME, ARCHIE ANDREWS, I'LL GO WITH REGGIE!
DON'T DO ANYTHING DRASTIC, RONNIE!
I'LL THINK OF SOMETHING... JUST GIVE ME A FEW MINUTES TO THINK!
2

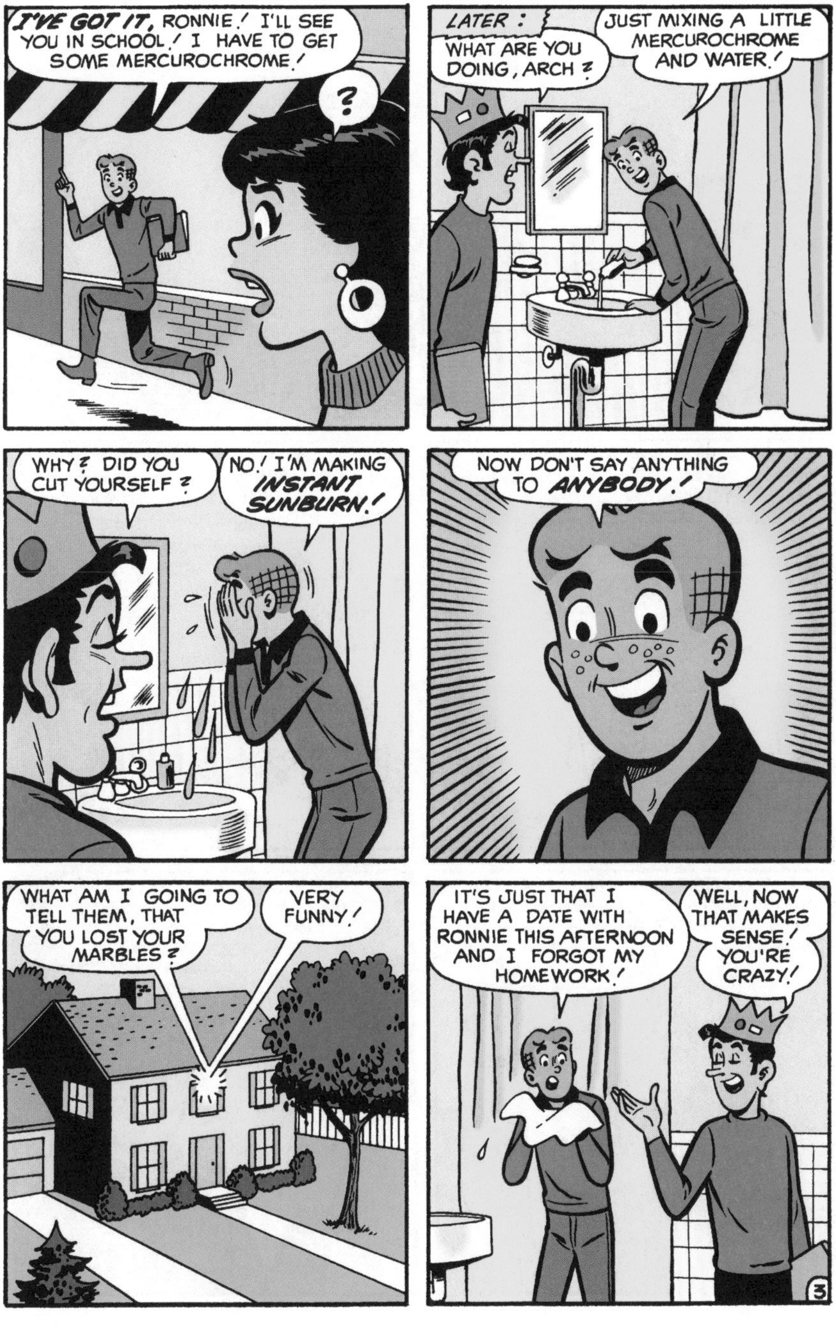
I'VE GOT IT, RONNIE! I'LL SEE YOU IN SCHOOL! I HAVE TO GET SOME MERCUROCHROME!
?
LATER:
WHAT ARE YOU DOING, ARCH?
JUST MIXING A LITTLE MERCUROCHROME AND WATER!
WHY? DID YOU CUT YOURSELF?
NO! I'M MAKING INSTANT SUNBURN!
NOW DON'T SAY ANYTHING TO ANYBODY!
WHAT AM I GOING TO TELL THEM, THAT YOU LOST YOUR MARBLES?
VERY FUNNY!
IT'S JUST THAT I HAVE A DATE WITH RONNIE THIS AFTERNOON AND I FORGOT MY HOMEWORK!
WELL, NOW THAT MAKES SENSE! YOU'RE CRAZY!
3

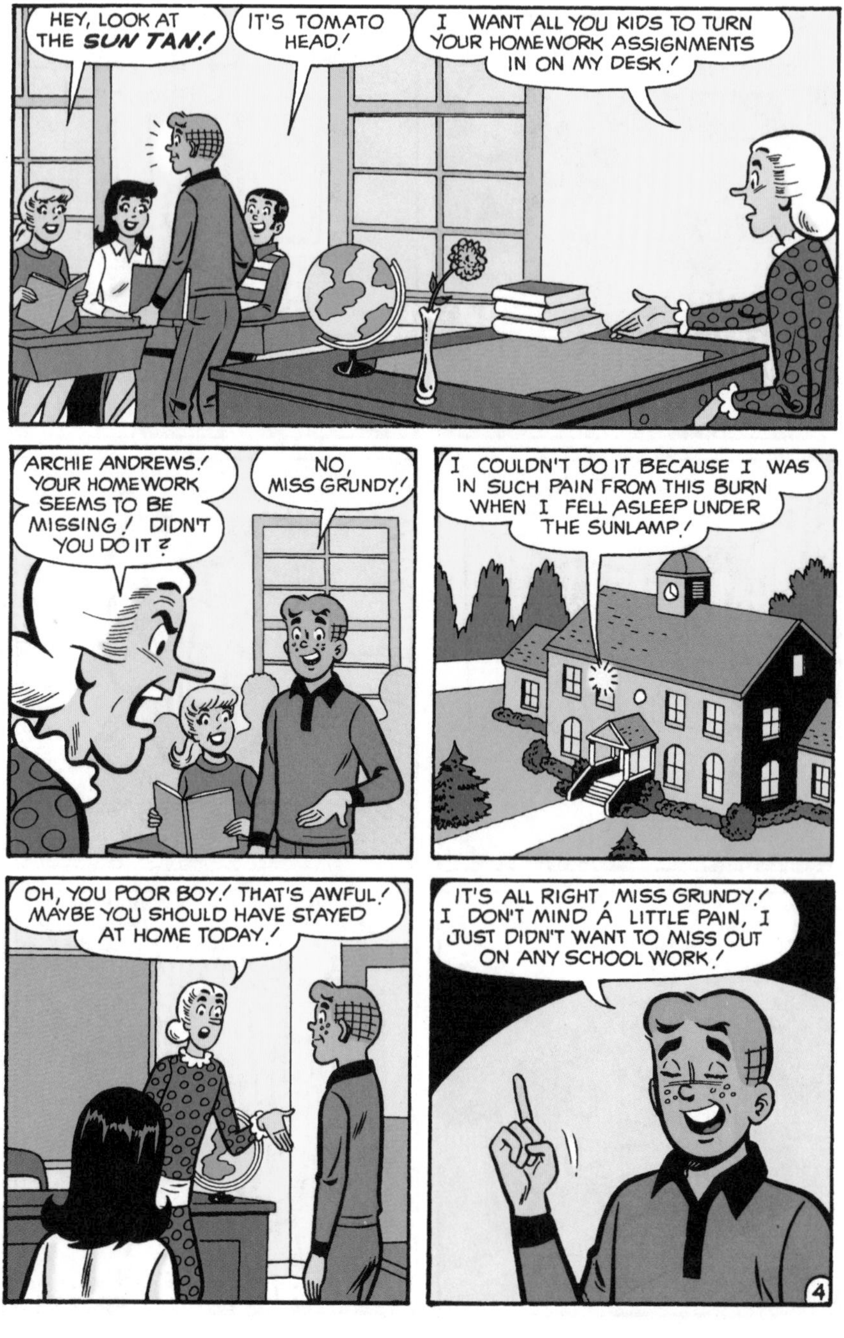
HEY, LOOK AT THE SUN TAN!
IT'S TOMATO HEAD!
I WANT ALL YOU KIDS TO TURN YOUR HOMEWORK ASSIGNMENTS IN ON MY DESK!
ARCHIE ANDREWS! YOUR HOMEWORK SEEMS TO BE MISSING! DIDN'T YOU DO IT?
NO, MISS GRUNDY!
I COULDN'T DO IT BECAUSE I WAS IN SUCH PAIN FROM THIS BURN WHEN I FELL ASLEEP UNDER THE SUNLAMP!
OH, YOU POOR BOY! THAT'S AWFUL! MAYBE YOU SHOULD HAVE STAYED AT HOME TODAY!
IT'S ALL RIGHT, MISS GRUNDY! I DON'T MIND A LITTLE PAIN, I JUST DIDN'T WANT TO MISS OUT ON ANY SCHOOL WORK!
4

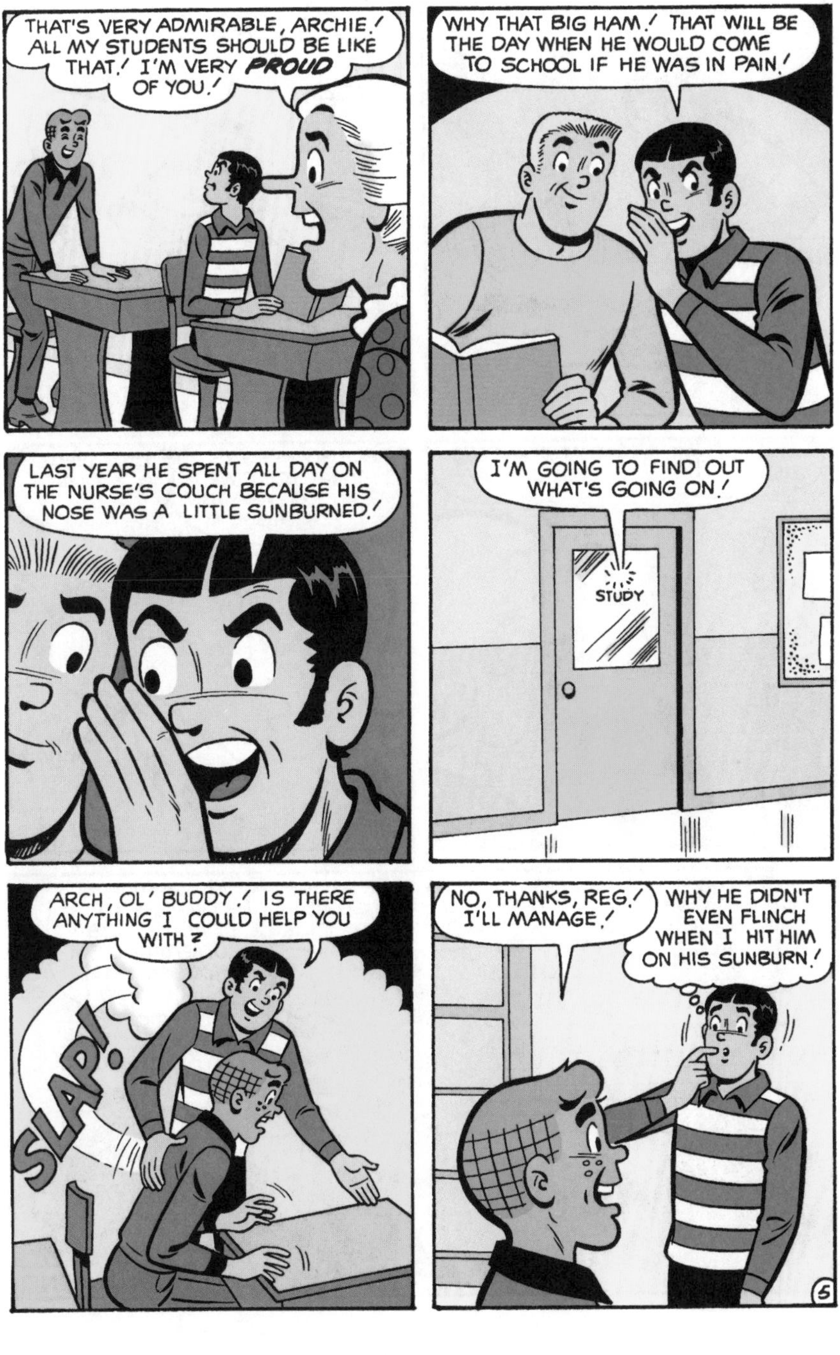
THAT'S VERY ADMIRABLE, ARCHIE! ALL MY STUDENTS SHOULD BE LIKE THAT! I'M VERY PROUD OF YOU!
WHY THAT BIG HAM! THAT WILL BE THE DAY WHEN HE WOULD COME TO SCHOOL IF HE WAS IN PAIN!
LAST YEAR HE SPENT ALL DAY ON THE NURSE'S COUCH BECAUSE HIS NOSE WAS A LITTLE SUNBURNED!
I'M GOING TO FIND OUT WHAT'S GOING ON!
STUDY
ARCH, OL' BUDDY! IS THERE ANYTHING I COULD HELP YOU WITH?
SLAP!
NO, THANKS, REG! I'LL MANAGE!
WHY HE DIDN'T EVEN FLINCH WHEN I HIT HIM ON HIS SUNBURN!
5

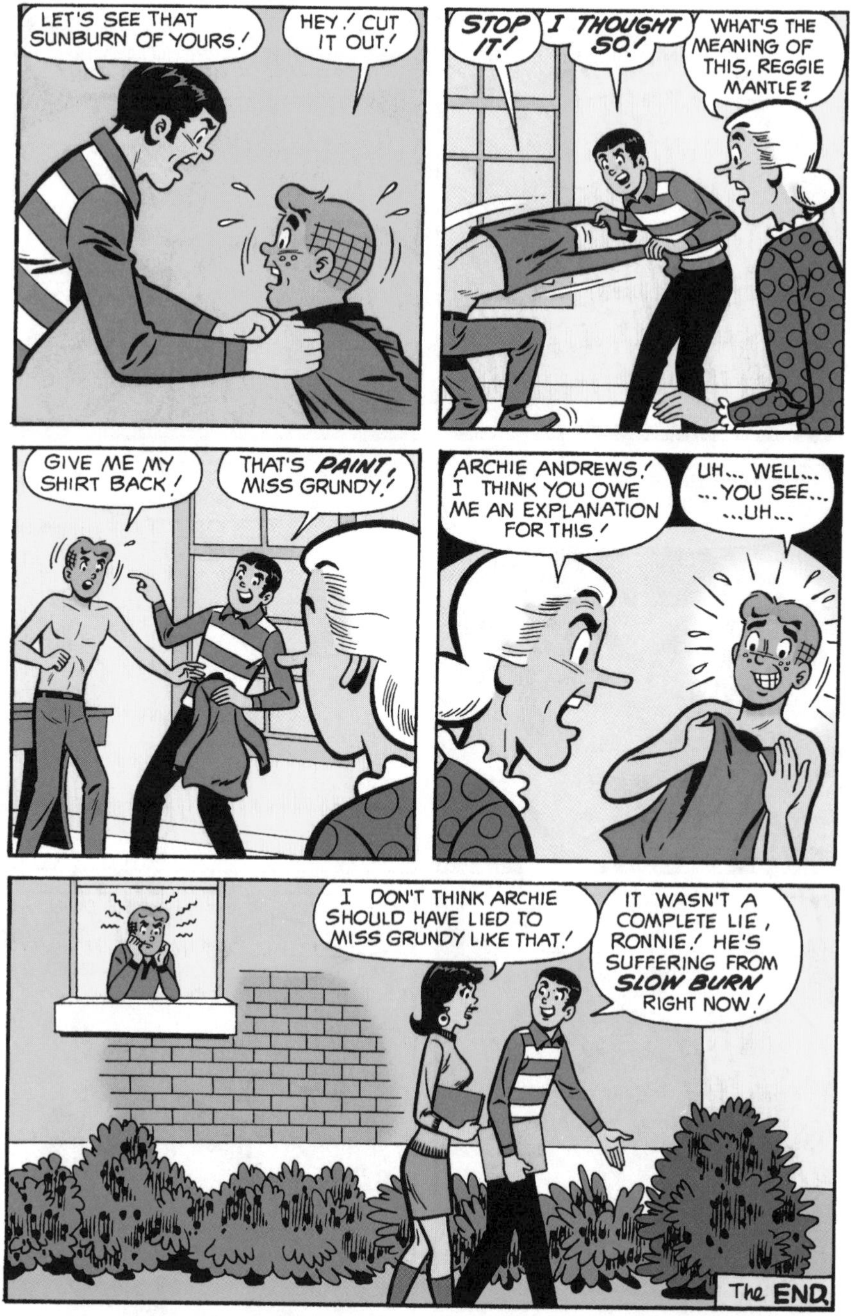
LET'S SEE THAT SUNBURN OF YOURS!
HEY! CUT IT OUT!
STOP IT!
I THOUGHT SO!
WHAT'S THE MEANING OF THIS, REGGIE MANTLE?
GIVE ME MY SHIRT BACK!
THAT'S PAINT, MISS GRUNDY!
ARCHIE ANDREWS! I THINK YOU OWE ME AN EXPLANATION FOR THIS!
UH... WELL... ...YOU SEE... ...UH...
I DON'T THINK ARCHIE SHOULD HAVE LIED TO MISS GRUNDY LIKE THAT!
IT WASN'T A COMPLETE LIE, RONNIE! HE'S SUFFERING FROM SLOW BURN RIGHT NOW!
The END

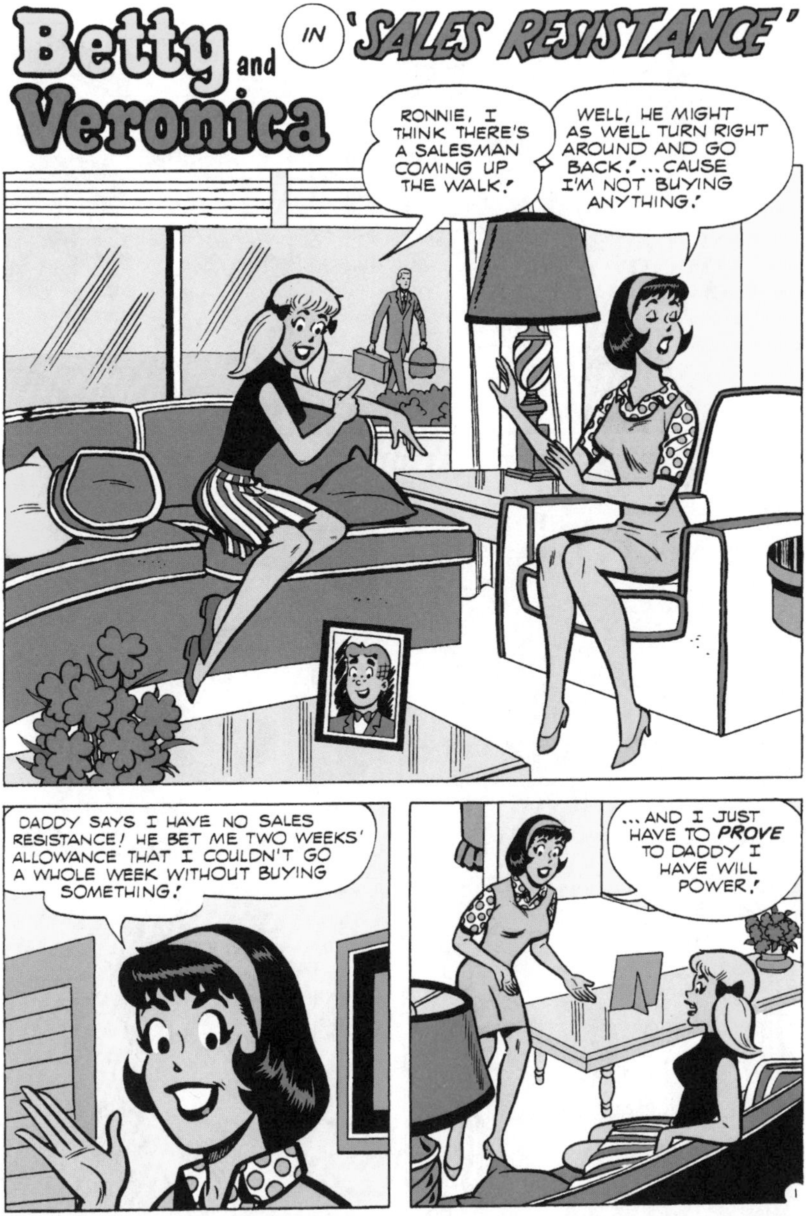
Betty and Veronica
IN 'SALES RESISTANCE'
RONNIE, I THINK THERE'S A SALESMAN COMING UP THE WALK!
WELL, HE MIGHT AS WELL TURN RIGHT AROUND AND GO BACK! ...CAUSE I'M NOT BUYING ANYTHING!
DADDY SAYS I HAVE NO SALES RESISTANCE! HE BET ME TWO WEEKS' ALLOWANCE THAT I COULDN'T GO A WHOLE WEEK WITHOUT BUYING SOMETHING!
...AND I JUST HAVE TO PROVE TO DADDY I HAVE WILL POWER!

Story & Pencils: Al Hartley Inks & Letters: Jon D'Agostino

Originally printed in EVERYTHING'S ARCHIE #13, APRIL 1971

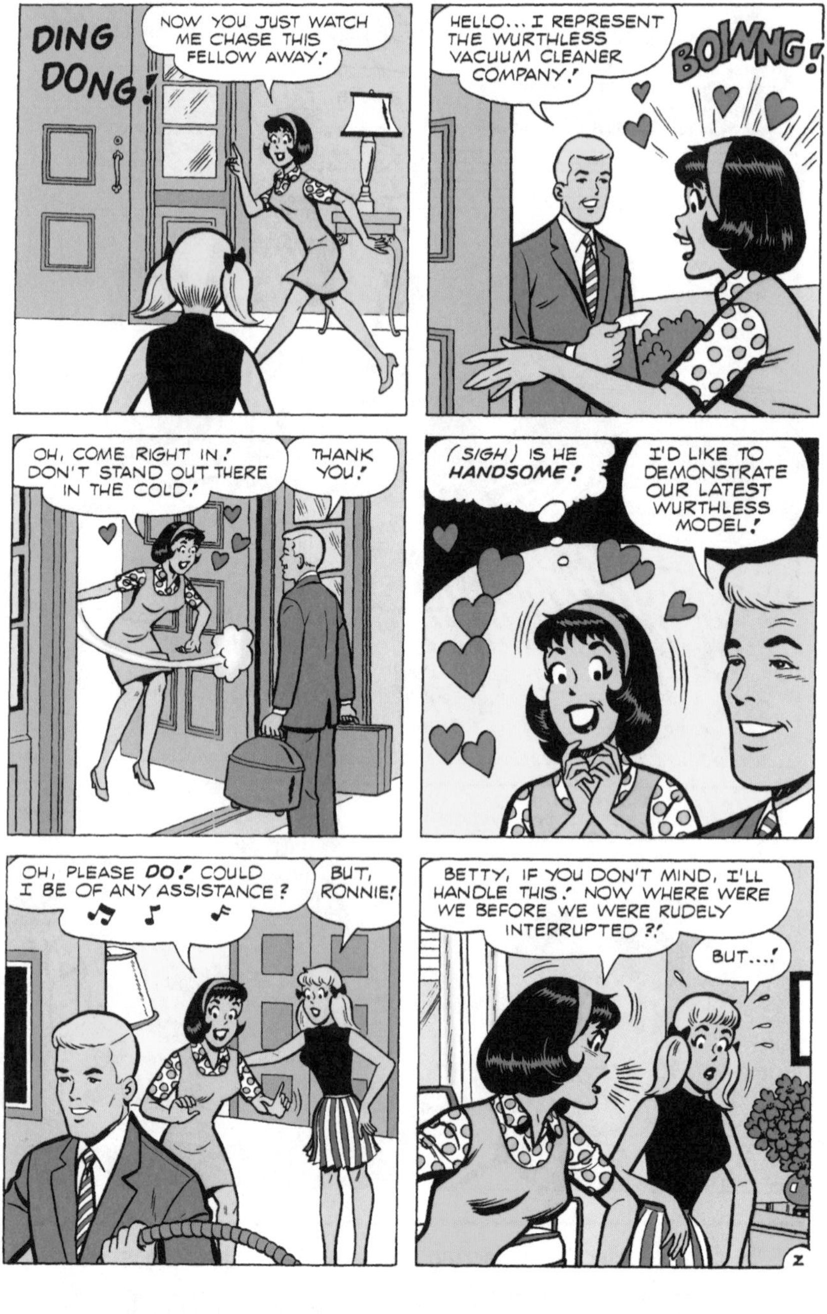
DING DONG!
NOW YOU JUST WATCH ME CHASE THIS FELLOW AWAY!
HELLO... I REPRESENT THE WURTHLESS VACUUM CLEANER COMPANY!
BOIWNG!
OH, COME RIGHT IN! DON'T STAND OUT THERE IN THE COLD!
THANK YOU!
(SIGH) IS HE HANDSOME!
I'D LIKE TO DEMONSTRATE OUR LATEST WURTHLESS MODEL!
OH, PLEASE DO! COULD I BE OF ANY ASSISTANCE?
BUT, RONNIE!
BETTY, IF YOU DON'T MIND, I'LL HANDLE THIS! NOW WHERE WERE WE BEFORE WE WERE RUDELY INTERRUPTED?!
BUT...!
2

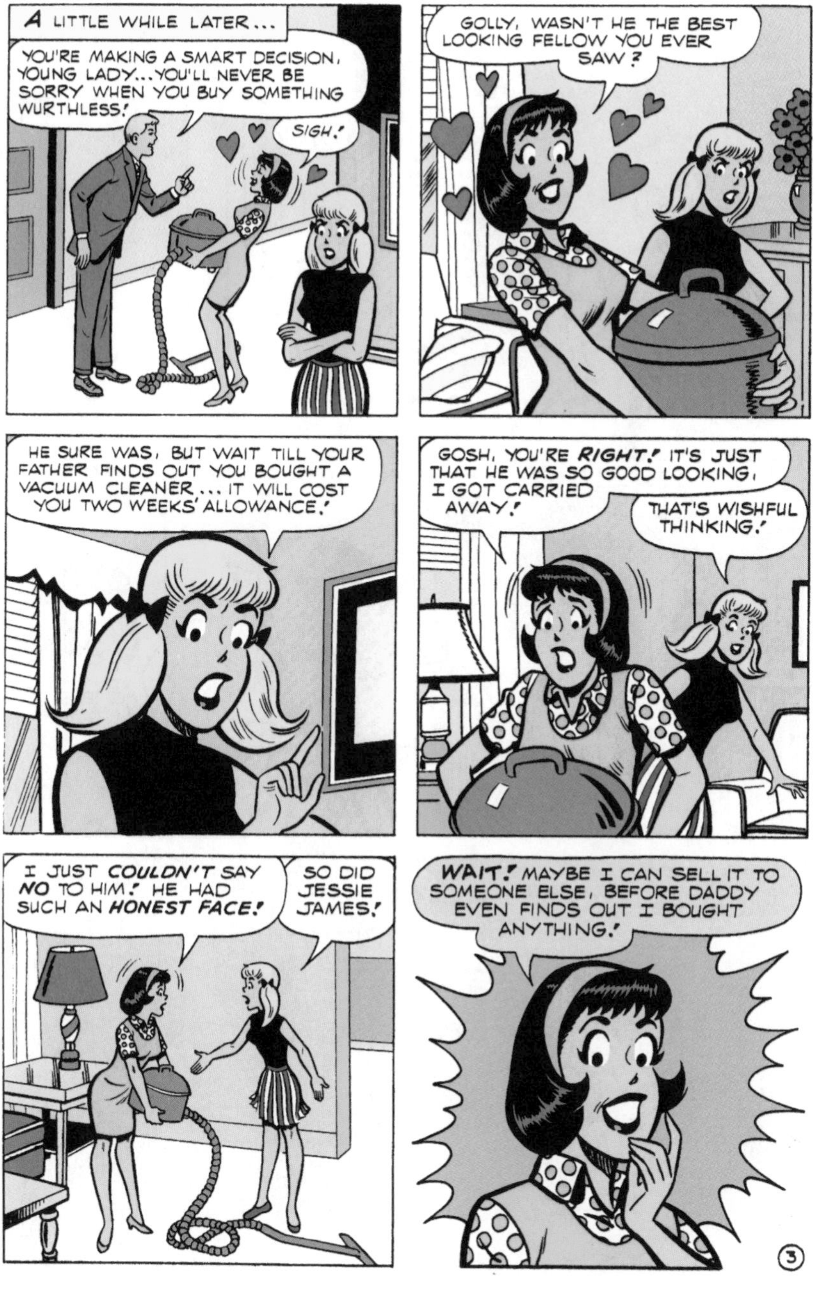
A LITTLE WHILE LATER...
YOU'RE MAKING A SMART DECISION, YOUNG LADY...YOU'LL NEVER BE SORRY WHEN YOU BUY SOMETHING WURTHLESS!
SIGH!
GOLLY, WASN'T HE THE BEST LOOKING FELLOW YOU EVER SAW?
HE SURE WAS, BUT WAIT TILL YOUR FATHER FINDS OUT YOU BOUGHT A VACUUM CLEANER... IT WILL COST YOU TWO WEEKS' ALLOWANCE!
GOSH, YOU'RE RIGHT! IT'S JUST THAT HE WAS SO GOOD LOOKING, I GOT CARRIED AWAY!
THAT'S WISHFUL THINKING!
I JUST COULDN'T SAY NO TO HIM! HE HAD SUCH AN HONEST FACE!
SO DID JESSIE JAMES!
WAIT! MAYBE I CAN SELL IT TO SOMEONE ELSE, BEFORE DADDY EVEN FINDS OUT I BOUGHT ANYTHING!
3

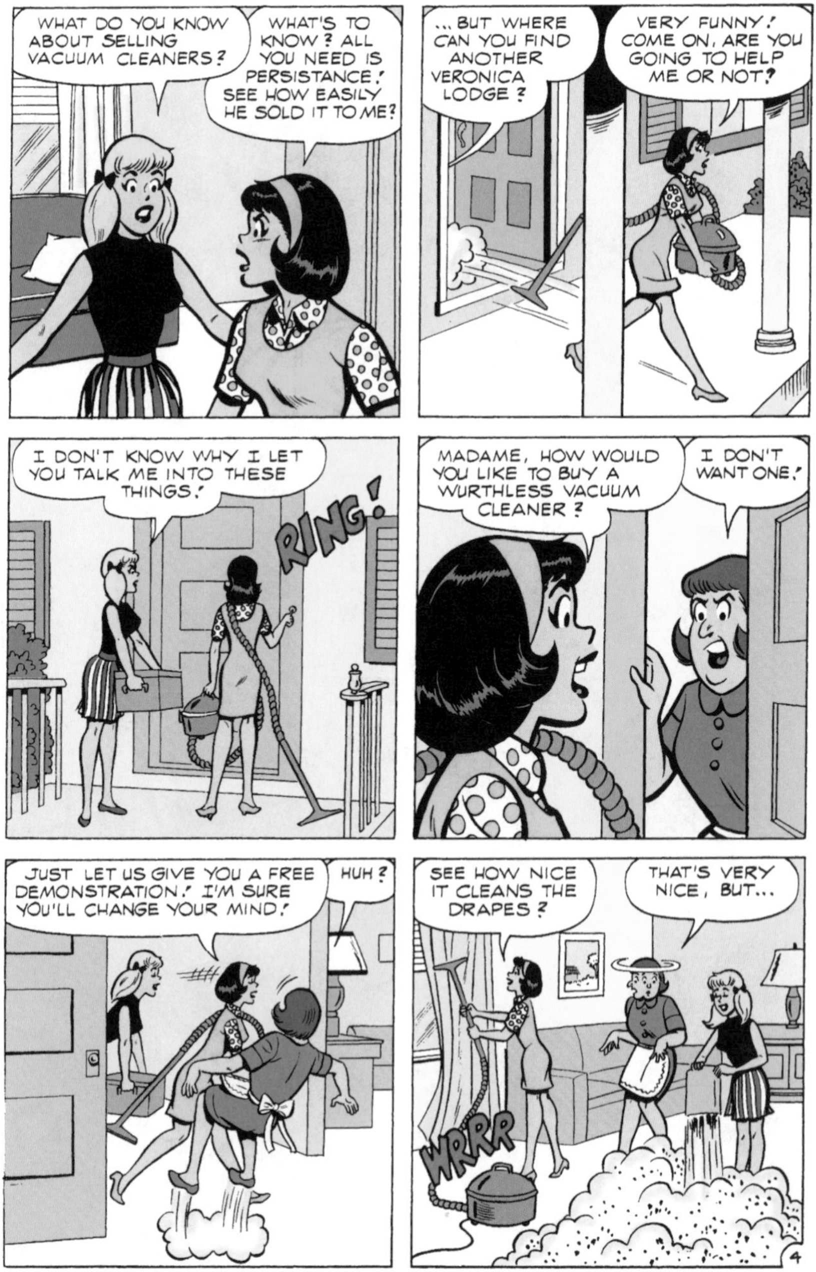
WHAT DO YOU KNOW ABOUT SELLING VACUUM CLEANERS?
WHAT'S TO KNOW? ALL YOU NEED IS PERSISTANCE! SEE HOW EASILY HE SOLD IT TO ME?
...BUT WHERE CAN YOU FIND ANOTHER VERONICA LODGE?
VERY FUNNY! COME ON, ARE YOU GOING TO HELP ME OR NOT?
I DON'T KNOW WHY I LET YOU TALK ME INTO THESE THINGS!
RING!
MADAME, HOW WOULD YOU LIKE TO BUY A WURTHLESS VACUUM CLEANER?
I DON'T WANT ONE!
JUST LET US GIVE YOU A FREE DEMONSTRATION! I'M SURE YOU'LL CHANGE YOUR MIND!
HUH?
SEE HOW NICE IT CLEANS THE DRAPES?
THAT'S VERY NICE, BUT...
WRRR
4

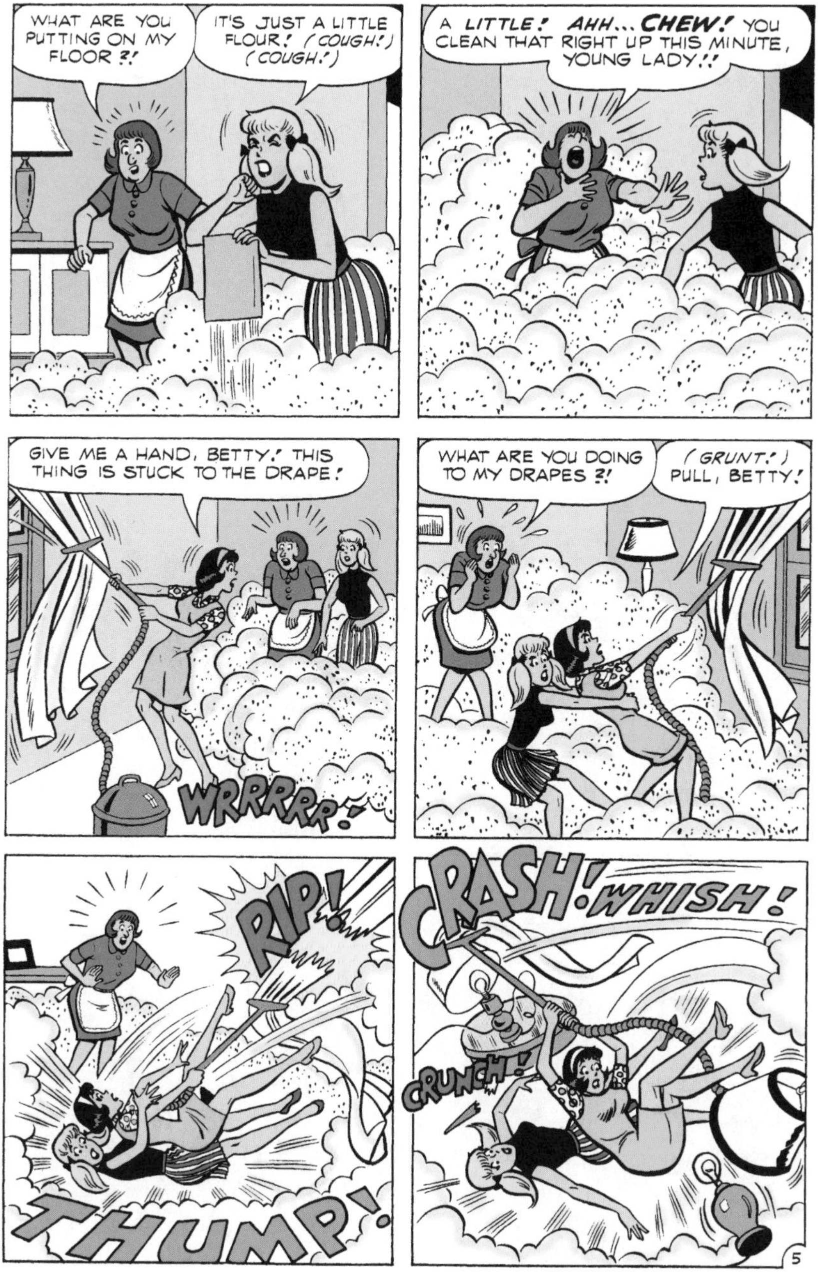
WHAT ARE YOU PUTTING ON MY FLOOR ?!
IT'S JUST A LITTLE FLOUR! (COUGH!) (COUGH!)
A LITTLE! AHH... CHEW! YOU CLEAN THAT RIGHT UP THIS MINUTE, YOUNG LADY!!
GIVE ME A HAND, BETTY! THIS THING IS STUCK TO THE DRAPE!
WRRRRR!
WHAT ARE YOU DOING TO MY DRAPES ?!
(GRUNT!) PULL, BETTY!
RIP!
THUMP!
CRASH! WHISH!
CRUNCH!
5

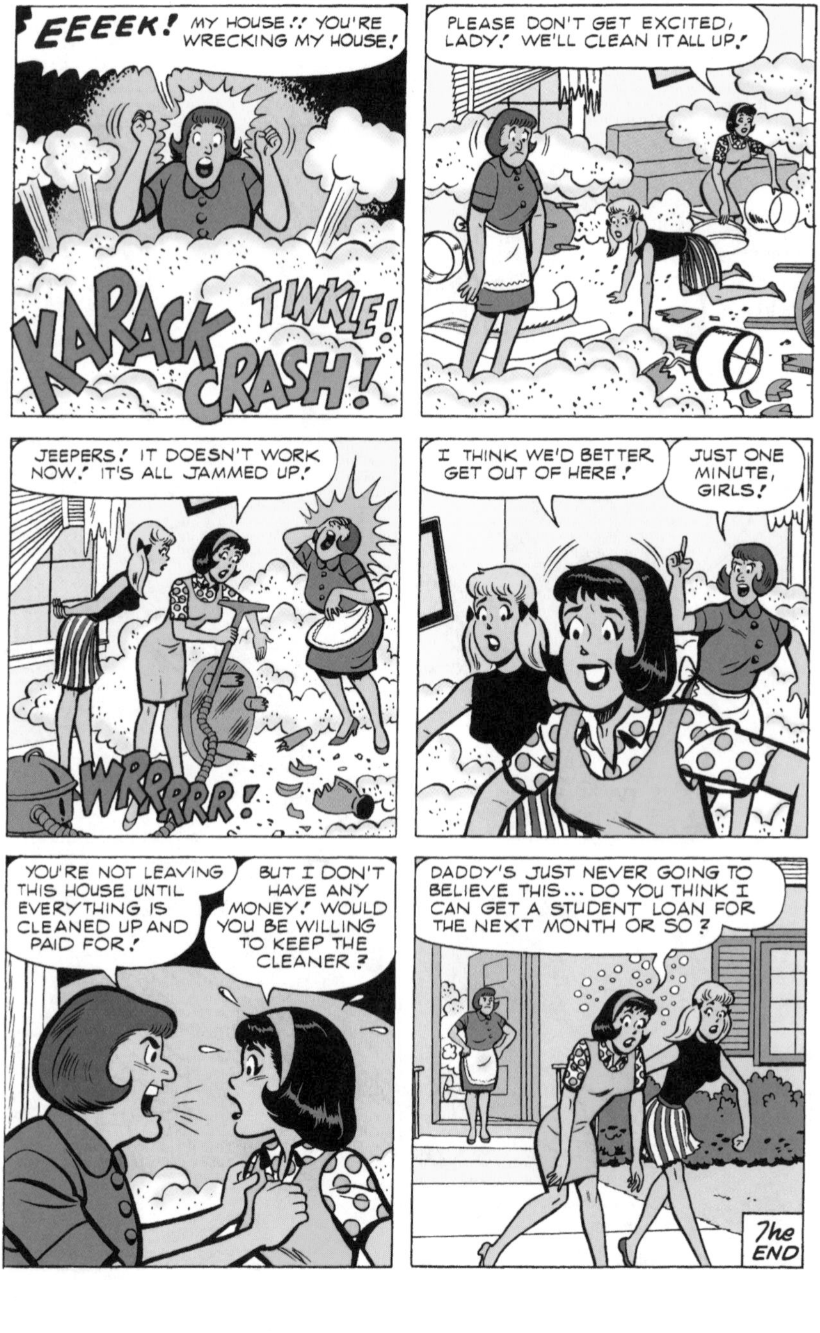
EEEEK! MY HOUSE!! YOU'RE WRECKING MY HOUSE!
KARACK
TINKLE!
CRASH!
PLEASE DON'T GET EXCITED, LADY! WE'LL CLEAN IT ALL UP!
JEEPERS! IT DOESN'T WORK NOW! IT'S ALL JAMMED UP!
WRRRRR!
I THINK WE'D BETTER GET OUT OF HERE!
JUST ONE MINUTE, GIRLS!
YOU'RE NOT LEAVING THIS HOUSE UNTIL EVERYTHING IS CLEANED UP AND PAID FOR!
BUT I DON'T HAVE ANY MONEY! WOULD YOU BE WILLING TO KEEP THE CLEANER?
DADDY'S JUST NEVER GOING TO BELIEVE THIS... DO YOU THINK I CAN GET A STUDENT LOAN FOR THE NEXT MONTH OR SO?
The END

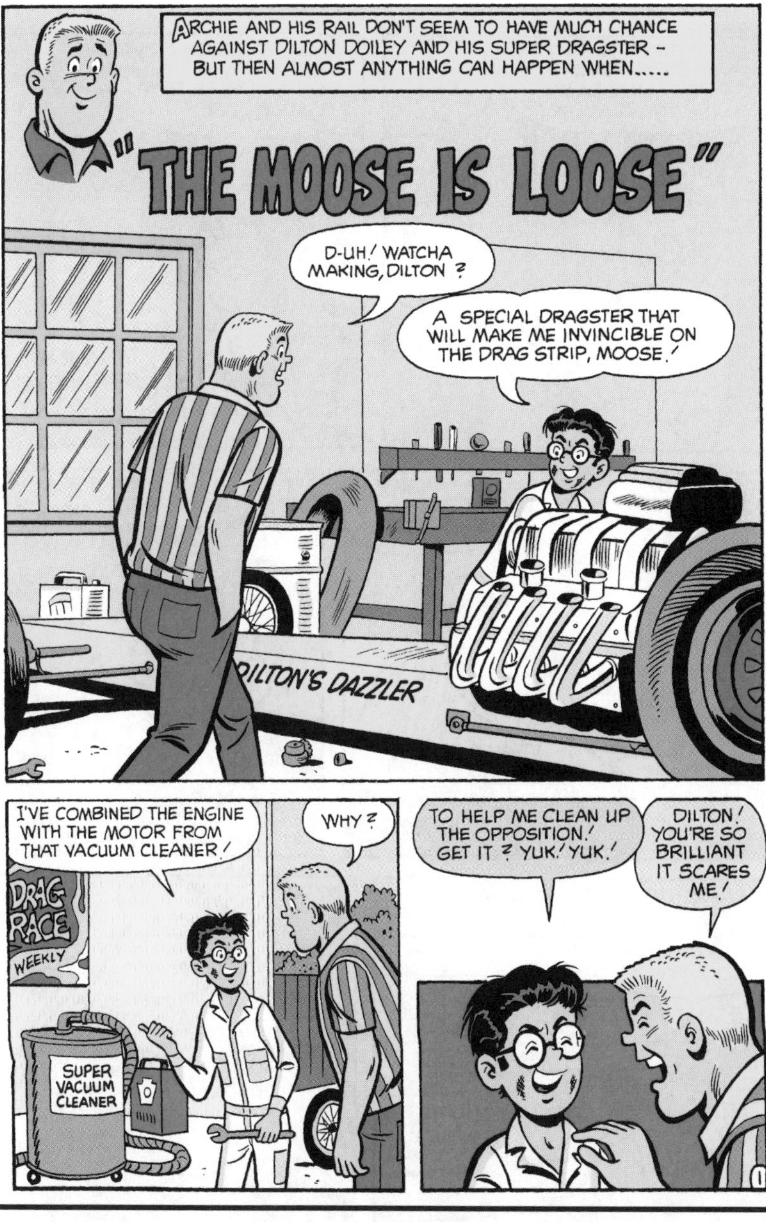
ARCHIE AND HIS RAIL DON'T SEEM TO HAVE MUCH CHANCE AGAINST DILTON DOILEY AND HIS SUPER DRAGSTER – BUT THEN ALMOST ANYTHING CAN HAPPEN WHEN.....
"THE MOOSE IS LOOSE"
D-UH! WATCHA MAKING, DILTON ?
A SPECIAL DRAGSTER THAT WILL MAKE ME INVINCIBLE ON THE DRAG STRIP, MOOSE!
DILTON'S DAZZLER
I'VE COMBINED THE ENGINE WITH THE MOTOR FROM THAT VACUUM CLEANER!
WHY ?
DRAG RACE WEEKLY
SUPER VACUUM CLEANER
TO HELP ME CLEAN UP THE OPPOSITION! GET IT ? YUK! YUK!
DILTON! YOU'RE SO BRILLIANT IT SCARES ME!
1

Story: Frank Doyle Pencils: Gus Lemoine

Inks: Jon D'Agostino Letters: Bill Yoshida Colors: Barry Grossman

Originally printed in EVERYTHING'S ARCHIE #13, APRIL 1971

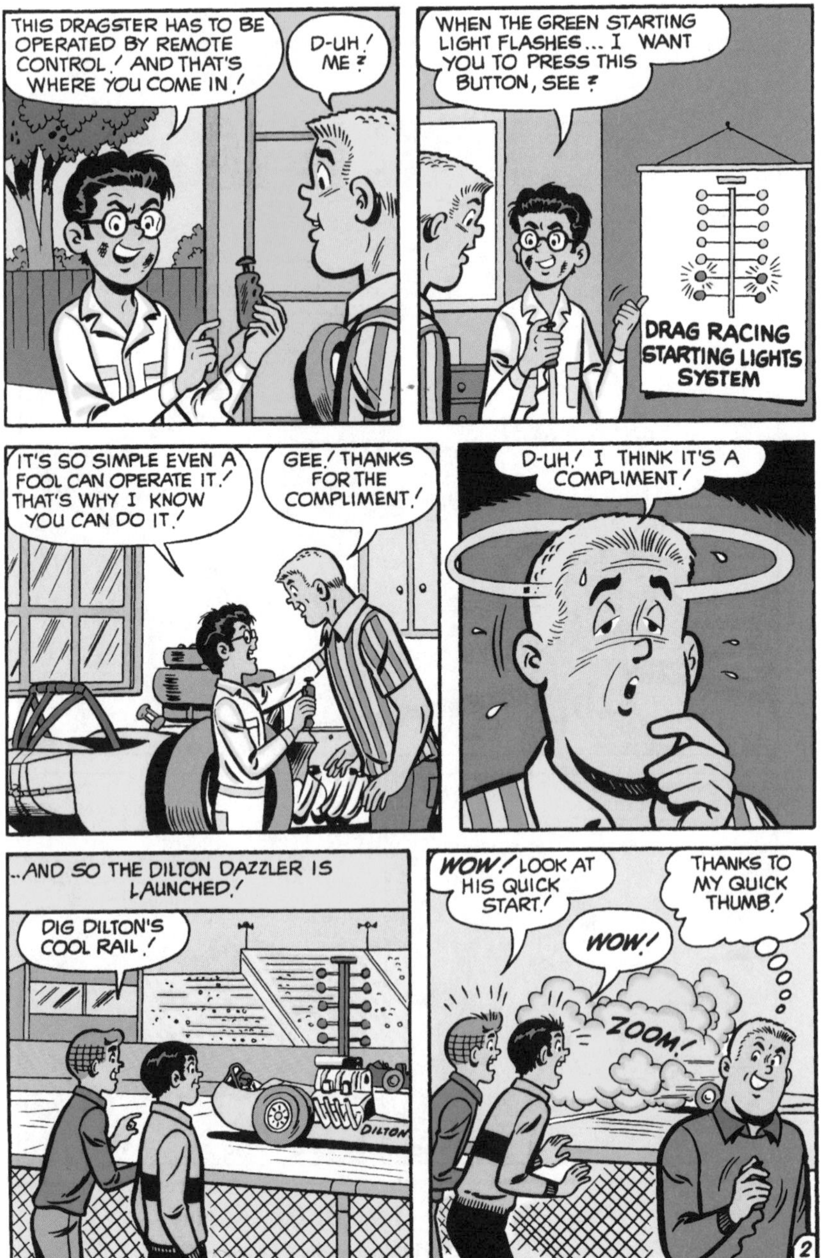
THIS DRAGSTER HAS TO BE OPERATED BY REMOTE CONTROL! AND THAT'S WHERE YOU COME IN!
D-UH! ME?
WHEN THE GREEN STARTING LIGHT FLASHES... I WANT YOU TO PRESS THIS BUTTON, SEE?
DRAG RACING STARTING LIGHTS SYSTEM
IT'S SO SIMPLE EVEN A FOOL CAN OPERATE IT! THAT'S WHY I KNOW YOU CAN DO IT!
GEE! THANKS FOR THE COMPLIMENT!
D-UH! I THINK IT'S A COMPLIMENT!
..AND SO THE DILTON DAZZLER IS LAUNCHED!
DIG DILTON'S COOL RAIL!
DILTON
WOW! LOOK AT HIS QUICK START!
WOW!
THANKS TO MY QUICK THUMB!
ZOOM!
2

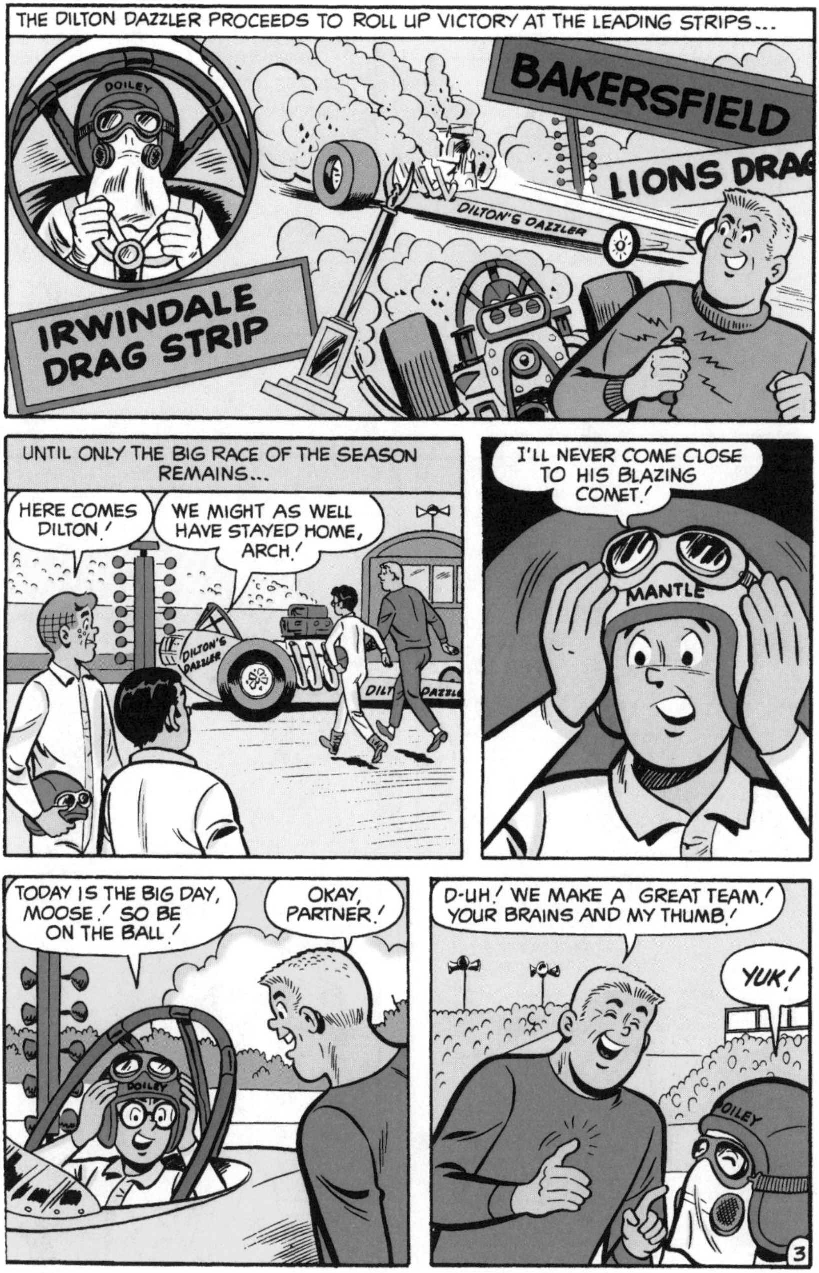
THE DILTON DAZZLER PROCEEDS TO ROLL UP VICTORY AT THE LEADING STRIPS...
DOILEY
BAKERSFIELD
LIONS DRAG
DILTON'S DAZZLER
IRWINDALE DRAG STRIP
UNTIL ONLY THE BIG RACE OF THE SEASON REMAINS...
HERE COMES DILTON!
WE MIGHT AS WELL HAVE STAYED HOME, ARCH!
DILTON'S DAZZLER
I'LL NEVER COME CLOSE TO HIS BLAZING COMET!
MANTLE
TODAY IS THE BIG DAY, MOOSE! SO BE ON THE BALL!
OKAY, PARTNER!
DOILEY
D-UH! WE MAKE A GREAT TEAM! YOUR BRAINS AND MY THUMB!
YUK!
DOILEY
3

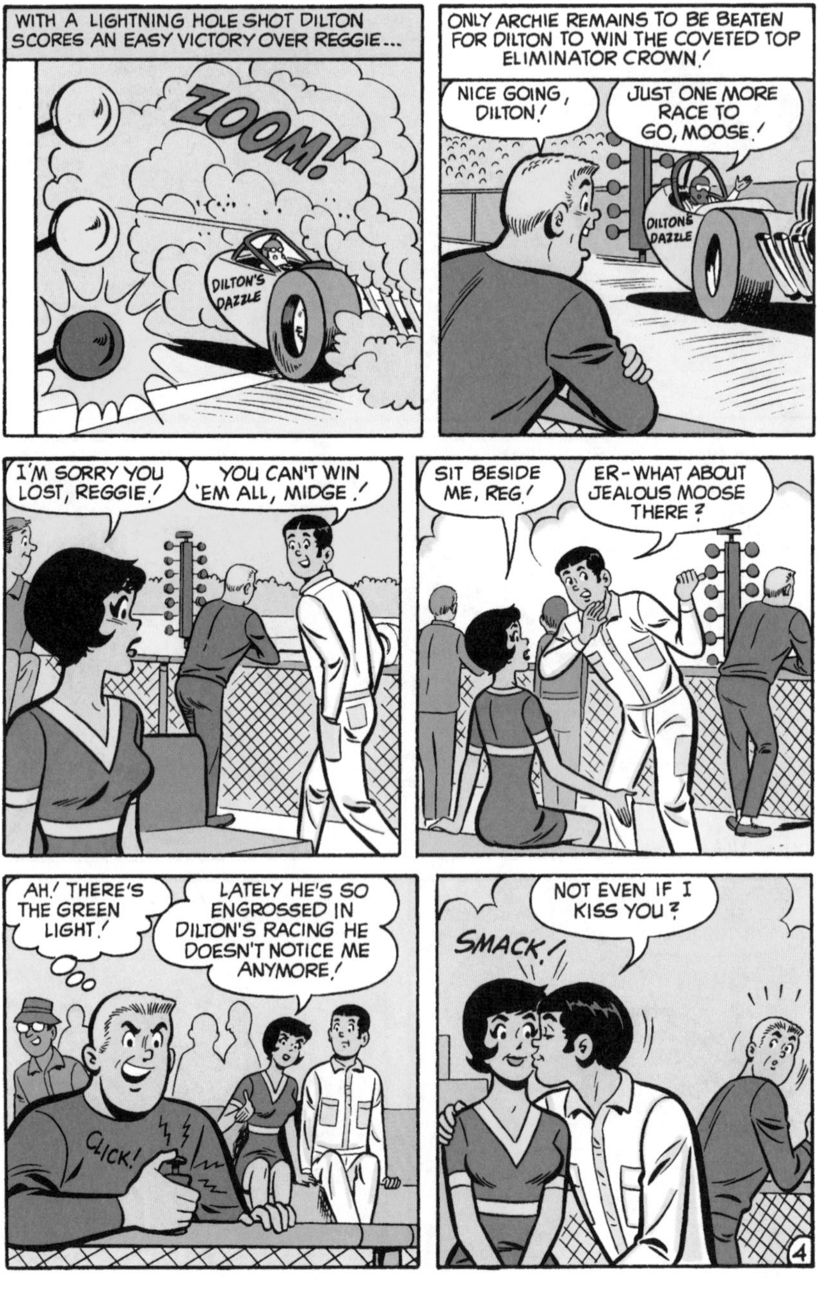
WITH A LIGHTNING HOLE SHOT DILTON SCORES AN EASY VICTORY OVER REGGIE...
ZOOM!
DILTON'S DAZZLE
ONLY ARCHIE REMAINS TO BE BEATEN FOR DILTON TO WIN THE COVETED TOP ELIMINATOR CROWN!
NICE GOING, DILTON!
JUST ONE MORE RACE TO GO, MOOSE!
DILTON'S DAZZLE
I'M SORRY YOU LOST, REGGIE!
YOU CAN'T WIN 'EM ALL, MIDGE!
SIT BESIDE ME, REG!
ER-WHAT ABOUT JEALOUS MOOSE THERE?
AH! THERE'S THE GREEN LIGHT!
LATELY HE'S SO ENGROSSED IN DILTON'S RACING HE DOESN'T NOTICE ME ANYMORE!
CLICK!
NOT EVEN IF I KISS YOU?
SMACK!
4

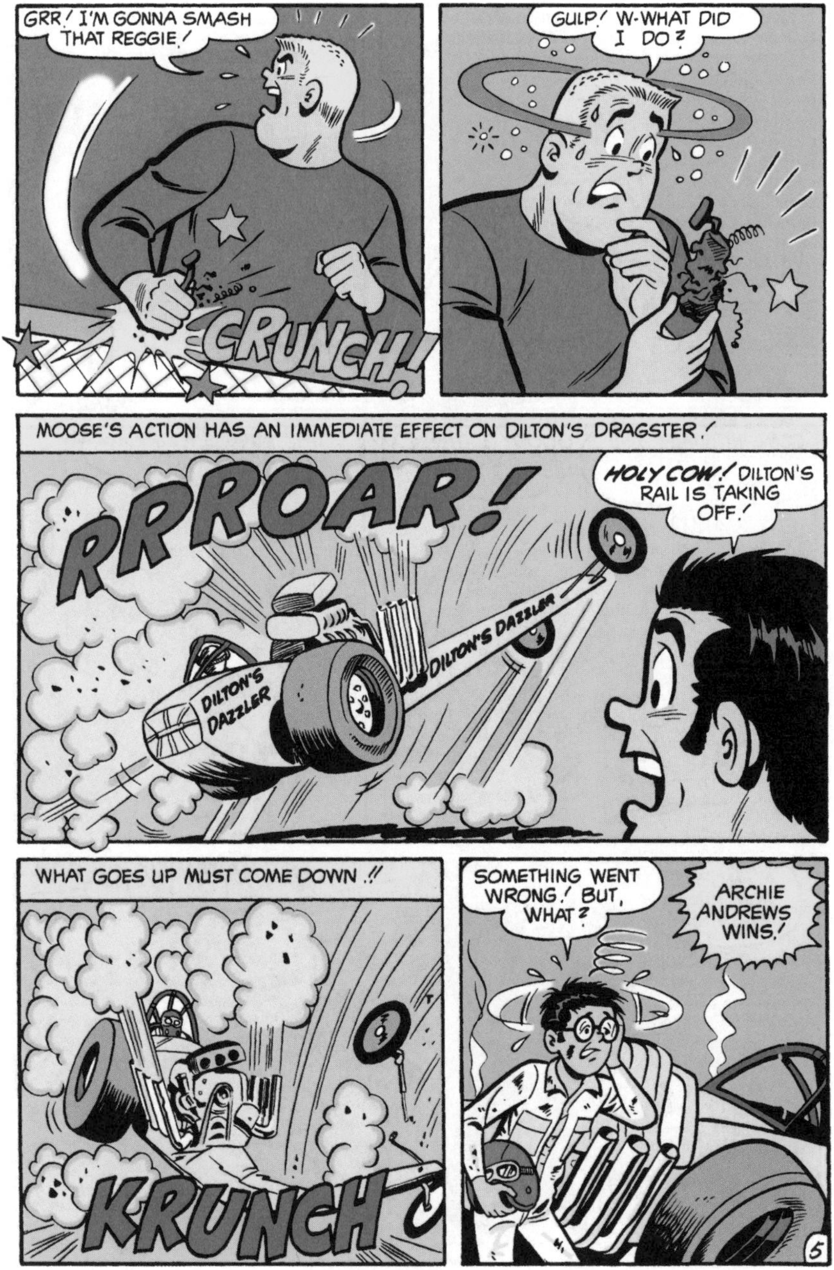
GRR! I'M GONNA SMASH THAT REGGIE!
CRUNCH!
GULP! W-WHAT DID I DO?
MOOSE'S ACTION HAS AN IMMEDIATE EFFECT ON DILTON'S DRAGSTER!
RRROAR!
HOLY COW! DILTON'S RAIL IS TAKING OFF!
DILTON'S DAZZLER
DILTON'S DAZZLER
DILTON'S DAZZLER
WHAT GOES UP MUST COME DOWN!!
KRUNCH
SOMETHING WENT WRONG! BUT, WHAT?
ARCHIE ANDREWS WINS!
5

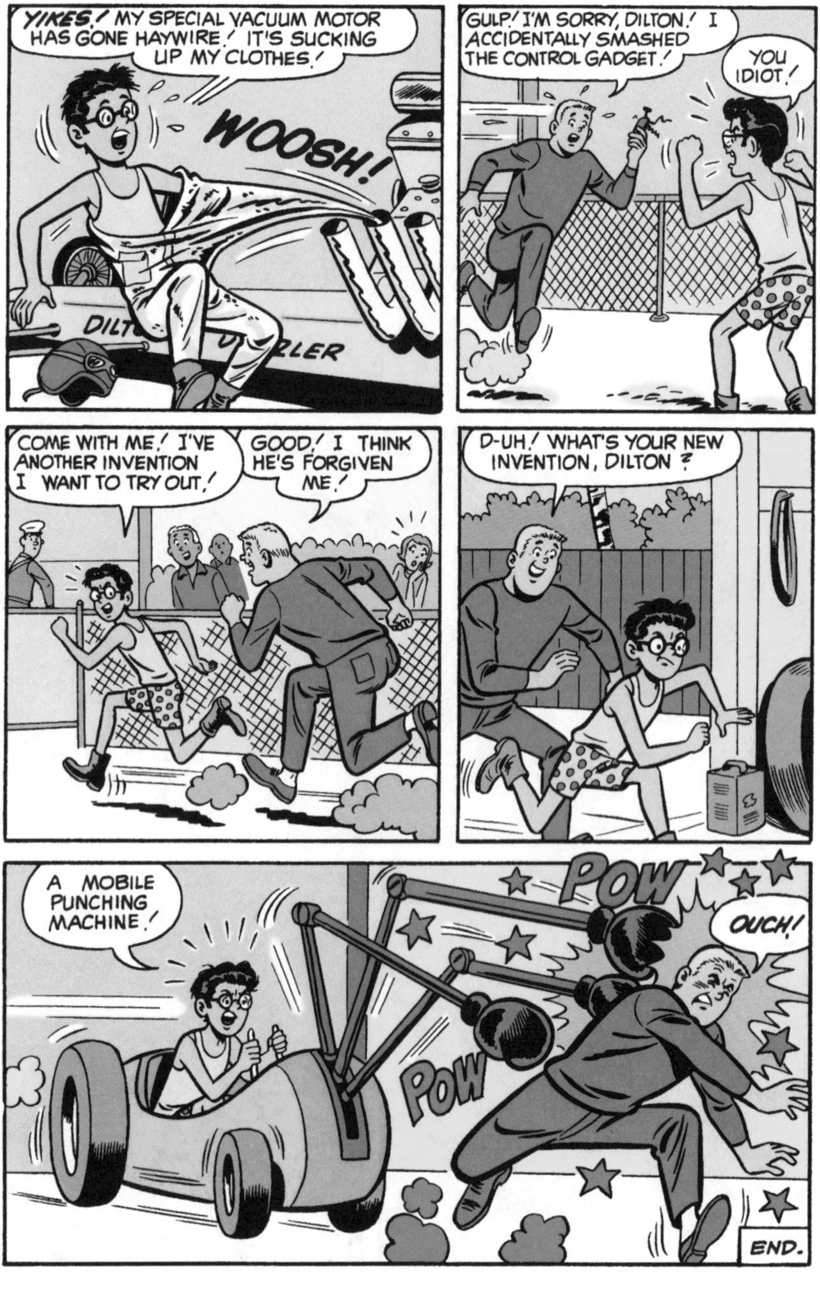
YIKES! MY SPECIAL VACUUM MOTOR HAS GONE HAYWIRE! IT'S SUCKING UP MY CLOTHES!
WOOSH!
GULP! I'M SORRY, DILTON! I ACCIDENTALLY SMASHED THE CONTROL GADGET!
YOU IDIOT!
COME WITH ME! I'VE ANOTHER INVENTION I WANT TO TRY OUT!
GOOD! I THINK HE'S FORGIVEN ME!
D-UH! WHAT'S YOUR NEW INVENTION, DILTON?
A MOBILE PUNCHING MACHINE!
POW
OUCH!
POW
END.

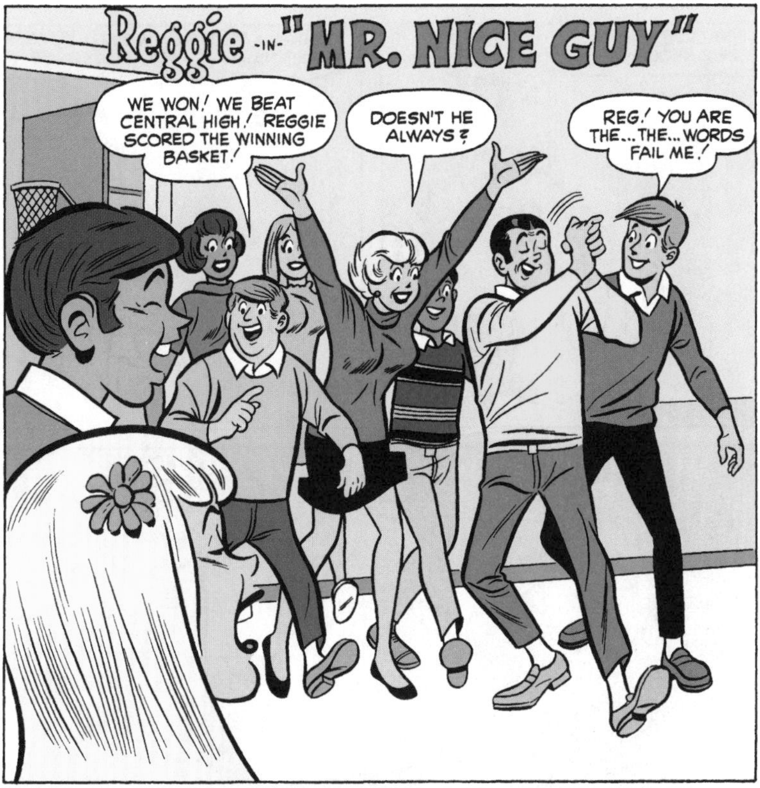
Reggie -IN- "MR. NICE GUY"
WE WON! WE BEAT CENTRAL HIGH! REGGIE SCORED THE WINNING BASKET!
DOESN'T HE ALWAYS?
REG! YOU ARE THE... THE... WORDS FAIL ME!

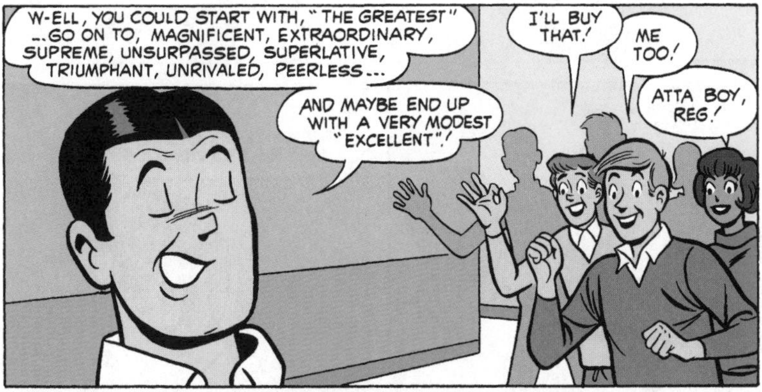
W-ELL, YOU COULD START WITH, "THE GREATEST" ...GO ON TO, MAGNIFICENT, EXTRAORDINARY, SUPREME, UNSURPASSED, SUPERLATIVE, TRIUMPHANT, UNRIVALED, PEERLESS...
AND MAYBE END UP WITH A VERY MODEST "EXCELLENT"!
I'LL BUY THAT!
ME TOO!
ATTA BOY, REG!

Story: George Gladir Pencils: Samm Schwartz
Inks: Marty Epp Letters: Bill Yoshida

Originally printed in EVERYTHING'S ARCHIE #13, APRIL 1971

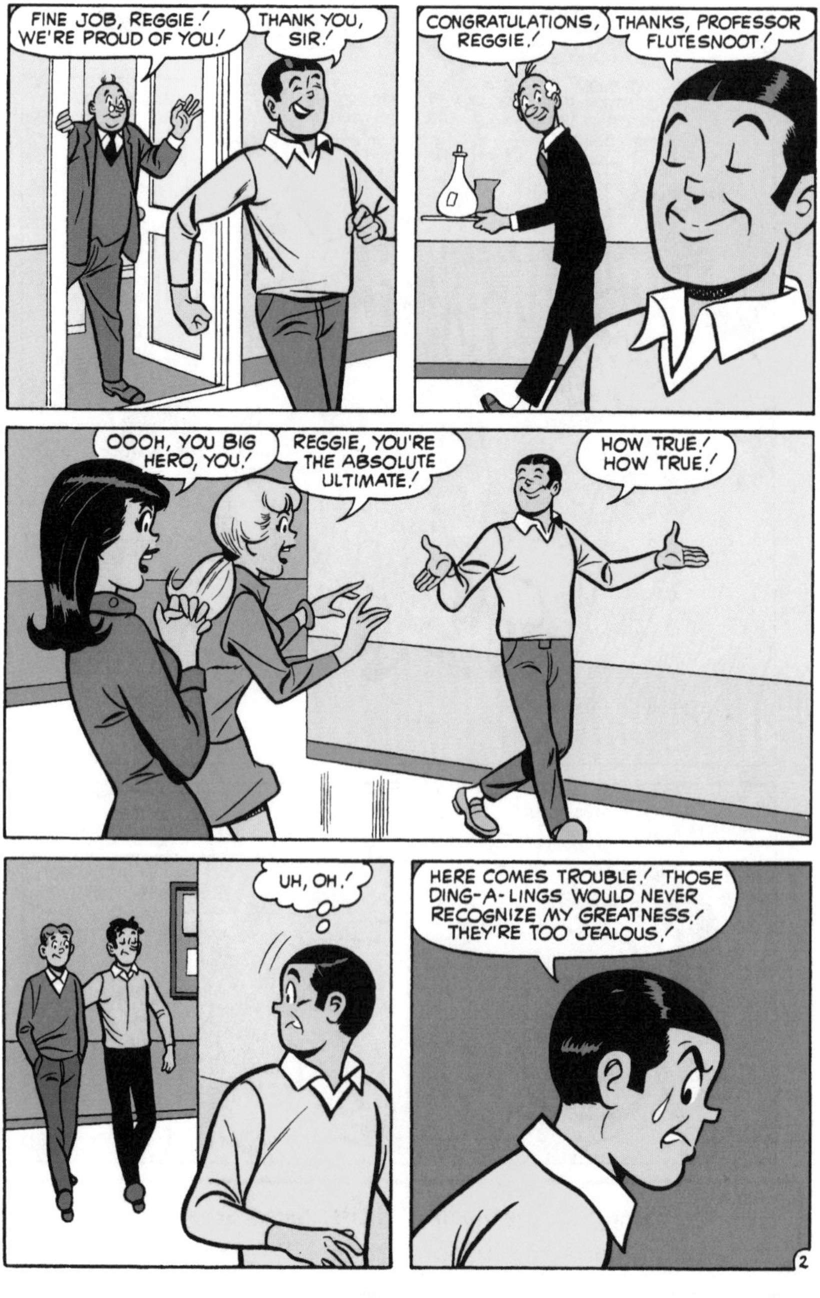
FINE JOB, REGGIE! WE'RE PROUD OF YOU!
THANK YOU, SIR!
CONGRATULATIONS, REGGIE!
THANKS, PROFESSOR FLUTESNOOT!
OOOH, YOU BIG HERO, YOU!
REGGIE, YOU'RE THE ABSOLUTE ULTIMATE!
HOW TRUE! HOW TRUE!
UH, OH!
HERE COMES TROUBLE! THOSE DING-A-LINGS WOULD NEVER RECOGNIZE MY GREATNESS! THEY'RE TOO JEALOUS!
2

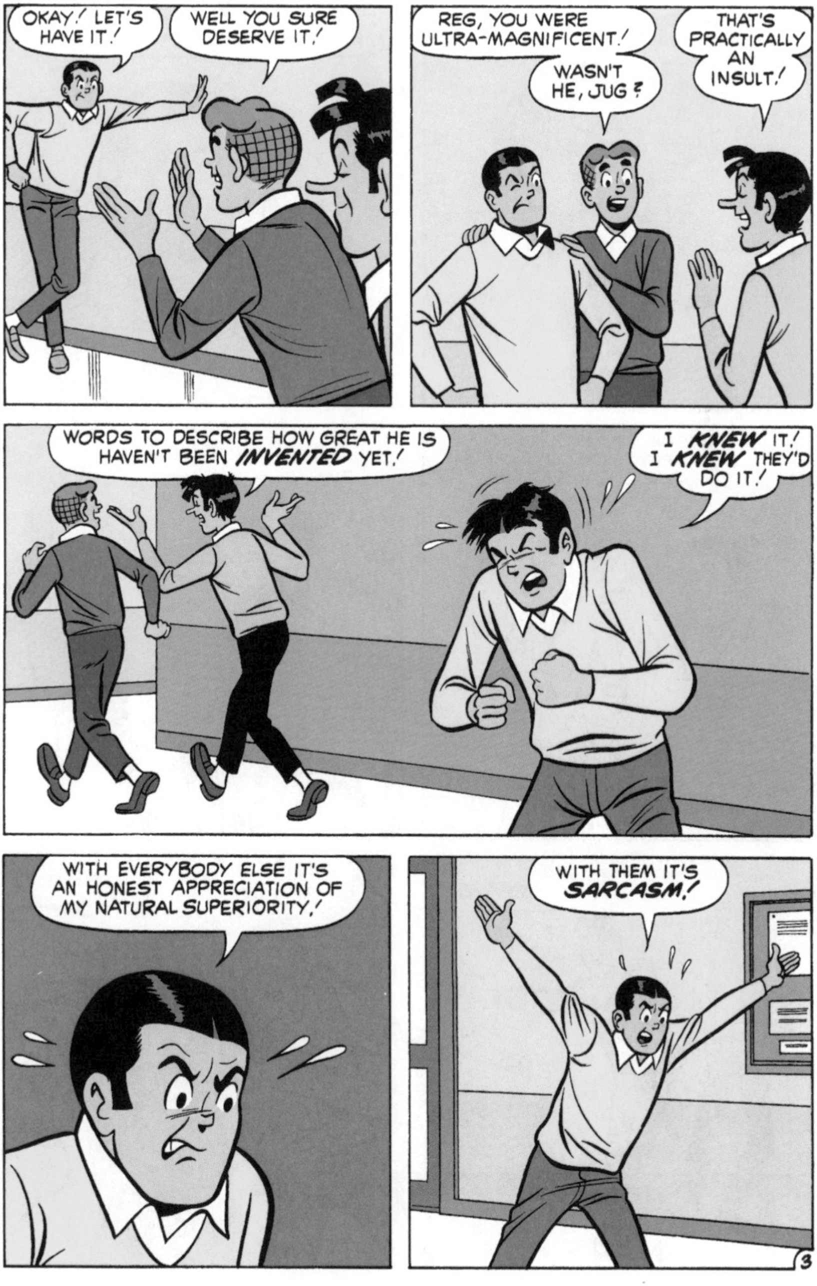
OKAY! LET'S HAVE IT!
WELL YOU SURE DESERVE IT!
REG, YOU WERE ULTRA-MAGNIFICENT!
WASN'T HE, JUG?
THAT'S PRACTICALLY AN INSULT!
WORDS TO DESCRIBE HOW GREAT HE IS HAVEN'T BEEN *INVENTED* YET!
I *KNEW* IT! I *KNEW* THEY'D DO IT!
WITH EVERYBODY ELSE IT'S AN HONEST APPRECIATION OF MY NATURAL SUPERIORITY!
WITH THEM IT'S *SARCASM!*
3

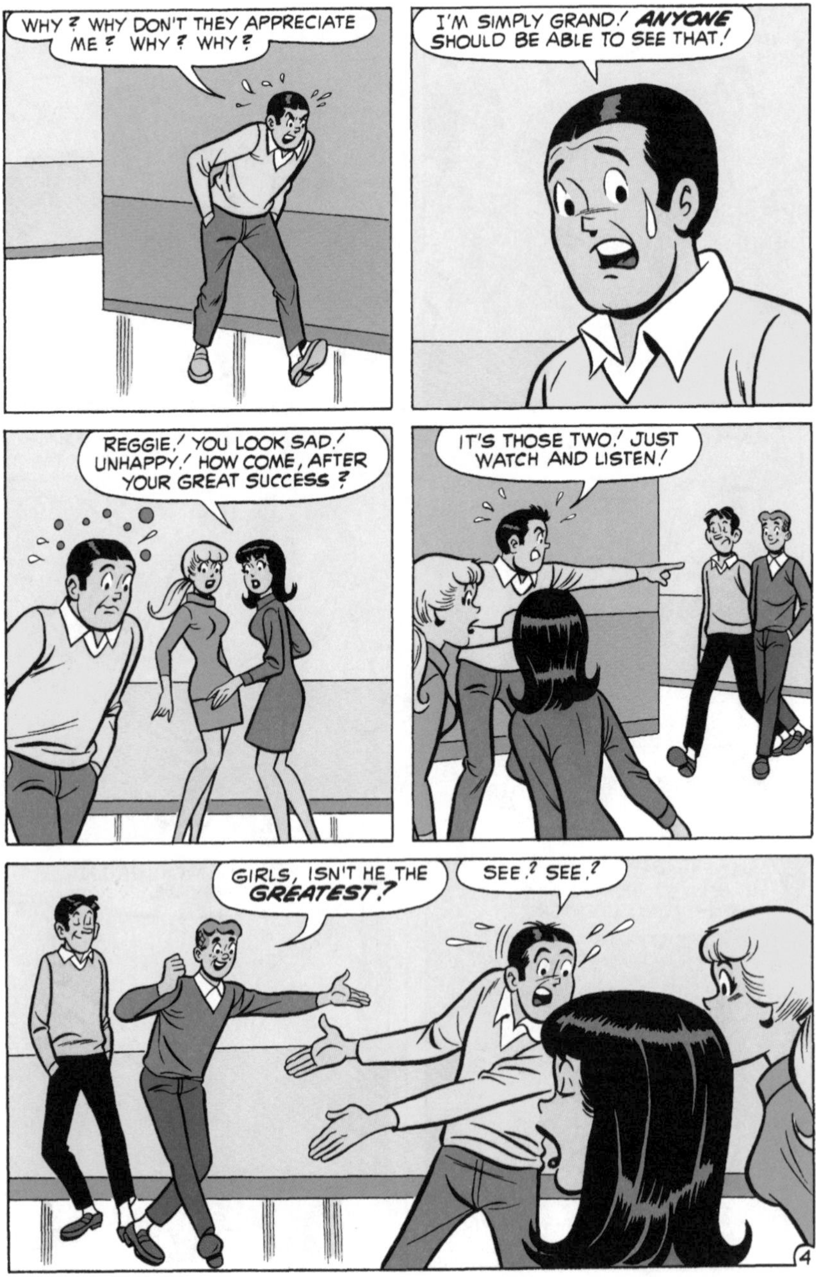
WHY? WHY DON'T THEY APPRECIATE ME? WHY? WHY?
I'M SIMPLY GRAND! ANYONE SHOULD BE ABLE TO SEE THAT!
REGGIE! YOU LOOK SAD! UNHAPPY! HOW COME, AFTER YOUR GREAT SUCCESS?
IT'S THOSE TWO! JUST WATCH AND LISTEN!
GIRLS, ISN'T HE THE GREATEST?
SEE? SEE?
4

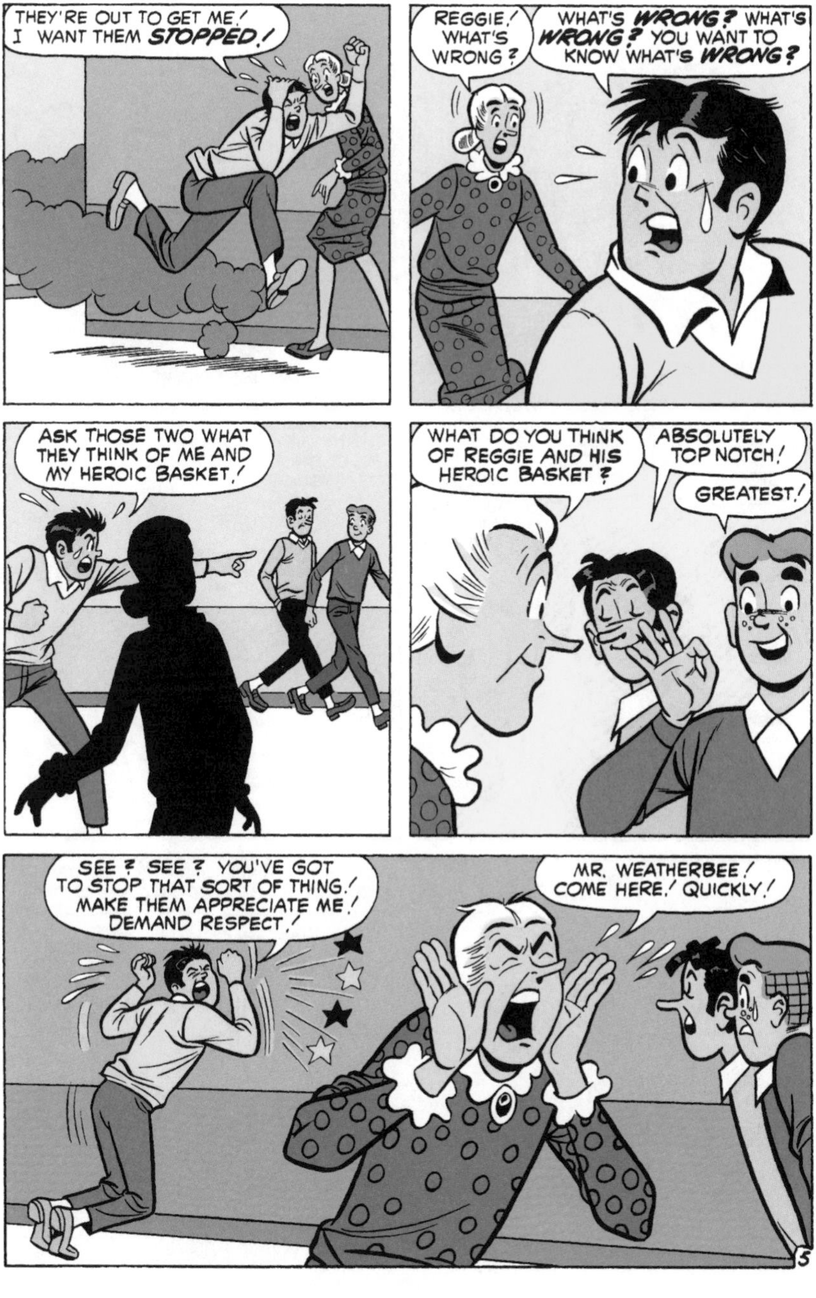
THEY'RE OUT TO GET ME! I WANT THEM STOPPED!
REGGIE! WHAT'S WRONG?
WHAT'S WRONG? WHAT'S WRONG? YOU WANT TO KNOW WHAT'S WRONG?
ASK THOSE TWO WHAT THEY THINK OF ME AND MY HEROIC BASKET!
WHAT DO YOU THINK OF REGGIE AND HIS HEROIC BASKET?
ABSOLUTELY TOP NOTCH!
GREATEST!
SEE? SEE? YOU'VE GOT TO STOP THAT SORT OF THING! MAKE THEM APPRECIATE ME! DEMAND RESPECT!
MR. WEATHERBEE! COME HERE! QUICKLY!
5

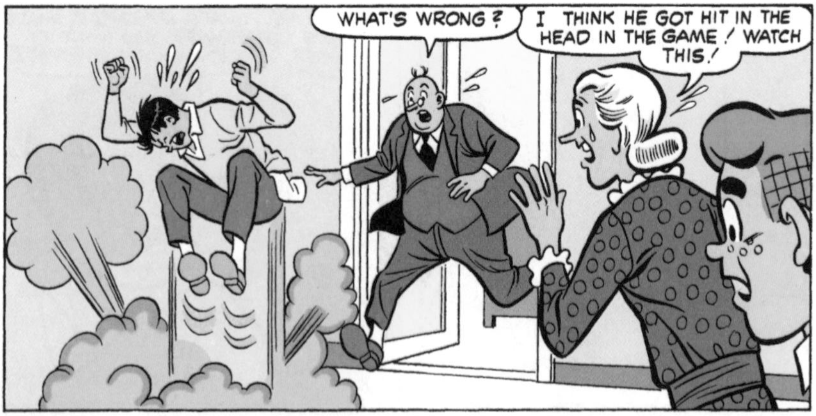
WHAT'S WRONG ?
I THINK HE GOT HIT IN THE HEAD IN THE GAME ! WATCH THIS !

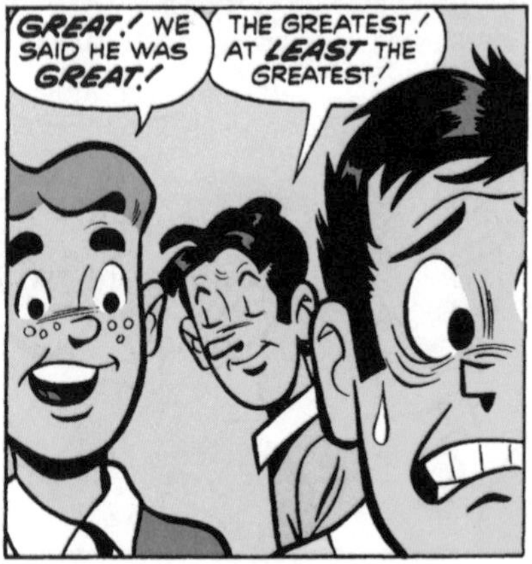
GREAT ! WE SAID HE WAS GREAT !
THE GREATEST ! AT LEAST THE GREATEST !

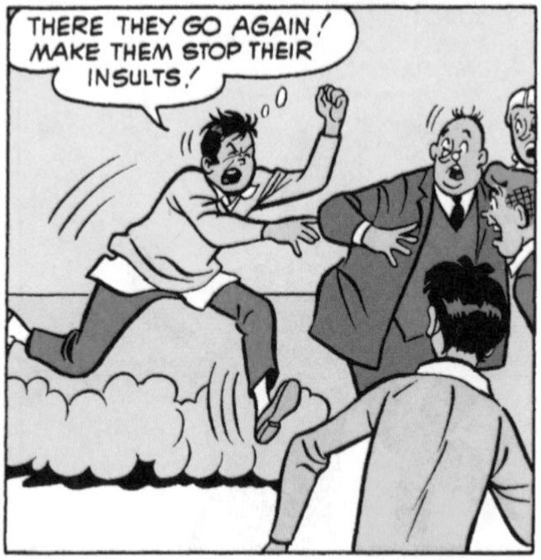
THERE THEY GO AGAIN ! MAKE THEM STOP THEIR INSULTS !

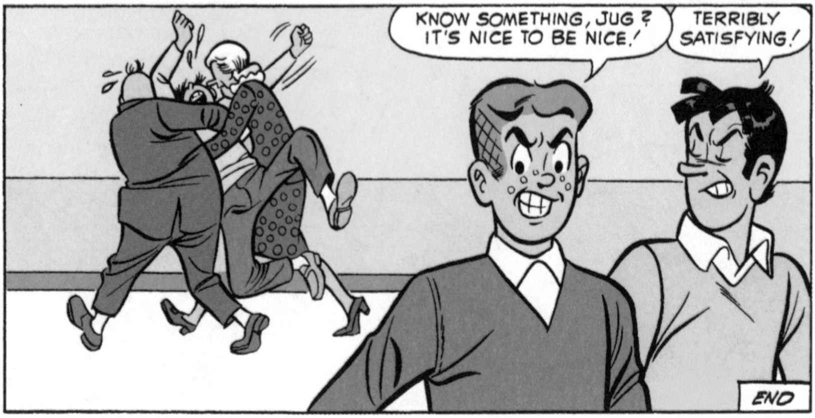
KNOW SOMETHING, JUG ? IT'S NICE TO BE NICE !
TERRIBLY SATISFYING !
END